Praise for *The Trade Off*

"*The Trade Off* possesses all the literary goodies that historical-fiction lovers will devour: rags to riches, love, loss, redemption, and my personal fave—girl power, during a time when women had none. Readers will fall deeply in love with the fiery, brilliant Bea, a young immigrant who believes in her own abilities against all odds. Woodruff takes us on a journey rich with history, female empowerment, and page-turning prose. A powerhouse of a novel, *The Trade Off* is blue chip all the way."

—Lisa Barr, *New York Times* bestselling author of *Woman on Fire*

"With a cast of characters so realistic that I swear some of them used to come to Rosh Hashanah dinner at my grandmother's house, Samantha Greene Woodruff has perfectly captured the Jewish immigrant experience of the early twentieth century in *The Trade Off*. Utterly satisfying and immensely enjoyable, with a nail-biting race to the conclusion, *The Trade Off* proves that Woodruff is an absolute powerhouse of historical fiction."

—Sara Goodman Confino, bestselling author of *Don't Forget to Write*

"Bea is the kind of well-drawn female character that you will root for from the very start, and the novel is an absolutely captivating read about one woman's trailblazing pursuit of the American dream for herself and her family."

—Jane Healey, bestselling author of *Goodnight from Paris*

"An unputdownable tale of one woman's inspiring rise from the tenements of old New York to the gilded floors of Wall Street, *The Trade Off* is a sweeping, evocative novel that kept me reading into the night. Lush with historical detail and brimming with insight, Woodruff's fast-moving novel presents the country's financial collapse through one woman's eyes, demonstrating just how hard she'll work to propel herself and her family to riches, even if it means sacrificing her own dreams. Don't miss this historical gem from an unforgettable writer."

—Brooke Lea Foster, bestselling author of *All the Summers in Between*

"Samantha Greene Woodruff has created a nuanced and captivating heroine who brims with courage, loyalty, and grit. Full of 1920s razzle-dazzle, engaging prose, beautifully complex relationships, and a high-stakes, suspenseful crescendo, this is a story that will draw you in from the first page and not let go until its stunning conclusion. A breathtaking look at one of the most dramatic moments in American history, *The Trade Off* is not to be missed!"

—Jacqueline Friedland, *USA Today* bestselling author of *He Gets That from Me*

THE TRADE OFF

ALSO BY SAMANTHA GREENE WOODRUFF

The Lobotomist's Wife

THE TRADE OFF

A NOVEL

SAMANTHA GREENE WOODRUFF

LAKE UNION PUBLISHING

This is a work of fiction. Names, characters, organizations, places, events, and incidents are either products of the author's imagination or are used fictitiously.

Published by Lake Union Publishing, Seattle

www.apub.com

ISBN-13: 9781662516467 (paperback)
ISBN-13: 9781662516450 (digital)

Cover design by Faceout Studio, Molly von Borstel
Cover image: ©Nicole Matthews / ArcAngel; ©Underwood Archives, Inc / Alamy; ©YuriyZhuravov, ©Net Vector / Shutterstock

Printed in the United States of America

For Lila & Alex

Finance in the financial centres of the country is still the citadel of the men, and to its innermost precincts women have not yet penetrated.

—Mary Vail Andress, *Banking as a Career for Women*, 1928

I am firm in my belief that anyone not only can be rich but ought to be rich.

—John Jakob Raskob, interview in *Ladies' Home Journal*, August 1929

PROLOGUE

October 29, 1929: Black Tuesday a.k.a. "The Great Crash"

Bea didn't have time to think. She dropped the morning paper the moment she read the headline and ran out the door. For the second time in a week, she was racing to Wall Street in a panic to try to help her brother. The crash had started last week, and today, the market finally hit what had to be the bottom. It was far, far worse than Bea ever could have imagined. She was sure Jake was on the phones and the wires like every other broker at every other bank, trying to sell anything he could. But selling was impossible. The lines were jammed. So were the streets. Bea was glad she planned to take the Lexington Avenue line instead of driving, because today the roads looked more like parking lots than busy thoroughfares.

When she emerged from the train downtown, she was stunned by what she saw. Wall Street was always bustling with people, but this was different. The streets were thick with dense mobs of men and women screaming, crying as they huddled over the papers with the latest stock updates. The ground beneath their feet was littered with red trading slips—sales orders that couldn't even make it into the exchange. Bea thought of Nate, who she knew was planning to spend today on the trading floor—had he made it inside? She tried to push through the crowds to get to the National City Building, where Jake was; until this moment she'd been certain there was something she could do to help her brother. Now that she was here, she realized she was wrong. This was a catastrophe beyond remedy.

It was immediately clear to Bea that she should go back home. Being here wouldn't help anyone and might even be dangerous. In addition to the distraught crowds, it seemed that people in the buildings above were hurling large objects from the windows. Bea pushed against the hordes to get out of the way. And then the screams of panic that had become the street's soundtrack were broken by a giant thud. The crowd parted to reveal a man on the sidewalk, unmoving. Instantaneously the horror of this moment transformed into tragedy. Bea hardly had time before she started to heave, her insides coming up in violent convulsions. She had to get control of herself. She had to get out of there.

As she slowly stood back up, her usually acute senses were distorted. The scene in front of her moved as if in slow motion. All she heard was a dull buzz in her ears. She didn't want to, but she knew she had to go look at the man. If for no other reason than to be sure he wasn't someone she knew.

She was momentarily overcome with relief. This was a stranger, not Jake, not Nate, not any of the men she had worked with at J.P. Morgan or National City. Then, like a set of violently crashing waves coming too quickly, her momentary relief was overtaken by the atrocity at her feet. No, she didn't recognize this man, but she easily could have. He was clearly a broker. And from the looks of his high-end suit, he was a successful one. Well, he had been. Before the market crashed.

She saw her panic and horror mimicked in the faces of everyone around her, felt her cheeks soaked with tears. Only then did she hear the percussive sound of more thuds. Only then did she take in the bodies that were coming from the highest windows of every building on Wall Street. Only then did Bea truly understand the magnitude of this day. Until now she had believed that any loss in the market would be purely financial. Now she saw it was so much more. Things had grown so bad that bankers were jumping from windows rather than face a financially decimated future.

She had to get out of here, to get home. She was worried about Jake. Maybe she could reach him on the phone. Given the sense of importance he derived from his recently earned wealth, she couldn't help but fear that he might be among the bodies on the street. She had to remind him that money wasn't everything. She had to tell him her secret. To assure him they still had a tiny thread of hope.

1926

Three Years before the Crash

CHAPTER ONE

Bea Abramovitz knew only a little about wealth. Mostly she knew that other people had it and her family didn't—and that her mother and her brother cared a lot about gaining it, and she, not so much. For her, Wall Street wasn't about getting rich; it was about numbers, and patterns, and strategy. And she knew a lot about that.

Bea wasn't yet an expert, but as she walked purposefully down Broad Street, she knew to ignore the curb sellers shouting offerings of nonsensical investments like "shares of a cocker spaniel for only one dollar." They hawked things only an ignorant speculator or pure gambler would buy. The stocks that mattered were the ones traded inside the actual New York Stock Exchange, not on the street corners outside. Behind those doors, ownership of the new America—railroads, steel manufacturers, and innovators like DuPont and Westinghouse Electric—could be bought and sold. That was the place where, if all went well today, the rest of her life would begin.

Bea thought she was used to the city's bustling streets, having spent her childhood helping her father sell fruit and vegetables at his pushcart on Orchard Street. She hadn't realized that her chaotic neighborhood on a Friday afternoon, with women hurrying to gather their last jars of schmaltz, bargain for extra bones with their beef, and collect a few more apples before the sun set, was like a peaceful sabbath Saturday morning compared to Wall Street.

People rushed in all directions: dense throngs of men in dark suits and bowler hats, women in smart drop-waist dresses with colorful cloches pulled tight over their bobbed hair. Bea sped with the crowds past the pillared marble facade of the Federal Building, preparing to make her exit from the steady flow of foot traffic. She stepped out of the rush at the place where the perpendicular street signs above her head read "Broad" and "Wall."

She had arrived.

Like its position at the physical center of the financial district at Twenty-Three Wall Street, the House of Morgan was, itself, the very symbol of the world of banking. So much so that it was this building that had been bombed to protest American capitalism six years before, killing thirty people and injuring hundreds. That didn't scare Bea because, while the building itself still bore a few pockmarks from the explosion, it remained the most prestigious and powerful place to be on all of Wall Street. And she, Bea Abramovitz, was the only girl in the entire Hunter College class of '25 lucky enough to get an interview there. Never mind that she was the only one interested in trying.

Bea had learned about the stock market from her father, Lew. She'd always loved numbers, unlike her twin brother, Jake. So, when she showed an interest in her father's hobby of studying the market in the financial pages of the daily English-language newspapers, he encouraged her to join him. He taught her about the Dow—an index of twenty of the most prominent companies listed on the stock exchange—and the two of them would discuss where it closed each day or the specifics of some company's stock that had risen exceptionally high or fallen precipitously low.

For Bea, what started as a way to spend time with her father quickly became a personal passion. The more she followed stocks, the more she recognized patterns and could predict what would happen. By the time she was in high school, she and her father had a running competition to see whose hypothetical investment portfolios performed better. Bea won more often than her father did, a point of pride for both of them.

Sure, the stock market wasn't actually relevant to immigrants on the Lower East Side who didn't have the time or money to buy shares of America's great companies, but for Lew, studying the markets was his way to dream of reclaiming all that her parents had lost in their flight from Russia to America. To imagine that he might be the economist he'd been studying to become back home, instead of the produce peddler on Orchard Street that he'd been all of Bea's life. For Bea, it grew from a thrilling game into a singular goal: by the time she started college, her intention was to make investing her job, as a broker on Wall Street.

This would have been realistic for Jake. He went to City College, the all-male school where finance classes were plentiful. But she went to Hunter, the all-female equivalent. And while both schools were renowned for academic excellence, the assumption was that most Hunter girls, if they didn't simply marry upon graduation, would become teachers or secretaries.

Bea knew she was lucky to have the opportunity to go to college at all. Unlike the other exclusive women's schools, such as Barnard or Smith, Hunter not only was open to young women of all backgrounds but also offered this education free to any girl who had the grades to qualify. Still, no matter how smart they were, no Hunter girl had ever worked as a stockbroker. If this was what Bea wanted, she'd have to create the opportunity herself.

School had always come easily to her, so from the start, she took the most challenging courses available. By the middle of her last year of school, Bea had taken every math, statistics, and economics class Hunter offered that might have relevance to the market, yet none of her professors had even mentioned the word *stock*. Bea wasn't one to give up easily, but her last semester of school was about to start, and she didn't feel any closer to her goal of becoming a broker than she had when college began. That was when Jake came home with news that would change everything.

"Hey, BB, too bad you can't take classes over at City College—some of my pals are studying investing there this semester. Apparently the professor's some former stockbroker who made it big before the war."

This was it. This was Bea's chance to really learn about Wall Street. "Are you going to take the class?" she asked hopefully.

"You know I'm awful at that stuff. I don't have your mind for numbers."

"But I could help you. I want to learn this anyway, so I would be happy to do your work for you. You'd just have to take notes so I could see the lessons."

"I can't. I've got a full course load already. I don't have time to go, even if you do all the work. I'm just trying to get school over with as soon as I can. I'm already more than a year behind you with your crazy double course load."

"Please, Jake, this could be my chance. And don't you think you owe me this? You wouldn't even be at City College if it hadn't been for me doing all your homework in high school."

"You're right." He chuckled. "Maybe I should've done it myself so I wouldn't have to be there now."

Bea shook her head and rolled her eyes. The fact was that Jake wouldn't have gone to college at all if their father hadn't insisted. Jake wasn't bookish like Bea. It wasn't that he lacked intelligence, but he didn't have the interest or discipline for schoolwork; his strength was with people. Jake had always been able to charm anyone into doing almost anything. Her mother, Pauline, loved to talk about how many more potatoes Jake could sell to Mrs. Millowitz than Lew or Bea ever could, "just with a few words and a smile." Still, their father insisted that he go to college because "a free education is a gift that will keep giving for the rest of your life."

"Listen, my taking the class isn't going to help you anyway. Don't you know it's connections you need to make it on Wall Street?"

Bea considered this for a moment. "Well, can you introduce me to the professor then?"

"Are you kidding? I don't know the guy. Let's see what my pals say about him after a few weeks of class; maybe then I can work something out."

Bea didn't want to wait. She had decided that this class, this professor, was her chance to get to Wall Street. And if Jake wouldn't help her, maybe her dean, Mrs. Bauer, could. Bea had met with Mrs. Bauer periodically over the years she was at Hunter, usually when the poet turned administrator called Bea in to discuss her peculiar course selection. While she didn't necessarily share Bea's predilection for math, she'd always been supportive of Bea's desire to challenge herself. Bea hoped that would still be the case. She went to Mrs. Bauer and proposed the unimaginable: that she go to City College and take the finance class herself.

CHAPTER TWO

A full week had passed, and the semester was already underway by the time Mrs. Bauer called Bea into her office to discuss her request.

"Well, Bea, I have some good news for you."

"I can take the class?" Bea leapt to her feet, opening her arms to embrace the dean as the woman held out an arm to stop her.

"Hold your excitement until you hear what I can offer you. As I expected, it would be impossible for you to take a course at City College in a classroom full of boys. However, it turns out that the professor, Harold Berkman, is an acquaintance of my husband's, and he has agreed to teach you in an independent-study format. You'll need to work around his schedule and commute to him, but he is willing to cover the material that is being taught in his course."

Bea clapped her hands excitedly and lunged again toward Mrs. Bauer to embrace her. With the dean a tall woman and Bea just a bit over five feet, she was engulfed by Mrs. Bauer's bosom as she gushed her appreciation. "This is incredible. Perfect. Even better than taking a class at City College. Mrs. Bauer, I cannot begin to thank you, I—"

"You're welcome, dear." The dean put her hands on Bea's shoulders and looked Bea in the face. "Just remember, this is no guarantee of anything at all. It is just an opportunity to learn."

"Of course. Of course." Bea nodded as she collected her things to go. She had to get to City College and meet this Harold Berkman immediately.

It took Bea over an hour to walk across the park to catch the El that serviced the part of Harlem where City College had its campus, but she hardly noticed. She would have swum up the East River if necessary. This was the big break she'd been waiting for, and nothing would stop her now.

City College wasn't like Hunter. Not only were there no girls in sight, but the campus, with its large lawns and numerous trees, felt parklike and open—a dramatic contrast to Hunter, which was decidedly part of the city, sandwiched between Park and Lexington Avenues. She wandered into three buildings before she even found the reception desk, and then she needed a map to find Professor Berkman's office.

When she finally found it, she peered in the window to see him animatedly talking to two young men. She positioned herself on a bench across the hall so she could catch him when this meeting was done. A few minutes later, Professor Berkman opened his door to walk the students out and immediately noticed Bea.

"Miss, may I help you? Are you lost?"

"No, sir—I mean *Professor*. I'm sorry to just show up like this. I'm here to see you. My name is Bea Abramovitz. I'm a student at Hunter. Mrs. Bauer, my dean, arranged for me to study with you?"

"Ah, Miss Abramovitz, I wasn't expecting to see you today." He smiled warmly at her, and her nerves immediately melted away. "Come on in."

Suddenly Bea's heart was pounding so intensely that she felt her whole chest cavity might explode. The boys who had been inside Professor Berkman's office looked at Bea as they left, one of them whistling under his breath. As they walked away, she heard him say, "I'd like to have a conference with her, if you know what I mean." And the two broke out in laughter. Bea smiled; it wasn't like this was the first time she'd gotten attention from a guy. But, at that moment, the comment was just what she needed to calm down and lighten up. If these juvenile boys were Professor Berkman's students, surely, she would be fine.

"Miss Abramovitz," the professor said as he signaled for her to sit in the wooden chair across from his desk, "I must say I was intrigued to speak to your dean. In all my years teaching at City College I've never had a request like this. Why, exactly, do you want to study with me?"

"Well . . ." Bea sat up, as if being more erect would make the professor take her more seriously. "I've been studying the stock market since I was a little girl. I love looking for the patterns in the numbers and picking stocks based on my analysis. And I'm good at it." She paused to make sure he was listening. "It's like a predictive equation in applied mathematics. Except, when you get the prediction right here, you get rich." She blushed and was suddenly flustered. *Why had she said that last part?* It wasn't about getting rich for Bea. While Jake got a rush when he had an extra dollar in his hand, no matter how he got it (in fact, Jake's usual sentiment was "the less work the better"), Bea's greatest thrill came from turning over a problem in her head until she found the solution. "I'm just fascinated by the puzzle of it all, and I want to understand it better—what drives the rises and falls? Why do prices land where they do? And how do they continue to soar and make our economy the greatest in the world?"

A smile spread across Professor Berkman's face. "Well, Miss Abramovitz, that is all very insightful. And I'd be happy to teach you more about that, but typically people who take my class do so to go on to work in finance. Surely you—"

"Oh yes! I forgot to mention that part. I want to be a broker." Bea turned her eyes to the oriental rug on the floor. Admitting this to him, a man who actually had the job she wanted, made her extremely nervous.

"I see." He looked at her kindly. "I assume you know that is quite an ambitious goal for a woman, yes? Other than a few trailblazers, there really aren't many people of the female persuasion on Wall Street." He pulled on his mustache as he pondered for a moment. "I have heard that some of the larger banks are beginning to create new ladies' departments to service their growing female clientele, but—"

"A ladies' department! That would be perfect."

"Yes, but they are very selective in their hiring, as far as I know. I certainly can't make any promises about a job even if you do study with me. At most I'd expect you might become a more attractive secretarial candidate."

Bea felt momentarily crestfallen, but she decided that was a worry for another day. "Professor Berkman, I'm not here because I want you to get me a job. Of course, that would be wonderful, but I certainly don't expect it. I just want to learn. The stock market is the driving engine of our economy. I've studied advanced mathematics and statistics, macro- and microeconomics, and I want to be able to practically apply my skills. I can do that in the stock market. It's dynamic and exciting and, even though I don't have the money to invest myself, I desperately want to learn how the professionals do it. Can you teach me that?"

"If that is your goal, Miss Abramovitz, I'm certain I can help."

Bea was so gleeful it took all her restraint not to leap out of her chair and kiss Harold Berkman on the lips. No matter what anyone said, she was one step closer to her dream. And nothing could take away her joy.

The way Harold Berkman taught Bea was essentially a more formalized version of what she'd been doing with her father for years. She constructed a hypothetical portfolio of stocks and kept a notebook recording what she would have bought or sold each day. Once a week, they met to assess her portfolio's performance and analyze what drove her gains and losses. With Professor Berkman's guidance, Bea started to see how to connect patterns she saw in the market to real-world events and economic forces, all of which made her stock picking even better than it had been before. Her record was impressive, even to Harold Berkman.

"Miss Abramovitz," he said excitedly as they sat together for their final meeting and calculated her overall rate of return for the semester.

"Do you know how unusual it is to be this accurate in the market?" She gave him a forced half smile as she shook her head with a tiny no. "Not only are you recognizing larger economic indicators but, also, if we annualized your rate of return, it would be nearly two hundred percent." He clapped his hands gleefully, as the tips of his mustache turned upward and the creases deepened in the corners of his eyes. His whole face radiated enthusiasm and pride. "You have a real gift for investing. Even seasoned brokers don't have results like this!"

"Thank you, Professor. I couldn't have gotten this far without your guidance." Her insides bubbled with excitement.

"Now, we haven't discussed this much, but it will be completely different for you when the money you're investing is real."

When the money she was investing? Was he saying he believed she could become a broker?

"Emotions—especially fear and greed—can cloud your thinking. Just remember to hold true to the most important lesson of the market. You know what that is, don't you?"

She shook her head, embarrassed.

"That's all right." He smiled again. "Now, Miss Abramovitz, listen closely: stock analysis is important and generally effective. You are an excellent analyst. But the markets are sly beasts, and you must never forget that, above all else, they will be driven by the forces of supply and demand."

"Supply and demand?" Bea asked, confused. This was the most elemental principle of economics. How could this be the most important lesson he had taught her?

"Yes. I know it seems simple, but let's think about it. If there is too much supply and not enough demand, what do stock prices do even when your analysis might indicate otherwise?"

"They fall." She nodded.

"Correct. And when there is more demand than there is supply?"

"They go up."

"So even if all of your statistical regression and charting indicates that a stock should soar, if there aren't people to buy it, the price will fall."

"Of course." This seemed obvious enough. But after months of studying with Harold Berkman, Bea knew there must be a reason he was harping on this point, so she wrote it down before asking the question she really wanted the answer to. "Professor Berkman, if I may be so bold, might I assume that if you're telling me this, it's because you think I might have a chance to work as a broker?"

His whole face lit up again in a smile. "Indeed I do, Miss Abramovitz. You remember that when we first met, I mentioned that some of the larger financial institutions are developing specialized divisions for women?"

Bea nodded; getting one of these jobs had been all she'd thought about since she learned they existed. "I remember. And I did some research, too, on some of the female executives: Virginia Furman at Columbia Trust, Mary Vail Andress at Chase National, Key Cammack at New York Trust."

"Yes, they've even formed their own organization, the National Association of Bank Women. Now, Wall Street is still primarily the province of men, but I daresay there is a new era dawning for women in finance, Miss Abramovitz, and I can't imagine a better young woman to seize the moment than you." He smiled at her proudly, and she felt so overcome with gratitude and hope her insides ached.

This was it. Her dream come true. Sure, she could have been a teacher or a bookkeeper, but that was a job. Wall Street would be a *career.* The chance for a truly different life not just for her, but for her whole family.

"So you really think I have a chance?" she asked, her excitement apparent in the smile that stretched across her face.

"Not only do I think so, I've already recommended you. I happen to have a contact at the House of Morgan who is arranging for you to be considered as we speak. You are a special talent, Miss Abramovitz. I can't wait to see what you do next."

CHAPTER THREE

February

For as long as Bea could remember, Sophie Romano had been her best friend. On the surface, beyond the fact that they lived in the same tenement, their apartments stacked one on top of the other, the girls were not an obvious match. First, Sophie was Italian and Catholic. Not that that was such a big deal—there were lots of Italian, Polish, and even some German people, living in her building. But Sophie was mild mannered and soft spoken, where Bea was opinionated and loud; Sophie was artistic and creative, where Bea had a head for numbers and business. They even looked like opposites, with Sophie tall and fair, and Bea small and dark. What the girls shared, though, was a driving determination to follow their dreams, as well as an intense loyalty to the people they cared about, and that mattered more than anything else.

From the time they had been allowed to run around their neighborhood alone, they'd spent nearly every moment together. They would do the shopping for their mothers, with Sophie carefully selecting the highest-quality items and Bea diligently comparing prices between vendors to ensure they didn't overspend. As they grew, despite their different paths—Bea went to college while Sophie worked with her seamstress mother—they remained devoted friends who leaned on the other's skills to complement their own. These days that meant that Bea was urging Sophie to stop doing piecework for her mother's neighborhood customers and start making and selling her own designs, and Sophie was creating chic outfits for Bea while reminding her to be polite, smile, and try to take a breath to let others catch up to her fast mind before she spoke.

Today Bea had her big interview, and she'd gone to Sophie's apartment as soon as the sun rose, so her friend could help her get ready.

"Oh, Soph." Bea squealed with glee as she admired her reflection in the length of the front room window. "You've outdone yourself. I really think this might be your best design yet!" Sophie had created a cream-colored light wool two-piece suit trimmed in brown and orange silk satin. The draped jacket was in the latest style, cutting across Bea's body at an angle to close with two bows at her left hip, and the box-pleated skirt was fashionably short but still office appropriate, hitting right below her knee. Sophie's mother had made Bea a simple blouse to complete the outfit in pale yellow imitation silk that tied at her neck. Bea couldn't imagine a more perfect ensemble for a new working girl. She was absolutely dizzy over it.

"She took those scraps of silk ribbon off the floor as soon as I cut them from my customer's dress, Beatrice. She wanted them badly," Sophie's mother said in heavily accented English, smiling warmly as she poked her head in from the kitchen to look at Bea and her daughter with pride.

"Well," Sophie added, "I just knew they would be perfect for your complexion! And I was right. Now, don't move, I need to run to the other room and grab one more thing to complete the outfit."

"What else could I possibly need? I already look like a model thanks to—" Before Bea could finish her sentence, Sophie was gone. Bea heard her shuffling in the next room, the place where Sophie slept, her bed directly above Bea's, like bunk beds separated by floorboards so thin they learned Morse code as kids so they could tap each other messages in the night. For most of Bea's life, she knew that when Sophie told her everything would be okay, she could count on her friend to help make it that way. And today that meant sewing Bea the perfect outfit, even though she had no money to spare for it.

Sophie returned with a cream felt cloche hat adorned with a large flower made from the same orange and brown satin ribbon that trimmed the suit. Sophie's face lit up as she placed the hat on Bea's head, carefully pulling out a few of Bea's curls, and holding up a hand mirror so she could see a proper reflection. "Now you are ready."

"Sophie." Bea welled up as she looked at herself and saw a modern, fashionable career girl looking back at her. "What would I do without you?"

"You'd get by, I suppose. But you'd look awful."

Bea laughed. "If I didn't already know how talented you were, I wouldn't believe you made this. Really, it looks like it came straight from a magazine!"

"It is perfectly you, Bea. Smart, sophisticated, and just a little bit fun." Sophie winked playfully.

"See, you already sound like a designer! Soon enough I'll be having to make appointments to see you at your atelier on Madison Avenue."

"Pshaw. You'll never need an appointment. Especially with that Wall Street salary you're about to have. Anyway, they don't rent space to immigrants up there. Just like they don't really welcome us with open arms where you're going." Sophie opened her eyes wide and looked down at Bea to express her concern.

"I'll be okay," Bea said, warmly touching Sophie's hand reassuringly. "I wouldn't have gotten this interview if they weren't open to people like me."

"I hope you're right. Still, I'm worried. Aren't all the Jewish bankers rich Germans, not Russian like you? Not to mention that they're all men . . ."

"Russian, German, rich, poor, men, women. You sound like my mother. Next thing you're going to tell me my short hair makes me look like my brother."

"I would never! I love your cut—and Jake is much more handsome than you, anyway." Sophie blushed at the mention of Bea's twin. Even though she'd long gotten over her childhood crush, Jake had always held a special place in Sophie's heart. "But really, Bea, be careful. This is a very different world."

"I know it's different. That's what makes it so exciting. And it's not like I'm going to some shady bucket shop full of lechers; it's the ladies' department at J.P. Morgan."

"I know, I know. Well, if this is anything like kindergarten . . . or sixth grade . . . or high school, you'll have the place figured out and everyone in your thrall by lunchtime. If anyone can make that place their own, it's you."

"Now that's what I needed to hear." Bea gave Sophie's hand a tight squeeze. She said her goodbyes to the rest of the Romanos before heading downstairs to show off her new ensemble to her own family. She had only a few minutes before it would be time to walk downtown to the fabled House of Morgan, a place that she was sure would change the entire trajectory of her life. She, Bea Abramovitz, was about to become a real professional broker. She had never been so happy to be alive in the 1920s, when a woman could do anything.

CHAPTER FOUR

Bea thought about Sophie's worries—the same ones she'd been hearing from her mother for months—as she stood in front of the iconic facade of Morgan Bank. Of course, she knew choosing to work in finance wouldn't be easy. Wall Street was still undoubtedly a man's world. But, as she turned to the street to take in the setting for another moment, a last glance at the crowds reassured her she would be okay. The streets were full of women. Scads of them. Sure, most were probably secretaries and receptionists, but some were more. Some had real positions of power at these banks. And if things went as she hoped today, eventually she would be one of them.

Bea climbed the five steps up to the Morgan building's imposing brass-and-glass doors. As she pushed through them and entered the lobby, she let out an involuntary gasp. The building felt like wealth, with its marble floors and grandly ornamented ceiling patterned with hexagonal coffers and crowned by a giant glass dome. The intensity of the street gave way to a hushed din as people bustled about with a directed sense of purpose. A calm frenzy, like the moments on Orchard Street when storm clouds started to move in, and everyone worked as efficiently as possible to restock their wooden carts and get them tucked in under the awnings of the larger shops before the rain diluted the herring or ruined the fresh babka.

Bea scanned the perimeter of the lobby; it was lined with men working behind low walls, and there wasn't another woman in sight.

Finally her eyes landed on a stunning girl, a doll of a female receptionist with blonde hair in a perfectly curled bob, heart-shaped lips painted a deep crimson and pursed coquettishly, hat pinned just so on her head. She was a dead ringer for Lillian Gish, and Bea wondered if she had been plucked from a silent film studio rather than a college classroom. As she stood up to collect some papers, Bea watched her subtly beaded sheath swish around her; she seemed to be dressed more for a night on the town than a day at the office. Bea looked down at her own simple suit: her sensible brown shoes, her ungloved hands. Moments ago she'd thought she was dressed at the height of fashion, but suddenly, she felt all wrong. Compared to this girl, Bea looked like a schoolmarm; she had no sparkles, no strings of beads around her neck, no bracelets clicking on her wrists.

She shook off her momentary self-consciousness. This wasn't about how she looked. It was her brain they were interested in, wasn't it? She walked with only a slightly forced confidence to not–Lillian Gish's desk. "Excuse me, can you direct me to Mrs. Halsey? I have an interview with her at—"

"Your name?" She cut Bea off, her red lips curved into a polite demi-smile as her eyes scanned Bea from shoes to hat.

"Beatrice—Bea—Abramovitz."

"That's a mouthful, isn't it?" She chuckled as she checked her list. "I see an Abram-o-veet-eez? That you, doll?" Bea nodded and was about to explain that the *v* was pronounced more like a *w*, and *tz* was pronounced more like a *ts*, when the girl continued, "Ah, all right then. I'll just ring Mrs. Halsey's office and see if she's ready for you."

Bea stood awkwardly, waiting. Other than the starlet receptionist, she really was the only woman in the lobby. Suddenly she felt a bit like an animal in a city zoo, an oddity placed smack in the center of an entirely unnatural world. Doubt overcame her. Was this a huge mistake? Maybe she was arrogant to think she could make her way here. Maybe she should have stayed in her own neighborhood "with her people."

No. She had landed this interview, and she was going to prove that she had every right to be here. She drew back her shoulders, straightening her spine to stand as tall as her five-foot-one-inch frame would allow. She might be feeling uncertain, but she surely wouldn't show it.

"Miss Abram-o-ve-teeez?" Another gorgeous woman, this one with darker hair in a bright pink chiffon drop-waist dress, came out of seemingly nowhere. *Is this a bank or a dance hall?*

"Yes, that's me. Pleasure to meet—" Bea reached out to shake the woman's hand just as she turned on her heel and started walking.

"Please follow me. Mrs. Halsey's on a tight schedule, so we've got to skedaddle."

Bea followed her through a maze of hallways, trying not to be distracted by the men talking triple time. If she closed her eyes, she might think she was listening to the clipped monosyllabic singing at the jazz club in Harlem she and Sophie had snuck out to once with Jake, instead of walking through the most prestigious financial institution in all of New York.

They rode an elevator to the top floor, where she was led behind a door marked "Ladies' Department." This space was decidedly different from the bank's lobby. It looked like a swanky sitting room in one of those mansions on Fifth Avenue that she'd only ever seen in glossy magazines. Large, upholstered chairs. Settees. Exotic rugs ornately patterned in vibrant jewel tones. A fire in the fireplace. A few women in elegant silk dresses, fur stoles, and sparkling diamonds sat around a glass machine that contained a ribbon of white paper.

"That's the ticker. They're waiting for the trading to start for the day," her guide whispered. Bea realized she had stopped in her tracks, staring.

This was incredible. Stock reports as the trading happened, like breaking news. Bea had only ever seen stock prices in the newspaper, long after they had come and gone. If she had thought about it, she would have realized that brokers would need access to more immediate information, but this was a room where even the clients could see it. She wanted to run over and study the machine, but her escort was moving too quickly.

"And here we are. Mrs. Halsey, Miss Beatrice Abromo-vee-teez, your next appointment."

"Bea Abramovitz," Bea corrected as she strode into the plush office, hand outstretched, shoving it in Mrs. Halsey's face before she even had a chance to stand from her desk. "Thank you so much for meeting with me."

"Quite eager, I see. Welcome, Miss Abr-rom-o—"

"Abramovitz, the sounds all kind of muddle together . . ." Bea flashed Mrs. Halsey her biggest, brightest smile and stood for what felt like an eternity but was more likely a few seconds as Mrs. Halsey read through some papers on her desk. Finally, she looked up at Bea.

"Please, have a seat, Miss . . . How about if I just call you Bea?" She laughed, and Bea nodded with an understanding smile even though she was beginning to feel her blood boil at each subsequent butchering of her name. It had never given any of her professors a problem at school. And in her neighborhood Abramovitz was as common as Smith or Jones would be in a place like this. Yet, somehow, within the sanctified walls of the House of Morgan, everyone approached it like it was written in Cyrillic. She knew that there weren't as many Jews at Morgan Bank as at some of the German Jewish ones like Kuhn, Loeb, and Company, but she had to assume there were *some*.

"So, Bea, you're interested in working in our ladies' department?"

"Yes, yes, I am, indeed," Bea responded. She realized that she may have been a touch too enthusiastic only when Mrs. Halsey's body withdrew into the upholstery of her chair. Bea took a breath and tried to continue more calmly. "I was first in my class at Hunter, graduating with honors in only three years, and even earning an A in applied mathematics. Plus, my independent study with Professor Berkman at City College . . . I am just fascinated by the stock market. I've made hypothetical bets at home with my father for years. My rate of return is excellent. I would have more than tripled my money by now if my investments were real. Of course, I know that true success in the market isn't only about studying the stock fundamentals, but I—"

"Well, Bea, you are clearly very passionate." Mrs. Halsey looked through her as if nothing she had said thus far had even registered. "Before we get into all that, I'd love to hear a bit about your background. You went to the Normal College, you say?"

"Normal? Oh, you mean Hunter. Yes, I forgot for a minute that it used to be named that." Bea nodded proudly until she saw that Mrs. Halsey wasn't asking the question out of respect but derision. Hunter might have been the "Harvard of the working class," but it was still a big step down from the Ivy Leagues and their Seven Sister schools in the eyes of many. Mrs. Halsey seemed to be among them.

"Oh, yes, they did rename it, didn't they? That happened after I was at Vassar."

"Right." Bea thought her cheeks might start to cramp from holding her smile so widely. She wondered if she'd start tap-dancing next. This was unexpectedly awkward.

"Your transcripts are impressive." Mrs. Halsey locked her small blue eyes directly on Bea, making her feel a bit like a mouse caught in the sight of an eagle when the strike was imminent. Somehow what she'd said was not a compliment. "Still, I'm not sure this is the right place for you." Bea felt as if she'd been slapped.

She hadn't been there more than a minute, and all she'd said so far was that she was first in her class and had perfect grades. And she was a woman talking to a woman about working in a department solely for women. Was it really possible that being a poor Jew from the Lower East Side would be enough to prevent Mrs. Halsey from even considering her? This was the 1920s. Women were voting. They were dressing how they wanted to. They were drinking. Dancing all night. Having affairs. She wasn't—well, except for the shorter dresses and bobbed hair—but she knew that some women were. And she'd assumed that, since she got the interview in the first place, the things that might have been against her in the past—being poor, going to a free college, living in the Ghetto—no longer mattered.

Mrs. Halsey made it clear that Bea was wrong as she continued, "I take it you didn't have a coming-out, Miss . . . Bea?"

"Coming-out?"

"You know, a proper presentation to New York society."

Bea recoiled. *This narrow-minded, condescending snob!* Bea was about to jump down her throat, but then she heard Sophie's voice in her head. She needed to stay calm, think before she spoke. This was her chance to make her dream come true, and she wouldn't be baited into ruining it. She also wouldn't make excuses and try to embellish her background to impress Mrs. Halsey. She was a college-educated girl and *more* than qualified to work here. She was meant for this job, and she would prove it. She looked at Mrs. Halsey with a gaze as sharp as the one scrutinizing her across the desk.

"Mrs. Halsey, if I may, I'll answer the question I think you're really asking?" Her interviewer stared back flatly. Still, Bea was undeterred. "No, my ancestors clearly didn't come over on the *Mayflower*, and I did not go to one of the Ivy League's Seven Sister schools. I couldn't pretend I did even if I wanted to—which I don't, by the way. I am who I am.

"But I studied one-on-one for an entire semester with Professor Berkman, and he believes that I have a gift for stock picking. I love numbers. I understand them. I have been balancing the books for my father's store since I was ten, getting the best prices on food for my family at the street market since I could talk . . . If you have a look at my school transcripts, my recommendations, I am certain you'll see that I'd be an asset to this bank." She took a deep breath, trying to remain calm even as she started to feel her face flush with agitated fury. "And as I mentioned before, I am not only a strong stock analyst, but I also have a good grounding in the way other forces affect the market. That is why I am here. *That* is why you should hire me."

"That is all quite impressive." Mrs. Halsey fumbled for a moment to find her words and then continued speaking in a slow and pedantic tone. "But our role in the ladies' department is to bring the bank new business. We are the liaisons between our wealthy female clientele and the rest of the institution. We make sure a certain kind of woman is comfortable, knowledgeable, and well guided in her investment decisions."

"I understand," Bea responded slightly more gently, trying to backpedal enough to turn this around. "And while I may not yet be that 'certain kind of woman,' I am sure I would be great at working with those who are." Her artificial smile was met with a scowl.

"While that might be the case, the most important part of our job is broadening our client base. And that, I'm afraid, requires connections—not calculus. You would be unfairly disadvantaged in a role here without a network in—as you so perceptively pointed out—the Seven Sisters or, at a minimum, membership to one of the Manhattan social clubs." Mrs. Halsey looked out the window, and Bea worried she was about to be dismissed. She felt foolish. She hadn't considered that being an investor meant finding people to give you their money to invest. And, like her, no one she knew had any to spare.

The silence in the room was the thickest, heaviest, most exasperating sound Bea had ever experienced. She started involuntarily tapping her foot as her frustration mixed with anger and panic, a tingling overtaking her body from ankle to crown. She couldn't possibly have reached the end of the line already. She was meant for this, and she wouldn't accept that her only shot was over before it began. "You invited me here for this interview, so you must think I have *some* potential. How about if you give me a month and see what I can do? I'll work for free?"

Mrs. Halsey was looking down at her desk, not acknowledging her, and Bea's heart sank. She felt her nose tingle with impending tears when Mrs. Halsey looked up and spoke again. "I admire your pluck, Bea, and Harold Berkman certainly holds you in very high regard, which is quite an accomplishment." She waved his letter of recommendation in the air, having clearly just read it for the first time. "However, I believe a mistake was made when you were placed into my candidate pool."

She paused and started looking through a pile of papers on the far side of her desk.

"I do have one thought." Mrs. Halsey smiled. Bea could tell she was trying to look kind but, having already shown herself so clearly, Bea knew it was really a smile of condescension. "I think you might quite like working in the wire department. It is a highly mathematical position that requires a keen, quick mind. And, with the market growing every day, I know they are hiring. If you have some time, I can have someone call down and see if they might be able to squeeze you in at some point today?"

Bea wasn't sure what the wire department was, but if it was a professional job at the bank, she'd happily take it. She knew enough to know that the first step was to get inside the door. Once they saw what she could do, she was certain they'd reconsider her up here on the fifth floor. Plus, she didn't want the small-minded Mrs. Halsey to think she could be intimidated so easily.

"That would be terrific. I can wait all day if I must. Mrs. Halsey, I can't thank you enough for giving me this chance. I promise you won't—"

Before Bea could finish, the same stunning brunette in the pink dress who had brought her in was standing at her side, ready to lead her back out.

"Miss Winfield will escort you downstairs, where you can wait until they have a moment to see you. Best of luck."

"Thank you, Mrs. Halsey. Thank you so much!" She put on her most affected and upbeat voice and tried to look back with one more smile, but Miss Pink Dress had already pulled the heavy wooden door shut behind her.

"You know what they say—when one door closes . . . ," Bea started to say. But she was talking to no one, as her chaperone was already halfway to the elevator. ". . . another one opens," she whispered to herself as she stepped inside the small box that would transport her down to the basement.

CHAPTER FIVE

As Bea walked home that afternoon, her usually focused brain was spinning like a dreidel. She couldn't quite make sense of what had happened at Morgan Bank today. She had been offered a job at the wire department (and immediately taken it), but did that make the day a success or a failure? She wasn't going to be a broker. At least not yet. Still, they hadn't thrown her into the administrative pool either. She would be working directly with stocks. That had to be a step toward her ultimate goal, didn't it?

She began to smell the distinctly pungent mix of salty fish, vinegary pickles, and too many people, and then looked up to see Seward Park before her. She was stunned. When had she crossed to East Broadway? She laughed. Wandering around the city oblivious to one's surroundings was usually Jake's department.

Her feet continued to carry her through the thick crowds on Orchard. Here, she didn't need to think—this was home. She smiled at Mrs. Levin haggling over a bag of walnuts. The seller, poor Mr. Klein, didn't have a chance against her fierce negotiating skills; this woman had managed to get at least a penny off every single bushel of apples she had ever purchased from Bea's father, and Lew Abramovitz drove the hardest bargain in town.

Bea had always taken pride in her father's relative success in America. When he and her mother, Pauline, had landed in New York City in late 1903, they were suddenly poor for the first time in their lives. Lew had never been wealthy, but as the son of a college professor, he had lived a comfortable life in Odessa. Pauline, on the other hand, had been truly rich. Her father was one of the biggest grain exporters in the city, and she had lived like an aristocrat in a mansion with a full staff. When Lew and Pauline fled the pogroms to come to America, she'd left behind not just her family but also this life of extravagance. She'd believed it was temporary. She'd been wrong.

The little that Bea's parents were able to bring with them from Odessa didn't go far. But Lew was industrious and immediately went to work, buying and selling basic food staples that he peddled door-to-door, from one edge of the neighborhood to the other. He used their paltry savings to buy his initial inventory and pay for a cot in the parlor of a crowded apartment, where they were one of three newly arrived couples squeezed into the room.

While Lew worked to make something of their lives in America, Pauline struggled to adjust. Their cramped accommodations were a shocking contrast to the stately home where she'd grown up, and Pauline didn't have the same basic skills as most immigrants. She didn't come from the shtetlach like so many of her new neighbors, so she didn't know how to cook, clean, or sew, having had servants to do those things for her. Her relative helplessness made Lew even more determined to succeed, to be able to properly care and provide for his wife. The love of his life. So Lew took more on himself, covering some of the other boarders' expenses in exchange for their cooking and washing for him and Pauline.

Lew knew the first step to success in America was to learn the language, and he held his head high when they placed him, an adult man with a university degree, in a kindergarten classroom with five-year-olds to learn English. It was a free education; besides, what other choice did he have? Thanks to his agile mind, he picked up English quickly and was soon able to discover inexpensive sources for excellent produce that many other immigrants, ones who spoke poorer English, couldn't find. He developed a reputation for the highest-quality produce at reasonable prices—round red apples without a single blemish or bruise, robust cabbages with only purple leaves (no brown scraps on the edges), and even more exotic delicacies, like sweet tropical bananas. His business thrived. Within two years, they had enough money to rent their own three-room apartment, provided they took in boarders to make the rent (and do the household chores). Once the twins were born, Pauline relied on the boarders to help take care of them too. By the time Bea and Jake were old enough to start helping around the house, Lew had grown his business to one of the largest produce stalls on Orchard, and they finally closed their home to others. This was a huge luxury for people like them and a mark of real success. But it was still not enough to compensate for all that Pauline had lost back home. It would never be enough.

Bea and Jake had heard the story of their parents' struggles, their father's triumphs, and his adoration of their mother so many times that they could recite it verbatim. They knew every detail about their mother's opulent life in Russia, when she was a daughter in the "House of Oppenheim," the phrase she would use to describe her family's standing in the Old World. They knew that she had lost not just riches but a baby during the passage to America and that, to this day, these losses undermined her happiness like a shard of glass lodged in her heart. Still, despite her pain, they knew that Pauline was as dedicated to their father as he was to her, and that his optimism almost neutralized her despair. Where she saw sacrifice and compromise, he saw opportunity and hope. Still, the twins were imprinted by her melancholy and grew up believing that, like their father, their duty was to make her happy.

Their history made the fact that Bea just got a job at Morgan Bank an even more significant accomplishment. Now, finally, after all that her parents had lost in Odessa, all that her father had worked so hard for in America was going to lead somewhere special. Thanks to her parents' sacrifices, Bea had landed a job at the most prestigious bank on Wall Street. No, she might not have been hired as a broker, like she wanted, but this was just the beginning. For the first time, she would be bringing in real money. She could truly help her family, and she was certain that, eventually, she'd turn this opportunity into her dream. She had taken the first step on the path to a whole new life.

She arrived at her father's pushcart, parked just a few doors from their building, sweeping up behind him, midsale.

"Yes, Mrs. Mandelbaum," he said in Yiddish, "the potatoes are fresh. No, you won't find any rot at the bottom of the sack."

"Mrs. Mandelbaum," Bea broke in, "are you giving my father a hard time? You know Lew Abramovitz has the best produce in the neighborhood."

"Beatrice!" Her father raised his eyebrows hopefully. She smiled back so widely he knew immediately that she had done it. She had been hired.

"So." He turned back to his customer, who was holding her stern expression in hopes of still getting a bargain. "I'll tell you what, just today, because my *shayna* Beatrice is apparently now a working girl, on Wall Street no less, I'll give you two extra onions with this bag of potatoes. Mind you, I am not doing this because the potatoes are bad, but because I need to pack up for the day and find out all about my daughter's new job. A real *yiddisher kop*, my Beatrice!" Bea blushed as her father patted her on the "smart head" he had just complimented.

Mrs. Mandelbaum walked away smiling at her victory, and Bea helped her father consolidate the items he hadn't sold back onto his cart to bring home. Anything close to rotting would be cooked in the next few days for their own supper, and the rest would be back on the street in the morning.

"Now, Beatrice, tell me everything. They loved you?"

"Well, Papa, I don't know if they loved me, but I got a job." She tried to wipe the smile from her face, but found it was impossible. "When they saw my school transcripts, they decided I would be better for the wire department, which is really just terrific, because that's the center of everything!" Saying this out loud to her father helped Bea to believe it. At the wire, she'd see every transaction that went through the bank, every purchase, every sale; she'd have a complete picture of every movement the bank made in the market and, the more she thought about that, the more she realized that would make her a better investor in the long run. Yes, this was a great opportunity for her, whether it was the one she had started the day hoping for or not. "I'll be taking down and transmitting every single transaction that the bank makes all day long. Every trade. Why I—"

"*Bite red shtatter*, Beatrice! Slower, please. I can't keep up when you speak that quickly in English!" Her father smiled sheepishly.

"Sorry, Papa, why don't I wait and tell you the rest when we get home?"

Bea followed her father to their front stoop and helped him carry his produce up the four flights of stairs to their apartment. When the last of the crates was in the hallway, she threw open the door into the kitchen.

"Say hello to the newest employee of the J.P. Morgan Bank!" Bea yelled triumphantly in Yiddish.

"Beatrice, it's about time. I've had to cook this whole meal by myself. Look at my hands, raw and stained from peeling so many carrots and beets. You're late."

"I'm sorry, Mama. They kept me most of the day, and I stopped to get Papa on my way home. I can help you now."

Bea's mother looked her up and down and shook her head. "No. You don't want to ruin your outfit, and I've done most of it myself anyway." Bea was surprised that her mother had started cooking without her. Maybe Pauline knew that, if Bea was working, things would have to change around the house. "Just set the table so we are ready when Yackie gets home. Any minute now, I hope."

Bea sighed. "All right, Mama. Where is Jake, anyway? Shouldn't he be home by now?"

"How should I know what that brother of yours is up to? Probably out with some of his friends after school. Yackie has so many friends, he is always off somewhere, you know that." She grinned at the mention of her son.

"Well, I have lots of friends, too, Mama, but I still make sure to be home—" Bea stopped herself. She knew this conversation wouldn't lead to anything but yet another petty argument with her mother about how unfair it was that Pauline treated her brother like a prince and Bea like a servant. She'd long learned to ignore it, mostly; anyway, this was a special day. She would be bringing in real money, and that meant she had something more important to do than be her mother's surrogate maid. Nothing Pauline said could change that.

In the room adjacent to the kitchen, where she and Jake slept, Bea changed carefully out of her dress, splashed her face with water from the basin, and then rinsed her hose in it before hanging them above her bed to dry. She smoothed her hat and stuffed it with the scraps of fabric Sophie had given her, so it would keep its shape. Then she slipped on a simple housedress and returned with dishes in hand to place them on the table.

"Well, you got a job? What will they pay you? They do know you are needed at home too?" Her mother peppered her with questions in a mix of Yiddish and Russian. Try as they might to convince her, Pauline refused to even try to speak English.

Bea took a deep breath so she wouldn't get angry. How could she not see what an incredible opportunity this was for Bea? How exciting and special it was?

"What do you think of our working girl?" Lew gave Pauline a kiss as he brought the box of delicate bananas and tomatoes into the kitchen to store for tomorrow.

"I don't know what I think. I haven't heard what she's earning yet."

"Mama, it's a good salary. I'll be able to help pay for things around here and maybe eventually even buy some new things for all of us. But—" Bea paused, watching her mother smile. She was pleased about the money, which made Bea now worry about the backlash that would come from what she would say next. "Mama, the hours will be long.

I'll be working in one of the most important departments at the bank. I won't be able to just leave because it's time to make dinner."

"They expect you to work until all hours in a women's department? I don't believe it." Pauline turned her head, giving Bea a sideways glance. "See, I listen when you tell me things!" She smiled.

"Okay, okay, you listen." Bea laughed. Her mother was teasing, still in a good mood even though she had been the one to make dinner and Bea had just told her she might be left alone to do that more often; this was a good sign. The closest Bea would get to her mother's approval. "You're right, though. I went to interview at the ladies' department, but they thought I was better suited to work the wire."

Bea knew better than to tell either of her parents, but especially her mother, about her morning with Mrs. Halsey. Pauline would never want her to go back to work if she knew that the most prominent woman there wouldn't hire a poor Jew from a public college. Her mother spent enough time bemoaning the life of privilege and prestige she had sacrificed when they came to America. The last thing Pauline needed was one more piece of evidence to support her belief that they would never truly make anything of themselves in this country. Her mother's often-told story began to play in Bea's head:

"We were robbed of our whole lives, just because we are Jewish. Did you know that, in Odessa, we had meals that lasted for hours, course after course, all served by butlers? I never touched a dish except to eat. My dining room walls were covered with important art. By Renaissance masters! I had wardrobes of dresses, drawers of jewels.

"But my parents knew, after the pogrom in Kishinev, that it was the start of something terrible. They worried for our safety—especially with a baby on the way—so they sent us here before the threat came closer and we couldn't leave. So many people were suddenly in a hurry to escape that we didn't even have time to pack proper trunks. We couldn't wait for first-class passage. Instead, we had to travel in steerage, with the vandals! These horrible men would steal whatever they could get their hands on when you slept! All we could take was what the servants could sew into the lining of

the clothes on our backs. And most of that is gone, sold off piece by piece for this little life we now live."

This was their origin story as told by their mother. From riches to rags, the Abramovitzes were now just another poor immigrant family in a Lower East Side tenement. When she finished, Pauline would always go to her mattress and take out the last remaining artifact of the once-prosperous House of Oppenheim—her prized diamond necklace with a flawless emerald in the center. It had been a wedding gift to her from her father, Bea's grandfather, and had become all that was left of Pauline's lost life.

No, there was no reason to tell her parents that today had been anything but a triumph for Bea. Thankfully, her father already saw it that way.

"I'm telling you it is *bashert*. Beatrice at the center of everything at the bank that is, itself, the center of everything!"

"I'm not sure it's that important, Papa. But it's true that all the transactions in the entire bank come through us." Bea felt a rush of joy as she said "us." She was now part of something so big. "And they only hire people who can work with perfect precision at lightning speed, because minutes mean thousands of dollars, and even a tiny mistake could cost the bank." She glowed as she recited almost verbatim what her new boss, Mr. Stanhope, had told her when he finally interviewed her earlier that afternoon. By then he hadn't needed to tell her that, because she'd spent the morning watching the fevered pace at which the department worked. It was exhilarating.

"It sounds like you have found your place, Beatrice. Not that I am surprised, such a clever girl. They would have been fools not to hire you with that brain, those grades, that *punim*." Lew squeezed Bea's cheek like she was a toddler.

"Papa." Bea swatted his hand away, smiling. "Everyone who works there is impressive. It's the top bank in the country."

"Maybe, but I bet none of them can solve equations in their heads as quickly as you."

"I don't know about that either. But I do know it will be hard work. And I can't wait!"

"Well, since she refuses to marry, at least she is going to bring in some money at that house of goyim. And she can help her brother get a job when he finishes school." Bea flushed with anger as her mother spoke. Just because she was a twin didn't mean that she had to share every one of her accomplishments. Her mother never gave Bea credit for anything. *Never.*

"Maybe," Bea said flatly. "Or maybe Jake can get his own job, by himself. He has other interests, other ideas. He—"

"Beatrice, you know these banks are really places for men. Would you try to prevent your brother from being as successful as he could be? Siblings should take care of each other. And their mother."

Bea opened her mouth to speak as her father gave her a pleading look, imploring her to let it go. It wasn't that she didn't want to help Jake, but this was her achievement, her dream. She had worked so hard to gain access to Wall Street, while Jake didn't even want to take a *class* with Professor Berkman. Sophie's mother never expected Sophie to pave the way for her siblings. No, Mrs. Romano encouraged Sophie to go after her goals and did all she could to help her children, working on her garments until her fingers were raw and her eyes bleary, and still finding time to make the most delicious food Bea had ever eaten. Bea knew Pauline had sacrificed everything to come to America, to give them safety, and that it pained her every day. But how did that justify that she was constantly worried about Jake's success and didn't care a lick about Bea's? Bea had managed to do the work all on her own that most wives and children in their neighborhood did together and finish all her coursework—with the highest marks, mind you—in nearly half the normal time. Her reward was that she could use her success to help her brother when he finally graduated? How was that fair?

Her answer came storming through the door, grinning from ear to ear.

CHAPTER SIX

Jake was the family's golden boy, one of those sparkling people who naturally brightened every room. He got the fair hair and blue eyes of their mother's side of the family, while Bea inherited the more typical browns of their father's. He was also surprisingly tall, almost six feet, which was really something since their mother was only five feet tall and their father five foot seven on a good day. Even his nose, made crooked by a run-in with a crate of turnips when he was five, somehow managed to give him character instead of detracting from his good looks.

Bea watched her mother fawn over Jake, taking his books and coat and kissing him on both cheeks. It had always been this way. She remembered the day they came home from middle school with their first real grades, back when she still hoped her hard work would earn the same praise and love from her mother that Jake got without even trying.

"Mama, Mama, I got all As!" She'd waved her report card proudly as she bounced into the kitchen, breathless from running all the way home.

"Beatrice, have some dignity! Don't storm into the house like an animal. I was taking my afternoon rest." Her mother shuffled sleepily into the kitchen. Her midday nap was as precious to her as her diamond-and-emerald necklace. Back then, Bea couldn't understand why they didn't sell it for a lease on a real store for her father, but whenever she asked, she was dismissed.

"Sorry, Mama. But look—my first real report card and all As!" Bea jumped up and down gleefully.

"Terrific! You got good marks. You work very hard. And you're a smart girl. Now"—Pauline smiled, looking at Bea with what Bea thought, for just a moment, was pride, before the expression vanished and her face became serious—"go get some water, please. I need a cup of tea. And you should start dinner soon." Bea looked at her feet to hide the tears of disappointment forming in the corners of her eyes. She placed her report card on the table in front of Pauline. Maybe her mother would look while Bea was getting the water downstairs in the courtyard. Why had she run home anyway? Now she was here before Jake, and fetching water was supposed to be his job. He got out of everything.

Bea fumed as she filled two large pots, carefully bringing one and then the other back to their kitchen. By the time she had settled the second one on the stove, Jake arrived.

"Yaacov, your sister is home before you again. Where were you?"

Good, let Jake get in trouble for once. Bea felt momentarily triumphant.

"She ran, Mama, I walked. I knew you'd still be resting, so didn't think I had to rush. Anyway, her grades are the ones you really want to see. She aced every course." He smiled at Pauline and gave her a kiss on both cheeks; Bea watched her mother instantly soften.

"Sweet boy. I want to see your report card too." Pauline put out her hand.

"All Bs thanks to the best study partner in the family!" He handed their mother his paper proudly and smiled at Bea with genuine appreciation. At least he recognized that she was the reason he was learning anything in school. During the day he was too busy cracking jokes and flirting, so when they were home at night, she taught him everything he hadn't paid attention to that day. She slowly explained equations. She rewrote his compositions. And she didn't mind; in fact, she liked it. It was easy for her. Still, she was glad he didn't pretend that his achievement was all his own. Maybe her mother would recognize her for that, at least.

"Yes, your sister is a smart girl, but smarts aren't everything. Beatrice." Pauline turned to Bea. "Is the water boiling yet? I want my tea."

Bea wanted to tell her mother to get up and get it herself or, maybe, ask her son for a change, when Jake jumped in.

"I'll get it, BB." He was at her side with a mug and the loose tea from the shelf. "You do enough around here," he muttered to her under his breath. And, just like that, her frustration melted away, replaced by appreciation for how lucky she was to have such a great brother. Sure, she did most of the hard work, and he got almost all of the attention, but he took care of *her*. This was just how they worked. And it suited them both just fine. More than fine. It made them both better than they would have been on their own.

"So, BB, did ya land the big job? Your charm and grace get them to open the locked doors of the boys' club to you?" Jake winked at her, teasing. She knew he was proud of her even if, maybe, a bit jealous that she would be the first one to make real money.

"Why yes, Jake, I did get a job. But it wasn't because of my charm and grace. Well, not only because of that," she clarified, never one to let Jake believe he had the monopoly in that department.

"Well, sure, you're a pint-sized genius. They'd be fools not to grab you while you're green. Still, my buddies at City College didn't have the nicest things to say about how the bankers at Morgan feel about people like us, so good for you for proving them wrong."

Bea shot Jake a sharp look. He knew as well as she did that this was not a topic to discuss around their mother. It was never a good idea to reinforce her worst opinions of their world. To give her a reason to launch, yet again, into her story of woe—her once fabulous life that the awful realities of anti-Semitism forced her to leave behind.

Bea felt for her mother. Pauline had given up so much. Bea and Jake wouldn't exist if she hadn't been willing to abandon everything in Odessa. And Bea knew that this was part of why she was so hard on Bea so much of the time, that she was wounded from the devastation of having lost so much. Still, today wasn't a day about the past. It was about the future. And, luckily, before Pauline had a chance to get lost in the despair of her history, Jake changed the subject.

"Looks like this is a double-win day for the Abramovitz twins." Jake took the plates from Bea's hands and set the rest of the table, which made her immediately suspicious. He never helped without being asked unless he needed her support for something he knew her parents would object to. Bea got a funny feeling in her gut, the way she did when Jake was in trouble. She was used to these feelings; they were a twin thing. She caught Jake's eye with concern, but he waved it away, smiling wide enough to reveal the only asymmetry in his face besides his nose, a dimple on the left cheek. "I have an exciting announcement too."

"Oh, Yackie, what is it? An engagement?"

"No, Mama, no engagement."

"Jake can't decide on just one single girl," Bea teased.

"How about we talk about this while we eat?" their father stated more than asked. The fatigue of a day on his feet revealed only by the fact that he was already sitting in his chair at the table.

"Sure, Papa. Let's eat." Jake sat in his usual seat. "You should be sitting down to hear this anyway."

CHAPTER SEVEN

As Jake carried the soup to the table, Bea tried again to get his attention. Usually he would talk to her before telling their parents anything important, good or bad. Or, even more often, he came to her with his wild schemes, avoiding their parents altogether. Like the time he decided he could easily make a quick buck selling bathtub gin and got on the wrong side of Lefty Moskowitz, who was running a large bootlegging operation in their neighborhood. Thankfully Bea had a friend who knew someone who was close with Lefty's cousin and was able to explain that Jake had made an innocent mistake. After she got him out of that jam, Jake had promised Bea there wouldn't be any more dangerous "get rich quick" schemes. So, if he wasn't getting hitched—and she knew he wasn't, because he had been out with three different girls in the past week—what was he up to?

When he finally sat down, she noticed the back of his shirt was wet with sweat. She couldn't tell if he was terrified or elated, because he was at an uncharacteristic loss for words. Jake was *never* nervous. Bea tried to make eye contact with him, to make sure he was okay, but he was staring at his plate. She wished they could go take a walk so she could find out what was going on, but it was too late; they were already at the table.

"Yackie, what? You look pale." Her mother reached across the table and gently patted Jake's hand.

"Funny you should say pale, Mama. Because I won't be for long . . ." He took a deep breath and looked at them with his brightest smile. And then everything he had to say came spilling out in a quick flood of words. "Mama, Papa, BB—I'm leaving. Heading west . . . to California to sell shares in oil mines!"

"California? Oil? How? When?" Lew barked out questions, looking as baffled as Bea felt. Jake was leaving, to go all the way across the country no less, and hadn't thought to tell her before now?

Her parents spoke over each other in confusion, while Bea was overwhelmed with hurt that Jake had kept her in the dark on something so huge. And couldn't he have picked another day to tell them this news?

"You know my friend Tommy? From school? I've told you about him, I'm sure. Anyhow, he's studying to be an engineer—"

"Must be a smart young man," their father interrupted, and Bea watched Jake suppress an eye roll.

"His uncle Mo—well, Maurice, but everyone calls him Mo—is a big deal at this oil outfit, Julian Petroleum. He's making a bundle selling oil mines—says it's the hottest ticket in town. The action is like nothing you've ever seen. Everyone who's anyone in Hollywood is trying to get in, and he can't keep up with the demand. It's like dollar bills are sprouting from the ground." Jake laughed nervously and then continued.

"Anyway, Tommy was telling me about how he's planning to head out west after school to help build the new movie studios, and when I told him I'd love to get in on the action out there, he introduced me to his uncle. He came to town to meet with some potential investors, and while he was here, he let on to Tommy that he was looking to hire a guy who could help him. He needs someone to be his right hand, to help with sales and customer service, someone young and hungry who could learn fast and work hard. Guess who Tommy thought of straight away?" Jake smiled. Bea did not. Neither did their father. "C'mon, Papa. You know I was made for this."

"So, this man wants his nephew to finish school before going across the entire country for a job, but he wants you to walk away from college with only one year left?"

"No, Papa, no. It's not like that. Mo pulled himself up from nothing. He's offering me a once-in-a-lifetime opportunity, and I don't have to do a thing except go along for the ride. I don't even have to pay to get there; we're going to take the cross-country train. First class! And he'll give me a place to live until I'm on my feet. Which he says could be as quick as a month. Can you imagine?"

"First class? Why do you need such extravagance?" Lew's voice was tight with anxiety and confusion.

"Because, Papa, Mo is a big shot, and he wants to make me one too. How do you think he got here in the first place? And when we head out tomorrow—"

"Tomorrow!" Bea finally broke her silence. Her brother was leaving *tomorrow*?

"Yaacov," her father snapped angrily. "You are lucky to have a free education at City College. And your luck will go much further with a college degree. You don't have that much time left at university. How could you not finish? Go with your friend later."

"No, Papa. I don't need a degree and the opportunity is now. Mo says I would be great at this, and the money is there just waiting to be collected. You don't understand how hot this market is. People are clamoring for shares of Julian Petroleum, and I'd get them for *free*. Just for working there! If I wait, I'd miss my chance. Bea is your college graduate. I'll just skip ahead to the part where I bring home the money."

"There is more to success than money, Yaacov. Don't forget about the learning and hard work along the way."

"I will learn. It'll just be from Mo instead of in a useless classroom. And I am a hard worker! Have I not spent every free moment of my entire life selling fruit and vegetables for you? BB?" He turned to Bea, expecting her to help convince their parents. "You know how hard I work. This is about taking an opportunity when it's there for you. Isn't that what you're doing right now at Morgan?"

Bea knew Jake was looking to her to defend his decision, and, if he had told her first, she might have been prepared to. She would, at least, have been able to ask the questions she needed answered to evaluate whether this truly was an opportunity worth leaving everything for, or not. She was so mad at him, so hurt. Still, in this moment he needed her support—that's what they did for each other, stood side by side. Maybe it was because they were twins, but they had always operated like two very different halves of the same whole. One there to balance the other out.

"Well, this sounds exciting, I'll say that, but it's so . . . sudden." She was struggling to put her own misgivings aside in front of their parents, as she ought to. "But oil? What do you know about oil?"

"C'mon, BB." He looked at her, his eyes hurt and pleading. "I'm not some dumb chump. I've been doing my homework. Mo already introduced me to a few of his money guys up here, and they all have friends looking for a way in. Two years ago, Mo didn't know a thing about oil, either, he just knew how to sell. I'm good with people, you know that. It's just that now, instead of selling carrots and turnips, it'll be the future of energy for our country. This is a once-in-a-lifetime chance. I'm telling you I can't lose." He really was born to sell.

Bea stopped herself from saying what she actually thought, which was that she didn't want her brother to risk going so far away to sell something that might just be speculative. These days "get rich quick" schemes were everywhere, and shares in some unseen oil mine sounded like it might just be one to her. She knew her brother was impulsive, especially if he thought it would make him money. Sometimes it worked in his favor, but she didn't know if it would this time. He didn't know anyone in California. Would he end up stranded with no friends or family? Would he have a place to live? A way to get back east to them if necessary?

"I think it sounds exciting, Yackie." Bea's worrying was interrupted by Pauline's enthusiasm. Her mother looked at Jake with a glint in her eye. "Go make us rich again."

"*Shefele*, we have enough. Yaacov will have more success in the long run if he finishes school. And there are plenty of opportunities closer to New York."

"*Feh*. You have a university degree, and where did it get us? Working yourself to the bone hocking fruits and vegetables in the neighborhood. Even with your success we can't afford a proper store."

"Mama!" Bea jumped in to defend her father. "We have always had enough. And I'm working now, so we will have even more."

"Yeah, but if I play it right, we'll have *everything*!" Jake stood from the table, pulling their mother out of her chair and twirling her around the room. "Things are going to change for this family, you'll see. Six months from now I'll have enough money to get you a big store, Papa. A new apartment with separate bedrooms and our own running water. Jewelry. Furs. A maid and a cook! Whatever you want. This is our ticket, trust me."

"Oy, Jake." Bea looked at him askance. He had the tendency to dream too big, and she was worried. "There's so much that you should understand before you go. Who are your customers? What is your competition? And what if you want to come back? How will you get here? We can't afford a train across the country period, let alone in first class." He rolled his eyes, dismissing her concerns.

"Listen, I've been talking to Mo all week. I know enough. This is about gut. Instinct. And everything in me says this is a winner."

Bea shook her head, defeated. She knew once Jake set his mind on something, there was no stopping him. "Sounds like you're going no matter what we say." Never mind that Jake was walking away from his degree; he was leaving her too. What would life be like without her other half?

She looked to their parents, watching Pauline move around the table sheepishly to take Lew's hand in her own. "Lewis, my *muzhik*, I didn't mean that about the store. I just watch you work so hard, and

I want you to get to rest. To have some of what my father did when he was your age. Yackie wants to help. We should let him. You, of all people, know what it feels like to want to try to make your way in a new world."

Lew's face softened. Bea could see that he, too, had acquiesced. "Fine, Yaacov, go chase your fortune. But make me one promise: if it isn't the place of your dreams, you make that Mo pay to send you back home, and you finish school."

"I promise."

Bea could tell by the way Jake was nodding, attempting to be earnest but holding back ever so slightly, that he was making an empty vow. No matter what his family said, he was sure he was going to succeed in California. She just hoped he was right, because he'd be too far away for any of them to help him if he wasn't.

Hours later, after her mother couldn't cry a single additional tear, her father was done repeating the same warnings and admonishments, and everything Jake planned to take was neatly (thanks to Bea) packed in a tattered valise for his departure in the morning, Bea was finally able to talk to Jake alone.

"How could you not tell me?" she yelled in a whisper as she sat cross-legged on her twin bed.

"I wanted to but, well, it happened so fast. And you had your big day. I didn't want you worrying about me."

"You know I am capable of worrying about you *and* still succeeding in an interview, right?"

"Of course." He laughed. "You're *capable* of anything you set your mind to. Still, I wanted you to have your moment all to yourself."

"Really? Do you think that was how it worked out? You know I did get the most important job of my life today, and then you came in and—"

"BB, I'm sorry. I really was trying to time it so that I didn't get in the way. But this morning Tommy told me that Mo was getting ready to leave. If I wanted in, I had to go see him immediately. So I went straight to his hotel—the St. Regis, by the way. I still wasn't sure I'd really go with him. But then I saw this place. The lobby all marble, his room was bigger than our apartment. And he used to be like us. He built all of this in the past two years. Two years! That's how hot this business is. So, when he said he was leaving tomorrow, I said yes. I'm not as smart as you, BB, but I know an opportunity when I see one."

"You're plenty smart, but still—" She took a deep breath. "Suddenly so many people want to own oil wells in California?"

"Ease off, Bea, why do you have to be so skeptical all the time? Can't you ever just trust me?" She looked in his eyes, saw how deeply he needed her to believe in him.

"All right, all right." She threw her pillow at his head. He was such a dreamer. She really hoped this dream would come true for him. "And I'm not skeptical, I'm practical."

"Fine. So, tell me, you liked Morgan Bank, huh?" he asked while stifling a yawn.

"It wasn't exactly what I expected, but—"

"Oh yeah?"

"Yeah, and you can't tell this to Mama and Papa, but the high hat who runs the ladies' department wouldn't even give me five minutes as soon as she realized I was some poor Jew without 'connections.'" Bea rolled her eyes.

"Didn't I warn you?"

"You did, but I figured she invited me to interview, they've created a department staffed entirely by women to serve women, maybe the place is more progressive than it gets credit for? Anyway, it doesn't matter. I still got a job. Tomorrow I'll be an employee of the fanciest of fancy banks, and I will do such a good job in my department that they will be begging me to join them upstairs."

"Well, BB, if anyone can rewrite the rules of the establishment, it's you." He smiled at her with genuine pride. He had always been her greatest champion. "So, while tomorrow you start shaking up the world of Wall Street, I'll be taking to the skies headed to the Great American West. Look at us, how far we've come!"

Her heart fell. Just as she was beginning a new life, she was losing one of the only constants that kept things in balance. How would she do this without her brother to have these late-night talks with? She hadn't thought she would cry, but suddenly she knew it was inevitable.

"Damn you, Jake, I'm gonna miss you. Couldn't you chase your fortune a little closer to home?" The tears were coming fast and heavy now.

"Aw, BB." He crawled next to her in the little corner where their beds met, and put his arm around her shoulders. "I'm gonna miss you too. But I'll write." He turned to look at her, tilting his head down and trying to suppress a smile.

"You, write a letter?" She started giggling. He hated writing almost as much as math.

"For you, I'll do it. For you, BB, I'll do anything."

"Even stay?" She knew it was a lost cause. Determination was one trait that they shared. And it was clear that Jake was resolved.

"There are limits to my generosity."

"I disagree." She hugged him tightly. "Now stop talking to me, we both have big days tomorrow. We need to get some sleep."

Jake pulled the curtain that divided the room, giving them a false sense of privacy, and they climbed into their beds, the frames squeaking and the thin mattresses sagging under their weight.

In near synchronicity, they both rolled onto their sides, backs to the curtain and each other.

"Night, BB."

"Night, Jake."

Bea tried to stay awake, to squeeze every moment out of what might be the last night she and Jake would ever share a room. But she was exhausted from all the excitement of the day, and, within minutes, she was asleep.

CHAPTER EIGHT

March

The wire room at J.P. Morgan felt like a miniature version of the New York Stock Exchange, at least what Bea imagined it to be: loud and frenetic, with data coming in and going out every moment the market was open. There was an organization to the space, with different functions grouped in different areas around the room. Most of the room was filled with rows of telegraph machines and their operators coding and decoding financial information, as this was the primary source of data at the wire. Bea had been disappointed to see that these operators were all men. In fact, the only women there were the two secretaries and three clerks who lined the far wall of the space, and seemed to be responsible for keeping papers organized and supplying bottomless cups of coffee to the men. Behind the women were four small phone booths, a quieter place for the brokers and traders who visited the wire room all day, to call in trades or discuss urgent market shifts with their clients. Finally, at the front, to the right of the door, were the ticker tape machines and the large boards where the latest stock prices and market trends were recorded for all to see. This was the part of the room Bea was most excited about and where she had sat for hours on the day of her interview, in a small chair in the corner, while she waited to meet her new boss, Mr. Stanhope. It had taken all her restraint not to get up and start studying the ticker herself.

Mr. Stanhope hadn't been specific about Bea's role in the department when he offered her a job, so she assumed, since he'd seen the recommendation from Professor Berkman and her nearly perfect transcript, that she would either be at the ticker or the telegraph. She felt like a fool when, on her first day, he gave her a seat in the back and told her that she would be filing order forms and paper records of stock trades. If she had wanted to do an administrative job, she would have tried to do one for someone senior at the bank, someone who might have the authority to eventually help her become a broker. She surely wouldn't have wanted to sit in the back corner of the basement, filing things after they happened. There was so much more she could do.

Bea first realized that she had a gift for numbers when she was eight years old. It was the day before Passover, and her mother had brought Bea to help with the shopping. From the time Bea could walk, it had been expected that she would help her mother with household tasks. Bea resented that she was cooking and cleaning while Jake, being a boy, was allowed to stay outside and play jacks with the neighborhood kids, but Bea didn't mind shopping. She loved the bustle of the markets. She made note of the prices at every stall and played a game of remembering how they changed from one day to the next. Bea didn't realize that, at her young age, it was unusual to remember what things cost, let alone understand what the fluctuations meant.

On this particular day, when she and her mother arrived at the butcher shop on Ludlow, it was already packed with holiday shoppers. Bea took in the lines of women stacked four deep across the length of the counter, all aggressively haggling for the best deal for their own seder meals. The butcher, Mr. Perlmutter, was frantically running meat from the glass counter in the front of the store, to the scale in the back, and then to his adding machine, and again to the front, trying to move his customers along as quickly as possible. He was one of Bea's favorite shopkeepers because he would often sneak her a lollipop, a hugely special treat and one that Jake didn't get, while she waited patiently for him to weigh and calculate her mother's order. Today she wouldn't get any sweets, though. He was much too busy.

Bea saw her mother growing uneasy and overwhelmed as she waited impatiently in line, frustrated by the pushing and the yelling. Bea, on the other hand, was energized by the excitement. The challenge of watching the scale and calculating the prices of each sale before the butcher announced them to the customer thrilled her. She was faster than he was. But she didn't say a word about it, until they finally reached the front of the line and Pauline gave him her order.

"Two chickens, three pounds of brisket, and one lamb shank."

"Ah, Mrs. Abramovitz, I've saved the very best shank for you." Mr. Perlmutter smiled and winked at Pauline. Despite her often-sour demeanor, Bea's mother was a very beautiful woman who took care to pull herself together whenever she went out. She wore her thick, sandy-blonde hair in a loose bun, with wavy tendrils hanging to frame her perfectly oval face. She dressed as well as they could afford, and better than many, because Sophie's mother, Mrs. Romano, made her fashionable outfits from less-expensive materials like imitation silk and velour, in colors that brought out the sparkle in her striking cobalt eyes. Bea noticed that the shopkeepers always worked hard to please her, hoping she would reward them with a smile. It was no different at home, where her father and Jake doted on Pauline like a czarina.

"All right, two and a half pounds." Mr. Perlmutter weighed the shank, and then typed the number into his adding machine. "So that is $1.50, plus the brisket at thirty-nine cents per pound, is $1.56, and the two chickens"—he placed them together on the scale, and Bea could see the wand move to a little over five pounds—"$2.05, so $5.11 total. On your account?"

Pauline had started to nod when Bea jumped in. "Mr. Perlmutter, sorry, but can you check again? I don't—" Bea paused, as the bustle of the butcher shop came to a halt, the eyes of every woman there suddenly on her. She stood taller, her cheeks turning red. "I don't think that's right. You said the shank is forty-five cents a pound, so two and a half pounds should be $1.13, and you're selling the brisket for thirty-nine cents per pound? On Rosh Hashanah it was only thirty-two cents. Why is the price different?" Bea tried to tuck behind her mother, embarrassed, while Mr. Perlmutter humored her and went back to his adding machine, an amused smile on his face. Pauline opened her mouth to chastise Bea for being disrespectful but, before she could speak, Mr. Perlmutter returned.

"Mrs. Abramovitz, you have one smart girl here. She's right. I miscalculated the shank. As for the price of brisket, the Beef Trust has me by the *kishkes*. They're charging more and more every day. I keep the prices as low as I can. As it is I barely make a profit." He leaned closer to Pauline, looking at Bea as he whispered, "But I threw in an extra calf's liver, free of charge, for my favorite customers."

Pauline thanked the butcher and, as she and Bea walked home, started peppering her with questions. Her mother's voice was softer than it usually was after a shopping trip—especially when her arms were full—and she seemed more interested in Bea than was typical. "Beatrice, where did you learn that trick?"

"Trick?" Bea didn't know what she meant.

"Doing those sums so fast. I couldn't do that even with an adding machine, at least not without a place to write it all down."

Bea looked up at her mother, confused. "I don't know." She shrugged. "I just see the numbers." Until this moment, she hadn't realized that what she saw in her head was unique.

"Really? And what about the price of brisket at Rosh Hashanah? That was so many months ago. How did you know that?"

"I remembered," she responded with another shrug.

"But did you write it somewhere and check it before we left?" Her mother stopped and looked at her, a gentle smile stretching across her face. "And what made you even think to compare the price?"

Bea shook her head. "I didn't think about it. I just knew it. It was more than before, and we're trying to save every penny, right? So we shouldn't spend more for the same thing."

"That is very true. We shouldn't." Pauline laughed with uncharacteristic gaiety and then started walking again. "But prices do change for the same thing for all sorts of reasons, just ask your papa."

Pauline patted Bea on the head in a rare demonstration of affection and, even though she was physically weighed down with a basket of trimmings from the butcher, Bea walked the rest of the way home floating on air. Pauline's rarely granted praise made her feel light and giddy. She resolved to keep doing whatever it was that she had done to make Pauline so happy. If only she knew what it was.

It took until her teenage years for Bea to really accept that both the speed with which she could calculate numbers and her precise memory for them was actually the "very special gift" her father had told her it was. But now, as an adult, Bea was not only comfortable with her unique abilities, she was also certain they could help her excel at the bank.

For her first two weeks on the job, she stayed quiet, did her work, and studied every piece of information that she saw. There were clear patterns in how orders to buy or sell stocks shifted based on the fluctuating stock prices on the boards (which came from the ticker), and she longed to be closer to the front of the room, where the data was actually coming in.

"Sure wish I could get a look at that ticker tape while it's hot off the reel, don't you?" she asked, by way of making small talk, to one of the other lady clerks. She was an older woman, and she held her finger in the air at Bea, indicating that she wouldn't respond until she finished what she was doing.

"Sorry, sweetie. Things move too fast in here for chitchat. I had to get these slips in the right client folder before the next paper dump hit my desk. Now what was that? Something about the ticker? We sure are lucky to be back here, where at least we can take an hour for lunch or a few minutes to powder our noses. Can't imagine how those guys do it."

Bea's heart sank. She had hoped to at least find like-minded colleagues in the other women at the wire, but each conversation she attempted had the same result. All the other gals in this room were either there looking for a husband or older women who needed a paycheck. They all seemed too frazzled by the pace of their work to have a moment to socialize, nor did any give the slightest indication of wanting to do more than they were doing. Bea, on the other hand, was bored. She could be much more useful to Mr. Stanhope and the bank overall if he'd let her; plus, she'd never become a broker if she stayed back here as a file clerk. She set a new goal: she would show Mr. Stanhope what she was capable of and get put on the ticker or the telegraph as soon as she could.

Her opportunity came unexpectedly a few weeks later. Scotty, one of the traders (she knew his name because the other girls talked about how they wished he wasn't the one always downstairs with them, his rotund shape, receding hairline and perpetually red face made him an unappealing prospect for marriage), stuck his head out of the booth and screamed: "Joe, what's Texas Oil at now? How much did it go up since open?"

Bea watched the board boy in the front of the room scramble through the rolls of tape to find the number Scotty needed.

"Joe? D'ya hear me? I need this now, right now. I—"

Bea knew the number Scotty was looking for; it had been on the board thirty minutes ago, which, to be fair, was like a week when numbers were coming in every second. She also saw that Joe didn't know, nor could he find it. Timing was critical in the market. She didn't want Scotty to wait. So she took a chance.

"It last hit the tape at forty-eight dollars, up 0.76 percent since market open and 0.96 percent since last night's close," she said quietly to Scotty. She didn't want to make poor Joe feel worse.

"What's that?" Scotty shouted at her. "What'd ya say?"

Bea repeated herself with more assurance and watched Scotty's face turn from panic to triumph, the tendons in his neck relaxing and the color returning from red to a soft beige. "Yeah." He smiled. "That's right. Thanks, doll."

"No problem," Bea said to no one. Scotty had already closed the door to the phone booth and continued his call.

Although she'd liked the momentary rush of being in the middle of the action, Bea thought that was the end of the incident. But when the market closed that afternoon, she discovered it was just the beginning.

"Bea." Mr. Stanhope was standing above her, looking serious. It was the first time he had spoken to her since her interview, weeks before. "I understand you had an interaction with one of our traders today?"

"Yes, sir. Well, I just . . . he needed a stock price and—"

"And you miraculously knew it off the top of your head?"

"Yes, Mr. Stanhope, I did. You see, I tried to explain to you at my interview I have what some people think is an uncanny memory for numbers."

"And the changes, you knew those too. Those weren't on the board."

"No, but I can also make calculations like that in my head." She watched Mr. Stanhope's brow unfurrow as he began to take in what she was saying. He ran to the front of the room and got some discarded ticker tape and started quizzing her about the prices of stocks that were in the Dow. The ones that would have been recorded on the board that day. She started to grow hopeful after she correctly remembered the fifth price, and she watched a perplexed smile grow across his face.

"Well, Bea. This is quite a talent you have here. I wonder, do you think you could keep track of all of this if you were working up front, helping the boys at the board with the ticker?"

"Absolutely!" Bea nodded so enthusiastically she realized she might look like a floppy puppet in a five-and-dime with her head moving so much. "I would love to watch the ticker, Mr. Stanhope. In fact, I was planning to talk to you about whether it might be possible for me to move up there. You see, I came to J.P. Morgan to be a broker and—"

"A broker," Mr. Stanhope started to bellow and looked around to see if anyone else in the room had heard Bea. "Surely you know that's not possible. You're a girl."

"Yes, but—"

"But we *can* make better use of a mind like yours down here. Starting tomorrow, you'll be up front. I'm sure the other girls can manage the filing without you."

Bea was thrilled. The opportunity she thought she would have to work for months to even have a chance to ask for had landed right in her lap, simply because she told Scotty a stock price. Sure, she didn't like Mr. Stanhope's dismissal of her ultimate goal, to become a broker, but she didn't pay it much mind. So far she found that every time she was dismissed, she managed to prove her detractors wrong. Why, a few weeks ago, he thought all she could do was file. She was sure that in a few months, if she worked hard enough, Mr. Stanhope would be personally escorting her back upstairs to the ladies' department, where Mrs. Halsey would welcome her with enthusiasm, realizing she'd made a big mistake.

CHAPTER NINE

May

Bea had been working for nearly three months and, this morning, as she moved through the congested streets of the financial district toward "the corner" (as she had learned the intersection of "Broad" and "Wall" was called by brokers), she bobbed and wove between the cars and people, like she'd always been here. Bea marveled at the fact that the rhythm of the crowds had initially seemed unusual to her; it had already come to feel so normal. So, when she stopped in the middle of the foot traffic to quickly look at her new wristwatch (a gift to herself after she received her first paycheck), she shouldn't have been surprised to be shoved out of the way with such force that she spun right around on her heel and nearly fell over. But she was.

"Hey, watch it!" she snapped.

"Sorry, doll. But this is Wall Street before the market opens, hardly a place for taking in the sights."

"Sightseeing? I'm on my way to work, just like you." She paused, fixing herself as she waited for his apology.

"My mistake. Didn't take a doll like you for a working girl." *How belittling.* She pursed her lips and turned to face him head on, so she could tell him just what she thought of his assumptions, but, as she brought her large brown eyes up, up, up to meet his, her words all but disappeared. She knew she had a weakness for a man in a suit, but this wasn't just any man. Square shoulders. Thick, dark wavy hair. Rich brown eyes, swirled with gold like the cat's-eye marbles she and Jake used to play with.

Her tongue suddenly turned to muslin in her mouth, and she stood, frozen, like a streetlight, as a second man catapulted her out of his way and into the first stranger's chest.

She bounced off him like he was a live wire.

"Sorry. I'm usually more stable on my feet." She looked down, overcome with embarrassment. He smelled divine.

"I'd think so, being so close to the ground and all." A wry smile spread across his face, revealing unnervingly straight white teeth. "You better get inside to safety, and I need to get to my desk, or I'll be out of a job. Pleasure to run into you, Miss . . . ?" His hypnotic eyes looked at her searchingly, and time seemed to stand still, even as she felt the energy of the street all around her.

"Abramovitz, Bea Abramovitz. I work at J.P. Morgan. At the wire." The flood of words came out in almost a whisper, very unlike her usually loud voice.

"Well, little Bea, I hope you're not the stinging kind." He tipped his hat and began to turn away before pausing and looking back. "The wire, huh?" Bea nodded. "Now that's something ya don't hear every day." He winked, grinned, and before Bea remembered she hadn't gotten his name, he was gone.

Bea stood breathless, her cheeks flushed, her heart pounding. This was ridiculous. It wasn't as if this was the first attractive man she'd ever met. So why had this guy rendered her speechless? And why, as she entered the bank to start her day, was she silently praying that she would bump into him again?

Bea allowed herself to indulge this frivolous thinking for the three minutes it took her to ride the elevator downstairs, and then she expunged the mysterious stranger from her mind.

Since Bea had moved up front near the tickers, the pace of her job during market hours was unrelenting. In addition to the constant updating of stock prices from the ticker, purchases, sales, transfers, and trades came across the telegraph by the second, and everything needed to be recorded immediately. From the opening ding to the final bell, there wasn't a moment for anyone to think about anything except documenting the information that was flowing through the room in a constant stream. Bea now understood why Joe, the board boy, had no idea the price of Texas Oil that day a few months ago. For most of the men in the wire room, it was natural to forget the numbers they wrote down seconds after they were recorded. They were stenographers, documenting and transmitting information, and it came much too fast to analyze it. Bea, on the other hand, remembered almost everything.

This morning sped past for Bea as she fell into her usual routine of dictating numbers from the ticker and the changes she calculated in her head to the board boys to write down; once every thirty minutes, she'd walk through the telegraph operators to collect their slips (and try to decipher the codes they were using) before depositing them to the women in the back to file. Any trader who happened to be in the room and needed a quote now knew to ask Bea. She always had the numbers at the ready. After the boys in the front of the wire room got used to Bea's presence, she became something of a mascot to them. In addition to being the only female in their ranks, she was also known as both the fastest and most accurate in the department.

The wire was the beating heart of the bank. Not only did they see every fluctuation of every stock traded on the exchange through the ticker, but they also chronicled every movement J.P. Morgan and its clients made in the market. Bea knew that this combination of information was invaluable. She just wasn't yet sure how to use it. In the first few weeks in her new role, the day's prices and trades would run through her head at night, keeping her up as her mind worked to tame the unwieldy streams of numbers. Bea was certain this data would give her an edge as a stock picker that might, eventually, earn her that place in the ladies' department. But she needed to see everything laid out in front of her to do more formal analysis. So she started to write it all down.

Bea got an hour each day for lunch, time she used to record and analyze the day's data in her little black notebook. The other girls at the wire never seemed to eat when she did, so she'd sit alone at a quiet table in the women's lunchroom, eating whatever small meal she had brought from home, and studying her data. Whenever she noticed an interesting trend or pattern, she'd make a note of it; she had even taken to graphing some of her observations. There was another gal who sat at the opposite end of her table with her head always in a book, and Bea had come to feel like they had a quiet companionship, even though they had never spoken. That all changed today.

Bea was puzzling over the fact that the market was weaker than it had been last month, flipping back to the same time period of the previous month in her notebook to see if she could understand why, when she was startled by a booming hello.

"So, what gives? You don't believe in chewing the fat at lunch?" Bea looked up to see a gorgeous young woman standing in front of her. "Hi, I'm Henrietta. We haven't really met yet." She smiled and put out her hand to shake Bea's. "Henrietta Brodsky. But you can call me Henny, everybody does."

Bea had seen Henrietta the first time she ventured on her own into the lunchroom. She was shocked, because she was sure she was the famous heiress to Brodsky's department stores, and Bea had no idea why she'd be at Morgan Bank. Henrietta's family was one of those aspirational Jewish success stories that everyone in the neighborhood talked about. She was a second-generation Jew; her father, Mordechai, had been born in this country and raised in the garment trade, eventually starting his own clothing store, which had expanded to become one of the biggest chains in New York. The Brodskys had moved out to Queens, where they supposedly lived in a house with a yard, multiple bathrooms with tubs and toilets, a bedroom for every kid (three in total), a maid to do the cleaning, and a cook.

Henrietta had no reason to work. She could have had a pampered life married to some successful man who wanted nothing more than to take care of her based on her family's reputation alone. Plus, she looked like a teenage boy's fantasy: lustrous auburn hair, plump full lips, and curves that even the fashionably shapeless drop-waist dresses she always wore failed to hide. And she wasn't all looks or money. She had gone to Barnard, which meant that she was both one of very few Jewish girls to come from a family who could afford to pay for college instead of needing to rely on the free public education at Hunter, and she was very smart.

"I . . . I know who you are, of course. Your family's famous in my neighborhood." Bea blushed as she stuttered her answer, embarrassed that she had yet to exchange much more than a smile with Henrietta, even though they had been eating lunch in the same room for two months. "I'm a dolt that I haven't introduced myself yet. The days are just so busy . . . time has slipped away from me. I'm Bea, Bea Abramovitz." Bea put out her hand to shake Henrietta's and was pulled up to stand.

"Nice to finally meet you. Now c'mon outside with me. Let's grab a ciggy. Even a cactus needs fresh air."

"I'm a cactus?"

"Well, I hope not, doll, but so far you're all prickers and spikes. At least Miss Milly over there has her book as an excuse." Henrietta tilted her head toward the quiet girl sitting at the other end of Bea's table, who was, as usual, hunched over a book. "Mildred Wentworth, this is Bea Abramovitz. I've decided the three of us are going to be friends."

Bea had heard the women in the wire room whisper about Mildred. She was a real upper-crust kind of girl. Grew up in Manhattan and Newport, went to Bryn Mawr. Her family purportedly had a key to Gramercy Park. She seemed like a perfect candidate for the ladies' department, if she were to work at all but, instead, she seemed to have some sort of clerical job. Bea had no idea why.

Well, she had an inkling; there was something slightly off about Mildred. Awkward. She was nearly six feet tall and clearly uncomfortable about it. She had terrible posture, rounding her spine downward, like a sunflower when there is no sun. Then, even though she clearly had expensive clothes, she always somehow looked like she had slept in what she was wearing the night before. Not that Bea cared how Mildred looked, she just couldn't get the pieces to add up. Truth be told, she hadn't spent much time trying. From the moment she'd started working, she had been so preoccupied she kind of forgot about making friends. Mildred would have been a lost cause anyway, as she seemed excruciatingly shy. Bea had accidentally caught her eye at the lunch table a few times, and Mildred always looked away before there was a chance for Bea to speak.

Clearly Henrietta didn't let that stop her. She hooked her arm in Bea's, dragging her to the other end of the table, where Mildred sat.

"C'mon, Milly, whaddya say?" Henrietta released Bea's arm and rested her elbows on the table in front of Mildred, staring up at her like a curious cat. "Come grab a gasper with me and Bea."

"Oh, um, I don't know, Henrietta." Mildred looked from the pages of *The Great Gatsby* and then turned away nervously. "A gasper?"

"A ciggy . . . you smoke, don't you? You've been working here even longer than Miss Bea's Knees, and you never leave the building. Why not make today the day—the lunchroom misfit trifecta?"

Bea was surprised to hear Henrietta lump herself in with Mildred and Bea. Bea was certain Henrietta typically ate at the tables across the room, where the gorgeous girls from steno and reception sat gossiping all hour long. Although, come to think of it, the first day she noticed Henrietta she, too, had been sitting alone.

"Oh, goodness, I don't know. I usually just read during lunch, I—" Mildred was chewing on her nail nervously.

"C'mon, sugarplum, your brain works better with a little fresh air. How 'bout this—if you don't want a smoke, we can make a quick trip to the soda shop. Wouldn't you rather be out in the real world tasting the best egg cream this side of Madison Park than reading about some party in West Egg?" Mildred shrugged. It looked to Bea like she'd actually prefer the latter.

"Hi, Mildred," Bea said gently. "I haven't properly introduced myself yet. Bea Abramovitz." She stuck out her hand, and Mildred took it tentatively. "I've been sitting with you at this table for the past two months. I'm awfully sorry that I haven't thought to do this before now. But Henrietta's right—it's about time we girls get to know each other. So c'mon?" Bea wasn't used to being a "misfit," and she surely didn't see Henrietta as one. But she'd already established that she had nothing to talk about with the other ladies in the wire room, and she was intrigued by Henrietta and Milly. Anyway, a girl needed allies, especially in this man's world.

"That's the spirit, Bea's Knees!" Henrietta cheered. "C'mon, Milly, I promise we'll be more entertaining than Mr. Fitzgerald's flappers and philanderers."

"Well . . . I guess . . . all right." Mildred sounded tentative but smiled appreciatively before putting in a bookmark to save her page. She bumped her elbow on the side of her chair as she went to put the book away in her leather satchel, and then smacked her knee on the edge of the table as she stood up.

"Honey, you're quite a klutz! Looks like I'm gonna have to teach you both a few things." Henrietta winked as she linked arms with Bea and Mildred and steered them past the clusters of chatting girls, to the elevator and out the door.

"Will we be able to go there and be back in thirty-five minutes?" Mildred asked anxiously. They got only one hour for lunch, and it was already well underway. Bea was glad she hadn't been the one to look like the stickler for the rules, even though she had been thinking the same thing. Well, that, and also wondering how much an egg cream was going to cost on this part of Broadway; she was trying to save every penny to help rent a proper store for her papa. She didn't really have the money to spare on frivolous treats like this.

"Of course, Silly Milly. This is Wall Street, everyone's in a rush. They'll have us in and out in a jiffy, don't you worry your pretty little pout." Mildred's cheeks turned crimson as she grinned, awkwardly adjusting her glasses. Bea wondered whether anyone had ever told her anything about her was pretty before.

Henrietta led the girls down a small alley to a soda shop. When they got inside, the crowds seemed to part in her path as she sidled up to the counter, revealing three stools, where the girls all sat down. Henrietta then waved to the waiter and ordered them all egg creams and slices of lemon meringue pie, before declaring that it was all her treat. Bea tried to insist on paying her way but, much to her relief, Henrietta wouldn't hear of it.

With the pie and drinks ordered, the three girls sat in a brief awkward silence. Mildred started folding her napkin into some sort of bird, and Henrietta looked into her handheld compact as she reapplied her red lipstick. *Why did she need lipstick to eat?*

"All right, so, where d'ya gals work?" Henrietta asked once her lips were coated in crimson.

"Um, Morgan Bank, where we were just in the women's lunchroom?" Mildred looked at Henrietta, perplexed.

"I think she means what department." Bea smiled, trying to sound kind instead of teasing. "I'm in the wire room."

"The wire, you must be really fast with numbers," Mildred said, a bit of awe in her voice. "I'm in the library."

"Seems like we're all over the place, the three of us."

"Where are you, Henrietta?"

"Call me Henny, please! Don't cha know? I'm the secretary for Mr. Driscoll."

"Wow." Mildred's jaw dropped open. She was even more in awe at this.

"Who's Mr. Driscoll?" Bea asked. She still didn't know the names of most of the bank's executives. She was much more interested in the companies they traded than the men themselves.

"Mr. Driscoll is a vice president at the bank. All the top boys work for him."

"You must learn so much being there where they are making the decisions. Does Mr. Driscoll have his own ticker?" Bea asked enthusiastically.

"Of course." Henny rolled her eyes. "When he's in meetings, I have to record what's coming out of the darn thing. What a bore."

"A bore? I think the ticker is amazing. We get to watch the stock prices across the whole market as they're moving! Although this month has been a little soft. Have you noticed? April was so strong and—" Bea spoke in a speed befitting of the nickname the boys in the wire had given her: "Lightning."

"Well, April was up a bit from March, but still down from the prior months. But the Dow looks like it's pacing to be flat for May," Mildred said matter-of-factly.

"Yes! I just calculated that before we left," Bea exclaimed, excited to have someone to talk to about this. "If automobile companies keep pace, they should offset losses in railroads. And the way things are moving right now, they will."

"How do you know that? I thought only the library and the chart room had that information?" Mildred asked, surprised.

"Oh, I keep my own notes. I—"

"Forget how you know. Why do you care?" Henrietta giggled and took a big slurp of the foamy egg cream in front of her.

"What do you mean? It's our job." Bea was confused.

"Not really. Our job is just to do what they tell us to do," Mildred said. "I save important information for later in case someone needs it. And you"—Mildred turned toward Bea—"take down what happens so the bank has a record of it. What you're doing is analyzing what you see. That's what the boys in Mr. Driscoll's department do. The brokers and the salesmen. Well, and the women in the ladies' department. I like that too." Mildred was nodding animatedly as she spoke. "That's where I wanted to work, but my father said I was too awkward for that job. So I'm here in the library instead."

"Really? The ladies' department didn't want me, either, but I thought you'd have been a shoo-in. Apparently you can't be awkward or poor up there." Bea laughed and suddenly felt an unexpected solidarity with Mildred. "Not that you're awkward, Mildred—sorry." Bea blushed.

"I'm sure they would have taken Miss Mildred Wentworth, but whyever would you want to go, Milly? What fun is the ladies' department? I'd much rather get to talk to the fellas and not have to worry about all that nonsense."

"What nonsense?" Bea wondered.

"You know, spending all day taking care of rude women with their noses in the air, thinking they're better than us just because they are Daughters of the American Revolution or something." Bea's eyes grew wide as Henny said this, and she motioned toward Mildred. "Sorry, Milly, I didn't mean you."

"But the fun is in the analysis. Don't you like the analysis?" Bea said innocently, Mildred nodding along on the other side of Henny. "Isn't that why you work at a bank?"

"Not really. I could have done analysis for my father; he wanted me to marry his partner's son, would have 'let' me keep the books for one of the stores, even said I could do some of the buying eventually. No. Thank. You." Henny shook her head so violently her hat nearly fell to the ground. "This Hen doesn't want to be a mother or a wife just yet. Nope! I wanted to be here in the new center of the world. Don't cha know, gals? The Wall Street boys are the ones to watch. Good to be able to bump into them all day with purpose, right?"

"I try to avoid bumping into anyone," Mildred said nervously. "And it takes effort because I'm not the most coordinated. A few days ago, my driver had to drop me a block from the office because the street was so crowded, and while I was walking toward the bank, I tripped and nearly fell on my face. Like one of those comedy actors on Broadway."

"I don't mean actually bumping into, Silly Milly. I'm just saying when I do get hitched, I want to land a banker for a husband. A real modern guy."

"Oh." Mildred suddenly looked sullen. "Oh right. I don't really think much about marriage. Haven't had much luck with men. My best prospect so far has been Montgomery Arlington, and he's three inches shorter than I am and always smells like gunpowder. For now I'd rather be alone. I have my books to keep me company."

"And now you have us!" Henny put her hand on Mildred's kindly. "And everything you're saying is ridiculous. When you want a husband, the boys'll be banging down the door. You just need a little . . ." Henny looked at Bea for help with the right word.

"Modernizing," Bea said.

"Mother says the modern style is garish," Mildred spurted out and before looking at Bea and Henny. "I mean, on you both it looks lovely. But me . . . I'm not the type who can pull it off."

"Phooey. I'll take you shopping. You'll see," Henny offered warmly.

"I have a friend who is a wonderful seamstress," Bea jumped in, realizing that this could be great for both Sophie and Mildred. "I'm sure she'd be happy to make you a whole wardrobe . . . if you want."

"Oh wow. Um, maybe? Mother typically takes me to her ateliers, but . . ."

"What fun! C'mon, doll, a makeover would be good for you! Starting with your name. From this moment forward, we will call you Milly. Yes, it's perfect!" Henny clapped. "Henny, Milly, and Bea—the Morgan girls three!"

Lunch was over before it had begun, and as Bea and her new friends walked back to the office, her mind was whizzing. She felt connected to Henny and Milly in a different way than she had with any of the girls at Hunter. These were women on the forefront of the new world, like her. She was excited. This was surely yet another sign that Wall Street was where she was meant to be.

CHAPTER TEN

June

"All right, Queen Bea—I don't see a ring on your finger, which means you don't have some boy from the neighborhood waiting to take you down the middle aisle. So how come you never hit the town with me?" Henny was standing at Bea's desk, holding the hand of a squirming Milly, who gazed pleadingly at Bea through her bloodshot blue eyes. "Milly's finally agreed to come out, so you really can't say no tonight!"

Bea smiled brightly at her friends as her mind searched for a reasonable response. Lunch for the three of them had become a regular thing but joining Henny for one of her many nights out on the town was entirely different. First, there was the fact that when Bea wasn't working, she had to be helping at home. As it was, once the market closed, she was racing to finish up her notes so she could get back before disappointing her mother by being late, yet again. Then there was the etiquette of the thing. Bea was expected to stay close to home, go out with boys her parents knew from the neighborhood. The only time she had ever gone anywhere even remotely adventurous was with Jake, who her parents felt could serve as a chaperone. And since he was across the country, she didn't have that option. Pauline and Lew still let her out occasionally if she was with Sophie, and if Pauline thought it might lead to marriage.

Lately, the target of Pauline's attempted matchmaking was Gerald Melnikoff, the "son" of Melnikoff and Son Appetizings. Bea and Sophie had known him since they were in pigtails, and he seemed to get only more boring the more time he spent on the planet. When they were kids, he used to spend hours trying to engage them in discussions about the way ants built homes with grains of sand, and now he exhibited equal passion for the various ways to cure a herring (he favored pickled, Bea creamed; Sophie thought they were both equally disgusting and suggested they try anchovies instead). Bea had recently agreed to go to one dance at the neighborhood hall with Gerald because Sophie had a date with her longtime crush Sal Delvecchio and begged her to join, but there was no way she was going to marry the man. Right now she didn't want to marry anyone.

She liked the idea of going out with her new friends, but three girls alone? It just seemed so scandalous.

"I'd love to. I mean, it would be swell to go out. But without an escort?"

"Escort!" Henny nearly dropped the lipstick she was reapplying. "Who are you, Bea Abramovitz? And what year is it anyway? Nineteen twenty-six. That's what year it is. And you come to work every day at the House of Morgan. In what world do you need an escort to spend a little time with your coworkers?"

"I had the same discussion with her ten minutes ago, Bea. You might as well give in now," Milly cautioned quietly.

"Well . . . where are you going?"

"Tonight we'll start at Chumley's. That's where the brokers like to go on Thursdays to 'mix it up with the artists and poets,' which works out swell for me, because I can change my getup, since I live right around the corner. Hey, I might have something for you too!" She looked Bea and Milly up and down, kindly but also making clear that their outfits weren't ideal for a night on the town.

"You live in Greenwich Village? By yourself?" Bea was stunned. She couldn't believe that she didn't know this already, either from their lunch conversations or from the neighborhood gossip. She was also green with envy. *How had Henny managed to get her parents to let her move out on her own?*

"You bet, honey." Henny giggled. "Well, I have two roommates—both thoroughly modern girls like us." Bea warmed at her words, being included in Henny's "us" made Bea even more determined to live up to her image of Bea. "In fact, one of 'em dances for Mr. Ziegfeld, so sometimes we end up at the Follies. C'mon! You gotta join us. It'll be such a hoot. Please? Do a gal a favor." Henny dramatically pouted and fluttered her heavily mascaraed lashes at Bea.

"Does that usually work?" Bea asked, laughing.

"Every time." Henny smiled. "At least with guys, they are so easy to manipulate. How d'ya think I got my papa to let me leave Queens and move to Greenwich Village!?"

"I was wondering about that, actually. Especially as I'm sitting here trying to figure out how I would even explain to mine where I was tonight . . . if I do go with you. Now that my brother moved away, he and Mama won't let me past Hester Street, except for work."

"I hear you, sweetie, but you just need to tell them to get with the times. If we women can vote, surely we can handle ourselves at a supper club or hooch joint!"

Bea considered Henny's point. She agreed with her—of course she did—but Bea was raised with a more traditional view of the world. Yes, her parents supported the suffragists and encouraged Bea to go to college, but that was where their progressiveness stopped. She had never considered that her dates might be unsupervised. Or that she might even meet a guy whom her family didn't already know. But hadn't she already started to change? She was working on Wall Street, surrounded by men. She was making her own choices. And if she really wanted to be a modern girl, she should be living a modern life outside of her job too. Shouldn't she?

"How 'bout this?" Henny's eyes, the color of perfectly golden-browned latkes, gleamed like a tiger setting sight on its next meal. "You come to Chumley's for just a little while—this time—and I'll make sure you get an escort back home before dark, or I'll bring ya myself. But, next time, you're coming to the Follies!"

"You make it sound so easy. I don't think you understand my parents."

"Or mine," Milly chimed in, seeming to sense an opening that might let her off the hook.

"Beatrice Abramovitz and Mildred Wentworth, it is time you both live a little. You're adults. Make your own decisions. All work and no play makes for one dull life!"

Bea looked at Milly and could see that part of her really wanted to go. Bea did too.

"Okay. I'll go . . . but just for an hour or so." Bea didn't want to press her luck at home.

"I'll take it!" Henny clapped her hands gleefully.

When the "Morgan girls three" stepped outside of their building, Milly tripped over herself as she stopped in front of a dark blue Cadillac parked on the corner, where a man in a driver's uniform was standing outside like a statue. "Oh my, I forgot about my car." She blushed. "Maybe I should just—"

"Don't even think it, Milly! You're coming with us, and that is the end of that. We can easily squeeze into this back seat like a bunch of sardines, and then your driver can take us all. Bea, have you ever been driven by a chauffeur before?" Henny raised her eyebrows enticingly.

"Ha! No one in my neighborhood has a car, let alone someone to drive it!" Bea said with a giggle as she shook her head.

"If you're really okay to squeeze?" Milly was so sweet. Bea wanted to give her a hug.

"More than okay! It will be part of the adventure."

As she and her friends drove off into the night, Bea thought about the morning, just a few months ago, when a chauffeur had come to pick up Jake to bring him to the train for his journey to California. He'd already written her twice and, if he was to be believed, his life out west was exceeding his wildest expectations, complete with lots of illicit alcohol and girls galore. If he could enjoy everything about his new life, there was no reason why she couldn't too.

CHAPTER ELEVEN

Bea had been to a real speakeasy once before, with Jake, but that was the one behind Ratner's Delicatessen so, while it had felt scandalous and a little dangerous, she still had a sense of comfort knowing if there was a raid her family's apartment was only a few blocks away. Tonight was different.

First, there was Henny's place. Bea wasn't sure what she had expected but, based on what she knew about Henny's childhood home, she had pictured something slightly more refined than what she saw when they entered. This seemed like some sort of flapper sorority house.

"Oh my, are those—" Milly whispered to Bea as she pointed to the garters and brassieres hanging on lines that crisscrossed the kitchen ceiling like party streamers.

"They sure are." Bea nodded, smiling in surprise. "Forget having Sophie make you a wardrobe, Milly, this kitchen has everything you'd ever need and more!" Bea walked to the rolling racks tucked in the small space between the stove and the washbasin. They were overstuffed with a rainbow assortment of dazzling dresses. The stove itself was stacked with accessories: hats, feather headbands, gloves in every color, and strand after strand of beads. "Where do you suppose they do the cooking?" Bea asked Milly as they both looked on, wide-eyed.

"Cooking? There will be no cooking in here," Henny decreed playfully. "Welcome, dolls, to the Greenwich Village outpost of Brodsky's department store."

"This is nothing like Bonwit Teller," Milly marveled as she moved tentatively toward the clothing.

"Get in there and have a look!" Henny laughed. "They aren't gonna bite you, Milly. Ooh, look at this one—" Henny pulled out a bright blue sleeveless dress with a beaded silver fringe. "This would be perfect for you."

"For me? I couldn't . . ."

"Why not? That's what these are here for."

"But they're yours. And . . ."

"They aren't really mine; a lot are from the girls' old Follies costumes . . . or gifts from patrons of the show. But we all share them." Henny winked as she sorted through the racks. She was taller and curvier than Bea, and shorter than Milly, yet she managed to pull out multiple dresses for each of them to try before she stripped down to her underthings to put one on herself.

"Whaddya say, will this do for tonight?" Henny looked the part of a perfect bohemian flapper in a green silk-and-lace number that made the red undertones in her hair pop.

"You look amazing." Milly pushed her glasses up her nose, looking on at Henny with awe.

"And so will you! Now, c'mon, try these already." She shoved two dresses at each girl, and while Bea started to undress to try on the salmon-and-gold one that she had been eyeing, Milly stood frozen.

"Milly," Bea asked quietly, "do you want somewhere more . . . private . . . to try it on?"

Milly nodded sheepishly as Bea scanned the railroad-style apartment. There were rooms on both sides of the kitchen. "Henny, which room is yours? For Milly . . ." She gestured to their friend, who was now holding a dress up in front of her as she fumbled to take off what she was wearing.

"Oh, goodness. Milly, doll, you don't need to be shy in front of us!" Henny took the dress from Milly's hand. "We've all got the same stuff underneath, ya know! But we'll turn our backs until you've put this on if it makes you feel better." She removed the dress from the hanger and held it out in her hand toward Milly, closing her eyes. Bea did the same.

There were sounds of minor struggle, and for a moment Bea was certain something had fallen on the floor when Milly finally said, "All right, you can look."

"Milly! You're a goddess," Henny cheered as she walked behind Milly and grabbed her shoulders, pulling them down and back to stop their friend from slouching. "Stand tall, honeybuns, you're the cat's pajamas!"

"You look gorgeous, Milly. Really. Wow." Bea was flooded with pride and awe at the transformation.

"You too, Bea's Knees. You're both just drop-dead gorgeous."

"Henny, you're incredible. Thank you, thank you so much," Bea gushed.

"Whatever for?"

"Getting us out tonight, dressing us up, showing us what life can be like."

Milly nodded along as Bea spoke.

"Please, this is nothing. I'm just thrilled to have you gals with me for a night on the town. Now let's scoot. Your time is running out!" Henny opened the oven and pulled out three pairs of pumps, grabbed a tube of lipstick from the silverware drawer, and then ushered the girls out the door.

Greenwich Village was a warren of angled streets and concealed doorways, nothing like the grid of Bea's neighborhood. As Henny led them confidently down Bedford, which Bea wasn't sure she would have been able to find on her own, Bea felt as if she had entered a magical other world. The magic continued as Henny gave a password to gain entrance through a hidden door. Once inside, the place unfolded through a series of windowless rooms, lined in deep walnut, and filled with people of all sorts; poets, flappers, sailors, and bankers all mixed together merrily, the free-flowing booze bonding them in revelry. As they walked, Milly grabbed Bea's hand and held on, like a nervous child waiting to get on the Ferris wheel.

"Oh my," Milly uttered in a whispered gasp.

"C'mon in, girls. The party's this way." Henny ushered them through the crowds, saying hello to nearly everyone, heads turning as they passed. Bea was pretty sure there wasn't a man in the place who wasn't looking at Henny, and why not? She was irresistible.

In the second room, at the bar, Henny nodded her head in the direction of a cluster of men at the far end. They were all in suits and surrounded by an assortment of women who were definitely not colleagues. "That group over there, those are the brokers. See why I made us change? We would have looked ridiculous in our office getups!"

"Would they have let us in if we weren't dressed like this?" Milly asked as she tugged at the bottom of her dress in a fruitless attempt to make it longer.

"Who knows? I've never tried!" Henny laughed. "Now let's go get these boys to buy us a drink."

Bea and Milly trailed dutifully behind as Henny moved closer to the bar. Bea took in every detail of the place as she walked: the women in colorful clothes, draped with layers of beads and spilling the contents of glasses into their mouths like it was water; the pungent, sour smell of stale liquor, sticky under her feet on the dirty wooden floor; the billows of smoke from cigarettes everywhere. It was intoxicating.

Henny draped herself seductively next to the cluster of brokers at the bar and, before Bea knew it, the girls had all finished a round of some delicious, sweet concoction of a cocktail. Henny was smiling coyly, batting her long eyelashes at the brokers when, suddenly, her demeanor shifted and she went from temptress to schoolgirl, standing on her tippy-toes, screaming and waving at someone across the room.

"Who's she so excited about?" Bea asked Milly, since she was too short to see through the crowd.

"Somebody handsome. Oh gosh, *so* handsome. And, oh goodness, he's . . . he's . . ."

"Milly? He's what?"

"He's coming straight at us," Milly whispered as she bit her lower lip nervously.

"Nathan Greenberg. Where have you been all my life?" Henny put her hand coquettishly on her chest before brazenly grabbing both of his cheeks to kiss the newcomer on the lips. "Nate, these are my friends. The little cutie-pie is Bea and that long tall drink of water is Milly." Henny giggled, and Bea began to wonder whether she'd somehow downed a glass or two of bootlegged gin when they weren't looking. Then she turned to shake his hand, and her heart stopped.

It was him. The man from the street. Of course. The first guy she was even inclined to think about for more than a minute, and he was Henny's. Bea took in the two of them together and got a chill. They sparkled.

"Hello again, Miss Abramovitz." Bea blushed; he remembered her! "And Miss . . . Milly. Nice to meet you." He grabbed Milly's hand, which was hanging limply by her side and, as he brought it toward his mouth to kiss it, she nervously shook it instead. Her whole body seemed to wiggle, like she was a wet noodle hanging to dry in the window of one of the markets in the Italian Quarter across Fourth Avenue.

"All right, then, we'll shake," he said gaily, clearly trying to put Milly at ease. "How about you, Bea? You prefer a handshake too?"

Before she could answer, Henny cut in, almost singing as she spoke. "Bea's Knees, aren't you full of surprises? How do you and Nate know each other?"

"We don't really," Bea spurted out a little too quickly. She didn't want Henny to know that Bea hadn't been able to get her boyfriend off her mind.

"We had a run-in on the street a few weeks ago." Nate flashed that smile again. That was one disarming smile.

"Yes, your beau almost knocked me over in front of our building!" Bea tried to sound confident and teasing, to hide her disappointment.

"Beau?" Henny laughed. "You hear that, Nate? She thinks we're together. Wouldn't that send the tongues wagging."

"Sorry, I just thought . . . well, the way you said hello . . ." Bea was flustered. Why did Nate make her so nervous?

"That kiss?" Nathan asked. "That's just Hen's version of a joke. When we were kids, our *bubby* Francis always made us kiss her hello on the lips. And she was always in the middle of eating herring or liver." He smushed his face to highlight his repulsion, which on him, just looked adorable. "Naturally we'd try to squirm away, so she'd grab our faces and hold them in place to plant one on us. My dear cousin here does the same to me whenever she can."

Bea's whole body suddenly tingled with excitement as she laughed, perhaps too gaily. Nate and Henny were cousins! Maybe that was why they looked so good together. They shared blood.

"It's true, although I still say I was a lucky girl to have this face as my first kiss." Henny squeezed Nate's cheeks like he was a baby. "Isn't he just drrrr-reeeeaaam-eee." She fluttered her eyelids teasingly.

"Uh-huh," Milly whispered under her breath, which made Bea and Henny roar with laughter. "What? Did I say that out loud?" She looked at them, mortified, her face the color of borscht.

"Don't worry, it's too loud in here for him to have heard you. Plus, he's used to the attention," Henny said reassuringly. "Right, Nate?"

"Um, yeah, sure." He leaned down and said just to Bea, "I didn't hear a word of what she said, but Hen likes to be right, so agreeing with her is usually a safe answer."

"Well, from what I know of her, it seems to me she usually *is* right."

"Yep, that too. I should have realized you might know her." *He should have realized?* Did that mean he'd been thinking about her too? Bea didn't want to dare imagine it. "But you're at the wire, right?" *He remembered!*

"Yes. Henny and I met in the lunchroom when she dragged me off for an egg cream."

"That makes more sense. So, the wire? Usually not too many gals there. You must be good with numbers. What d'ya think of it so far?"

"It's terrific. Absolutely divine." Henny handed them both a drink, thanking Nate for buying, and then disappeared.

"You mean the choice of men, like my cousin? Look at her making a beeline for the broker crowd."

"No! Not at all. If I wanted a husband, Mama has a list of boys in the neighborhood I could marry. I have no time for eligible bachelors right now." *Except maybe you.* "I just love the work. The pace of the day. The patterns in the stocks."

"Patterns?" A dubious smile crossed Nate's face. "What kind of patterns?"

"You know, like today. People were selling steel all day long. It closed at its lowest price in weeks. When steel goes down, railroads usually go up. So I imagine those will open high tomorrow."

Nate nodded. "Yes. Smart."

"Is he boring you over here, trying to talk business?" Henny draped her arm over Bea's shoulder and around Nate's waist.

"Not at all. Bea was just making some very astute observations about the market."

"Market-schmarket. We're off the clock. Can't we discuss something droller than stocks? What about Stanley over there?" Henny waved her pointer finger, now wrapped in a gold snake ring, in the direction of another handsome man in a suit. "Has he asked about me?"

"I keep telling you, these guys aren't good enough for you, Henrietta," Nate said. "They don't value a gal the way they should."

Nate was gorgeous and a protective cousin. Was he too good to be real? Bea's heart pounded, and she felt the room start to spin. *Surely this man didn't have that much power over her?* She looked in her hand and noticed that she had finished her second drink. And she hadn't had any lunch today. Her stance started to wobble, and suddenly Nate grabbed her under the arms.

"Whoa there. How much giggle water have you had?" He turned her to face him, handing her glass to Henny. *Those eyes.* "I think she needs some fresh air. Let me take you outside for a minute."

"No. No. I'm fine. Just haven't eaten in a while's all." Bea was so embarrassed. She wasn't an experienced drinker, for sure, but it wasn't like this was the first time she'd ever had alcohol either. She needed to get out of there before she humiliated herself further. "I'm so sorry, but I just realized the time. I really should head home."

"Do you need a ride?" Nate asked sweetly.

Oh, how she wanted to say yes, but she couldn't risk being with Nate in this state. She felt too out of control. Plus, what if her parents happened to see her emerge from some strange man's car. They'd never let her out of the house again. "That's all right. Milly and I are going together. Right, Milly?" She caught Milly's eye and motioned for the door. Milly shook her head, entranced by Nate, but Bea was now determined to leave. She nodded yes, and Milly hung her head like a chastised toddler.

"Henny, thank you for tonight. I'll clean your dress and bring it back to you in a jiffy." Bea gave Henny a squeeze.

"Don't you dare. It looks so good on you, it's yours now, honeybuns. Don't ya think, Nate the Great?"

"It's berries." Nate smiled at Bea. A ripple of delight ran through her like a current.

"Nate, nice to actually meet you." She tried to stay composed as she held out her hand to shake his.

"Not as nice as it was for me, I bet." He pulled her arm toward his mouth and bent over to deposit a soft, perfect kiss on the back of her hand.

Bea was certain she was actually swooning when Milly pulled her out of the way and gave her own hand to Nate. "Bye, Nathan," she said in a blissful gasp. "And thanks for everything, Henny. It's been just swell!" Milly kicked up a heel in a clumsy imitation of dancing, and then followed Bea to the stairs leading up to the street.

When they got outside, Milly insisted on giving Bea a ride home. As they settled into the back of Milly's car, she grabbed Bea's hand and turned to her. "What a magical night. Didn't you think?"

"It sure was." Bea smiled as visions of Nate swirled in her head. Maybe it was the gin.

"Thank you for getting me out of there. Mother and Father would be appalled if they knew I was downtown at a speakeasy." She emphasized the last word like it was a curse. "They're still dragging me to every possible society ball, hoping I'll find a suitable husband."

"Is there no one that you like?"

"There have been a few, but the feeling was never returned. And I refuse to get married to someone just to merge our two families. I might be more old-fashioned than you and Henny, but if I marry at all, it will be for love."

"I couldn't agree more. We have enough in our lives. Our jobs . . ."

"You really love the bank, don't you?"

"Yes." Bea was surprised by the question. "Don't you?"

"Sure, I think the market is fascinating. But some days I just wish I could spend all my time lost in a book."

"Couldn't you?"

"I could if I had a husband. But if I did that now, Mother would surely fill my days with plots and plans to marry me off. I much prefer using my brain and being with you gals."

"Good for you!" Bea cheered. "There is plenty of time for guys and marriage. Now is our time."

The car pulled up to Orchard Street, and she gave Milly a tight hug. "Thank you tons and wish me luck!" She was certain there was a fight waiting for her when she got upstairs, but as she closed the door to the car, she realized that was okay. Tonight was worth it.

CHAPTER TWELVE

Bea's first surprise, when she walked through the door of her family's apartment, was that the kitchen was both dark and empty. The second was the faint sound of music and laughter coming from the other room. Bea was starving. She really hadn't eaten a thing since breakfast, and she'd anticipated that her mother would be sitting at the table with a cold plate of stuffed cabbage and a scowl. She never dreamed that there would be no food out for her, nor anyone to greet her when she arrived at this unexpectedly late hour.

She made her way down the hall and into the front room, which served as both a parlor and sleeping quarters for her parents. She found her parents inside, dancing. They were wearing the nicest clothing she had ever seen. Pauline had on a beaded dress, her hair curled and piled high on her head, her lips red, and her neck sparkling from the glow of her diamond-and-emerald necklace. Her father, meanwhile, was in a modern double-breasted suit, his worn and dusty black boots replaced by shiny leather spectators. It was like they were headed to a ball in a modern fairy tale. And as if that wasn't enough of a shock, Bea suddenly realized the reason they were dancing—there was music coming from the corner of the room. Since when did they have a phonograph?

"Beatrice! Finally, you're home!" Her mother almost cooed at her.

"Yes, I'm so sorry, Mama. I had a last-minute obligation after work and—"

"Never mind that. Today it doesn't matter. Today we are celebrating!" Pauline giggled and twirled around Lew. Bea looked at her parents and then at the room again, still stunned.

"Papa, what . . . what is all of this?" Bea opened her hand to indicate her parents in their fancy clothing, her giddy mother, and the music.

"Yaacov! It's Yaacov!" Pauline answered for Lew. "Your brother is a real *macher*! He sent gifts! They were delivered this afternoon. There is something for you, too, Beatrice." Pauline motioned to a large box in the corner of the room, and Bea crossed to it, excited to see what was inside. The dress Jake had sent for her looked like something one of the girls on the other side of the lunchroom at the bank would wear. It was clearly store-bought, and from the feel of the silky green fabric and the detail of the ornately embroidered roses down both sleeves, it was expensive. She loved it. But it was surely not something she needed.

"He sent all of this? But how could he afford it? His last letter said things were going well, but . . ."

"It seems we were wrong to doubt his decision to go west. Yaacov has obviously found a great opportunity in California." Bea studied her father's face as he spoke, waiting for a sign that he remained skeptical—a twitch of his mustache, a downward slant to his eyebrows—but she saw nothing. Lew just smiled proudly, marveling at his wife as she basked in the joy of their son's success.

Bea knew she had gotten lucky by choosing to go out on this particular night; on any other, who knew what the consequences would have been for coming home when she did, gin on her breath, no less. She also knew that now that she'd gotten a taste of the true modern lifestyle, she wanted to keep living it. She wasn't a liar, so she'd need to find a way to make her going out okay for her parents. It seemed like success would help. Her mother was happier than Bea had possibly ever seen her, just from a few gifts from Jake. They were particularly lavish presents, but also, Bea could feel the mood of her house had shifted. It was like her mother lived every day with her hands balled into fists, clinging for her life, and now, suddenly, with this taste of luxury, her grip began to relax.

She had never believed before that the lack of money was actually the problem in their house but, watching her parents tonight, she suddenly saw things differently. Bea started to imagine how free her life might be if Jake really made it in California. Being rich would take the burden off her in a way she hadn't considered before. She'd be able to stop taking care of things at home and focus solely on chasing her dreams. And then their family's success wouldn't just come from Jake. She was getting so good at picking stocks that, once she started to invest, she would surely make her own fortune. She just had to get from the bank's basement to the fifth floor.

Bea felt her stomach rumble and remembered that she was in desperate need of a meal.

"Is there anything to eat?" she asked her father quietly. She didn't want to remind her mother that she hadn't been there for dinner.

"I set a plate on top of the stove for you, *ziskeit.* Go, eat, before your mother remembers that she was less than happy with you before these gifts arrived." Lew winked at Bea. "And, Beatrice, I know that working girls go out when the day is done, but please be careful. You are a nice girl from a good family. Remember that. Wherever you are."

"I will, Papa. I promise."

Bea breathed a great sigh of relief and went back to the kitchen. She lit the flame under the teakettle to boil water for all of them, and then, while she waited, she sat at the table and quickly ate the two knishes her father had left her. He must have done a barter with Yonah Schimmel today. Another lucky break for Bea.

Bea sat with a gigantic smile on her face. A smile for Jake, for her parents, for her, for Nate. Nate. She wondered when she would see him again. She'd try to casually ask Henny. She didn't want to seem too eager. But there was just something about him. The water in the kettle started to boil, and as she stood to pour the tea, she became aware of the silence. The music in the front room had stopped, and the apartment was quiet. Bea peeked her head in and saw Pauline and Lew lying side by side, still fully dressed, holding hands, and fast asleep. She quietly, carefully, removed the necklace from her mother's neck and put it back in its black velvet box, took the shoes off both parents' feet and lined them up neatly under the bed, draped a blanket on top of them, and turned off the lamp. Smiling in disbelief, she went to her own room to get ready for bed. This had been an entirely unexpected day. She wondered what might possibly be coming next.

CHAPTER THIRTEEN

When Bea got to work Friday morning, Henny was waiting at her desk, with a smile and a cup of coffee in hand. Bea was used to being the one who did things for other people, so she was particularly moved by this small gesture.

"Finally! I've been wondering how early you get here and now I know, not as early as I thought." Henny threw her head back, laughing, her bobbed red-brown curls shaking as she did. "Gotcha a cuppa joe. Did you have an all right time last night? You didn't get into too much trouble at home, I hope?"

"Actually, it was a small miracle." Bea gratefully took the coffee Henny was holding out to her and rested her hips on the edge of her small desk, right next to her new friend. "My brother sent some gifts to us, and they arrived just in time to properly distract my parents. Well, my mother, anyway. And she was the one I was really worried about."

"More worried about your mother than your father?" Henny raised her eyebrows, genuinely surprised.

"Yes, it's complicated, and growing up how you did, you wouldn't understand. We don't have anyone to do the household work, so that falls on me." Henny looked stung as Bea spoke. "Don't get me wrong, I'd give anything to have someone to take over my chores. I'm just saying that you grew up lucky. And Mama has very high, or maybe low, expectations of me."

"She can't possibly still . . . now that you're here and all? It's not every girl who gets a job at the Morgan Bank!"

"I know that, but she doesn't. Or she doesn't really care. Well, she cares that I have a paycheck, but the way she sees it, my work shouldn't interfere with taking care of her at home. So, missing dinner last night, that would have been trouble if Jake hadn't saved the day."

"Wow, that's awful. I thought I had it bad with my papa and all his 'expectations' of me. But Mama, she always encouraged me to do what I wanted—within reason, of course."

"Yeah, well, it's easier with a maid and a cook." Bea looked at Henny and realized how rude her comment was. "Oy, my foot seems to want to live in my mouth today. It's just that my mama . . . she means well. Most of the time. But she grew up living like royalty in Odessa, and she's never completely adjusted to her life here. She'd do much better with a maid and a cook."

"I understand. I think that's how it was for my mother with my grandmother. She didn't want us, my sisters and I, to feel that pressure. And she was lucky because by the time we were born, the family was established. My parents lived their whole lives here. Still, you're doing so much out here in the world. You're making money. You have a right to have your own life. Maybe you should move out?"

"Oh no. I couldn't. She needs me. Especially with Jake gone, it would be too much for her. For both of them."

"You're a better girl than I, Bea. But remember, what you need matters too." Henny nudged Bea's hip with her own. "Now tell me more about this Jake. A brother who sends gifts. Sounds divine!"

"Oh yes, the divine Jake." Bea laughed. "He's my twin. Although basically my opposite in almost every way. He's in California now."

"You don't say? Is he in the pictures? Oh, I'd love to be on that silver screen."

"Really? I can't think of anything more dreadful. But no, he's at a big oil concern. Seems they've found some really rich land out there."

"Oil schmoil. Next you'll start talking about investment returns and all that jazz. Then I'll get bored and have to walk away like I did at Chumley's last night." Henny waved her hand dismissively.

"I know you don't think much of investing, but don't you think the new financial world is even a little bit fascinating? A person can make or lose a fortune every single day, depending on how they read the market."

"I mean, sure, I recognize that there are all sorts of new opportunities for all sorts of people to get rich. That's why I'm working in banking, you dolt. Still, it's not my passion or anything. I'm here because it's a good job in the new economy. And even if it was, talking about work is not what a night on the town is about! I'm trying to teach you how to have fun. To turn off that buzzing brain of yours every once in a while. In fact, I'm headed to the Follies tonight. You should come. Now that will take your mind off everything!"

"Tonight? On Shabbat? I couldn't possibly . . . it's hard enough to explain why I have to work Saturdays. I couldn't miss dinner too!" Bea saw a strange expression come across Henny's face and suddenly felt uncomfortable. "Don't you have dinner with your family on Friday nights?" she asked awkwardly.

"Well, I used to . . . I mean, not always . . . I guess . . . now that I'm on my own in the Village, I do what I want with my weekends. No religious shackles to hold me down."

"Must be tops to have so much freedom. Although I can't imagine not having Shabbat dinners. We're not so religious, but that's when we see Tanta Isabella, and Sophie and her family usually come too. We have Sunday supper—macaroni and gravy—at theirs, and they have Shabbat at ours. It's no night at the Follies but, I don't know . . ." Bea felt like a simpleton for relishing this old-world tradition. Henny's family was clearly more assimilated and sophisticated; she must think Bea was so provincial.

"Sounds nice. All right, another time then," Henny said, sounding surprisingly wistful before turning to Bea with a bright smile and abruptly changing the subject. "Now, you and my cousin Nate, what an absolute hoot that, of all the guys on the street, you and he ran into one another? This big old world really is so very small! He's a cutie-pie, right?"

"I think it's fair to say he is undeniably handsome." Bea felt her face getting warm. She didn't want to admit to Henny how often Nate had entered her thoughts in the weeks since she first met him on the street. "Just ask Milly." She giggled, hoping to deflect any suspicion.

"She was a gas, wasn't she? Need to teach that girl how to act around guys. She's got a lot more going for her than she realizes, just needs to learn how to use it! Not like you, Bombshell Bea, seems you know how to flirt." Henny winked at her. "You and Nate'd make one swell pair."

"You think?" Bea tried to seem nonchalant even as her insides started to flitter like they were filled with butterflies.

"Absotively! Too bad he's still tomcatting around right now. He's gonna be an important man at National City one day, and he's too focused on that to get serious about a gal. Even one as spectacular as you!"

Bea's heart dropped. She, too, was dedicated to her career. Still, she had felt like there was something electric between her and Nate. A connection. She was embarrassed to have been taken in by what was apparently his standard flirtatious charm. This was a good reminder, she needed to stay focused. No distractions. Her attention should be on working hard and learning any and everything she could about the market. If she kept at it, she was sure before long she would actually be investing herself.

CHAPTER FOURTEEN

September

Bea couldn't believe how much had happened in the year since she was last preparing for the High Holidays: it felt good to be doing something so familiar.

"Do you think your mother would approve of this one?" Sophie laughed, holding up a card that was clearly from another shopkeeper's old Christmas stock. They were shopping for cards that her mother insisted they send to relatives in Russia, even though it was unlikely they'd ever get them. In this one an image of a Torah was sloppily pasted over a tree, and the tips of the star of Bethlehem, plus some of the green branches, still peeked out from behind the new image.

"That one is perfect, Soph. Why don't *you* give that to her?"

"I have a better idea; I'll peel off the picture and use it next year myself . . . for Christmas!"

"Now that's a-good-a thinking! Such a clever girl-a," Bea said in an exaggerated mimic of Sophie's father, thick Italian accent and all.

Sophie grabbed Bea's hand and looked at her, suddenly serious. "I've missed this."

"You've missed fighting the crowds in the street markets to help me shop for my High Holidays?"

"Bea, you know what I mean. And yes. I have. I miss spending time with you like this. You always have something to study or somewhere to be these days."

"I'm working!"

"I know. And that's terrific. But sweet Milly doesn't seem as preoccupied as you are all the time. And Henrietta—"

"You can't compare me to Henny! She's like Dr. Jekyll and Mr. Hyde—perfectly professional, well, mostly, when the market opens, and when it closes, she becomes 'Bohemian Brodsky.'" Bea batted her eyelashes and kicked her feet in Henny's exaggerated style.

"Bea, you know I think you working on Wall Street is great. Just—"

"Just what?" Bea suddenly felt an ache in her chest. She missed Sophie, of course she did. But she didn't have time to dwell on that. Sophie had no idea what it was like to do what she was doing, how hard she had to work. Henny and Milly didn't seem to care if they were taken seriously, given a chance to do more, but Bea did. Every day she worked, her desire and determination grew. She was watching this new era of finance develop, watching people make so much money, and she was sure she could do it. But the longer she was at the wire, the less confident she became that anyone would let her. It was so frustrating.

"Just remember that you don't always have to reach for the next thing. That's all."

"Why shouldn't I? You should too. With your talent and my connections—Milly loved what you made her! We can help you get your own clients . . . Why won't you set up your own business?"

"I will, someday. But I'm not ready yet. And Mama needs me to help her. My time will come. I don't have to force it too soon."

"How are you always so calm and patient?" Bea cracked a small smile.

"And how are you always such a hothead?" The girls burst into giggles and moved on to the next shop. Bea knew how lucky she was to have a friend like Sophie, someone who was so loyal she'd spend her precious afternoon shopping for a holiday that she didn't even celebrate, just to help keep Bea company. Jake wouldn't have done that.

Jake.

Bea's heart hurt at the thought of enduring the upcoming week without him. She and her parents understood that it was too hard for him to come home for such a short stretch; still, this time of year had always been Bea and Jake's together. He was her constant companion for all of the holiday's rituals. They cast off their sins together during the *tashlikh* on the Williamsburg Bridge. They entertained each other through the long hours of prayer on Yom Kippur, and competed to see who could last longer before breaking their fasts. It was during the High Holidays years ago when Jake had shown Bea just how far he would go to protect her, even if it meant getting in trouble himself.

They were thirteen. Jake hadn't yet had his growth spurt and Bea had blossomed early, so this was the year where she was the one getting attention for her looks. It was also the year of Samuel Eisenberg, or as Jake called him, Smeisen. Smeisen had been Jake's best friend in elementary school and was a fixture in the Abramovitz house when they were young. Like Bea, Smeisen was incredibly bright but, when they were kids, he used his intellect to invent elaborate pranks that he and Jake would play on her. He was decidedly annoying. Until he wasn't.

The fall of eighth grade, Bea walked into her advanced math class and saw the handsomest boy she had ever seen. His hair, previously a frizzy mess, was tamed with pomade into perfect waves, his formerly chubby face suddenly all angles. He towered over her at nearly five foot seven, his broad shoulders straining the seams of his shirt, and if she looked closely, she swore she could detect the slight curvature of muscles on his arms and chest.

"Bea? What's wrong with you?" he said, smirking. She realized she had stopped in her tracks, staring at him.

"Sm—Smeisen?" Bea couldn't believe it was him. She hadn't really paid much attention to boys in general, so this feeling was unfamiliar to begin with. And the fact that she was feeling it for Jake's jokester pal was such a shock she almost couldn't make sense of it.

"It's Sam now." He smiled at her and winked. Bea was a goner.

Sam walked Bea home after the first day of school, and they soon became inseparable. Jake wasn't thrilled that he had lost his best friend to his sister, but in truth, with Sam in all of Bea's accelerated classes and Jake in the regular ones, the boys had already begun to drift apart. Bea had never felt about a boy like she did about Sam; she wanted to be with him constantly, and when she wasn't with him, she was thinking about him. Bea would do any and everything for Sam and, that fall, it was like the usually good, rule-following Bea had been replaced by a Sam-obsessed risk-taker. That was how it happened that Sam convinced Bea to sneak out of temple in the middle of Yom Kippur services to go kiss in the alley.

Leaving during services was strictly forbidden. They weren't even supposed to go to the toilet, except during designated breaks, so Bea sneaking out in the middle of prayer to have her first kiss was pure scandal. Under normal circumstances she'd never have done something so brazen, but Sam made her bold. Plus, the idea of getting to put her lips on his made Bea feel giggly from the inside out.

"So, when they start the viddui, you grab your stomach like you're in pain and come out to the alley, yes?" Sam confirmed the plan with Bea.

"The viddui? If our parents find out, they will kill us! You can't leave during such an important prayer."

"Bea Abramovitz, you're such a good girl, you have nothing to atone for. A few minutes outside of temple won't matter and, anyway, no one will see. Everyone has their eyes closed then."

Bea was nervous about the plan, but her desire to kiss Sam was more powerful than her fear. So, when the appointed time came, she slipped away from her mother who, as Sam predicted, was lost in her deep contemplation and didn't even notice. Bea ran around the corner to the alley, where Sam grabbed her by the wrist and pulled her toward him.

"Finally we are alone." Bea had imagined this moment feeling like a beautiful dream—horns would start to play and the clouds would part, and she would be warmed from the inside out. Instead, it was uncomfortable and awkward. Sam lurched toward her, lips puckered and, when they landed on hers, they felt slimy and damp. Then he pushed his tongue into her mouth, and she felt like he had deposited a piece of gravlax and just left it there. Her empty stomach turned, and she was about to pull away when she heard Jake.

"Bea! What the heck? . . . Smeisen?"

"Jake." Bea pushed Sam away. "We were—"

"Shh. Save it. I see what you were. Are you trying to get killed? Mama was mulling around in the front, looking for you."

"She was? But it's not time for a break yet. It's—"

"Yes, it is. You two are idiots. You wanna kiss, be my guest, but today? Here? You'll both be—"

"Yaacov? Beatrice?" Pauline rounded the corner and saw the three of them in the alley. Sam had moved away from Bea and toward Jake, leaving Bea standing alone. "How dare you two leave shul in the middle of viddui. Have you no respect?"

Bea braced herself for Jake to tell Pauline the truth. That Bea had snuck out and Jake had only come to find her, but instead he said: "I'm sorry, Mama. Smeisen and I were just so hungry. We are growing boys, you know, so I suggested we come out to play marbles for a few minutes to distract us." He pulled a sack from his pocket and shook it while he turned to Bea and gave her a look that said, *go along with me*. "BB just came to look for us when we weren't in front."

Bea stood still, stunned and appreciative that Jake was lying this way for her when he had absolutely no reason to. Pauline was furious with him. The angriest she had ever been. For the next two months, she made him come straight home from school every day and pray for forgiveness every night. Bea offered to confess, but he wouldn't let her.

"BB, you're always so good. And yet you're always the one punished for my *mishigas*. I more than owe you this."

Bea had learned two important lessons that day. First, that all the fuss about boys was really in the anticipation, not the reality, of being with them. From now on she would put her energy into things she could count on. Like knowing that if she had fewer than five problems to do for math homework, she would be done so quickly that her mother would expect her to make dinner alone. She also learned, or maybe recognized more clearly, that as annoying as Jake's seeming perfection in their mother's eyes could be, he selflessly had her back when it mattered. The High Holidays had been cemented as Bea and Jake's from that day on. And this year, for the first time, she'd have to do it all alone.

"It's going to be hard without him home this year, yes?" Sophie asked gently.

"I was just thinking that Mama is going to be a wreck. Not to mention the many hours of torture I will have to endure without any entertainment."

"You have friends at temple. Too bad Sam Eisenberg moved away." Sophie laughed. Bea's recounting of that awful first kiss had given them hours of squeals as girls. "At least you can sit with Gerald Melnikoff and talk toppings for bagels."

Bea rolled her eyes. "Not funny."

"If you want, I'll come with you. God forgive me." Sophie genuflected in an exaggerated sign of the cross, laughing. They shared a lot, but their time at their respective places of worship wasn't one. "Okay, what else do we need? These bags are getting heavy."

The girls finished shopping and walked home, turning the corner onto Orchard Street to find their block in complete chaos—well, even more than the normal chaos of the day before the start of the High Holidays. As Bea looked around to make sense of what was happening, she realized there was a car driving slowly down the street, weaving in and out of the pushcarts and honking its horn. "What in the—"

Bea wasn't sure who saw him first, but before she knew what she was doing, she started running toward the car in disbelief. The street was so crowded she caught up with it quickly, and when she got level with the passenger in the back, she thought she might start to cry. "Jake! You're here! It's really you!"

"BB! I was hoping to get all set up in front of the building and surprise you there, but I guess this is just as good. Hop in, Wally here'll drive you to the door."

"Since when do you have a driver?" Bea took in the swanky black Cadillac, which looked especially out of place among the pushcarts on her street. She had opened the passenger door to climb in with Jake when Sophie caught up with them.

"Jake, you came back!" Sophie flashed Jake a wide, genuine smile. "Bea, I tried to collect your bags, but I couldn't carry it all. You should probably go grab them before everything gets trampled."

"The bags!" Bea shut the door of Jake's car. "We were shopping for Rosh Hashanah. I'll just run back and grab them and then hop in?"

"Sure thing, little sis. I'll wait for you right here."

"How 'bout you get out of your throne and help me?" Bea rolled her eyes but was smiling. "And I am only your 'little sister' by sixty seconds, so don't you go pulling rank on me."

"Sixty seconds, sixty days. I'm still older!" Jake winked and got out to help Bea with the bags. Once the three of them were sitting inside, the car moved in a slow crawl down Orchard Street. The driver was honking his horn and Bea couldn't tell if it was more to clear the way or if Jake had instructed him to so that everyone in the neighborhood would see him arriving in a chauffeur-driven car. Either way, she thought, it was pure Jake.

CHAPTER FIFTEEN

When the initial excitement over her brother's unexpected arrival had dissipated, the family sat in the front room of their apartment, eating slices of the oranges Jake had brought back from California.

"Fruit? Why did you bring me fruit, Yackie? I can get more fruit than we can ever eat from my suppliers, you know that!"

"I know, Papa, but even you can't get this. These are Valencias. Best in the world. Just taste one and you'll see."

Bea watched Lew wrinkle his nose dismissively as he bit into a slice. All at once his entire face changed. "Yaacov, this is like liquid honey! It's *geshmak*."

Bea took a bite and couldn't believe her mouth. It was, as her father had said, truly delicious. She'd had oranges before, but they were always a little sour and bitter, and usually left a hint of acid burning down her throat. This was different; it was pure sweetness with a twist. It tasted like . . . sunshine.

"Slow down, BB! There's more where that came from." Jake laughed, clearly happy that she was enjoying his gift so much.

"It's just so good!" Bea wiped the juice that was dripping down her chin.

"Yackie, you are a wonder. Seven months ago, you left us. Seven months. And look at you now. Handsome like a movie star in the finest suit! Arriving by first-class rail and chauffeur-driven car! Bringing us manna from the heavens! You might be an Abramovitz, but there is no doubt that you hail from the House of Oppenheim!" Pauline beamed at her son. Associating him with her wealthy family was the greatest compliment she could give, and while Bea had long learned to ignore these moments, today she felt just a hint of that old familiar jealousy creeping in.

"Well, Mama, I told you it was a gold mine down there in California. And this is just the beginning."

"See, Lew, you should trust Yaacov. He always knows what he is doing." Pauline turned her nose in the air. A tiny vestige of the time in her life when she was an aristocrat. Bea imagined this was how she behaved as a girl.

"Ah, but it was never about trust. It was about making the best choices. Still, yes, it seems that leaving school has been all right for you, Yaacov. A good decision."

"You have no idea. Every Hollywood honcho wants shares of Julian Pete. I'm taking calls from Louis B. Mayer, Cecil B. DeMille, they can't get enough! And I get a bonus each month that I sell more than the quota. Which, I might add, is every month. And they pay it in shares of the company, which are skyrocketing. So my money is growing like weeds!"

"That's fantastic," Bea said. "But you know you really should spread out your investments. Maybe before you buy more clothes or cars, or plow more money into Julian Petroleum, you should think about investing in shares of some other companies? Diversify your risk?"

"Diversify schmiversify. Listen to you, all Wall Street. How would it look to our investors if I didn't put my own money where my mouth is? Oil is going to make us millionaires before the year is done. Mark my words!"

"Look at him, such a *macher*. He looks like wealth for sure." Pauline patted Jake's hand, gazing at him adoringly. "Beatrice, *this* is making money! Yaacov can buy a car and gifts for us. He can take off all ten Days of Awe. This bank of yours isn't even closed for the High Holy

Days. I just don't see why you keep doing this work, especially at that place."

Bea had opened her mouth to snap back at Pauline when Jake jumped in. "Mama, do you know how hard it is to get a job at the House of Morgan?" Jake sat up taller and shook his hands in the air as if he were referring to a holy site. "Let alone a Jewish girl from our neighborhood? Bea might not be making money as quickly as I am, but what she has accomplished is truly amazing." Bea watched her mother sink inside her skin, surprised to be chastened by Jake.

"Well, I just . . . I'm just saying that she works so much, she's almost never home, and I don't really see what she has to show for it."

"Mama, I'm just starting out. It's different at a bank. J.P. Morgan is an old and formal institution. There are rules and processes. Anyway, material things aren't the only signal of success. I am learning so much about the markets. I'm the only girl in the wire allowed at the ticker. Soon I will be a broker and then—"

"So then they're going to let you do that after all?" her father asked excitedly.

"Well, not on the trading floor, or the regular brokerage desks, but at the ladies' department. I'm building the skills at the wire to work there one day. Maybe I'll even invest for you, Mama."

"You think we have money to gamble away? Psht," Pauline snapped at her, laughing dismissively.

"It's not gambling," Bea responded defensively.

Jake threw his arm around her, and Bea's whole body relaxed. She had missed him. "For now I'm all tied up, but when I'm a millionaire, I'd be happy to let you make me more millions!"

"How gracious of you, Jake," Bea said with a smirk.

"All right, enough. Your mama and I couldn't be more proud . . . of both of you." Lew looked at Bea with the earnest pride that had fueled her all her life. The small reminder that he saw her, even if her mother didn't. "This is the start of another new year for our people, and for our family. And what a fantastic way to begin, with all of us together again under one roof!"

"Amen." Pauline grabbed Lew's hand, smiling as if nothing had happened.

Yom Kippur arrived too fast. For the first time in their lives, they would spend the Day of Atonement in a big, fancy auditorium. Jake was so flush with cash that he had bought the whole family tickets to services at the Grand Theatre. Pauline was thrilled to be able to parade along Chrystie Street in another new dress. And, while Bea liked the small community of their makeshift temple, she had to admit that a day of fasting was much more pleasant when sitting in cushioned, velvet theater chairs, instead of squatting on wooden stools in their cramped shul.

When the long day's services ended, everyone's spirits were high despite their gnawing hunger. Jake had ordered platters from Katz's to break their fast, so that Bea and Pauline didn't have to worry about cooking; this meant that instead of having to finish preparing the meal while already famished, the Abramovitz women could eat immediately, just like the men.

"Well, Jake." Bea linked her brother's arm in her own as they walked quickly home. "I've gotta say, I'm kind of liking your big new life. All these extravagances are surely more than we need, but I can see what Mama liked about living like this."

"This? This is extravagant to you? This is nothing, BB! Wait until you see it in Hollywood. Now that is living big. These are just small things to make life a little more comfortable. Just the beginning, you'll see."

"It's incredible how much money you've made so quickly . . ." Bea gave Jake a side-eyed glance to underscore her unspoken question: Was this all on the up and up?

Jake nudged Bea with enough force to almost knock her over. "C'mon, BB, this is real. It's a booming business, part of the new economy. I'd think you, of all people, would understand that."

"I do, I do. I just . . ."

"You just what?" he asked sharply.

"I just want you to be careful. In my experience, when things seemed too good to be true, they usually are."

"Ah, yes, in your vast experience with new businesses and places." Jake nudged Bea with his hip and looked at her with a teasing smirk. "This is happening for me, BB. For us. Just let yourself enjoy it for once instead of worrying about some invisible problem that you're going to have to fix. I promise, I've got this."

Maybe Jake was right. Just because Bea had always been the one to take care of things in the past didn't mean she had to now; if Jake could go across the country and make a fortune, she surely could do the same right here on Wall Street. Then she could get her parents what they truly wanted—a real store for her father, household help for her mother. She and Jake had always been one kind of team: he saw her for who she was and stood up for her, but she did all the work. She had always been the good girl. The one who behaved. The one who made everything okay for everyone. Maybe, finally, even that was changing between them. She felt herself relax into the idea of not being the one to carry the whole burden of the family on her shoulders. It felt good.

Pauline had invited as many neighbors and friends as they could cram into their small apartment to show off and share the lavish spread; it was nearly two hours before everyone left. When the family was finally alone, Jake suggested that they all take a walk and Bea had that uncanny twin feeling that Jake was up to something.

"What are you doing?" she asked him in an anxious whisper after he chose a different path than their usual one toward the East River.

He just smiled and kept walking. One block later Jake stopped in front of a vacant storefront that served as the ground floor of a five-story building. Now Bea had a strong idea of why Jake had insisted on this walk, and she was overcome with a wave of conflicting emotions. Jake had leased a store for their father. She was suddenly certain. And while this was an objectively wonderful thing, her joy for her father hit right up against her own disappointment. Bea had wanted to be the one to finally give Papa his own store. She'd even been quietly saving money for it; that was one of the reasons she hadn't bought more superfluous things for her mother. She hadn't told anyone because she didn't have nearly enough yet, and she didn't want to make false promises. Now here was Jake, coming in out of nowhere and making a big splash, and here she was, yet again, about to get lost in the wake.

"What's this, Yaacov? Why are we stopping here?" Pauline asked, clearly not yet realizing what Jake had done.

"It's a nice building, isn't it?" Jake opened his palm toward the facade like he was a real-estate broker and they, his customers.

"Very nice. Excellent street. I always told your papa that this was where we should be. But, of course, that's not how things worked out."

Bea watched Jake's mouth stretch into a grin so wide it looked like it hurt. She stood in silence, trying to calm the jealousy that was welling up inside of her.

"Papa, what do you think of this place?" Jake asked eagerly.

"Would be a wonderful shop for someone with a business big enough to afford this kind of rent," Lew said dismissively.

"Or someone who happened to be related to the landlord."

"Jake?" Bea asked, stunned. "Landlord? What did you . . . ?"

What Jake had done was more than Bea could even have anticipated. For the past week, when he said he was meeting with potential investors, he was actually scouting real estate to find the perfect place to buy for their family; not to lease, to purchase. And this was it. The building had running water in each apartment, telephones, and the vacant storefront that would soon become "Abramovitz Grocers." Bea and her parents would live in the best apartment in the building and collect rent from the remaining units. Bea was stunned that Jake could do something this big this quickly. Before she could ask, her father broke her shocked silence.

"Yaacov, you didn't talk to me before you did this?" Lew was surly, not quite angry but not elated and appreciative. Bea was surprised by his reaction but not nearly as much as Jake, who seemed to have been gut punched.

"Why should he have, Lew? This is everything we ever wanted and more!" Pauline chided. Jake stood a bit taller.

"Maybe ten years ago. Or even one, before Jake moved across the country and Beatrice began her own career. But now . . . a store is a more complicated business. I know what I need for my cart, exactly how much produce to buy so I don't end up sitting on bushels of rotten food at the end of a week. Why should I expand now, take on more risk, spend more money that we don't have, to build a store that will have no legacy?"

"Of course you will have a legacy! Beatrice can come work with you. They don't need her the way you do. She should use that head for numbers to help her family."

How dare she? Bea wasn't just some doll that could be picked up and placed in whatever room suited her mother.

"I am helping the family in my job now, Mama. I am making money too. I—"

"Well, sure, but nothing like Yaacov. What are we really getting from your job? A few new dresses? That's helping the Romanos more than your own family. Since you've started 'working' I've never been more tired."

Before Bea could tell Pauline about her new savings, the money she had planned to put toward a store, or remind her of all the small things Bea paid for, the debts they no longer had all around town, her father stepped in to defend her.

"*Shefele*, stop. Beatrice has made our lives more comfortable. And she is entitled to her own dreams. We are fine the way we are."

"But, Lew, if we own this building and the shop below, we will have a real family business. You and Beatrice downstairs . . . and I can collect the rent!" Pauline cracked a slightly wicked smile. "Finally, other people will be giving me their money instead of always taking it from me! The 'House of Oppenheim' will rise again."

"More like the new 'House of Abramovitz,'" Jake corrected, nudging his father as he grinned.

Bea hated the idea that her father didn't want to grow his business because neither she nor Jake were there to follow in his footsteps, but why did she have to be the one to make everything okay? Jake buys a building and she's supposed to give up her career? She wanted to be furious, but there was nothing she could say because, of course, Jake buying this building was a great generosity. He was so earnest and proud of his success. And it was remarkable. He had done so well so quickly. It was almost too good to be true.

"Jake, can you really afford this? We'd have to buy furniture for the apartment, displays for the store. Not to mention the increase in inventory. And Papa would need to hire at least one salesperson . . ." Was she really concerned about these things? Or was it that, for the first time in their lives, she was truly jealous of her brother?

"BB, stop worrying. I've got it covered. All of it."

"You have this much money?"

"Well, no. Not yet. But I can borrow until I do. I worked it all out."

Of course. Borrow it. Bea knew that borrowing had become a popular way to buy. In the markets, investors would put down a little money for a stock and buy more shares on "leverage," borrowing from the bank to cover the difference. And it wasn't just for stocks; regular people were buying cars, radios, household appliances on "time," paying a little bit each month until they owned the thing outright. Jake hadn't made this money yet any more than Bea had; he was just willing to do things she would never do to get ahead faster. Her mind started spinning.

She knew she tended to be cautious. Maybe she needed to take more risks. This was a new era. The new economy. And if she didn't need to be the one to provide a store for her father, she was free to invest her savings. She could start her next chapter on Wall Street.

"Papa, you've always wanted this, haven't you? I can work with you on Sundays. And after work at night. And I'll help you find a full-time shop assistant."

"Exactly! Papa, don't give up on your dream just because BB and I have new ones. Let's all reach for the stars together," Jake chimed in.

"I don't know." Lew shook his head. But as Bea watched him take in the storefront, the building, the street, and the glow of excitement in Pauline's eyes, she knew that he was going to do it.

And that meant that she better start working as a broker as soon as possible. Now more than ever, it was time to take her shot.

CHAPTER SIXTEEN

October

Bea had always been able to achieve her goals by following the rules, instead of bending them, unlike Jake, and she knew her first step toward being an investor was her boss. Mr. Stanhope might have laughed at the idea of her being a broker before, but now he knew what she was capable of. She'd developed a reputation in the wire department for her instant recall, and had become the first person anyone in the room asked if they were looking for a specific number. One week, she counted how many times one of the guys yelled "Hey, Lightning" and asked her for a piece of data. The average was seventy-five per day.

Mr. Stanhope knew how much she added to the wire room with her unusual memory and quick analysis. Surely he would see how that could translate to investing. Maybe she couldn't work with the men inside the exchange, but she'd be a perfect broker for the clients upstairs in the ladies' department. Having Stanhope in her corner as witness to her excellent work at J.P. Morgan would surely more than compensate for her inherent "drawbacks" in Mrs. Halsey's eyes: being Jewish and from the wrong part of town. She just had to talk to him. Unfortunately, that was harder than she thought.

Bea had tried three times to get on Stanhope's calendar for a meeting, but his secretary insisted he had no availability. She'd tried casually stopping by his office (always before the market opened or after it closed), but he was rarely there. She was at her wit's end trying to find a way to get his attention when he walked by her desk one morning, on the way to the coffee kitchen. She stood and followed him.

"Morning, Mr. Stanhope. Getting your own coffee today?" she asked as she walked behind him into the small kitchenette down the hall.

"My girl is out sick. So now here I am. Good thing the pot isn't empty, or I'd be in trouble." Bea smiled in sympathy even as she was slightly annoyed. This was 1926. Did he really not know how to make a pot of coffee?

"What do you think of what's happening with Westinghouse?" Bea said to demonstrate that she was always analyzing the market, even as she helped the guys record it, unlike the others at the wire. She was surprised how slowly he prepared his coffee, considering that they got backed up if they were away from their desks for one single minute.

"Westinghouse?" He looked at her askance.

"Yes, everybody's been buying the past few days." *Maybe step aside while you add your sugar so a girl can get a cup?* "I wonder if they are planning some sort of acquisition or something."

"Acquisition? I don't know what would make you think that," he said dismissively. He looked at Bea like she was speaking another language and continued to move as if he had nothing to do but relax by the coffeepot. Bea was taken aback. She needed to try harder to impress him, and fast.

"Well . . . I've just noticed that trading volume on RCA has slowed considerably, while orders to buy Westinghouse are suddenly coming in in droves. Seems like something is about to happen."

"Do you know someone at RCA?" Mr. Stanhope stirred his coffee and finally stepped aside for her to get a cup herself. "Someone telling you something we at the bank might want to know?"

"Oh no, it's not like that, sir. No, not at all. It's just, well . . . you know . . . we have such a unique position here at the wire . . . we've got so much insight into the market, recording movements as they happen."

She lifted the pot to pour her coffee, only to find it was now empty. Of course. "But I don't need to tell you that, you know it better than I do," she said sweetly as she turned back to face Mr. Stanhope with what she hoped was an appropriately deferential smile. This conversation wasn't going as she had planned. He met her gaze with an expression that was either perplexed or irritated; she couldn't tell which.

"Every position at the bank is unique. What we are counted on to do is record things as quickly as possible, with perfect accuracy. The 'insight' you mention is for the brokers to think about."

"Yes, well, sir, I actually wanted to talk to you about that. I've tried to set an appointment, but you are a busy man." Bea wasn't usually nervous, but Stanhope was so casual and dismissive she suddenly felt less certain she would have his support. "Do you remember when you first moved me up from the file desk in the back?"

"Of course. Was a genius idea on my part. We've never been more efficient."

"I'm glad to hear that. Glad that I am helping. The thing is, I think I can do more."

"What now? Do you want to learn the codes so you can operate a telegraph?" He chuckled as he took a sip of his coffee.

"Actually, I want to be a broker. Up on the fifth floor."

"You, in the ladies' department?" His chuckle turned into a guffaw. "Did the boys put you up to this?" She smiled at him tightly. This wasn't a prank. "Come now, Bea, I thought you understood when you first came down here. There's no place for you up there."

Bea felt like she had been about to get comfortable in a chair and Stanhope swiped it out from under her. She wanted to reply, to make her case, but the words had momentarily been knocked out of her.

"You're quite a find for us here in the wire. I'd never have imagined it, a girl who could keep all these numbers straight all day; apparently word of our gal 'Lightning' has even spread to other banks. You should be proud. I see a long career for you down here with us." He patted her shoulder patronizingly. "Oh, and the coffee's out. Probably want to make some more before you go back to your desk." He motioned back toward the kitchen and then turned and left.

Bea was furious. The wire was the first step toward her goal, not the end point. She was meant to be a broker, and whether she had Stanhope's support or not, she would find a way to do it.

When Bea told Henny and Milly about her conversation at lunch, she got an earful from them both.

"Jeez, Beez, don't you know Stanhope's not gonna help you get ahead? Long as I've been here, the only place a girl has gone in this bank is back home to be someone's wife. I keep telling you, the closest you're going to get to being a broker is to get into bed with one!" Henny flashed Bea a mischievous smile and Bea slapped her hand.

"Henny, I'm being serious. And, really, my goal and the bank's goal work together, right? If I'm as good at being a real broker as I have been theoretically, then I'll make the bank and its clients lots of money. Everybody wins. Are you really telling me that there is no chance I could do that here? It just doesn't make sense. It's irrational. Unfair."

"Honey, listen, I don't know for certain, because I haven't tried. I like my gig just as it is. I make good money, get to flirt with the cuties, and leave it all behind at the end of the day. But I know a lot of people, and fair or rational has nothing to do with it. The House of Morgan hasn't ever put a girl like you upstairs anywhere, except maybe in steno." She took a bite of her sandwich and looked at Bea, a glint in her eye. "But look, it's 1926, and we are modern gals charting our own path. Hell, I'm an unmarried single gal living in Greenwich Village with showgirls. So, if you want to be a broker, I say do it! If not here, then somewhere else."

"Somewhere else? Like where?" Bea was agitated. She knew that there were a few other large banks that had departments dedicated to female clientele and staffed by women, but she had no connection to any of them to even get an interview. When Professor Berkman had been helping her last year, he'd felt Morgan was her best chance.

"I don't know off the top of my head. Because I've never cared to pay attention, hon," Henny said soothingly, trying to calm Bea down. "But the one thing I do know is all the secretaries for all the big honchos' offices around town. So how's about I make some calls and see what we can find out?"

"And I'll ask my mother," added Milly. "Most of her friends have allowances that they invest. It was part of why Father was comfortable with the idea of banking for me in the first place." Milly rolled her eyes. "Bea, you're too smart and too strong to accept defeat. If you want this, you must go get it. And we will do everything we can to help!" Milly sat up tall and pounded on the table with uncharacteristic bravado.

"I don't know what to say." Bea felt a flood of relief and hope. As she looked at her new friends, women she hadn't even known six months ago yet were willing to go out of their way to help her, she welled up. "I think I am just the luckiest gal on the planet to have friends like the two of you."

"As my grandma Doris used to say, 'The feeling is municipal.'" Henny laughed as she spoke. "I know you'll make us proud."

CHAPTER SEVENTEEN

December

Mary Vail Andress was a symbol of what it meant to be a successful female in banking. She was an officer at Chase National, the first woman to hold an executive role at any bank in the country, and a founding member of the National Association of Bank Women. She was known to be a fierce advocate for females in the industry, and Bea had pinned all her hope on the meeting that Milly had helped Bea secure today, thanks to her mother's social network.

Over the past two months, Bea had pursued her dream with renewed vigor. Henny was able to use the name of her boss, Mr. Driscoll, to get Bea interviews in the women's departments at most of the major institutions on Wall Street, and at least once a week Bea left work the moment her tasks were done to run to an interview. Unfortunately, while she went into each meeting hopeful, by the end of each she received the same frustrating feedback: It didn't matter how smart or skilled she was. It was all about connections. This was the last meeting on her calendar for the year, and while it wasn't an interview exactly, she hoped that Mrs. Andress would have some other ideas or leads for her search. She was wrong.

Bea hadn't known what to expect of Mary Vail Andress, but it wasn't the person sitting across from her now. This woman didn't match the trailblazer Bea had pictured. She looked more like the clients Bea had seen at Morgan's ladies' department on the day of her first interview all those months ago—a society lady in a fur stole, diamond earrings sparkling on her ears, a large sapphire ring on her finger.

"Mrs. Andress." Bea's heart was pounding when she entered her office. "Thank you so much for taking the time to meet with me. It is truly an honor. You've done so much to open doors for women in banking."

"Yes, yes. Well, of course. I am always happy to help provide direction for young women at the start of their careers. There are many opportunities available to the right type of young lady. Now let's see what might be interesting for you . . ." She paused to look at the résumé Bea had handed her when she entered her office. "I'm not sure I understand, Miss Abramovitz. You already work in the wire department at Morgan . . . a very impressive job. You must be quite sharp and quick."

Bea warmed at the compliment. None of the other women she'd interviewed with seemed to care at all about her work at the wire.

"So, are you interested in working here instead? Because I don't know that I'd recommend it. J.P. Morgan is a fine institution. And you've only just started there." Mrs. Andress looked at Bea, her eyes narrowed in confusion and her lips set in what might have been annoyance.

"Yes, it is. Of course. I am very lucky to have the job I do at Morgan. But I was hoping you might have some advice about moving into a different kind of role."

"What type of role, dear? I oversee all the branch managers and the cashiers. Is that the type of thing you'd like to do?"

"No," Bea answered quickly. "I want to be an investor."

"An *investor*?" Mrs. Andress smiled, looking at Bea like she had grown a second nose.

"Yes, well, a stockbroker." Bea had begun to launch into her now-well-rehearsed pitch about her lifelong interest in stocks and her hypothetical track record when Mrs. Andress cut her off.

"Miss Abramovitz, for a girl who is clearly very bright, you don't seem to understand the basic facts. I didn't have any intention of becoming a banker, you see. I was very active in war relief overseas. I started working at Bankers Trust, in Paris, after the war because they were impressed by my fundraising efforts. Also, we were good customers of the bank. Eventually I was brought here, to Chase. Do you see what I'm getting at?"

"Well, yes, you more fell into the job than directly pursued it, thanks to your background. But thanks to women like you, I can go after what I want." Bea wasn't ready to concede, because if Mrs. Andress didn't think Bea could become a broker, then her dream would be dead. "I'm a really good stock picker, I'm faster than any of the men in my department at calculations and my analysis . . . I just see the market and recognize what is going to happen. A lot of the time, anyway."

"I'm afraid you aren't hearing me." Mrs. Andress began to organize the papers on her desk, signaling that their meeting was already coming to an end. "We all have our place in the bank and the world. You have found a wonderful position that is perfectly suited to your strengths and background. Now, I'm sure you know that the trading floor or a broker's desk is simply not a place for a woman. Why, they don't even let us inside the exchange. That's not where we are useful to the bank."

Bea felt this was an antiquated way of thinking, but she didn't dare say as much; instead, she tried one last time to find a ray of hope. "But what about the ladies' departments? Working there is essentially acting as a broker."

"Possibly but . . . dear, you went to Hunter." While she didn't say this unkindly, like the other women Bea had interviewed with, her implication was still that this was a problem. "I assume, from your name, that you come from an immigrant family? Jewish?" She asked this without judgment, a simple clarification of facts.

Bea nodded.

"Yes, well, then as I said before—you've already found a job that is a wonderful fit for you. Surely you understand that, to work in the investment arm of a bank, it doesn't matter *what* you know, it is *who* you know that counts. So, you see, you'd simply be of no use to any ladies' department."

Bea felt all the blood drain from her face. Her head began to spin. She didn't remember what she said for the remaining time she spent in Mrs. Andress's office. All she knew was that the woman she had hoped would offer her the best perspective on how to reach her dreams had, instead, confirmed what everyone else had already told her.

For the first time in her life, excelling at something wasn't enough. It didn't matter how good she was at picking stocks if she didn't have access to people with enough money to make the picks matter. In less than a year she had already gotten as far in banking as she ever would. This was all there was. And, apparently, there was nothing she could do but be happy with that. Or, at least, that's what she was being told.

"Can you believe she said that? I mean, she wrote a pamphlet called 'Banking as a Career for Women' for goodness' sake!" Bea slurped her martini. Henny had gathered the girls, even Sophie, to take Bea out and cheer her up.

"Yes, Bea. I can," Sophie said gently. "And you can believe it too. You just haven't wanted to."

"She's right," Henny said. "I just wish it wouldn't get you so down. Jeez, most gals would be over the moon having accomplished what you have in less than a year. A respected job, fabulous friends—" Henny threw her arms around Sophie and Milly, drawing them in tightly so their faces took up Bea's entire field of vision.

"I know. And that is all terrific. I'm so lucky to have you gals. I'm just not sure where I go from here."

"Why do you have to go anywhere? Can't you just try to be happy where you are?" Henny asked.

"She wouldn't be Bea if she did that," Sophie said teasingly.

"I'll figure something out. I just don't know what, yet."

"Milly, you're awfully quiet," Henny said.

As the girls turned their attention to Milly, Bea realized that she had an odd expression on her face. She almost looked like she was going to cry.

"Mil, you okay?" Bea asked gently.

Milly put down her martini, took a deep breath, and then began. "Oh, Bea. I just feel awful, so awful. I was going to tell you about this today after you had a great meeting, but things didn't go well for you, and now it just seems cruel and, well, it's so unfair . . . and I can just say no, on principle—"

"Mildred Wentworth." Henny clapped her hands in front of Milly's face. "What in the world are you going on about?"

"They've offered me a position in the ladies' department." Milly spat out the words as fast as she could and then stuffed an olive in her mouth.

"They offered you—" Bea felt her stomach plummet.

"Oh, Bea, I'm so sorry. I know we had this solidarity that they didn't want either of us. But, well, it's thanks to the two of you, and Sophie, of course, that things have changed for me." Milly gestured at her latest dress, one that Bea had watched Sophie spend hours pleating. She saw Sophie's cheeks turn pink. "I told Father that I like working in finance and want to focus my efforts on growing here at the bank instead of using this as a placeholder until I find a suitable marriage prospect. If I find a man, fine, but I have you gals and my books and work and that's a lot. Somehow he heard me. He made a few calls, and I met with Mrs. Halsey and, well, they've offered me a position. I don't want you to hate me—you girls really are just the best friends I've ever had. But now that he's gone out of his way, Father will kill me if I don't do it and"—she looked down sheepishly—"I also kind of want to."

Bea hated that she felt envious. It wasn't that she didn't think Milly deserved this job, she did. She was smart and sweet and kind and connected. But it rankled Bea that all it took for Milly to achieve Bea's dream was to polish up her appearance and ask her father, while Bea would have to invent a whole new life.

"This is wonderful for you, Milly. Congratulations! Really. You deserve it." Bea meant it, as much as it hurt her.

"Oh, Bea, I wish I could bring you with me. You'd be so terrific at that job. Maybe once I'm settled . . ."

"Don't be silly. It is abundantly clear that they'll never want a girl like me up there."

"Me either," Henny jumped in. "Not that I'd wanna go."

Suddenly Bea had an idea. "Maybe that doesn't matter."

"It doesn't?" Milly looked at Bea, perplexed.

"She has a new idea. I can see it," Sophie said hopefully.

And she did.

Bea had been looking at her situation all wrong. Reaching for the wrong thing. No, maybe she couldn't be a broker. But what she really wanted to do was be able to use her analysis to invest. Until now she hadn't been able to do that because the only people who would take her money were the bucket shops, and they robbed you blind. But with Milly at the ladies' department . . . "I have a little money saved up. It isn't much, but do you think you could take me as a client, Milly?"

"Gosh, I don't know for sure, but I don't see why not." Milly looked pleased to be able to help Bea, but then her face contorted into concern. "Oh nuts. We do have investment minimums for clients. I wonder if there is a way I can get around that."

"Milly, you're not going to start a new job by breaking the rules. Do you know what the minimum is? Maybe I can find a way to get enough." Bea's mind immediately went to Jake.

"Or maybe I can chip in from my own allowance," Milly said, sounding more cheerful. "Really, you'd be doing me a favor. You're so much better at stock picking than I am, I wanted to ask you for some pointers anyway, but I felt so awful about the circumstances."

"Milly, never feel awful about what you achieve. You deserve every bit of your success!" Bea smiled at her friend, and she meant it.

"What a devilishly divine idea!" Henny chimed in. "Maybe I'll even scrape together something extra to add to the pot."

"That's the spirit." Bea smiled, raising her glass. "To Milly, the ladies' department's new rising star!"

"To Milly," Henny cheered.

"And to Bea, the strongest girl I've ever met who doesn't let anything get her down." Milly smiled sheepishly.

"And Sophie, the best dressmaker in all of Manhattan." Bea tipped her glass in her best friend's direction. She never would have expected this particular group of gals would come together to feel like one big family. But suddenly they did. No, things weren't happening the way Bea would have predicted, but they were happening nonetheless. And that was good enough for now.

1927

Two Years before the Crash

CHAPTER EIGHTEEN

January

DOW MONTHLY AVERAGE: 156, –1 POINT FROM DECEMBER

It was a new year, and everything was looking up. Bea and her family had moved to the new place on East Broadway, every other apartment in the building was rented, and Abramovitz Grocers was officially open. The store was beautiful with its neat rows of wooden bins, filled to the top with fruit and vegetables. Lew made sure that the shop assistant kept the displays tidy and appealing, restacking apples, oranges, and lemons into small mountains several times throughout the day as inventory was sold, and spritzing the greens with water to keep them from wilting. For all his concern about running a whole store, Lew was a natural. He quickly adjusted his inventory to fill his much-expanded space, and his customers had grown so much that, most days, he was left with almost no extra stock.

Bea wished Jake were here to experience the joy that had become the primary emotion in their house, instead of the bitterness and frustration that they had grown up with, but he was across the country, making the fortune that made their new lives possible. At least they had their own telephone in this new apartment, so she could fill him in on their weekly Sunday-evening phone calls.

"You should have seen Mama yesterday, Jake. She floated into the store like some grande dame, all dressed up in one of her new outfits, and made small talk with the customers as they were browsing."

"Small talk? Mama?"

"Yep. For a minute I thought you had possessed her body."

"If I were going to choose a vessel to possess, I'm not sure that would be the one I'd pick." Jake laughed and Bea felt a pang. She missed her brother. "So how's life on the Street? How much did you make this week?"

"My little portfolio is doing great. I just wish I had more to put in it. You know what they say: 'You need to have money to make money.'"

"Can't you buy on margin? That's what most of our investors do. Things are going up so fast, it's essentially free money!"

"Sure, as long as things keep going up. But that's a bet I'd rather not take." Bea didn't like unnecessary risk, and had no interest in borrowing to make a small investment stake larger, no matter how popular this use of leverage had become on Wall Street. She wanted to invest only what she had, not a penny more. "Say, as long as you've brought this up, though, I did have another idea."

"Yeah, what's that?"

"How about if you invest with me? Put some of your money into my portfolio? I'm really good at this, Jake. If I had a bigger nut, I'd have so much more to show for my efforts." Bea still didn't care about getting rich for the sake thereof, but it was an irrefutable fact that the measure of success in finance was how much money you made. And success was what she wanted more than anything.

"I can't," he said dismissively.

"You can't?" She was surprised and hurt. All he did was brag about how rich he was getting; did he not trust her with his money? "Or you won't?"

"You know I'd get in with you if I could. But I don't have the greenbacks."

"What do you mean you don't have the money? I thought you were raking it in? What about the rent on the other apartments in the building?"

"I'm using that to pay the mortgage."

"All of it?"

"Of course. Most of my salary is paid in stock. The little cash I do get goes to necessities for my life out here. Dinners, new suits . . . you know—gotta act like money to make money."

"But . . . you don't have anything more?"

"Nope. Not even a peanut. But don't worry, BB, soon as I'm allowed to sell my stock, you'll be the first to know."

"And when is that?" Suddenly Bea was less worried about her own desire for success and more concerned about her brother. She didn't like the idea of everything Jake had being tied up in the stock of a single company, no matter how well it was doing.

"I can take out the first bit at the end of the year. But it's a good thing, BB; the longer it's there the faster it grows. I've already made ten times what I started with!"

"Ten times. That sounds wrong, Jake. Almost unreal." Bea paused before saying anything more. Her instinct was that something wasn't right about this investment. That Jake's riches were more precarious than he realized. Or was she being extra hard on Jake because she was jealous of what he had achieved and because, despite it, he couldn't help her get closer to realizing her own dreams? For the first time in their lives, she needed him for her success more than he needed her for his.

"Almost unreal. But not. It's real, BB. I see the statements. We don't have enough shares to satisfy the demand. This company just keeps growing, and there is no end in sight. I'm telling you, it's all upside."

"Maybe, but it never hurts to have a backup plan. If you could get some of your payment in cash, and I invested it for us, you'd have another way to make money. My stock picking has gotten so good, Jake, and you know I wouldn't say that lightly. I think I can make you—us—some real money."

"Bea, I don't think you understand the kind of money I'm making here. There is no way your little investments could come anywhere near it."

Bea nearly dropped the receiver. Jake had always been arrogant, but he didn't have to be condescending.

"Of course, what I'm doing is small and petty, and what you're doing is big and important."

"Look, BB. I don't know what you're getting so upset about. I don't have money to invest right now, and I can't get it, and that's the honest truth. I would love to help you, but I can't. I already got you your own bedroom. How about if instead of asking for more, you say thank you."

"Thank you? Just because you delivered the big prize to Mama and Papa doesn't mean I'm not doing my part too. Before you came along with your big windfall, I was paying off all of Mama's credits around town, and helping Papa refurbish his cart. Now I'm reinvesting every extra penny I can so that I can make enough money to be taken seriously as a woman on Wall Street. And, let me tell you, that is almost impossible for a girl like me. But you wouldn't understand any of this, because you're not here! So just forget it. It's late and I need to go. So sorry I bothered you."

Bea slammed the earpiece back on the receiver. Yes, she had allowed herself a few tiny indulgences with the money she made, the occasional lunch out, a few extra dresses, but she still bought them from Sophie, not at a store. She was careful with her money and put every extra dollar into her portfolio. She would just have to do what she always did. Work hard, follow the rules, and make do with what she could provide for herself. She was foolish to think she could ask Jake to do something like this for her. She knew better. She was on her own.

CHAPTER NINETEEN

February

DOW MONTHLY AVERAGE: 162, +6 POINTS FROM JANUARY

Bea had left work at a reasonable hour for once, but the sky was already midnight black, stars sparkling as if to taunt her. How could they be so relaxed hanging there in the sky naked in this intense cold? There was no escaping winter this time of year. She tucked into herself, pulling the fur collar of her coat tighter around her neck to shield her from the East River chill, which somehow seemed to intensify as it snaked between the buildings and directly into her bones. Bea walked double time to generate heat, which was probably why she didn't notice that someone had joined her on the sidewalk, keeping pace with her exactly, matching each step stride for stride.

"Are you going to ice me out all the way home?"

Bea turned, surprised to see Nate, of all people, walking beside her. "Goodness, Nate! I didn't notice you there."

"Well, that makes me feel a little better. I can't say I've never done something to make a gal ignore me like that, but this time I don't think I deserved it." He tilted his head to look down at Bea with an innocent smile, and she suddenly felt very warm.

"Hmm, let me think." Bea touched her gloved hand to her cheek, pretending to ponder. "Nope. You're safe. This time."

"Scout's honor, I'll do my best to keep it that way." He held up his two fingers and crossed his heart. "Funny running into you on the street again. I was kinda hoping to see you somewhere more comfortable. I keep looking for you out on the town but no luck since the summer. Where have you been hiding?"

"Not hiding. Just busy with work is all." She slowed her pace and looked at him out of the corner of her eye. *He had been hoping to see her again!* "Plus, I've gotta be home to help my parents most nights. We moved recently, and Papa now has a proper grocery store, and the bookkeeping and inventory management is time consuming so . . ." *She was babbling. Why did he make her so nervous?*

"Moved? Not far, I hope."

"Not far at all. Just a few blocks away from where we were." She giggled. *He was such a flirt, and she was helpless in his presence.* "My brother bought a building, and we've moved into the top apartment. Papa's new grocery store is on the street level. It's all very exciting." *And she was babbling again.*

"That sounds like a big change." He smiled earnestly. *That smile.* "Brother bought a building, huh? He in real estate?"

"No." Bea laughed. "He's across the country. In California."

"You don't say. So he works in the pictures?"

"No, no—he works for a big oil developer out there. Got involved through a friend, and the company is going gangbusters."

"Hmm, oil's a tricky business. Lots of charlatans looking to swindle people out of their money. Tell him to be careful."

"Funny you should say so. I have been worried because his returns are unusually high, yet he's not getting any of the money in cash. Just stock. Know anything about that?"

"I know too much, really. My team follows the oil stocks pretty closely. Hey, listen." He stopped and gently placed his hand on her shoulder. She could feel goose bumps run down her spine, and it wasn't from the weather. "It's colder than a witch's kiss out here, but I'd love to keep talking. Can I buy you a cup of coffee?"

"Coffee?"

"Well, I'd offer gin, but you seem to be in a hurry, so I figure coffee is a safer bet."

Bea knew she should be getting home, but everything in her body wanted to stay longer with Nate. She peeled off her glove to check her wristwatch. "I suppose I could spare thirty minutes for a quick one."

"Thirty minutes, huh? I'm honored."

"Well, if you're good company, maybe next time I'll give you forty-five." *Next time?* Why had she said something so presumptuous?

"I'll take what I can get. But be warned, next time"—he paused for emphasis, and she felt the blood rush to her face—"I'm looking to earn at least ninety. And maybe a drink too."

"You'll have to be an excellent conversationalist for that."

Nate made a right off Broadway and led Bea to a cozy café almost directly under the Brooklyn Bridge. The proprietor gave them a warm greeting, calling Nate by name, and waved them to a small table in the back, right next to a roaring fireplace.

"May I take your coat, m'lady?" Nate asked, bowing like a prince. *He could be Prince Charming from a fairy tale.* Bea felt almost powerless in his presence, like she would do anything this man asked of her. But that was his game, wasn't it? Hadn't Henny said he had the gals falling at his feet but no interest in marriage? Not that Bea was looking to get married anytime soon. Except with Nate, she could picture it. She could see forever. She needed to stay guarded.

"I think I'll keep it for now." Bea sat down quickly, before Nate's outstretched hand could touch her. She needed to at least try to remain impervious to his charm.

"Whatever makes you comfortable." Nate sat, too, ignoring the slight rebuff. "So tell me all about yourself."

"There's not much to tell, really. What do you want to know?"

"Well, I already know from Henny that you live on the East Side with your parents. But now you're somewhere new. How's that?"

"Oh, the new place is really fantastic. I finally have a little space for myself. And we have a telephone. And running water." Bea suddenly felt a wave of remorse about her fight with Jake. They hadn't had a good conversation since then. And he really had done so much for them all. She should apologize and thank him.

"That's swell. I still remember carrying water up the stairs to our apartment when I was a kid. Awful chore."

"You lived in a tenement?"

"Yep, was on Essex until I was six, then my pops got a big new client, and we moved out to Queens."

"Kew Gardens, like Henny?"

"Yes, ma'am. Although my old man's plant is in Long Island City."

"Plant? What does he do?"

"Printing. That's my dad's family business."

"Oh, not Brodsky's stores?"

"Nope! Henny's mom and my mom are sisters. They both married well." He laughed.

"Every girl's only dream," Bea said teasingly.

"Well, most anyway. Not you?"

"Not me. I want to be able to take care of myself."

"Look at you. Only our first date and already telling me where to stuff it." He grinned at her mischievously.

"Is this a date?"

"Isn't it?"

"From what I understand, Nathan Greenberg, you aren't interested in dating."

"From what you just said, Bea Abramovitz, neither are you." He raised his eyebrows at her, looking more adorable than ever.

"I didn't say that. Just, I'm not counting on a man to take care of me. That's all." She looked up at him and felt her cheeks turning crimson.

"Well, good for you. Anyway how, exactly, do you know that I don't want to date?" Bea watched a smile slowly grow across Nate's face. "Asking about me?"

"Hardly." Bea looked away. "Your cousin warned me about you."

"She did, did she? And what exactly did she say?"

"Nothing too bad, really. Just that you aren't interested in getting serious. That your tastes tend to run toward more of the flapper types—you know, the kind of girls who don't believe in settling down."

"That's not true; it's just that right now I don't have a lot of time and I—" Suddenly he looked embarrassed.

"No need to defend yourself. I understand. I'm focused on my career too. I just don't have the luxury of dallying around on the side while I try to make my way on Wall Street."

"Well, that's unfair for you, isn't it?" He smiled. "You seem much more serious about your work than Henny."

"That's a fact. I'm at the wire for now, but I've got my sights set higher."

"You don't say? So what's next for you, Miss Abramovitz?"

"I don't know yet. I'd love to do what you do. Make the decisions about trades. Be in the market instead of just recording it."

"Big dreams. Not such an easy road for anyone, but especially a gal."

"I know." Bea didn't mean to, but she knew her frustration came through in her response.

"Look at you. A regular little Hetty Green."

"Well, hopefully I'm slightly more pleasant than the woman they called the Witch of Wall Street!"

"Without question. Just . . . I'm impressed, that's all. All this," he gestured at her face, "and brains too. You're pretty special, aren't you, Miss Bea Abramovitz?" He looked into her eyes, and she was sure that she was going to dissolve into her seat like the sugar cube she had dropped into her coffee.

"I suppose that's for me to know—"

"And me to find out." He tipped his cup up to his mouth, taking the last sip. "Time for a refill?" She wanted to say yes. Oh, how she wanted to say yes. But she had to get home. And, furthermore, she worried that even ten more minutes with Nate and she would be in his thrall for eternity.

"Not today. I've really gotta go."

"All right then." He tossed a dollar on the table and got up, walking around to pull her chair out for her as she stood. "Well, if you need help carrying crates of produce into your papa's grocery, you know where to find me."

"Why do I have a feeling that manual labor isn't really your strong suit?"

"Hey! Don't let these pretty-boy looks fool you. I've done plenty of heavy lifting in my day. Pops used to make me move reams of paper around the plant after school."

"Okay, okay. But you're not a child anymore."

"That's for sure. Now I get to go on dates with smart and beautiful women." He nudged her and, when they exited to the street, linked his arm in hers. "At least let me walk you home. It's dark and I don't like the thought of you walking alone."

"I do it myself every night, you know."

"Well, tonight you don't have to. And this way I get to spend a little more time with you."

The conversation flowed freely on the walk, and Bea was sorry she didn't live more than ten minutes away. When Nate left her at the steps of her building, he reached for her hand to kiss, as he had done that night at Chumley's, but it was gloved. She found it took all her restraint not to lean in and substitute her lips. No one had ever made Bea feel this way before. Was it possible she had truly met her match?

CHAPTER TWENTY

April

DOW MONTHLY AVERAGE: 165, +8 POINTS FROM JANUARY

"I swear, I've never seen him like this. He's crazy about you," Henny said, smiling, as she clipped a barrette into the right side of Bea's hair above her ear and pulled her curls down more on the opposite side, over her left eye. "Good?" She held up the mirror for Bea to see.

"Perfect," Bea said, admiring her reflection. "I don't know why I can't get my hair to look like this when I do it. I always end up with a lopsided mess instead."

"Stop, you always look adorable, but tonight, we want you to look flawless."

"Do you know something about tonight that I don't?" Bea asked, trying to sound casual despite her churning nerves on the inside. She had been spending a lot of time with Nate lately, but mostly in a group. She was trying to be all right with their undefined relationship—she was a modern girl, after all, with her own life and dreams—but she found herself yearning for more. It wasn't that she was in a hurry to get married or anything, but there was something special about Nate, and it wasn't just that he was heart-stoppingly handsome. In the past, the guys she had spent time with (usually boys from the neighborhood selected by her mother) liked her for her "cute" looks and her "spunk." When they found out she was smart, it was a novelty that typically grew tiresome. Nate was different. When Bea talked with Nate about the market, he listened intently. He asked questions. He treated her like an equal. And on top of all that he was fun, and funny. And kind. He was a friend. An extremely good-looking friend.

Tonight they were going out on a proper date, just the two of them, and Bea was hoping this would be the beginning of an actual relationship between them.

Nate picked Bea up at Henny's apartment at her request, so she didn't have to explain herself to her parents. When the buzzer sounded, Bea grabbed her bag and spun around for Henny, the handkerchief hem of her green silk dress floating in the air. "How do I look?"

"Divine." Henny kissed her on the cheek. "Don't do anything I wouldn't do!"

"That's not much of a guideline." Bea laughed as she skipped down the stairs.

Nate was standing at the bottom, looking up.

"Wow," he said, his eyes fixed on Bea. "Aren't you a sight! I should have come up to get you. That was rotten of me."

"Don't be silly. Why waste your energy coming up four flights of stairs, when I am perfectly capable of walking down them myself?"

"You're really something, you know that?" Nate nudged Bea with his hip.

"You're not so bad yourself," Bea shot back, smiling.

"Ready to go? We have a seven thirty reservation, and if you're late, they make you sing for your supper." Nate laughed and Bea wondered whether he was kidding.

It was only a short walk from Henny's place to Adolph's Asti, a new Italian restaurant that had become famous for waiters who broke out into operatic song midmeal. Bea had heard about the restaurant from Henny, who said it was a hoot, but she hadn't mentioned anything about the patrons having to sing. After putting so much time into looking her best, she didn't want to ruin the evening with her terrible singing voice.

"Do you think they sing arias to you while you're actually chewing?" Bea asked Nate. "Will I be slurping spaghetti to the tune of 'Figaro, Figaro, Figaro'?" She laughed, but she was actually wondering.

"From what I've heard about this place, anything's possible."

"You haven't been?" Asti had fast become a popular date spot and, while Bea hoped Nate hadn't been there with another girl, she had no way to know for sure.

"I have not. I was saving it."

"For someone who knows opera?"

"Well, no, not exactly. But do you?"

"Do I what?"

"Know opera?"

"A little. Mama and Papa like to listen to it on the phonograph. Reminds them of home, I guess."

"My parents too. Maybe it's an immigrant thing."

"To be honest, I usually associate opera with sadness; you know, loss and death? But Henny said this place is an absolute gas."

"I've heard the same." He stopped at the door and held it open for her. "Guess we're about to find out."

Once inside, there was no question that the restaurant was designed for fun. The room resonated with the sounds of lively conversation, laughter, and the clinking of heavily filled wineglasses. The walls were haphazardly covered in framed drawings and photographs of famous sopranos, altos, and tenors (many of whom were supposedly among the patrons), and the red-clothed tables were so tight up against one another it was hard to tell where one group ended and the next began.

"Looks like this place is going to live up to its reputation." Bea smiled, wide-eyed as she took the seat the waiter held out for her at one of the more intimate tables along the wall.

"And then some. I just hope we'll be able to have some conversation too."

"What was that?" Bea asked mockingly.

"Ha ha." Nate looked at the menu. "So what looks good to you?"

"What doesn't?" The menu was large and overwhelming, and Bea, who was not accustomed to eating out, was at a bit of a loss.

"I remember the first time I went to a restaurant for dinner. It was right before I started working at National City. Papa took me to Keens. He wanted me to know what it felt like to eat at a 'formal dining establishment,' since he said that was the kind of thing banker types did all the time. I couldn't believe how many choices there were on the menu, and that was mostly steaks. This is so much more. How about if we share a few things? I can order?"

"Sounds perfect." Bea usually liked to make her own decisions, but in this case she was relieved. "Your family must have been very proud of you when you got the job on Wall Street."

"Not really. My mother was so mad that I wasn't apprenticing with Papa to take over the printing plant that she didn't speak to me for a month."

"A month?"

"Yep. And when you meet my mother, you'll know that that was not easy for her. She likes to talk. Kind of like Henny." Nate laughed and Bea felt her insides flip. *When I meet his mother?* "But Papa was happy for me. He always encouraged me and my sister, Lizzie, to make our own path. In fact, for a while, he even had Lizzie working with him at the plant. She wanted to try it, and he said there 'should be more women in printing.'"

"What did your mother think of that?"

"She thought it was ridiculous. But it didn't last, anyway. Lizzie got married, and now she lives down the street from our house and spends every day with Mama shopping and going to the beauty parlor and such."

"Sounds awful . . . I mean . . . sorry . . . I know that's what lots of gals hope for but . . ." Bea looked down, embarrassed. Who was she to criticize Nate's sister's life?

"Don't apologize to me, Bea. I know you're not the typical girl. It's one of the many things that makes you so exceptional."

"Jeez, Nathan, you better be careful, or I might think you're actually serious about me." Bea tried to sound like she was teasing, but when she looked up, Nate was staring at her intently across the table. The flickering candles made his eyes look like they were dancing. And he opened his mouth to respond, only to be overpowered by a booming "O Sole Mio." It was their waiter. He was singing to them. They both started to giggle, and then Nate joined in. And, to Bea's surprise, he could sing. He could *really* sing. The waiter pulled him up from his seat, and the two men started to sing together as the diners hummed and clapped along. A moment later another patron stood and joined them, and suddenly Bea was watching her date belt out an aria in perfect three-part harmony. When the spontaneous show was over, Nate bowed to the uproarious applause and then, as he rejoined Bea, he came around to her side of the table, lifted her out of her seat, and kissed her. Smack dab in the middle of the restaurant with everyone looking.

All of Bea's senses blurred into one and the room went silent; or at least it did in Bea's head. His sweet spicy smell, his soft lips, his strong arms around her waist. And then he drew back and looked at her, and she suddenly heard the crowd roaring even louder. Cheering for Nate. For her. He kissed her hand, a signal that the show was over, and sat back in his seat.

"Sorry about that. I got caught up in the moment," he said sheepishly. "Although I have been wanting to do that for a very long time."

"Sing opera?"

"Why yes. It's been a lifelong dream . . . no, Bea, kiss you. Since the day I ran into you on the street."

"Well, what took you so long then?"

"I dunno. You're just . . ."

"I'm just what, too intimidating? All five feet of me?"

"A little. I mean, you're special, Bea. You're such a looker . . . and then . . . you're so smart . . . When we're together I feel like I'm with my best pal. Well, if all I could think about was how badly I wanted to kiss my best pal, that is." He laughed. "I . . . look, before I say anything more that I'm really going to regret, I need to know. Do you think you could be serious about me, Bea?" He looked at her so earnestly she wanted to leap across the table into his lap and shower him with kisses. "I wasn't looking for a gal. I'm still building my career. But then you came along. You—beautiful little Bea, with your fast mind and your quick smile. And every day that I don't see you feels like a year. I know you're a modern girl. You want to keep things light. But I want more. I want you, Bea. Would you ever want to be my girl?"

"Would I ever want to?" Of course she wanted to be Nate's girl. This was Nate. He was kind and he made her laugh and her insides turned to mush when he touched her. He was one of the smartest people she'd ever met, and he seemed to really understand her, to appreciate her for her brain. She had been trying to control her feelings because Henny said he wasn't looking for something serious. "Nathan Greenberg, I would love nothing more."

He reached across the table and kissed her again. "I've been so worried that you weren't interested in me like that," he said quietly. "I've wanted to come call on you properly, to meet your parents. To introduce you to mine. But I didn't want to scare you away."

"You just sang an aria in three-part harmony in front of a room of strangers, and you're worried about scaring me away?" She grabbed his hand and intertwined his fingers in hers. "I think it's safe to say that I'm not easily scared. Now if I'm going to be your girl, I do have one very important question for you." Bea made her face as serious and menacing as she could and watched the panic come across Nate's.

"Where in the world did you learn to sing like that? And when are you going to do it again?"

The rest of the evening was perfect. Nate sang a second time and tried to get Bea to join in but, unlike Nate who, she learned, had a long history of singing in public, having been the cantor's pet at temple for years, she refused to risk ruining this night with her decidedly awful voice.

"So when do I get to see you again?" Nate asked when he dropped her at home later that evening.

"Whenever you call."

"So can I phone you at home?"

"You can if you're willing to meet my parents."

"I'm not just willing, I'd love to. I need to thank them for bringing someone so extraordinary into the world."

"Did you really just say that?" Bea rolled her eyes. "I thought you had better lines."

"Oh, I do, but I save those for the important girls." Nate placed his hand gently under Bea's chin and tipped her jaw upward so their eyes met. "Bea, I would like nothing more than to officially declare myself to your parents." He grinned and bent down to land a gentle kiss on the tip of her nose. She thought she might faint right there on East Broadway.

"Well, all right then. But don't say I didn't warn you."

CHAPTER TWENTY-ONE

May

DOW MONTHLY AVERAGE: 173, +17 POINTS FROM JANUARY

When Nate found out Bea had never been to Coney Island, he insisted they go as soon as possible, which was the first Sunday in May. It would still be chilly to sit on the beach, but they could stroll and enjoy the rides and attractions at Luna Park. It was also the perfect way for Bea to introduce Nate to her parents. He could stop in for a quick cup of coffee and a pastry before they went on with their day. Pauline wasn't thrilled with the informality of the meeting, but her joy that Bea had a beau, and a Jewish banker at that, made up for it.

Bea wasn't quite sure what to wear for a day on Coney Island. Sophie had never been, either, and Henny had been no help when she said "easy, comfortable, and cute," so Bea had chosen something that felt right for the water: a sailor-style dress in crisp white poplin with a navy shawl collar and matching tie. She topped the getup with a broad-brimmed straw hat. She felt good about her choice of outfit when Nate arrived dressed casually, with a sweater replacing his usual suit jacket and a newsboy cap instead of a fedora. Bea thought, if it was possible, he looked even more handsome than usual. Bea had never brought home a boy she actually cared about before, and she'd been nervous waiting for him to arrive. Her jitters disappeared the moment he walked through the door with a box of rugelach and a stunning arrangement of flowers. As usual, he was immediately engaged, charming, and perfectly at ease.

"Nathan, please excuse our humble surroundings," Bea heard Pauline say in Yiddish, as Bea brought coffee and a platter of pastries to the living room. "I know this is probably nothing like the home you grew up in, in Kew Gardens." Bea was about to translate for Nate when he responded, in Yiddish.

"Your home is lovely. Much bigger than the apartment I lived in when we were on the Lower East Side." His Yiddish was perfect. Possibly better than Bea's. "I especially love the fabrics in this room. Did you select them yourself?"

Bea raised her eyebrows as she looked at him, eyes wide. *Yiddish? Fabrics? Was there anything he couldn't do?*

"I did. It was such a relief to have a formal sitting room again. We had several in my home in Odessa," Pauline replied, smiling in approval.

"That must have been very hard to give up," Nate said sympathetically. "My grandparents left a lot behind when they came to this country from Poland. It is a tragedy, what our people have had to sacrifice."

"It is. But we've made our way. Haven't we, *shefele*?" Lew chimed in.

"You certainly have, Mr. Abramovitz. I couldn't help but peer in the window of your shop before I came upstairs. You must be the biggest grocer in town!"

"Maybe not the whole city but, yes, in the neighborhood I am." He smiled proudly. "I even have a large storage room with refrigeration in the back so nothing spoils. Of course, I'm known for the freshness of my produce, so I never sell anything past a few days unless it's intended to last, like potatoes or onions. My customers know they can count on that. If you have time, we can go downstairs and see—"

"Papa, let's save that for another day," Bea said gently.

"I would love to spend a whole afternoon in your shop, Mr. Abramovitz, if you'd let me. But today I'm worried about the Sunday traffic heading to the amusement park."

"You'll come another Sunday then," Pauline said enthusiastically.

Nate charmed Bea's parents through one refill of coffee, and then she stood and said it was time to go.

"You'll come back soon, Nathan. For Shabbas?"

"I'd love to, Mrs. Abramovitz. I'll just have to clear it with my mother."

"You're a good son." Pauline held his face in her hands, and Bea could almost feel the ache of Jake's absence leaking from her mother's heart.

"Probably not as good as you think. But I do my best."

Coney Island was a brightly colored, candy-filled, exotic dream. Nate held tight to Bea's hand as he led her from one unusual attraction to the next. There was an Egyptian village, a display of China's Fairy Fountains, a Wild West show, and even performances by hula dancers. Bea felt as if she'd traveled the world in a single hour. And then there were the rides.

"You have to go on this one with me!" Bea insisted to Nate as she got in line for the Tornado. "It says it's the newest one in the park." Bea heard the screams of riders as they mounted each hill and plummeted down the other side and could feel her stomach rising and falling. She was tingling with excitement.

"I didn't take you for a daredevil." Nate laughed. He looked nervous.

"And I didn't take you for a chicken. C'mon. It's just a canned thrill. I promise I'll hold your hand the whole time."

Bea had never experienced exhilaration like riding a roller coaster. She was either screaming or giggling the entire ride, and when their little cart finally slowed to the finish, her heart was pounding so fast she felt like she'd just run from one end of Manhattan to the other. "That was incredible." She smiled at Nate as she climbed out of the cart. "Oh my, you look a little green."

"I'll be fine in a minute. Soon as I get my feet on solid ground again," Nate said weakly.

"Finally, something you aren't perfect at!" Bea laughed as she wrapped her arm around Nate's waist to stabilize his wobbly legs.

"I'm not sure riding a roller coaster counts as a skill to perfect but, if it does, I definitely failed. Can we sit for a bit?"

They settled on a bench away from the park's attractions. Nate got them both Coca-Colas and a soft pretzel, which they shared. When the color had returned to his face and he looked like his handsome self again, he turned to Bea, suddenly looking serious. "Listen, there is something I want to talk to you about. I know this isn't the right time, but it's eating me up, and I'd rather just get it off my chest . . . it's a little uncomfortable, but . . ."

"What is it? You can talk to me about anything." Bea waved her hand in the air, trying to seem light and easy even though she was suddenly sure this was very bad. *He looked nervous. He hated her family? He had changed his mind about her? He forgot to tell her that his parents had already made a match for him, and he was getting married?*

"It's about your brother, in California."

"Jake?" Bea wasn't sure whether to be relieved or even more worried. Ever since their big fight at the beginning of the year, things had been strained between Bea and Jake. She tried to apologize for getting so angry. And he had apologized for being so dismissive. But he still seemed distant to her. She had begun to fret that he was getting too enamored with the fast life out west. Too big for his britches now that he fancied himself a minor oil baron. But what would Nate know of any of this?

"Yes, your brother. Well, you know my team trades a lot of commodities . . . so my boys follow the oil companies closely?"

"Yep, you've said before." She smiled nervously.

"So . . . one of my guys—very smart, almost never wrong—thinks something's off about Julian Petroleum."

"Off? What do you mean?"

"The amount of stock that's trading, the returns they are paying, it just doesn't add up. You know that even the best stock will level out at a certain point. But this company . . . the price just keeps going up, and more and more shares are sold. It isn't following the logic of the market. The only way this could happen, unless Julian Petroleum is better at finding good oil fields than any other company in the history of the industry, is if it is some kind of con." Nate looked at Bea with a pained expression on his face. He and Bea had spoken enough about Jake for him to know how close they were. He also knew how much of her family's new life was funded by Jake's stake in Julian Petroleum. If he was right, this wasn't just a huge deal for Jake; it would impact her whole family.

"I don't . . . I can't . . . are you saying that my brother is a con man? Jake is impulsive, he gets carried away, but if this were all a fraud . . . He wouldn't do that." Bea was suddenly defensive. It was one thing for her to have her own suspicions, but how dare Nate suggest such a thing?

"No, no, you don't understand. I think he might not know."

"But selling shares is his job. How could he not know?"

"Listen." Nate grabbed Bea's hand and held it tightly as he looked at her. Their eyes met. The gold in his shone brighter than usual with the reflection of the sun off the water. She wanted to forget what he was saying and just get lost in his gaze. She wanted to keep having a frivolous day. For the pit in her stomach to be only from the rides. But no. She could see it pained Nate to say what he was saying to her now. "Bea, I'm not telling you this to upset you. I am trying to help you. To help your family. I think Julian Pete might be a castle built of sand. If Jake can get out, he needs to do it now. Or as quickly as possible. I want to help if I can." His hand held firmly on her now shaking fingers. "Will you let me help you?"

"How? How can you help?"

"Well, I can talk to your brother? Tell him what we're seeing. Try to get him to sell. Maybe help him transfer some of his funds to more stable commodities."

"But why . . . why would you do all of that for him? For someone you don't even know?"

"Because I care about his sister very much. I—" Nate looked sheepishly at Bea.

"You what?"

He looked at her, cupping her face in his hands. "I love you, Bea." And then he kissed her. And her body was flooded with an unfamiliar intensity. She yearned to be closer to him. To feel his hands all over her. To feel their bodies come together. If they hadn't been in public, she wasn't sure what she would have let him do to her. But they were. So they simply kept kissing, alternating between small, loving pecks and longer, lingering ones. And, as they kissed, Bea was overcome with an unfamiliar feeling. It was hopeful and exhilarating and terrifying. It was love.

The sun was setting when they crossed the bridge back into Manhattan, and reality came as sharply into view as the New York City skyline. It was Sunday night and Jake was sure to call. Did Bea know enough to tell him about Nate's suspicions? She hated how she felt after her last fight with Jake, his cold distance from her. Was she prepared to feel that again?

As she kissed Nate goodbye, she asked for one last bit of clarification. "So, when Jake calls tonight . . . should I—" Bea shuddered, thinking about the conversation that she would have to have. Hoping Nate would tell her they had time to come up with a plan.

"Tell him, Bea. Tell him to sell as much and as fast as he can. When something like this starts to stink, it's never long before the rot takes over."

Bea nodded.

"Call if you need me." Nate leaned over to give her one last kiss, and then Bea went inside. As she climbed the stairs to her apartment, her body was rocked by a cyclone of emotions. The most incredible man she'd ever met loved her. And she loved him. She was elated. And filled with dread.

How would she tell her brother that his newfound fortune might disappear? That he might be part of some sort of scheme like the one perpetrated by that horrible man Charles Ponzi? Would he believe her? Would he be able to save himself and them?

How was it possible for the very same day to be both the best and worst of her life?

CHAPTER TWENTY-TWO

When the telephone box began to ring at seven, Bea let Pauline answer it. She thought it would be better for her mother to have a nice talk with Jake before Bea got on and ruined everything. Bea heard Pauline telling Jake about their tenants, the women at the new temple she wanted to join, and all about Bea's "very impressive new beau." Bea smiled to herself, thinking that, for once, she and her mother felt exactly the same way about something. Pauline started to wind down her conversation with Jake, and Bea returned to the kitchen to take the receiver. Lew rarely talked to Jake when he called on Sundays beyond a quick hello, so Bea knew it was her turn.

"Hey there, golden boy." Bea infused her voice with so much ersatz sweetness she thought she might choke.

"How's my favorite sister?"

"Oh, you know. Just going about my days as always."

"That's not what I hear. Sounds like there's a new man in town! And one that is not only Jewish but rich. Mama's already planning the wedding."

"Of course she is." Bea sighed. "In the six hours since she met him, she's probably already purchased everything we need."

"You sound happy. I'm glad. You deserve to be happy, BB."

Bea's heart broke a little. Jake hadn't been this kind on the phone in months. And after she was done with this call, she wasn't sure he would be again.

"He's pretty swell, I can't lie." Bea smiled despite the impending doom looming over their call. "And what about you? Haven't heard much about the girls in California lately."

"Oh, you know me, BB, I'm having fun. But nothing serious. No time. Too busy selling."

"How are things going anyway?"

"How're they going? They're going great! Stock keeps soaring and people just want more."

"Sounds like a good time for you to sell."

"BB." Jake's tone changed sharply. "Not this again. Please. Can't we have one conversation where you don't try to tell me what to do with my business? I know that you're used to helping me out, but I don't need it anymore. How much money do I have to make before you'll have a little faith in me?"

"It's not about faith. I do have faith in you, I really do. It's just . . ."

"Just what? I'm sorry I couldn't stake your little investment. I wish I had enough cash to do it. But I'm taking care of the rest, right? So you've got something of your own to invest now. And this way, we both grow the family pot. Me my way and you yours. I just don't get why you can't let up on this."

"Jake." Bea took a deep breath. She was glad that she had started to invest her own money with Milly. Her wealth was growing much more slowly than Jake's, but the fact that it was growing at all gave her a sense of pride and independence. That wasn't what this was about. "Do you ever wonder how the price of Julian Pete just keeps going up? No other oil companies are moving that way all the time."

"You mean like Standard Oil? That's an ancient business. This is the new world, BB. You can't compare."

"Fine, but . . . are you actually seeing new wells drilled? New land discovered?"

"Of course not. I'm a salesman for goodness' sake, not a prospector. I don't have the time or the need to be out in the fields. Speaking of which, I have to skedaddle to get to a dinner. So unless you have something better to talk about, I think it's time for goodbye."

"Wait, Jake. Don't hang up. There is suspicion that Julian Petroleum is a scam. A Ponzi scheme."

"A what?"

"You know, a money pyramid like that guy Charles Ponzi ran? Is it possible that the money you take in for new shares is getting paid out to older investors, as dividends?"

"You've lost your mind. I swear—"

"No, listen. Nate just told me that's what they think at his bank. He said to tell you to sell everything you can before it all collapses. Jake, do you have *any* cash? Anything saved?"

"The company gave me a car and, I guess I need to remind you, I own a building."

"You don't own the building. We pay for it every month."

"Well, yeah, but it's guaranteed by my stock. Bea, you don't seem to get it. I am worth over five hundred thousand dollars!"

"I know. It's incredible, really. But it's only on paper. Please, Jake, turn some of that into cash. Even if you have a penalty for selling early. Please, protect yourself, protect us. If Nate is wrong, it will just mean a smaller profit for you. If he's right . . ."

"He's not right. And I'm not going to listen to this insanity for another minute. Get yourself together, Bea. This new jealous side of you is not attractive. Do me a favor and don't get on the phone when I call next week. Don't get on the phone again until you're ready to eat crow. Because I can't listen to your crazy talk anymore."

"I'm not crazy, Jake. I'm . . ." She was going to say *sorry*. That she was just trying to protect him. Them. But he was gone.

The following week, as Julian Petroleum stock continued to soar, Bea did some research to see if she could figure out what was going on for herself. What she discovered did nothing to assuage her fears. Apparently this wasn't the first time investors had been wary of Mr. C. C. Julian. In 1924 his oil business almost shut down before it was saved by a reorganization. There were some allegations that he was a charlatan in the business news then, but Bea was certain Jake knew nothing about the checkered history of the company he had uprooted his whole life for.

Jake needed to understand the risk of his situation. But he wouldn't listen to Bea. She had to find another way to warn him. To hopefully get him to open his eyes. She saw only one option, and it was risky. But the risk to their lives if this business collapsed was worse. She knew what she had to do, and she needed Nate's help.

CHAPTER TWENTY-THREE

"Let me get this straight: you want me to come for my first Shabbat dinner and, during this same meal, tell your parents that their son is likely embroiled in an enormous con? I thought you wanted them to like me?" Nate raised his eyebrows at Bea in a teasing smirk as he walked beside her. Every night this week she'd left work to find him waiting for her, on the corner of Broad and Wall, to walk her home.

"I see your point." She pulled at her lower lip, thinking as they walked. "But I don't know what else to do. Mama won't believe me. She'll just think I'm jealous and don't understand the business. Papa might listen, but it won't matter if Mama isn't convinced. And you're the one who thinks that time is running out."

"You really think that I will have a better chance of convincing your mother than you will?"

"Oh, I know it. You're already the anointed one in my house."

"I'm not sure I want to sully my status so quickly." Nate started to smile, and then he looked at Bea. She couldn't hide the panic she felt. "All right. I'll do it."

"You will?"

"Of course I will. If you need me to. Whatever you need, Bea, I want to give to you. So, if you think I'm the only way you can get through to your parents, to save your brother, I will sacrifice myself." He lifted his eyebrows as he waved his hand across his throat in mock execution.

Bea smiled. "You truly are an amazing man, Nathan Greenberg." She leapt up and gave him a grateful kiss.

"Tell that to your parents on Shabbat."

Bea felt an unusual sense of pride as she prepared the house for Friday-night dinner. For the first time in her life, Bea didn't feel a pinch of resentment that she, never her mother, had always been the one to do this in her family; because, suddenly, she realized it meant that she could keep a good home. She was a working girl, and she could be a good Jewish wife, and, unexpectedly, the latter seemed to please her too. She couldn't believe she cared. But Nate did this to her. Made her think differently.

Nate made her mother act differently too. Instead of complaining, yet again, that they should hire a girl to help in the house, do the cooking, Pauline was alongside Bea in the kitchen, preparing all the family's favorite recipes. She even thanked Bea for rushing home from work as early as possible. Bea could really get used to this.

Nate arrived right before sunset with two bouquets of roses. "One for you and one for your mother. I would've brought wine but didn't want to ruin your parents' impression of me," he whispered to Bea as they made their way to the living room.

"Henny didn't even consider such a thing when she came over." Bea laughed. "But they don't mind. Papa thinks prohibition is anti-American. Not that he's a big drinker or anything. But he says that the country decreeing what we can drink feels like Czarist Russia."

"I see his point. Mr. Abramovitz, so good to see you again." Nate crossed the room to shake hands with Lew. "And Mrs. Abramovitz, are you sure you're not a fashion model?"

"It is a new dress." Pauline preened. "Now that I can finally afford some nice clothes, I should wear them, don't you think? My Yaacov is really providing for all of us." Even as Bea was annoyed that Pauline seemed to have forgotten that Bea was the one to take her shopping for that dress, she was hit with a wave of nauseated dread at the conversation about Jake that was to come.

"I can see that you are very fortunate in many ways. Mr. Abramovitz's store and Bea's job too." Bea beamed at Nate; how did he know just the right thing to say?

"Fortunate indeed," Lew added proudly. "We have more than we need! Yaacov has given us a great gift with his success. This wonderful apartment. The grocery, full of customers every day. And Beatrice—not just working in the stock market but earning money on her very own investments!" Bea warmed at her father's words, even as she wondered how he never felt belittled by her mother. "Nate, these women have made you a feast. Let's eat."

As Pauline and Lew peppered Nate with questions, she realized that this was the first time a boy—well, a man, really—they knew nothing about was joining them at their dinner table. Any other "suitor" who had eaten with them had been from the neighborhood, invited by her mother, not Bea herself. She was enjoying watching Nate interact. He was so at ease, so natural. Like he was meant to be there. Like he was part of the family.

Her mind shifted to Jake. Sometimes she felt his absence like a missing limb, a sense that something wasn't as it used to be. Right now she felt it more as a stabbing ache. If he were here, at this dinner, living in New York where he belonged, he wouldn't be messed up in this risky business across the country. She shuddered at the thought of what was coming next.

It had been such a lovely evening. Watching Nate with her parents was just making her fall even harder for him. She found herself imagining things she had never contemplated before. Where they might live. How many children they would have. Who would take care of them if both she and Nate were working. Sure, she knew she was getting ahead of herself, but she couldn't help it. Before Nate, she wasn't sure that any man in the world would feel like "the one." Now, the more she knew of Nate, the more certain she was that her "one" was him. She was tempted to just let the night end this way—happy, hopeful. But she had a responsibility to her family, to Jake; she couldn't let Nate leave tonight before they had told her parents about Julian Pete.

"You know that Nate specializes in commodities. His desk is one of the best on the exchange."

"I'm not surprised. You are a very bright young man." Lew smiled warmly. Bea's heart started to pound. Her father was so kind, so welcoming. How would he take the news they were about to deliver. "Wait—commodities, so you're involved in oil then?" Lew had taken the bait. Bea couldn't believe it.

"I am, sir. We study it closely."

"I'll tell you; I didn't know from that business before Yaacov got involved. But seems like a good investment. You own a lot of it, I bet."

Nate looked at Bea, his expression mirroring the pain she felt in her stomach as she anticipated what was about to happen.

"Well, we own some companies . . . others seem too good to be true. There is a lot of room for fakers in the oil world."

"Well, there are bad people in every business," Lew said, unaware of the anvil that was about to drop. "It's a good thing Yaacov is in with a legitimate one."

Nate looked at Bea hesitantly. It seemed he didn't want to hurt her parents any more than she did. But this was for their protection. She nodded for him to continue.

"As a matter of fact, Bea was hoping I would talk to you about that . . . Julian Petroleum has actually got us a bit concerned. We—"

"Concerned? But it is so successful," Pauline cut in. Bea felt for her.

"Not exactly, Mrs. Abramovitz. I—"

"Nate's team thinks that Julian Petroleum might be a scam," Bea blurted out in one staccato stream. She couldn't let this drag on longer, and she couldn't let Nate be the one to take the brunt of what was to come.

"A scam?" Lew looked at her, puzzled.

"Yes, Papa. The stock doesn't move in normal patterns. It never goes down. No one ever seems to sell except the directors and, according to Jake, there are always more people desperate to buy than there are shares to be had. This doesn't happen to even the most successful company. Something isn't right."

"Beatrice, this is too much!" Pauline pushed away from the table and stood, her eyes flashing with fury. "I knew you were envious of your brother, but this is just hateful. Yackie is too smart to get fooled by a fake business. Besides, if it's not real, how do you explain this building? Our apartment? The grocery? You have no idea what you're talking about, and I won't—"

"Enough!" Lew stood, too, but his ire was directed at Pauline. Bea had never seen him angry at her like this before. "Pauline, let her speak. This is her world and Nathan's job. If there is something we need to hear, we should hear it. Pretending doesn't do anything for anyone." Lew moved around the table and put his hand on Pauline's shoulder, gently encouraging her back into her seat. She complied, sitting back down as he gently pushed in her chair. "Beatrice, Nathan, continue," he said stiffly as he, too, sat back down.

"Believe me, Papa, Mama, I am hoping with all my heart that this isn't true. But after Nate told me his concerns, I started to do research. This C. C. Julian—he's been in trouble before; he was almost shut down for selling fake shares of an oil company in '24. And Jake keeps telling us that he's rich, but all his money is in Julian Petroleum stock. I've been begging him to sell some, to convert some of it into cash, but he won't listen."

"Well, he is there, Beatrice. He should know what is really happening with the business, yes? If he believes the stock is good, shouldn't we trust that?" her father asked.

"Mr. Abramovitz, the problem with these types of schemes is that sometimes only the men at the very top know the truth before it is too late."

"Exactly. We are afraid that's what's happening with Jake. That he doesn't know."

"It just doesn't seem possible. All of this"—Lew opened his palm and waved it around the room—"all of this is real. My store is real."

"It is only as real as whatever Jake put down on this building, plus the value of Julian Petroleum stock, Papa. And if Nate's right and it's a scam . . ."

"No. Yaacov wouldn't be that foolish. And he's no crook! He wouldn't give us all of this if it could just disappear."

"The thing is, Mr. Abramovitz, he doesn't think it will disappear. In this type of scheme, as long as the con is working, everyone involved believes they're getting so rich that no one cares to wonder how or why," Nate responded for her. "But it isn't real money. It's stock. A promise of money someday. And the only people turning that artificially inflated stock into cash are the ones at the top of the pyramid," Nate explained gently.

"Yes. And Jake is not at the top," Bea added. "I tried to tell this to Jake . . . he got so mad he won't speak to me at all now." Bea's eyes unexpectedly began to fill with tears. "I just want to protect him. And both of you. And I don't know how to do it." Bea looked at her mother, who was motionless in her seat.

"But these are just your suspicions? Yes? The new economy is growing exponentially. How can you be sure Julian Petroleum isn't part of that growth?" Lew asked, his voice quiet now.

"We can't know with certainty unless the scam is exposed. And I hope we are wrong," Nate said calmly.

"But even if they are wrong, it makes sense for Jake to sell his stock now. To turn his theoretical wealth into cash. To protect himself. And us. I've told him this, several times, but he won't listen. He doesn't believe it. He just keeps watching his paper fortune grow as the stock rises."

"So what can be done?" her father asked. "It is his money."

"But it's all of our lives," Bea said emphatically.

"Maybe you can help him, Nathan?" Pauline asked.

"I'm happy to try, but the most important thing is for him to sell as much of his stock as possible. Before it's too late."

"And since he won't listen to me," Bea jumped in, "I thought . . . well . . . he might hear it differently coming from you." Bea looked pleadingly at her mother.

"Me? What do I know from this? I'm not accusing my son of being a criminal just because his resentful sister thinks he might be. I know he is not!"

Bea should have expected this reaction, but it still stung. She sat in silence, feeling embarrassed in front of Nate, defeated, and unsure of what to do now.

"Mrs. Abramovitz. No one, especially not Bea, is saying Jake is a criminal. But it seems like he might be mixed up with some men who are. And—"

"And he needs to open his eyes or have them opened for him before he ruins us all!" Bea snapped. She couldn't believe she had just said this to her mother. Nate's support made her bold. Sort of how she used to feel when Jake was in her corner. She couldn't believe how much had changed in such a short time.

"I . . . I . . . I wouldn't even know what to say." Pauline lifted her teacup, and Bea saw her hand was shaking.

"Shefele." Lew touched her arm gently. "I will talk to him. I will ask him to sell his stock, but you know he also needs to hear it from you. We need to do this together."

Pauline stood on shaky legs, turning away from them to obscure her face. "I've had enough for tonight," she said quietly as she exited the room. "I'm going to get in bed. Good night, Nathan."

"I'm sorry, Mrs. Abramovitz," Nate called after her.

"You're just trying to help." Lew looked at them with an understanding but pained smile as he followed Pauline out of the room. "We will think about this with clearer heads tomorrow."

"Well, that went about as poorly as it could have," Bea said to Nate once they were alone. She tried to laugh, but the mood in the apartment had become so heavy, nothing came out.

"I really am sorry for all of this." Nate held Bea's hand tentatively.

"Don't be. You didn't do anything but point out the truth. Well, the likely truth."

"Still I—"

Bea cut Nate off, grabbed his hand, and brazenly pulled him in for a kiss.

"Where did that come from?" he asked, smiling.

"Thank you. For caring. For protecting me and my family."

"I've met a lot of gals in my day, and never have I met one with such a pure heart. You don't care about my money—or even your own—you care about succeeding on your own terms and doing what is right. For everyone in your life. You're one of a kind, my sweet Bea." He gave her a tender kiss goodbye. She wanted to ask him to stay a little longer, but she was exhausted, and she had a big weekend ahead of her.

CHAPTER TWENTY-FOUR

Bea's sense of dread grew throughout the weekend and, by Sunday, she had such a bad feeling, she couldn't bear to be in her house. It wasn't just that her parents were going to talk to Jake that evening; it was something more. That almost visceral sense that her brother was in trouble. Waiting all day to speak to Jake was driving her mad, so she went for a walk back to their old building to visit Sophie.

"Maybe it's not as bad as you think?" Sophie said calmly after Bea explained why she was in such a state. "I know Jake hasn't always had the best judgment, but could he actually do something like this?"

"I don't think he knows he's doing it. That's almost the worst part. If we're right and he doesn't know—will he even survive the embarrassment? Not to mention how we'll pay for this new life he's 'bought' for us."

"But you can still afford the new place, can't you? You're making extra money, too, from your investments? Milly can't stop talking about how good you are at picking stocks. Says you're almost never wrong. You must have made a bundle."

"Hardly a bundle. I've made some, but you need to have money to make it, and I didn't start with much. Sure, what I have is growing. The problem is, I need to keep investing for it to grow more . . . I don't know how much of the building Jake owns or how much he pays each month. Every time I ask him, he just tells me it's under control. So I've left it alone."

"I know how much that must kill you."

"Yep." Bea rolled her eyes. "And now all I can think is that if I had forced the issue, maybe I wouldn't be in this predicament now."

"Stop! There is nothing you could have done and nothing more you can do. And maybe Nate is wrong. Maybe your parents will talk to Jake today and you'll discover that he really does have everything worked out. Have a little faith. It's not like he's some dummy. You know what my Nana says: 'Worrying may keep you moving, but it doesn't get you anywhere.'"

"I know. I know. I just have a bad feeling . . . Okay, distract me. Tell me about your week."

"Oh, Bea, I've never been so busy! Really, Milly is such a doll. She had me come to her house to fit her mother for some dresses."

"Sophie, that's terrific."

"I know. And some of Milly's mother's society friends want dresses too. Apparently my style is the perfect mix of classic and au courant."

"You do have impeccable taste. This is so exciting. And . . ." Bea smiled mischievously. "If you're in demand with the Gramercy Park crowd, you can finally open your own studio!"

"I might have to. That or get a car to fill with fabrics and trimmings. These women like to see a lot of options!" Sophie's eyes lit up, and Bea was overcome with excitement for her. This was what she was meant to do. "And there's one more thing."

"There's more? Goodness, Soph, hasn't it only been a week since I last saw you?"

"Two. You've been busy," Sophie teased. Bea had been spending most of her free time with Nate, and while Sophie wasn't the kind of friend Bea needed to see or speak to every day to feel close to, she was the kind who would tease her endlessly for getting lost in love.

"Okay, so what else?"

"I think Sal is going to ask me to marry him!"

"Marry you! Soph, I can't believe you let me go on and on about Jake, and you were sitting on that news. Sal Delvecchio. The two of you have been circling each other for years. I'm so happy for you! Our first wedding." Bea squeezed Sophie's hand excitedly.

"Well, it hasn't happened yet. But I have a feeling."

"I know you, and if you have a feeling, it is going to happen."

All Sophie's good news turned Bea's mood around, until she got back home to find her parents in the kitchen. Pauline was dressed like they were going out somewhere, her hair done and lipstick on. But they were just sitting there, staring at the phone, looking distressed.

"What happened? Did you speak to Jake?" Bea asked, surprised. It was only four o'clock, and he didn't usually call until after supper.

"We did not speak to Yaacov. Do you think we would just be sitting here if we had spoken to him?" Pauline barked at her.

"I don't know what you'd do, Mama. But I think it's too early for him to call." She turned to her father. "Why don't you go for a walk? Get some fresh air?"

"I think that's a good suggestion. Come, let's go outside for a few minutes. Clear our heads." Lew reached for Pauline's hand, but she snapped it back from him. "Do you want to try to reach him now? So we don't have to think about it anymore?" he asked. "Bea, you know how to call him, yes?"

"I do, Papa. But it's only early afternoon for him there. He'll surely be out at the beach or somewhere."

"As usual, Beatrice knows it all. So we wait." Pauline's voice was cold and sharp as she stood to go situate herself somewhere else.

"Don't get up. I'll go." Bea didn't know how she had become the villain in this situation, but she was also too drained to defend herself.

"Beatrice, you've done nothing wrong," her father said softly. "This is just hard for your mother. For both of us. To think that Yaacov might be mixed up in something like this, have gotten us all mixed up in it—"

"I know, Papa. I know." Bea decided the best thing she could do was to try to take care of her parents while they waited, so she busied herself cooking. Her mother loved Tanta Isabella's blintzes. They took some time to make but, right now, all they had was time. Bea got to work.

Blintzes were a smart choice. By the time they were done, it was past seven o'clock. They ate in the kitchen, near the phone. It didn't ring. Seven thirty came and went. They had tea, still huddled around the table, waiting. No call. By nine, Bea and Lew went to ready themselves for bed. He had to rise with the sun for work in the morning. Bea changed into her nightclothes and washed up with her ears pricked, hoping the phone would finally ring. It did not.

"Can you try to call him?" Bea jumped to find Pauline standing at her door in her robe and slippers, her father behind her. They both looked the way Bea felt—frustrated, worried, and weary. "He is already two hours late, and we need to put this day to rest." Her father sounded defeated as he spoke. Bea nodded and went back to the kitchen, her parents right behind her.

She tried the number she had been using to reach Jake, but it just rang and rang. She contacted the operator to make sure she had dialed properly. Again, the phone just rang. "He doesn't seem to be home." Bea tried to sound light in her tone. It wasn't like Jake to miss his weekly call, even if he was still mad at Bea. The nagging unease she'd been feeling all day blossomed into a panic that she didn't want her parents to see. "You know Jake," she said with a forced laugh. "He probably had plans with some girl or another and lost track of the time."

"The girls do love him." Pauline smiled. "Well, then, we won't be talking to him tonight. Time for bed." She stood.

"Good night, *shayna*. Try to get some rest," Lew said softly, kissing Bea's head as he followed Pauline to their bedroom. Bea knew his face too well to miss the troubled expression he was trying to mask with a smile. She wanted to tell him he didn't have to hide it from her. She was feeling it and then some herself.

The answer to why Jake hadn't called was in the evening papers the next day. It was a small piece, but the weight of it was enough to shatter them all:

SUSPECTED SHARE OVERISSUE LEADS LOS ANGELES STOCK EXCHANGE TO HALT TRADING ON JULIAN PETROLEUM CORPORATION

Friday evening, all trading of JPC stock was frozen when the exchange learned that the company had falsely sold close to 4,000,000 nonexistent shares to unaware buyers. Allegations assert that a small cadre of insiders were issuing shares to cover their own redemptions. The actions are particularly egregious because many shareholders of Julian Pete, as it was colloquially called, were not sophisticated investors, but small-time innocents who have been swindled out of their life savings to line the pockets of crooked fat cats. An investigation is underway but, if true, this will be one of the biggest criminal scandals in the history of modern finance.

CHAPTER TWENTY-FIVE

June

DOW MONTHLY AVERAGE: 166, +10 POINTS FROM JANUARY

The next few weeks went by in a blur. Jake had disappeared and, with no way to reach him, Bea now feared for his safety. The papers claimed that some very dangerous men had lost millions, and Bea knew enough to know they would be looking for revenge. All she could hope was that Jake was out of harm's way.

Unfortunately, Jake vanishing was only the beginning of the family's worries. A week after the Julian Pete story broke, the loan officer who held their mortgage visited Lew at the shop.

"It is even worse than you feared, Beatrice. Yaacov didn't pay for this building at all." Lew didn't even try to hide his panic, his voice shaking as he recounted the details to Bea. "He used stock in Julian Petroleum for the down payment and took a loan for the rest. How could he be so foolish?" Bea felt as if the ground underneath her had begun to sway as she watched her father pace the length of the stockroom. "What are we going to do? Your mother—she can't find out about this. She's so happy now. Here in this new apartment. Being landlords and shop owners. I can't take this from her. I don't know if she will survive."

Bea was devastated and furious with both Jake and herself. She had worried about Jake spending too much too soon. Why hadn't she asked more questions about how the building was financed? Why didn't she keep nagging him to sell some of his stock when he might have had a chance? Had she set aside her concerns because she, too, was enjoying the benefits of his success? Or was there nothing she could have done to stop her brother? At this point she'd never know. What she did know was that if her mother had to, yet again, go from some semblance of riches back to nothing, while not even knowing if her son was alive or dead, it would break her. And that would break them all.

"Papa, did the banker tell you how much we need to pay to keep the building?"

"It's too much, Beatrice. More than we have."

"There must be something we can do. Let me try talking to the bank. I have my investments. Maybe that will be enough to pay them off for now."

"But that's your money, *shayna*. We can't ask you to—" The desperation in her father's eyes was so intense it almost cleaved her in two. He wanted her to do this, to give up the little she had earned in the market to save them, but it pained him.

"You don't have to ask. I insist. Let me call the banker and see what can be done."

That night a telegram arrived from Jake. The good news was that he was alive. The bad news was that, as she suspected, he had lost everything. Her family was on the precipice of collapse. Abramovitz Grocers was doing well, but the shop's small profits were only enough to cover their basic living expenses. The rent from other tenants in the building would cover the interest on the loan but, again, didn't leave any extra to put toward the additional debt with which they were now saddled. The family's financial situation was dire. Bea's money was the only chance of saving them, and that wasn't nearly enough to cover the entire down payment on the building.

Bea tried to work out a payment plan with the loan officer. If she could give him a small sum to start, she could at least keep a portion of her money growing in the market. He refused. As far as he was concerned, they didn't own this building at all. The best Bea could get was thirty days. Thirty days to come up with nearly ten times what she had earned in her small portfolio so far. It was almost impossible; still, she had no choice but to try.

For the first time in her life, Bea was consumed with the need to make as much money as she could, as quickly as possible. Her life had suddenly gone from nearly perfect to teetering on the verge of Greek tragedy, and she was determined to do everything she could to prevent the precarious balance from falling in the wrong direction.

When Bea first started investing with Milly, she did so cautiously, with a long-term view. Days of analysis went into every stock she picked to ensure that she took only the safest positions. Now was different. Bea's sole mission was to grow her stock portfolio every day, and she devoted any moment she wasn't actively working to achieving her goal. Thanks to her job at the wire, she was often able to anticipate temporary swings in stocks before they happened, and she'd call Milly multiple times a day barking directions to "buy" or "sell." It was a good thing that Milly was Bea's broker, because if not, they wouldn't have spoken much at all. Bea had stopped going out to lunch with the girls, instead using all her free time to study her notebooks for investment ideas. They understood. Henny even made sure to pop by her desk with a slice of pie or an egg cream after lunch most days.

Nate wasn't put off by Bea's preoccupied state either. Nearly every night, he waited to walk her home after work. No matter how late she stayed at her desk, when she left the building, there he was. Standing patiently, calmly offering companionship, whether she was talking him through her latest investment ideas or silently lost in her own thoughts.

He let her lead the conversation. He had stopped asking for news of Jake after a few days, when it became clear Bea would tell him if she heard anything more. He also never pushed her to talk about the specifics of the money she owed.

But, when it was just two weeks away from the loan officer's deadline and he could see Bea's growing desperation, Nate finally spoke up.

"Bea." He stopped walking, gripping her arm gently to stop her too. "I know you want to handle Jake's debt by yourself but . . . if I could help you . . . we could call it a loan—"

"No." Bea shook her head. "It's too much money. I can't ask you to do that."

"But why not? If I have the money—and I'm not sure whether I do, because I don't know how much it is—I can't think of a better way to use it. I love you. I want to help."

Bea knew that Nate had already done well for himself. He had his own apartment and a car. But he was only a few years into his career too. He was saving for a bigger life. Why should he have to give up his honestly earned money for her brother's mistake? Sure, if he had enough to cover the rest of the down payment on the building, she wouldn't have this burden. She could keep investing with less pressure and pay him back slowly. But what if things didn't work out between them? Six months ago, he was a guy who wasn't ready to settle down with anyone. It would be one thing to rely on him that way if they were engaged, although even then she wouldn't like it, but now? It was too much of a risk.

"You're wonderful for offering, but I don't want to complicate things between us. Not when this is still so new."

"New or not, what I feel about you is real. That's not going to change. And I just want to help. You're working so hard to make this money so quickly."

"And I'm getting closer. I just need a few really big ideas."

"How many? How much more money do you need?" Bea hadn't let herself think about the figure, because if she did, she was afraid she'd lose hope.

"When we found out about Jake, I had one thousand dollars in my portfolio. In the past three weeks, I've doubled that."

"Wow." Nate looked impressed. "That's terrific. Wish I could have you on my team."

Me too, Bea thought.

"So, how much more do you need?"

"Eight thousand." She watched Nate's face fall as she blurted the number out loud, and she could read on his face what she'd refused to accept. There was no way she could make that in two weeks.

"Whoa. I don't have that kind of cash lying around."

"I didn't expect you would, nor, as I already told you, would I take it from you if you did."

"But I have some. I think I could get you about two thousand . . ."

"I don't want to take your money, Nate. And even if I did, we both know it's hopeless."

He didn't answer right away. He just walked beside her quietly as her stomach tightened in on itself. His silence told her all she needed to hear—she couldn't do it. She couldn't make this money. Her family really was going to lose everything.

"There is one other way that might work," he said tentatively.

"There is?"

He nodded and started walking faster.

"Well, what is it?" she asked impatiently.

"Leverage."

"Leverage?"

"Yes, you buy stock with a margin loan, put down a small amount of cash, and borrow the rest. If the stocks go up, you can exponentially increase your returns."

"I know what buying with leverage is, Nate. I just can't believe you're suggesting it. It's the surest way to lose your shirt."

"Look, I'm not particularly warm on the idea, in general. I've seen it go really wrong . . . why just the other day I had a client who was long Sears & Roebuck with ninety percent leverage. The way the stock was moving, it should have been a home run. But then there were rumors that they were lagging in sales for the quarter, and the stock dropped a dollar in a flash; we had to call his loan. He lost everything."

"Exactly. The risk is significant. Too significant."

"In general, I agree with you. But when it works, the reward is even bigger. And in this particular instance, where you need to make this much money in just two weeks, we might want to consider it."

"We?"

"Yes, I'll add my two thousand to your two thousand. Bigger starting point, faster to the goal."

"Or faster to complete desolation if I pick wrong."

"Yes. But you haven't been wrong so far."

Bea contemplated Nate's suggestion as they walked. There was some inherent risk to the stock market, although less and less every day, as everything just seemed to keep going up. But taking a margin loan on the little money she had invested was true gambling. The idea made her stomach fall like she was back on the roller coaster at Coney Island. Still, her time was running out. If she didn't use leverage, it was almost impossible that she would be able to make enough to keep the building. And if that was the case, what she had made wouldn't matter anyway. So, really, this might be her only shot.

"If I took your money, we would be partners. So if we bought on margin, and it worked, I would pay you back whatever your returns should have been as soon as I can. On a payment plan."

"Bea." Nate smiled. "I'm not looking to make anything here. I just want to help you. Help your family."

"But that's too much. I can't just take a handout like that. Especially when I could lose it all."

"Will you take my money if I say no to your conditions?" Nate cocked one eyebrow, to make clear that he thought Bea was being silly.

"I wouldn't want to."

"Then fine. I agree to your terms."

She held out her hand to shake on it, but instead he pulled her tightly into his arms. Encircled in the safety of his strong frame, Bea felt the tension of the past weeks melt away, like an icicle in the midday sun. She started to cry.

"Bea? I was trying to make you feel better, not worse."

"You have." She laughed through her tears.

"You sure have a funny way of showing it."

Bea was overwhelmed with gratitude for Nate and her friends. She wasn't used to having people in her life who wanted to help hold her up when she was falling. This wasn't all on her shoulders, and for the first time since this whole Julian Petroleum debacle began, Bea felt real hope.

CHAPTER TWENTY-SIX

The next day Henny and Milly were standing in front of Bea's desk at noon.

"Enough is enough. You need a break. Just for an hour, kitten," Henny said firmly.

"It's true, Bea. Sometimes the best way to make sense of a problem is to step away from it for a little while," Milly added.

"I wish I could, but I have less than two weeks to make this money, and I need every idea I can get, and—"

"Psht!" Henny held up her hand and opened and closed her fingers like the mouth of a duck as she walked behind Bea's desk, collecting her handbag. She wasn't going to accept no as an answer. Bea had so much to do. She was studying every stock she could to come up with the right ones to buy on margin. But just having the girls here with her made her feel calmer. She decided she could use the break.

The minute they got outside, Henny planted a big red kiss on her cheek, and she and Milly enveloped her in a tight hug.

"Oh, girls, I'm sorry. I know I've been a rotten friend lately. I just—" Bea apologized, feeling increasingly guilty as they started walking briskly to their favorite luncheonette. She had really missed this time with them.

"Please!" Henny waved her hand as if clearing away Bea's words. "You're goin' through something awful; we know that. We just want you to know we're here for you, s'all."

"I know that. You've been wonderful." They arrived at the luncheonette and slid into what had become their usual booth in the back corner. "But the truth is the only thing I can do right now is find the best ideas, so my money makes bigger returns, faster. It's not complicated—"

"Your returns have been exceptional," Milly said reassuringly.

"Maybe. But they're not enough. I think my only chance now is to buy on margin."

"I would have suggested it, but I didn't think you believed in leverage." Milly didn't even bat an eye as she spoke.

"Well, it's dangerous, don't you think?" Bea asked, surprised.

"Not really. Most of my clients do it. It is the best way to grow your portfolio fast. And your stock picking is so good . . ."

"Nate said the same thing. And I'm considering it. I could certainly use the boost. But the risk . . . if I'm wrong—"

"Honey . . ." Henny joined the conversation, speaking with surprising authority. "If you're wrong, which you won't be, you'll be in more debt than before. You'll be in a pickle. But you have a steady job with a good paycheck. Your father will have customers whether he's in a store or a pushcart. If you don't take this risk, you're not going to have enough money to keep the store anyway, right?"

"That's what Nate said." Bea laughed.

"Well, good thinking runs in the family, I guess." Henny grinned.

The girls' encouragement was the push Bea needed. Nate had already given her his money, which made her feel physically ill. She'd never even taken a blouse for free from Sophie, yet here she was accepting more money than she'd ever seen in her life from Nate. But they had their partnership agreement. She'd even written it up on a piece of paper and had them both sign it.

There were eleven trading days left for her to make the big stock purchase, and she finally had her plan.

"Chemicals," she said to Nate on their walk home that night. The evening before she'd given the purchase order to Milly, and even though she'd analyzed it every way possible, she wanted Nate to reassure her that her logic was sound. He'd been doing this a lot longer than she had anyway. "The *Wall Street Journal* hinted that Union Carbide might be eyeing an acquisition. Trading volume has started ticking up for it, and some of the smaller chemical companies, today. But the stocks haven't moved much yet."

"Okay, so you'll buy tomorrow, and we will all pray for an acquisition announcement in the next week."

"That's what I'm thinking. Do you agree?"

Nate squeezed her hand. "I think if you were on my team, I'd tell you to pile in. This is gonna work, I can feel it."

For the rest of that week, Bea, Nate, Milly, and even Henny were more interested in stocks than ever before. Bea tried to concentrate on the rest of the data coming through the ticker, but her brain would freeze every time she saw a quote for UCC. So far, her prediction had been right. Several more articles came out in the business news that week, hinting at an acquisition, and the stock had risen 20 percent. By the time the market closed on Saturday afternoon—just three days after she'd put her plan in place—Bea and Nate's $4,000 had turned to seven. If the stock continued to grow at this pace, and there was no reason why it shouldn't, she would have hit her goal two days before the down payment on the building was due. It was a miracle.

And then Monday came. For no discernible reason, Union Carbide dropped dramatically, and with it, Bea's profits turned to losses. Over the course of a day, the value of her portfolio fell to where it had been before Nate even added his own money. She got a panicked call from Milly.

"I don't know how to say this, but . . . ," Milly stammered. "I need you to put more money in your account. The bank is insisting that we get collateral to cover the losses."

"But I don't have any more money!" Bea snapped at her friend.

"I know you don't. I've been racking my brain to come up with a solution, but I can't think of one, Bea."

"All right." Bea took a long, ragged breath, her heart racing so fast she thought it might pop right out of her chest. "How long do I have before they call the loan?"

"Forty-eight hours," Milly whispered. "I'm so sorry, Bea. I—"

"It's not your fault. But I have to go. I have to see if there is any way out of this mess."

For the rest of the afternoon, Bea made herself crazy with analysis. She combed the papers and asked every trader who came by the wire room whether they'd heard anything about Union Carbide or other news in chemicals. There was nothing. The drop was inexplicable. And if it didn't correct itself, and then some, in the next two days, Bea would be ruined.

That night Bea told Nate she had to stay late and not to wait for her. She was too ashamed to face him. When she got home, she collected all the business papers from the past week (her father had a habit of keeping them around much longer than they were relevant) and read them cover to cover to see if there was anything she had missed. Any tiny detail that might have caused the stock price of one of the most promising stocks on the exchange to suddenly falter. She didn't sleep a wink, puzzling out scenarios for her and her family if the worst happened on Friday. Until now she had kept these ideas at bay, focusing only on turning things around. But she could no longer escape what seemed inevitable. She pictured a fire sale in the grocery as her father desperately tried to make as much money as he could before he was kicked out of the store. She pictured men with batons standing at the door of their apartment, waiting while they tried to collect their things, marching them to the street. Where would they go? She pictured her mother, clinging to her diamond necklace, weeping.

She went to work the next morning in a daze. The market opened, and Bea tried her best to stay focused on her job. It was about to be all that she had. She was looking at the latest tapes when UCC popped up. The stock had jumped. It wasn't where it had been when Bea bought it, but it was moving in the right direction. And then the midday paper came out, and she saw the news she had been waiting for. Union Carbide was acquiring two smaller chemical companies to nearly double their output. This was it.

For the rest of the day, Bea watched. The stock kept rising. She was even on her loan. There was no margin call coming. And then, in the last hour of the day, it skyrocketed. In a twenty-four-hour period, Bea went from having lost everything to having made more money than she'd ever seen in her entire life. The next morning, when her position was worth $14,000, she sold it. She had done it. Her family was saved.

As the flood of Bea's relief dissipated, she began to reflect on her experience investing over the previous few weeks. She knew that her success was a result of taking an extreme risk, and she was grateful it had paid off. She was also reminded of Professor Berkman's lesson, back when she was only investing hypothetically and the exchange was just a dream: no matter how good she was at analysis, success in the market still came from a combination of skill, timing, and plain old luck. This time, all three had ended up on her side.

Oddly, though, even if they hadn't, a part of Bea would have still appreciated the experience. Being an active investor was exhilarating. She knew that, if she'd made these calls as a broker for someone else, the emotional intensity might not have been the same, but she also knew this was undoubtedly the best part of Wall Street. In a matter of weeks, she'd succeeded in making enough money to pay off their debts on the building and pay Nate back, plus his return on the investment. She'd saved their house. The store. Her parents would be all right.

Being so close to losing everything had changed the way she thought about money and about the markets. Never again, she vowed, would she let her family be in a position of such precariousness. And as long as she could keep investing, they never would be.

CHAPTER TWENTY-SEVEN

July

DOW MONTHLY AVERAGE: 181, +25 POINTS FROM JANUARY

Spring turned into summer and, while not a day passed that Bea didn't worry about Jake, she was comforted to know that she'd put her and her parents' lives back together. She had saved them, and she did it so quietly that her mother never knew how close they had been to losing it all, again.

Nate had become a regular presence at the Abramovitz house, which gave Pauline something to focus on other than Jake's disappearance. That's not to say that she didn't regularly break down worrying about her son, who hadn't called or written another letter or given them any indication at all that he was even still alive, but the pain was mitigated by a new adoration for her daughter's suitor, and a relentless nagging about when they might be engaged.

Bea was head over heels for Nate, but she was too busy to think about marriage right now. Thankfully, her mother was the only one who didn't seem to understand that. With the market on a steady upward trajectory, Nate was also busier than ever, and Bea fully supported his desire to put his career first. Bea was trying to do the same. She'd come to believe that her job at the wire was actually beneficial to her own investments, and she was in the process of slowly rebuilding her portfolio with Milly. After coming so close to losing everything, she was determined to make enough money to never put her family's welfare at risk again. She and Nate had plenty of time for the rest, eventually. Life had settled into a rhythm, a new normal, and it suited Bea just fine. And then Jake came home.

Bea felt Jake's presence before she realized he was back. It had been a huge day in the market, Bea's portfolio was beginning to grow again, and she was practically skipping home when an odd, uneasy feeling came over her. A tall, skinny man in dirty rags was pacing in front of her stoop. She was momentarily worried for her safety, but then she was flooded with that feeling of familiarity that told her almost immediately who he was: her twin brother had returned. She ran, throwing her arms around him as he shrank into her embrace.

"Jake! Is it you? Is it really you?" She pulled away from him, reaching on tippy-toes to hold his cheeks in her hands. She was stunned at his appearance. Her magnetic, handsome brother, the shining star who always landed on top and looked the part, was diminished almost beyond recognition. His hair was shaggy and so caked with grease it looked brown. His skin was tanned and leathery, his eyes sunken. If they didn't share a birth date, she would have assumed he was ten years her senior. Still, he was here. She tucked her concern and shock away and gave him her most dazzling smile. "You're alive! You're home!"

He nodded as tears streamed from his eyes. "BB, I'm sorry. I'm so, so sorry." He started to sob. "I should've listened to you. I should always listen to you. I was afraid you wouldn't be here anymore—in this building. That the store—" He gestured to the window of Abramovitz Grocers, dark for the evening but with shelves full of produce that made clear it was thriving.

"We're still here. We're doing well, actually. It's all okay, Jake." Bea rubbed his back to soothe him like she had when he was young and failed a test. "Let's get you upstairs and into a nice bath and some clean clothes." Bea noticed that Jake didn't have anything with him, not even the tattered valise he had left with last year. "We probably have some of your old things, or you can borrow something from Papa until we can take you shopping." Bea smiled, the image of six-foot Jake in their five-foot-seven father's pants running through her mind. "Or maybe you can borrow something from Nate. I can ring him."

"Nate?" Jake looked at Bea, perplexed as he used his dirty sleeve to dry his eyes.

"Oh, Jake, you've missed so much. Don't worry, once you're settled in, I'll catch you up on everything!"

Bea decided that seeing Jake as he was now might be too much of a shock for her parents, so she animatedly entered the apartment, distracting them with a story while he snuck directly into the bathroom. She then made a big stink about needing a bath herself and disappeared to run the tub and find Jake something to wear. The next thirty minutes seemed like a year and then, finally, he emerged in an old pair of pajamas. His body was unusually muscular, but also alarmingly thin. He was holding the waist of his bottoms to keep them from falling off. Bea stifled a gasp, forcing a broad smile. "I think you're ready for Mama and Papa. And some food!"

"That's for sure. Can you tell I haven't had much to eat lately?" Jake smiled and winked, trying to make light of his thinness as he followed Bea into the kitchen. Pauline and Lew were at the table, drinking tea before bed.

"Mama, Papa. I have something for you."

"Beatrice—what is it? I thought you weren't buying gifts, saving up for your 'portfolio.'" Pauline's voice was edged with annoyance; she had no idea how much Bea had given her the past few months, and she never would. She stepped aside as Jake entered the room.

"Yaacov!" Pauline's teacup fell with a clatter from her hands. She leapt up, screaming, and ran to encircle Jake in her arms. "My baby boy! It's a miracle!" Lew stood up as well, and Bea saw his eyes glistening with the seeds of tears as he, too, embraced Jake closely.

Suddenly the room felt lighter, freer. Bea knew how hard it had been on all of them to be without Jake. To have no idea where he was or what he was doing. But, until this moment, Bea hadn't realized how tightly they'd been holding themselves in his absence. All at once, she felt everything in them begin to relax.

They stayed up late that night, feeding Jake until he was ready to burst and filling him in on all that had happened while he was gone. Bea was anxious to get Jake alone, so she could hear the details of his story and explain what her mother did and didn't know about the family's financial situation, but Pauline seemed unable to pull herself away from Jake's side. It was almost midnight when Lew finally stood, insisting they all go to bed. Bea got herself washed and ready for sleep and then made her way into Jake's bedroom, hoping they could talk like they used to in the old place, when they shared a room and would whisper about their secrets until they drifted off to sleep. But by the time she got to his door, the sound of snoring told her the truth would have to wait another day.

Jake was still asleep when Bea left for work the following morning. As usual, her day at the office distracted her, so much so that she hadn't even had a chance to tell Nate or the girls that the prodigal son had returned, until lunch. Sophie would find out at Shabbat. *Shabbat.* Bea had completely forgotten that she was supposed to join Nate and his family tonight. Nate had been so understanding about how hard Jake's disappearance was on Pauline that when they spent time with family, it was usually with her parents. She'd met Nate's only once. This dinner had been planned for weeks. Still, she couldn't possibly go now, not with Jake just home. She didn't want to disappoint Nate, but she had no choice; she just had to hope he'd understand. If Nate was miffed that Bea canceled on him, she couldn't tell. Instead, he sounded thrilled for all of them that Jake had returned safely and hoped to meet him soon. Bea thought, not for the first time, that she couldn't believe her luck at finding such a good man.

Jake was in the kitchen, cooking, when Bea got home.

"What in the world?"

"BB! You're home! I figured with you working all day and it being Shabbas and all, I'd make dinner. I'm just basting this chicken before I put it back in the oven to roast longer. Then I'll go downstairs to help Papa with the end-of-week rush."

"Jake? Did you suffer a blow to the head?" This was not her brother, no matter how down on his luck he had been.

"No! I'm just grateful, BB. So grateful. I don't know how you did it, but you saved us. You saved us all."

Bea blushed. Even though it was nice to be recognized, Jake's raw vulnerability made her feel awkward instead of proud. Particularly now, seeing him so reduced. "I'm just glad it all worked out."

"How did you do it, BB? Exactly. I mean, my stock was worthless. So there was nothing to pay for this building. And you said you only had a little savings . . . where did you get the money?"

"Forget about that for now. I still don't know what really happened to you. What have you been doing since May? Where have you been? And how did you get home?"

"It's a long story."

"I've got time."

"Okay. Well, after you warned me that last time about Julian Pete, I decided to ask Mo about it, just to be sure. 'Course Mo said I was being nuts, that everything was great. Why look a gift horse in the mouth, you know? Less than a week later, trading was stopped altogether. I was kicked out of the apartment—the company'd been paying for it. I thought I still had my car, at least; it was supposed to be a bonus from the company. Turns out even that was a lie and it was repossessed. Mo was suddenly unreachable, so I tried Tommy, you know, Mo's cousin? And when I finally got a hold of him, Tommy said his family had lost everything they invested with his uncle, and Mo had disappeared."

Bea imagined things had been hard for Jake, but somehow, she hadn't anticipated what that really meant. "So you were swindled and left with nothing—collateral damage, just like all the others whose stories I've been reading in the papers. I had hoped . . ."

"Yeah. I was the ultimate sucker. I wanted to come home, but I had no money. And after I'd been so rotten to you, I was too ashamed to ask for help. So I started to work my way back to New York. I hitched rides and spent weeks at a time working on farms and taking any other day-laborer job I could get. Sometimes they gave me a bale of hay to sleep on; sometimes I slept in the dirt on the side of the road. Truth was, I didn't really sleep much at all. I sent you guys that one telegram before I left LA, but I didn't want to spare the pennies to send another one. Plus, I didn't know when or if I'd make it back to you. And when I got here . . . I was worried you'd all have been put out on the street thanks to me. But you saved us. How?"

"I made the money to pay off your debts in the market." Bea felt an involuntary smile creep across her face.

"In the market?"

"Yep. I got a thirty-day extension on the loan, and then I got really aggressive with my investments. I took more risk than I ever had before, or ever want to again." As she spoke, she started to relive the stress of those weeks. The constant worrying. Her brother had had it hard, but so had she. And he had no idea.

"Okay, so you're telling me that you are so good at stock picking that you could make enough to put a cash down payment on a building in just thirty days?"

"Yes."

Jake started shaking his head. "Then I don't get it, Bea. If you're so talented, why are you hiding in the shadows? Why isn't this your job?"

"Because"—Bea looked around to be sure her mother was out of earshot before she spoke—"nothing has changed at the bank. They wouldn't even consider someone like me for a job like that."

"Then leave. Go somewhere that will."

"There's nowhere. I've accepted that. It's backward and unfair. But I've talked to everyone at every semirespectable bank in New York, and this is just the way it is. I've come to terms with it. I'm growing my own investments. Making my own money. The good news is that working in the wire room helps me refine my picks. I get insight into what is happening in the market that I wouldn't have otherwise. More transactions come through Morgan than almost any other bank, and that gives me a huge advantage."

"If you say so," Jake replied, suddenly pensive. Bea could see the wheels spinning behind his bloodshot eyes. What, she wondered, was he thinking?

Bea had never seen Jake this broken. Any residual anger or resentment she had toward him evaporated. She had to help him. But how? Lew wanted him to go back to school, which Bea didn't think was an altogether bad idea; she was making money, and with the market climbing daily and things stable at home, she had begun to see a path toward making a lot more. If Jake would be around to help at home and at the store, then she would be free to focus on her job. Sure, that was the last thing Jake would have wanted, but for the moment, he had no choice. She had sacrificed long enough for the good of the family; now it was his turn.

CHAPTER TWENTY-EIGHT

August

DOW MONTHLY AVERAGE: 190, +9 POINTS FROM JULY

Jake had been home for a month, and his initial willingness to do anything possible to help Bea had diminished. He refused to take summer classes at City College, so he had nothing to do but shuffle around the house and begrudgingly work in the grocery. Physically, his body looked better—steady meals, comfortable sleep, and no manual labor helped him fill back out to his natural size—but his eyes gave away his misery. For all their lives Jake had had the eyes of a dreamer; when you looked at him closely, you couldn't miss that flicker of enthusiasm. He was perpetually working on a scheme, a new idea, always excited about something. Often those somethings were flights of fancy, winding maps ending in pots of fool's gold, but the energy they gave Jake was contagious. It was part of his charm.

Since coming home, this fire was gone. Jake's eyes were flat, dull, the blue suddenly more like the sky on a dreary day than on a bright, clear, crisp one. Jake was so unhappy all the time Bea had been afraid to introduce him to Nate, Henny, and Milly. What would they think of this shadow of a man who now inhabited the space her brother used to occupy? Even Sophie was stunned by how different Jake was. She tried to tease and innocently flirt with him; now that she was marrying Sal, everyone knew it was only in jest, but he couldn't even engage in that. Something had to be done to pull Jake out from under his cloud of failure and misery.

Bea wasn't sure that a ritzy night out would lift Jake's mood, but Nate and Henny thought otherwise (even though they had yet to meet him). They convinced her that getting all dolled up and making the trip uptown to the swankiest jazz club in Harlem would be just the thing to remind any man that there was still a life to be lived. When Bea proposed the idea to Jake and saw his face come to life for the first time since his return from the West Coast, she knew they were right.

The night felt like a true celebration. Even though the Abramovitzes lived on the other side of the city from Harlem, the group had decided to start the evening at their apartment. Everyone—Milly, Henny, Sophie, Sal, Nate, and Lowell (one of Nate's banker friends, whom he brought to even the numbers between gals and guys)—gathered in the living room. Pauline had squealed with delight like a schoolgirl when Jake came out of his room dressed in the new double-breasted suit Bea had bought for him. She might have felt resentful that on top of everything else she had done, she was now buying him fancy clothing, since it was because of him that her portfolio was wiped out. But her brother needed this. She could feel his heaviness in her own body. And she was in the process of slowly rebuilding what she had lost, now with the goal of buying their building outright as soon as possible.

Before he even entered the living room, Bea sensed a shift in Jake. When she saw him, she momentarily lost her breath; with his hair greased and combed, face clean shaven, Jake looked like a million bucks again. Henny, who was never shy around Lew and Pauline, poured everyone champagne, and her parents even joined in a toast and then headed downstairs to pile into Milly's and Nate's cars for the ride uptown. Bea didn't know if it was the bubbles or the moment, but she was overwhelmed with the feeling that this, finally, was a much-needed new beginning for their family.

It was a long ride to Harlem, but they passed the time gleefully sipping more champagne. Jake was in such high spirits he started telling Nate and Henny stories about nightlife in Hollywood, where, apparently, it was as if prohibition didn't exist at all. Bea had grown much more sophisticated since Jake left, but she hadn't experienced anything like what he was describing—starlets jumping into swimming pools naked, actors betting hundreds of dollars on single hands of poker. She wasn't surprised; the old Jake had always been the center of the fun. Maybe tonight, their first at the ultraglamorous Cotton Club, he would be again. And Bea was thrilled that, this time, she got to be there to participate.

The group arrived at 142nd Street and Lenox and nearly fell out of their cars, already heady from all the champagne. As they walked inside, Henny linked arms with Jake.

"Do a girl a solid and hold me up, will ya?" she asked, directing her most seductive smile at him. "I think my legs went to bed already, curled up like they were in the back of Nate's roadster."

"Happy to hold you up as long as you need me. Even longer if you want." Jake drew Henny's waist in closer, giving her a little squeeze. Bea was surprised. She had assumed Lowell, Nate's broker friend, was there for Henny. But when she turned behind her, she saw him engrossed in conversation with Milly. He was a beanpole of a man, and Milly was standing up straight to meet his gaze. Bea smiled to herself; they made a nice pair. Now Henny and Jake . . . that was something she simply hadn't contemplated. But tonight, tonight was for letting go, so she decided to stop making a puzzle out of everything and everyone, swung Nate's hand playfully in hers, and let herself get lost in the immersive world of Harlem jazz.

The Cotton Club was elaborately themed. The club's door looked like the outside of a log cabin, smack dab in the middle of Manhattan. The walls inside were covered with detailed depictions of stately grand southern plantations, the room lined with exotic plants to feel like a jungle. Oddly, the patrons were all white. Bea was surprised. The one time she, Jake, and Sophie went to a jazz club before, it was more like a typical speakeasy, with all sorts of people mixed up together. The Cotton Club felt like what she imagined a black-tie affair at a very white club might, except that it was set to the music of Duke Ellington and his band, who were the only Black people in the room. It struck her as odd that there were no Black patrons, but she just added it to the list of unexpected things happening tonight.

When they sat at their table, Henny made sure to be next to Jake and whispered to him constantly during the show. After the first act, they finally ordered dinner, and the group began talking.

"So, Jake, I hear you got mixed up with that Julian Pete disaster. Tough break," Lowell said innocently. Bea's fingers tightened around Nate's hand. Why would Nate have told him about that?

"It was a great thing until it wasn't," Jake said with a forced laugh.

"Aw, honey, you were just trying to find your fortune. I admire that." Henny stroked Jake's arm. *Could she actually like Jake? He wasn't her type. Still, she seemed so taken with him. Maybe she was just being nice. She knew how down in the dumps Jake had been, and she always wanted to cheer people up.*

"For a minute there I really had a fortune. If only it wasn't all in bad paper." Jake picked up his martini glass and drained it in a single gulp. "Guess it serves me right. My sister knew better, of course. Little genius can smell the stink of something foul three thousand miles away."

"That right?" Lowell asked curiously. "More than I could do. I lost a nice chunk of change in that deal myself. It looked like a winner to me."

"Are you in commodities too?" Bea asked Lowell, trying to shift the subject.

"He's a bond salesman. Mostly railroads," Milly jumped in. "But he's in the market with his own money too."

"What are we, at a job interview? Next we're going to ask Sal to tell us all about building houses, for goodness' sake. Aren't we here to have fun?" Henny asked, pulling out a cigarette. Jake nearly dropped his fork on the floor, racing to light it.

"That we are, and we know with you here, Hen, we surely will." Nate nodded at his cousin playfully. "So tell us, Jake, what secrets should we know about our angelic Bea?" Nate asked teasingly. "So far sweet Sophie here has been too loyal to tell us anything good."

"I stand by my friends!" Sophie giggled. "Unlike you, apparently." She smirked playfully at Nate, and Bea was overcome with a wave of joy. Her best friends, her boyfriend, and her brother out together and teasing one another like they were all family. It was incredible.

"Hmm . . . Bea was always pretty perfect. There was that time that she tried to become a blonde." Jake looked at Bea and winked.

"A blonde? Her hair is darker than the waiter's tuxedo jacket!" Henny laughed.

"Yep. But Yale Schwartz liked blonde girls, and that summer, Bea wanted to get his attention any way she could."

"Not true!" Bea said with a smile. Yale Schwartz had been very cute when they were fifteen. He hadn't grown up so well, though.

"That I can tell you is true." Sophie giggled.

"Yep. So Sophie told her that there was an ancient Italian secret to turn hair blonde: lemon juice. Lucky for us, Papa had lots of rotting lemons."

"Jake Abramovitz, how dare you blame that on me!" Sophie gave Jake a fake evil eye.

"It was you, Soph. Anyway, Bea spent hours squeezing those lemons into a pitcher and soaking her hair in it. Then she sat outside in the sun for the rest of the day. By the time she came in, she had a full head of . . . fried brown hair."

The group broke into uproarious laughter as another round of drinks arrived at the table.

"Well, Yale Schwartz noticed me after that."

"He did, and he called you 'Frazzle' for the next three years."

The orchestra came back on, this time with dancers dressed in nothing but leotards adorned with sequins and sky-high headdresses with gigantic feathers atop their bobbed hair. Their act mesmerized the entire club and, thankfully, distracted the group enough that "Frazzle" slipped from their minds. When the dancers cleared the floor to make way for the patrons, Henny pulled Jake out of his seat and corralled the whole group onto the dance floor. Bea had never seen Jake so in his element—he shined.

"I think Henny has met her match," Nate said to Bea as he pulled her in for a twirl.

"You don't think she's just being nice?"

"Henny doesn't do *this* kind of nice to someone she doesn't like. You think it was an accident she ended up in the car with us instead of Lowell? She was gaga for Jake the minute she walked in the door."

"But she's only interested in bankers?"

"Don't you know the heart works in mysterious ways?" Nate pulled Bea in and kissed her. "Look at me, determined not to fall in love until you came along—and now, I'm so head over heels I can hardly stand up!" Nate did a jelly-legged Charleston, making Bea laugh so hard her stomach hurt. The next song was slower, and Nate drew her in to dance.

Bea looked around the club and was flooded with joy; all the people she cared about the most in the world suddenly seemed happy: Milly and Lowell awkwardly and unabashedly doing a poor version of the Black Bottom, Sophie and Sal giggling to the beat in the most basic two-step, and Jake grinning admiringly at Henny's sultry shimmy and then suddenly pulling her into a passionate kiss. It was a perfect evening. She had found her way in the world. Hopefully tonight was just the thing to break the spell of misery that had fallen upon Jake and set him on the right path too.

CHAPTER TWENTY-NINE

November

DOW MONTHLY AVERAGE: 198, +42 POINTS FROM JANUARY

That fall, Bea's life was ostensibly lovely. She and Nate were going strong. She had a steady job where she was appreciated for her talents (even though she knew that her potential was unfairly limited). She was slowly making money in her investment portfolio with Milly. A year ago, she would have been thrilled with the progress she'd made but, after that summer, something inside of her shifted. As horrible as it had been to be teetering on the edge of losing everything, the excitement of having found a stock, investing big, and making all that money was hard to forget. When she started working on Wall Street, she wanted to be a broker because she thought it was the natural objective for someone who loved the puzzle of the market. Never mind that women didn't do it. But now, after everything she'd been through, she realized that there was more to it. There was a rush to being in it as the market moved. To knowing that everything you had hung in the balance of your choices. Suddenly she found herself looking at her job in the wire and her small portfolio that, due to her conservative investment approach, felt like it was growing slower than Sophie's father's grapevines in winter, and wondering: *Is this all there is?* She was twenty-two years old, and she couldn't accept that she'd already achieved everything she was going to in her career.

While Bea felt like she was walking in place, professionally, Jake was going backward. He'd made good on his promise to Lew before he went to California and was back at City College, but after the pace and energy of Los Angeles, he was bored and miserable. Bea's and Jake's personal lives were much more exciting than their professional ones. Bea had never seen Jake or Henrietta get serious with anyone, but since that night at the Cotton Club they were inseparable. Nate and Henny became regular fixtures at the Abramovitz house, the fact that twins were dating cousins lost on no one. Pauline delighted in having both a Brodsky and a successful banker at her table, and insisted on Henny and Nate joining them for dinner as often as possible. It was during one of these casual family dinners when Bea had the idea that would change all of their lives.

"The market is the strongest it has ever been in history," Nate said when Lew remarked on the constant upward trends he had been seeing in the papers. "I've never seen people make this much money this quickly. It's really extraordinary. And there doesn't seem to be an end in sight."

"Sounds like a dream," Jake said glumly.

"Well, it's hard work keeping up with all of it. We can't hire new guys fast enough to meet the increased demand from our clients."

"Wish you could hire me," Jake said.

"You don't like the markets, Jake," Bea replied. "You wouldn't even take Professor Berkman's class when I asked you to."

"That was school. I think we all know how I feel about school."

"You have too much going for you to be wasting your time in a classroom, if you ask me," Henny added.

"He could always join Papa at the grocery," Bea jabbed.

"But really, Nate, do you think they'd hire Jake?" Henny seized on the idea.

"I dunno." Nate looked at Bea. He knew how badly she'd wanted to be a broker herself, and it seemed he understood that this might feel like a real insult to her. And in the first instant Jake said it, she did feel that way. How dare her brother, who had never shown an interest in anything that made one good at stock picking, suddenly want to do the one job she had wanted more than any other, and could never get? But Bea knew Jake. She knew he wouldn't do the kind of analysis she did to select stocks. He wouldn't have the natural instinct for the market that Nate did. But he was great with people. He could surely land clients.

Suddenly she had a crazy idea. "You should try it, Jake. National City is one of the best banks in the country. If they are hiring like mad and Nate thinks you could get an interview, why not?"

"Because he needs to finish school, that's why not," Lew jumped in.

"Papa, I'm twenty-two years old. The time for me to be in school has come and gone."

"But doesn't he need a college degree to even be considered, Nathan?" Lew asked.

"Actually, no. We have training programs to teach the specifics of the market. Jake is actually just the kind of guy we're looking for: smart, confident, eager to learn and make money, and great with people."

"Yackie is wonderful with people," Pauline chimed in. As Bea expected, she followed up with one of her standard brags about Jake. "Since he was a little boy, he could sell a rotten turnip to Lew's pickiest customer. And since he's been helping at the store in the afternoons, sales have never been better. Isn't that what you said, Lew?"

Lew nodded.

"He's always been a terrific salesman," Bea added. She no longer felt resentful when her mother lavished praise on Jake. She knew the facts: Jake had strengths, and he had limitations, and Pauline couldn't see that because it would hurt her too much; she needed her son to be perfect. Bea was fine to maintain that illusion for their mother. "Would you want to be a broker, Jake?" Bea asked.

"Are you kidding? You heard Nate, Wall Street's the hottest place to be these days. I'd kill for a chance like that."

"Oh, that would just be berries, wouldn't it?" Henny squealed. "Jake on Wall Street. Nate, whaddya think? Can you get him an interview?"

"I don't see why not."

"Well, I still think nothing can compare to a university degree, but if the banks don't care . . . ," Lew said, resigned to be overruled.

"Nate, I'd owe you for life if you could get me in those doors. I'd work harder than anyone National City has ever seen." Bea could tell Jake was in salesman mode; she felt his nerves underneath his pitch for the opportunity. But she knew how to make his worries disappear. And she couldn't wait to start.

"It's settled then. Nate will see what he can do. Now let's have dessert. I spent hours baking this sponge," Bea joked as she went to get the cake Henny had brought over from a local bakery.

When Henny and Nate had left and their parents went to bed, Jake followed Bea into her room. "D'ya really think I can do this, BB?" His bravado had evaporated, and now he was so worried he looked almost gray.

"Of course I do. Wouldn't have said you should if I didn't."

"And you wouldn't be mad? I know this was your dream and—"

"*Was* my dream. I have new ideas now. And you being a broker might help me achieve them."

"Oh yeah? How's that?"

"It's simple, really. I'm the one of the two of us who should be a broker. No offense." She looked at Jake apologetically; she wasn't trying to insult him.

"None taken. I agree. So go on."

"But we know I can't get hired because of who I am. A female. But we're twins. We are like two halves of a whole. So why not use that to our advantage on Wall Street?"

"You want to dress up as me?"

"Of course not. What I'm saying is that I've been studying and working in the markets for a while now. I've got my notebooks with historical trends. My job at the wire gives me context on everything coming across the ticker. You and I live in the same house. So you can be the face at National City, but I can be the broker behind the scenes."

"I see how this is good for me. But what do you get out of it? I'd feel like I was taking advantage of you."

"But you wouldn't. I want to be in on the action. You'd give me the chance to make decisions for multiple clients, and a cut of your profits. Hopefully, if you do well enough, you'll get a bigger job, and then you can bring me in to work with you."

"So you're saying, if I get this job, then for a percentage of my profits, you'll do the stock picking, and I just have to land clients and keep 'em happy?"

"Exactly. You do what you're good at, I'll do what I'm good at."

"And we'll both make a bundle, as a team. I love it, Bea. But . . ." Jake suddenly looked concerned.

"But what?" Bea got nervous. She finally saw a real path to achieve her goals, and she didn't want to hear Jake say anything that would interfere with that.

"I don't think we should tell anyone about this."

"Well, we can tell Mama and Papa. Henny. Nate."

"No. Definitely not Nate. So not Henny either. What will they think if I need my sister to be able to do my job? Mama and Papa, sure. They'll hear us talking."

"But—" Bea wanted to object. She hated the idea of any kind of lie or deception, especially from Nate and Henny.

"But it's not like this will be forever . . . right? So, for now, we just keep this in the family? I'm a broker and you are, too, in secret."

Suddenly Bea had hope again about something bigger in her career. She saw a path to her and Jake making the kind of money that would give them financial security for life. And it wasn't so much a deception as a small omission. She thought keeping it secret was a ridiculous request, but if it was what Jake needed to have the confidence to move forward, something she knew would be better for them both, she would agree. For now.

"A secret broker." Bea laughed.

"Almost the same as a broker, right?" Jake said encouragingly.

It wasn't exactly what she wanted, but it was the closest she'd come yet. Maybe, just maybe, this would be a perfect partnership. Maybe being a stockbroker's sister was just as good as being a stockbroker. Maybe it could even be better.

1928

One Year before the Crash

CHAPTER THIRTY

January

DOW MONTHLY AVERAGE: 199, +42 POINTS FROM PRIOR JANUARY

201. That was where the Dow closed at the end of 1927. It was the highest level in history. Just one year before, Bea's first year on Wall Street, the world was elated when the Dow peaked at 163. But all through 1927 it just kept going up. Investors heralded it as a new era in the market: a state of permanent expansion. The economy was growing, new industries were emerging, so it followed that stocks and bonds would grow too.

It was into this heady market that Jake, who had been hired by National City on the spot at his interview in December, started his banking career. His first two weeks of work were a cram course on stock market basics; by late January, he was set up with his own desk and a small list of customers. He had been working on Wall Street for less than a month and was already advising clients on securities purchases worth thousands of dollars. Even though this was what Bea had hoped for, after what she'd been through to try to work as a broker herself, it was hard to see how easily Jake became one. He was no more a part of elite New York society than Bea, and he didn't even have a college degree, but he was a man, and that was enough. Well, almost enough. Without her help he couldn't have done this. Likely couldn't keep doing this. And his gratitude and reliance on her, coupled with the belief that this was her surest path to financial stability and, possibly, a new way in the door on the brokerage floor, made up for any jealousy she might feel.

Beyond the obvious new innovator stocks like General Motors, DuPont, and American Telephone & Telegraph, Jake had no idea what to buy. Bea did. So, each evening, after work, she sat with Jake and her notebook, pointing out the trends and movements in the market and predicting how she believed they would impact the following day's stock activity. Jake needed a lot of help to understand how to use patterns and relationships across stocks to his advantage. That was where Bea came in.

"So you see how RCA can make traditional stocks move? Here"—she pointed to her chart—"RCA went up and, as a result, American Chemical, U.S. Steel, American Locomotive, they all went up too. Because RCA is driving movement in certain traditional sectors in the market. Conversely, if RCA is going up, Paramount goes down. And the other way around. So, if Paramount goes up, what do you do?"

"Sell RCA?"

"Exactly." Bea was pleased. Jake was much more attentive to her lessons about the market than he had ever been to anything she tried to teach him when they were in school.

"Okay. But how can I possibly remember all of this? I mean, during the day when things are coming in so quickly?"

"After a while, you just know it."

"You just know it, BB, because you remember everything. You know my mind doesn't work like that. I can tell you the names of every guy in a room after I meet them once, but numbers, that's your thing."

"We can train you to do it with stocks."

Jake looked at her skeptically. As much as it pained her to see how someone so confident in other areas of life could be so insecure about this, it was also reassuring. This was the balance between them. This would be the key to their success.

"Okay, how about this?" Bea said. "I'll make you your own notebook and, at the end of each day, we can look together and come up with a strategy for the following day's trades."

"Sounds like a lot of work for you. But if you're willing."

"I am." This was the part Bea loved; it wouldn't feel like work. And even if it did, this was the work she wanted to do anyway. She and Jake had already agreed that he would cut her in on all his commissions, and since she was the one actually making the stock picks, she had essentially become a broker. Even if no one knew it.

Now that Bea was basically investing with Jake, she decided it was more efficient to have her portfolio at National City than at J.P. Morgan. Jake could invest her money and treat her investments as one of the many he was managing. As Bea expected, Milly was understanding when she told her. Milly had plenty of clients and was doing well at the bank. She'd miss the daily phone calls, but they'd still have their lunches. Bea couldn't believe her good fortune; now that she had adjusted her goals, everything was falling into place.

CHAPTER THIRTY-ONE

February

DOW MONTHLY AVERAGE: 195, –4 POINTS FROM PRIOR MONTH, +38 FROM PRIOR YEAR

Bea had a lot less time alone with Nate since Jake had started working at National City. Their nights out were frequently group affairs now that everyone was coupled off. Sophie and Sal were planning a small wedding, while trying to save every penny for him to set up his own construction business and her to lease a small studio. Milly was a goner for Lowell, who, with his unusually tall stature, always sunny demeanor, and slightly awkward social skills seemed to be a male version of her in nearly every way. And Henny and Jake were going stronger than ever. Bea was still surprised about them as a couple. She understood why Henny had captivated her brother—she was everything a guy could want and more. But Jake didn't have the success or money to take care of Henny the way the boys she usually ran around with did. Sure, if things kept going well in the market, and with Bea's help, he might soon. But he didn't now, and Henny was more devoted to Jake than to any guy Bea had seen her date. As predictable as some things were, love clearly operated by its own set of rules.

During the week, Jake waited for Bea after work, so they could walk home together and discuss the market. It was the first time she and her brother had something like this in common, something external and intellectual that they were both interested in, and she loved it. Nate sometimes tagged along, but it wasn't the same for either of them with Jake there. Bea missed her time one-on-one with Nate. This Saturday, he'd planned a date just for the two of them, all alone, to go ice skating in Central Park. She wasn't particularly coordinated and had never been skating; still, if it meant time alone with Nate, she couldn't wait.

Saturday was chilly but, somehow, it felt warmer in Central Park than it had downtown. Maybe it was because there were no buildings to block the sun from shining on them and intensify the biting breeze, or maybe it was just being here with Nate, cuddled together, shuffling in circles on the ice.

"I miss this, you and me, alone," Bea said as she held tight to Nate's elbow, nearly falling for the third time.

"Me too. Clearly, since I planned this whole day."

"Yes, this is very romantic." She stopped moving and grabbed his arm again, to steady herself. It didn't help much—he was as off-balance as she was. "But why, exactly did you pick skating if you don't know how to do it either?" She smiled.

"You make a fair point. I wanted to do something frivolous and fun. Something where I could hold you close. And I didn't really think through the actual skating of it all. Do you want to stop?"

"Just when we're getting the hang of it?" She pushed off him gently to glide a little on the ice, giggling. And then her ankle started to wobble, and she grabbed back on in a panic, nearly taking them both down. "All right, I'm reconsidering. Maybe some cocoa on the bench would be safer."

"I have a better idea."

They took off their skates, and after Nate bought them both hot chocolate, he steered Bea toward a horse-drawn carriage parked on the road near the frozen pond.

"Your chariot." Nate gestured grandly for her to get inside. She giggled as she excitedly climbed into the back. She'd never been on a carriage ride in the park before. It was something she thought was reserved for much fancier people. Nate followed behind her, handing her their cocoas before pulling the thick fur blanket over their laps. And then they were off.

Bea was lost in the magic of the moment: the park's trees covered with snow, glistening in the bright sunlight; the soothing, rhythmic sound of the horses' hooves hitting the road below; the luxury of being snuggled up in the cab with the man she loved.

"This is the most perfect afternoon. Maybe I should stay too busy to see you more often," Bea said teasingly.

"Please don't do that," Nate said, suddenly serious. "I know it's silly, but I've felt so lonely without our nightly walks. I love our whole gang, of course, and it's just tops that things are working out for your brother at National City, but I miss being with just you, alone."

"I do too. We'll have it again. Once Jake is settled at the bank, I'm sure he won't want to walk home with me every night. And I know Henny wants her time with him just as much as I want mine with you. We just have to be patient. It makes these moments even more special, anyway."

"I was thinking of a different solution." Nate turned to face Bea, reached his hand in his pocket, and took out a small red box, which even Bea knew was from Cartier. "Nate? What are you—" *Was he about to propose? Could this really be happening?* She was excited and anxious at the same time. She loved Nate, couldn't imagine a better husband someday, but now?

"I love you, Bea. You're so much more than I ever imagined any gal could be—independent, caring, brilliant, beautiful." He opened the box, and the ring inside was exactly what Bea would have picked for herself. A stunning squarish diamond set in a simple gold band. It was elegant but not flashy. She was overcome.

"Beatrice Abramovitz, will you marry me?"

"Oh, my goodness, it's stunning." She grabbed his face and kissed him. His pillowy lips met hers softly, and then pried them open with enough authority for her to simply succumb as his tongue found hers inside her mouth. He paused for a moment and then cupped the back of her head to draw her in even more. She was dizzy with delight. Lost in his embrace. Dazed at the idea that she could do this with this man for the rest of her life.

And then he went to put the ring on her finger and, suddenly, she started to panic. She wasn't ready for this. It wasn't that she hadn't dreamed of marrying Nate, of course she had. But everything would change once they were engaged. She was just getting started with Jake, and she'd promised not to tell Nate about her involvement. How could she call this man her fiancé to the world when she was keeping this secret from him?

"Bea?" Nate looked at her anxiously.

"Nate. I love you. And I absolutely, desperately want to marry you. But are you sure now is the right time? I thought you wanted to be a vice president at National City before you even considered those domestic things, you—"

"I still want that—to be as successful as I can at the bank, to move into the executive ranks, to make as much money as possible so I can make the world a better place—but I want it with you. I want you to be by my side for the rest of our lives. Don't you want that too?"

"Yes. Of course I do. More than anything. But I'm worried about the timing. I want to make enough money to buy my family's building, and sort things out with my career before Mama makes every waking moment of my life about a wedding."

"With Jake working as a broker, you should have that money in no time. As for your career, isn't it sorted? You're a maverick at the wire. And once we have kids, maybe you won't even want to work."

"I'll always want to work," she snapped. He knew this about her.

"I know, I know. That was a dumb thing to say. I wouldn't expect you to stop. At least not anytime soon. But I thought once we're married, we'd fatten your investment portfolio and maybe you'd be satisfied investing with your own money."

"Maybe, but that's not what I want right now." Bea didn't want to be a housewife playing in the markets with her portfolio, especially not now that she was responsible—behind the scenes, of course—for multiple portfolios across many different investors. She was just starting to get a taste of what being a broker felt like, and until she could talk about that with Nate, she didn't think it was fair to wear his ring.

"Nate, I love you. I am yours, forever. But I'm not ready for a big wedding and a new house and all that comes with marriage. Not yet. Not while Jake is just getting back on his feet and I'm finally rebuilding my own portfolio."

Nate's face fell, and his brow contorted into a concerned furrow. He looked like a child who'd been told he couldn't have ice cream.

"Don't you see, I'm not saying no? I'm just asking if, maybe, I can say yes to marrying you, but we don't tell anyone yet?"

"Keep it a secret?"

"Yes, you keep that stunning and perfect ring. And in a few months, when everything is more settled, you'll put it on my finger for real."

Nate's mouth curled into the charming grin that had lit her up from the moment they met. And then he laughed. "You don't do anything the easy way, do you, Miss Abramovitz?"

"What would be the fun in that?"

"All right. Long as I know you're mine, I'll wait as long as you need to tell the rest of the world. Or at least a month or two." He winked and flashed her a smile that made her want to take him home to her bed that very instant.

"I love you, Nathan Greenberg, so very much."

"And I love you, too, Beatrice Abramovitz soon-to-be Greenberg."

CHAPTER THIRTY-TWO

May

DOW MONTHLY AVERAGE: 220, NEW ALL-TIME HIGH, +8 POINTS FROM APRIL, +21 FROM JANUARY

By the spring of 1928, with Bea's stock picking and Jake's natural ability with people, he was already being recognized by the top brass at National City as one of their best. The market helped, too; the way it just kept going up, it was almost impossible to pick wrong. Everyone on Wall Street was minting money and the Abramovitz twins were no exception. Over the course of just a few months, they had become truly rich, at least by the standards of their life so far. Pauline had a monthly shopping allowance, and they had hired a girl to cook and clean the house for them.

Bea had made this new life possible for her family when she paid off Jake's debts last year after almost losing everything. She never wanted to feel that level of uncertainty again. She'd gained a more nuanced understanding of her mother's preoccupation with her lost childhood wealth; it wasn't simply the material things, it was the security of having money, knowing you had a comfortable place to live, food to eat, the ability to take care of yourself. And, if she was honest, Bea had also begun to get used to their new standard of living. She could buy clothes and go out without worry. Her mother finally had a more comfortable life, her father had a real store, Jake was making a name for himself on Wall Street, and she was rebuilding her own savings.

Because Jake was giving Bea only a fraction of his overall commissions, his money had grown exponentially faster than hers. Suddenly he had enough to do what Bea had hoped to herself, pay off the loan on the family's building. He even had excess money for a down payment on a new apartment.

"A real swanky spot uptown. With a doorman and an elevator." He had even suggested that their parents move out of the Ghetto to a more upscale neighborhood but, for all of Pauline's desire to live like royalty, she wanted to do it in a place where everyone spoke Yiddish, and that meant staying on the Lower East Side. Instead of feeling jealous, Bea took comfort in knowing that not only did they now own their home, but also, she still had a sizable stock portfolio that she could continue to grow. Money that was really all her own.

Still, as the months went on, Bea grew more and more bored at the wire. She wished she could work with Jake, for real, but she knew the industry hadn't changed enough to accept a woman at a brokerage desk. And then Jake had an idea.

"You know, BB, once I'm living uptown, we aren't going to be able to have our nightly market talks."

"I know. I assumed once you moved out, we'd just start talking on the telephone. Although it will be tricky during market hours. I don't really have time to talk. I guess at lunch. I—"

"Actually, I had a different idea than the phone."

"And that is?"

"Well, at National City I've become the guy with the Midas touch. I'm doing so much better than the other new brokers that they're expanding my coverage. I'm getting a promotion, BB. I'll be running a whole desk, managing bigger clients."

"Running a desk?" *Maybe he could hire her to work for him.*

"Yep. Soon enough, I'll be as big as your boyfriend." Bea couldn't imagine that Jake's early success could even come close to what Nate had accomplished in his years at National City; thinking that it might brought up a host of conflicting emotions. On the one hand, she was proud—Jake's triumph was due in large part to her skill. But, at the same time, Nate was her almost-fiancé now. His career was important to him and to her. If Jake started to do better than Nate, that would put her in a terrible spot, almost as if she was choosing her brother over her future husband. She didn't think she should have to choose. But the only way not to was if Bea's helping Jake was no longer a secret. If she could talk about the markets as freely with Nate as she used to, without worrying about revealing too much about her involvement with Jake, then she'd be making the same observations to Nate as she did to Jake. Whether he decided to act on them or not would be his business. *How terrific would it be if Jake gave her a junior job on his desk? It would be the perfect payback for all that he put them through with Julian Petroleum last year.*

"So, with this promotion, I get my own secretary. And a private office. So if you came to work for me, you'd be there by my side, all day long. We can make trading decisions on the spot."

"Came to work for you how?"

"As my secretary, obviously."

She felt foolish to have hoped for more. She should know better by now. "You want me to leave my job and come be your *secretary*?"

"I sure do. Hey, why do you sound disappointed? You'd only be a secretary as a cover—you'd really be my co-broker."

She contemplated the idea. Being Jake's administrative support was the last thing she would have chosen, but with their arrangement, it had its benefits. She'd get a good salary as an executive secretary, and she'd be there, in the brokers' pit, advising Jake as things happened. She'd made such an impression at the wire that she was the first female to get to work up front with the ticker and the trades. Maybe she could do the same at National City and become a broker after all.

"BB? Whaddya think? Would this be the fox's socks or what?"

"You know what, Jake, it just might." She smiled slowly.

"You're in?" Jake looked at her with a goofy grin.

"I'm in." She raised her eyebrows, surprised at how excited she suddenly felt.

He lifted her in the air. "Hooray! I promise, BB, this is going to be the best decision you've ever made in your life! There's just one thing." He paused, looking suddenly serious as he set her feet back on the ground. "You know what we're really doing still has to stay between us, right?"

"It does?"

"Yeah. At least for now. As far as everyone except Mama and Papa are concerned, you'll be my secretary."

"I guess, but . . . Jake, we can't keep this a secret for much longer. It's been really hard to keep this from Nate, and with me at National City it will be even harder. We've always talked about investing. Also, I'd hope that eventually I might be able to start making stock picks out in the open, as a broker myself. But if no one at the bank knows how well I've done, I'll never have that chance."

"BB, I don't know if you'll have that chance under any circumstance. But if there is a possibility, you know I'll do whatever I can to help you. Just give me a little more time to impress them. Then we'll be so stinking rich we can do whatever we want anyway."

CHAPTER THIRTY-THREE

June

DOW MONTHLY AVERAGE: 210, –9 POINTS FROM MAY, +12 FROM JANUARY

At first, working for Jake was pretty awful. She'd never been a secretary before and, even though the work was relatively brainless, she still had to learn the job. In the first weeks, while she was settling in, she was so busy answering the phone, scheduling meetings, and learning whom to call for the best table at every important restaurant in the city that she almost didn't have time to stay on top of the ticker. Within a few weeks the administrative tasks became routine, and she finally had the space to study the market again. It turned out that she was one of the few people on the floor who could actually "read" the ticker, discerning patterns and their implications as they happened, and now, without the distraction of another job, she started exploring more complicated methods of investing. One of these was short selling.

The strategy of playing both sides of the market was a common one: investors turned into bears when they thought the market was going to drop, taking short positions on specific stocks by borrowing them at their current (too high) price to repay later, when the price had hopefully fallen, and pocketing the difference. These same investors turned back into bulls when they anticipated growth, at which point they would buy stocks that they thought would continue to rise. Until now Bea had stayed away from this approach. It was one thing to sell a stock that you thought was weakening; if you were wrong and it went up, all you lost was opportunity. But shorting a stock, this meant directly betting against a company. Not only was it risky, but it felt mean-spirited. Still, she knew that the biggest investors relied heavily on it because it optimized returns. Plus, there was more strategy to investing on both the ups and downs, and that excited Bea. She wanted to try it.

Until now, Bea's approach had been to buy stocks in sectors that she believed, based on a combination of news and company performance relative to stock price, were temporarily undervalued and therefore poised to go up. Those kinds of bets were easy for Jake to understand and pitch to his clients—it made logical sense to buy, for instance, American Telephone & Telegraph, when there were whispers of a large-scale urban telephone installation. But betting against the market, when the market was generally on a steady climb and showed no signs of weakness, this was much harder for Jake to support. June had been a down month so far, so Bea took it as her opportunity to experiment.

"I've got the shorts!" Bea blurted out as she walked into Jake's office. "Bethlehem Steel, American Locomotive, and General Railway Signal."

"Railroads? Are you kidding?"

"No, I am not kidding. General Motors is announcing their new production schedule on Monday."

"So I should buy GM."

"Well, yes. But everyone will do that. I've been studying this"—she started pacing back and forth in front of his desk—"and the railroad sector takes a dip when automotive announces new production."

"No, it doesn't. Does it?"

"Well not always, but often. And Bethlehem Steel, American Locomotive, and General Railway Signal are all way too high right now. They are poised to drop."

"Okay, so I'll just sell them."

"Jake, I've explained this to you. If we get short in advance of an expected drop, we make more money."

"Yes, but—" Jake looked at the paper Bea had handed him, with the specifics about the positions she wanted to take. "The size of these positions, the amount we could lose—"

"Or the amount we could earn." Bea looked at Jake, hoping to see the understanding in his eyes that usually came when she was this insistent about something, but it wasn't there. "You don't have to do it for your clients if you don't believe me, but at least short these stocks in my portfolio."

Bea expected this to be enough. Jake was too competitive to let Bea be the only one making money. She was incorrect.

"I just don't see it right now, BB. It feels wrong."

"Since when do you have a feeling one way or the other?" Bea snapped, caught by surprise that he was suddenly standing his ground.

"I see. Right. I'm so stupid that, even though I have been working here for months now, buying and selling stocks all day long, there is no chance that I have learned a single thing?" Jake's reply was cold, and she watched his face tighten. "Do you actually think that I am just your marionette? That every move I make is because of a string you pull?" She had pushed too far. Hit him where he was most vulnerable.

"No. No. You're not stupid at all, Jake. I didn't mean it that way. It's just—I've spent so much time on this lately and I think this is a real opportunity for us. This could be the biggest Wall Street win we've had yet and, yes, it feels like a risk . . ." Bea spoke with all the confidence in the world, even though inside she was terrified. The only part of investing that she didn't like was risk. Especially given what they had been through after Julian Petroleum. They were doing so well, her money had grown dramatically already, and she was certain that they'd be able to stop hiding their arrangement at the bank very soon. If she pushed this and was mistaken, not only could they lose a fortune, but also she'd be set back even more from possibly becoming a broker. Still, this was part of how the big winners won on Wall Street. If they were really going to play the game, they had to go all in. "But aren't you the one who always says 'bigger risks, bigger rewards'? This move could catapult your career, and mine."

Jake sat silently, considering Bea's statement. "All right, if you believe in this, I trust you. Let's be short sellers."

Two weeks later Jake called Bea into his office and, as soon as she shut the door, he lifted her in the air, spinning her around three times.

"BB, do you know what we've done? In two weeks, two weeks, I've personally made thirty thousand dollars!"

Bea grinned, triumphant.

"And guess what?" Jake put her gently back on the ground and looked at her like an eager puppy dog. She'd never seen him this excited.

"What?" she asked, genuinely curious, and slightly nervous.

"I told them to stuff that dinky two bedroom on Park Avenue and put down a deposit for one of the new apartments at One Sutton Place."

"You what? Jake, that deposit was the equivalent to a year's rent on our old tenement. And wasn't it nonrefundable? This is two weeks of profits, none of it is locked in yet. Shouldn't you wait before—" He always went too far too fast.

"Oh, BB, you're such a worrier. What can go wrong for me when I have my own secret weapon by my side?" He bowed to her like she was a queen. "You've gotta see this place, BB." He pulled out a pamphlet for the new co-op along the East River and began to read. "Protected, unobstructed views. Parklike setting. Every unit flooded with light."

"It looks fabulous, Jake. Still—"

"And you know what else? I'm gonna buy a ring for Henny. Now that I'll have a proper place for us to live, I'm gonna ask her to marry me."

"Marry you? Oh, Jake! Really?" Bea squealed with joy. Henny, wonderful Henny, would be her sister. She hadn't expected this. At least not yet. But it was marvelous. With things moving at such a fast pace, she'd be out on her own and officially engaged to Nate before the end of the month.

CHAPTER THIRTY-FOUR

July

DOW MONTHLY AVERAGE: 216, +6 POINTS FROM JUNE, +17 FROM JANUARY

Bea stood in front of the full-length mirror in her new dressing room—a converted bedroom that was part of the suite that was now hers alone in her family's expanded duplex home. She was wearing the most elaborate and expensive dress she had ever owned, purchased at Bergdorf Goodman instead of commissioned from Sophie, because she needed it in a hurry and Sophie was backlogged with orders.

"So what do you think?" She turned to face Henny and Sophie who were, respectively, reclined across her new brocade settee and perched at the edge, pincushion in hand. "Is it too much?"

"Oh, Bea, it's stunning," Sophie gushed as Bea began to spin around, showing off every detail of the exquisite dress. It was made of a delicate lilac silk chiffon that was embellished with glimmering silver beads and, as Bea swirled in the flowing skirt, she looked like she was floating. A sheer flutter of the chiffon fell in a loose drape off the top of the shoulder, giving just a suggestion of a sleeve, while revealing enough skin to still undoubtedly be a summer dress. Bea couldn't believe she had been able to afford something so special.

"It really is something. So beautifully made, and it fits you impeccably—except for the length. I think maybe it needs to be shortened a bit, right?" Sophie asked, looking at Henny.

"More than a bit! Little Bea's hem should graze her knees, not her shoes! But . . . my oh my . . . it's the cat's pajamas! Perfect for a party at a place like the Livermores'!" Henny cooed.

"I'm sorry I'm not wearing one of your pieces, Soph. This is a perfect crowd to show them off to."

"She can show one off herself!" Henny suddenly sat up, excited. "You must come with us, Sophie! The invite is for 'the more the merrier'—long as you're a stunner. And you more than qualify!"

"Oh, I wouldn't know what to do at some swanky summerhouse like that." Sophie blushed. She was happier behind the scenes.

"It's simple, really: you drink the champagne, slurp the oysters, kick up your heels on the lawn, and go gaga over the ocean views." Henny spoke like she had been at many of these parties, but Bea knew it was her first time too. At least at a place like the one they were going this weekend.

"I don't know. I don't really have anything to wear. And Sal wouldn't like me going out without him."

"I'm sure you can bring Sal, right?" Bea turned to Henny. She would feel a lot less out of place at this party if Sophie was there with her. "And you have that sample you just finished? That's perfect for you. All wrong for me, but for you . . ."

"It's settled then! They say Dorothy likes to start her parties with a sundown toast, so we'll meet here on Saturday, ready to go, by six." Henny clapped her hands gleefully.

"I don't know, it's such short notice and . . . ," Sophie said as she circled Bea, pinning the hem of her dress to the almost scandalous knee length that was all the rage this year.

"And nothing! You're coming. It'll be a hoot," Henny urged.

"You should just give in," Bea said with a pleading smile. "Once Henny gets an idea in her head, resisting is hopeless."

"Who is Livermore, anyway?" Sophie asked tentatively.

"Jesse Livermore?" Bea said excitedly. "Why, he's only the most famous speculator on Wall Street, an investment genius. He's made millions in the market, often by selling short, and he is completely self-made. He started as a board boy, then made a small fortune with the curb sellers until they cut him off because his profits were too good. Has his own firm now. And it is all very hush-hush. His offices are supposedly more closely guarded than the US Mint, and no one who works for him is allowed to discuss what goes on inside," Bea said authoritatively.

"Forget all that, that's not the good part." Henny laughed. "His house in Great Neck is directly on the sound. They say you can see all the way to Connecticut. There's a huge private beach, and he has his own yacht, which he supposedly takes across the sound to go to work. Can you imagine being so hoity-toity that you hop on your yacht to go to work?"

"And how are you all invited to this man's party?" Sophie looked even more nervous than she had when their discussion began.

"His wife Dorothy was a Ziegfeld dancer before they got married. She really knows how to have a good time. Her summer parties are supposed to be berries, and her husband likes her to fill them with pretty girls. So anyone who dances for Mr. Ziegfeld is welcome with their friends. My old roommate Sally was a Ziegfeld girl you know? And she and her husband are going—he's another Wall Street guy; she moved up to Park Avenue when they got married. Anyhoo—she insisted I come along with a crowd. Milly and Lowell and Bea and Nate have already agreed, and of course me and Jake . . . and now you and Sal. Oh, it will be divine!"

"Soph, I've never been to a party like this either," Bea chimed in. "But Jesse Livermore! There's a whole book about him, and now we get to be at his house. I wonder if I'll be able to ask him about his trading strategies. You know he's a numbers investor; his whole philosophy is about the patterns in the data. He sees the market the way I do . . . but much better, of course. The clarity of his trading rules is astonishing. I keep telling Jake to read the book *Reminiscences of a Stock Operator*—it's supposedly fiction, but everyone knows it's about Livermore—he is just so fascinating and—" Bea rambled enthusiastically until Henny cut her off, amused.

"Sophie, you *must* come. If for no other reason than to keep Busy Bea away from Mr. Livermore!"

"Well, if I'm needed, I'll try to convince Sal. I'm sure he'd love to see how the other half lives." Sophie still sounded tentative, but Bea could tell that she had been swayed. They were going to have the night of their lives.

CHAPTER THIRTY-FIVE

At seven fifteen Saturday evening, Nate's and Milly's cars entered a long bluestone driveway, dramatically lined with trees, that ended in a large circle in front of the grandest house Bea had ever seen. Sal immediately commented on the high quality of the materials—a combination of brick and limestone, with a slate roof and four chimneys. "Imagine if I could build you a house like this someday, baby?" he said to Sophie, awestruck.

A team of valets were on hand to park the scores of cars, and the group was ushered through the imposing entrance hall and out to a terrace, where they were momentarily stopped in their tracks by the scene. The terrace itself was one of a pair that sat on either side of the back of the house. They were covered entirely in blue, yellow, and white tiles set in the most beautiful patterns and framed by carved granite balustrades.

"Mediterranean style," Milly said, "very popular in Palm Beach."

Bea and Henny raised their eyes at each other and giggled. Milly was so unassuming that they sometimes forgot she was born and raised in this moneyed world.

Beyond the grand terraces lay the true sight to see: a sprawling lawn that rolled in tiers all the way down to the water, with panoramic sight lines across the sound. Bea had never seen a view this stunning, period, let alone in someone's private backyard. Between the terrace and the beach, each section of the expansive grass was filled with some form of merriment: a dance floor that was already packed with revelers enjoying a jazz band in full swing; cocktail tables surrounded by gilded chairs for sitting to rest tired feet, overflowing with fresh, exotic flowers, and set with magnums of champagne; a tent, under which was laid an elaborate spread of every imaginable kind of seafood, plus two towers of champagne coupes, down which the bubbly wine flowed like a fountain.

The women were a sea of sparkling jewels and feathers; men wore everything from sports jackets to white-tie tuxedos and top hats. There was no other word for it than *spectacle*. And while Bea was both overwhelmed and slightly repulsed by the ostentation of it all, she also couldn't believe she was lucky enough to be a part of it.

"All right, kittens and bulls, no fun to be had standing up here. Let's go make our entrance and get this party started!" Henny linked arms with Jake.

"I think you're a little late for that, doll. This joint is already hopping." He laughed as they strode together boldly into the fray.

Milly and Lowell followed behind them, and Bea noticed that Milly seemed more at ease in the extravagance here than she did at the speakeasies they frequented.

"Have you been to parties like this before?" Sophie asked her as they walked.

"Not really." Milly shook her head. "This is a lot looser and more modern than the events Mother and Father drag me to, but in some ways, they are all the same." Milly turned to Lowell, who was nodding in agreement and asked, in a way that was really telling him, whether he wanted to secure a table while there were still some free. As usual, he followed her dutifully. "Don't be intimidated by all this," Milly said softly to Sophie and Bea, "it's a lot of show, but they're just people."

Bea was proud of how confident Milly had become. She was dressed in the most youthful and fashionable dress Bea had ever seen her wear, she had left her glasses at home, and she'd even put on makeup: rouge on her cheeks, a dark line of kohl on her eyes, and a bright red lipstick that perfectly framed her deep cupid's bow. Bea didn't know what it was, her successful job in the ladies' department, having such a devoted beau, or maybe, finally having friends appreciate her for how wonderful she was, but something really seemed to have brought her out of her shell.

"Have you ever seen a place like this?" Bea asked Nate as he took her hand to lead her, too, into the party.

"Only in the papers. It's a little much, don't you think?"

"It's a lot much. But fun to pretend for a night that this is our life." Bea chuckled as she pulled Nate's hand in the direction of the tent. Sophie and Sal followed behind them and went directly for the giant tower of lobster tails on silver platters. Bea and Nate joined Jake and Henny, who were already refilling their coupes with a second glass of champagne.

"You've gotta taste this." Henny handed glasses to Bea and Nate. "I swear it's liquid heaven."

Bea and Nate clinked their glasses. Bea's eyes popped open wide as she took her first sip, stunned that something could taste this good. It was sweet, yet tart, with tiny bubbles that perfectly tickled her tongue as it went down. "If this is champagne," she said to the group, "what have we been drinking for the past two years? Soda water?"

"Basically. Soda water with a kick." Nate laughed and took another sip. "Might as well enjoy the good stuff while we can."

They all drained and then refilled their glasses, and then Henny corralled the group onto the dance floor.

"Do you think we'll actually get to meet Mr. Livermore?" Bea asked Nate excitedly, as they walked.

"I dunno. It's possible, rumor has it that one of the only times he comes out from his office is for his parties."

"Oh, I'd love to talk to him." Bea clapped her hands together excitedly. "He's such a visionary, and an outsider who made such a name for himself and all. Maybe he'll have some advice for how a gal like me can do the same."

"I wouldn't count on it. He's not such a hero, you know."

"Whaddya mean? You don't think Jesse Livermore has the markets figured out? He's an investment genius."

"Possibly, but he's also a plunger who plays both sides and the middle to his benefit."

"But isn't that what makes him so good? That he can see the shorts as well as the longs?"

"I'm not so sure. First, the way he invests is pretty selfish, un-American even. He takes huge risks, and his bets are so big he has single-handedly nearly brought down the whole market more than once. He has been penniless multiple times."

"Are you telling me you never take a short position?"

"I'm not saying that. I'm just saying that when you've been investing as long as I have, you know that guys like Livermore, who seem too good to be true, are doing less than aboveboard things to make the market move the way they want it to. And if you're short when that happens, it can be a disaster. I know Jake just had a windfall with a short sale, but it's always a dangerous game."

Bea was shocked. Since she and Jake had done so well with their first short, she had started shorting any opportunity she could get. Jesse Livermore had been one of the investors she studied the most to understand how to do it. Was he a fraud? And un-American? She was selecting shorts based only on where the stocks were priced compared to company performance and industry trends. It wasn't as if she was wishing for companies to fail. She couldn't ask Nate any of this, of course, because he had no idea that she was making investment decisions at all. Maybe if she found him, she could ask Livermore himself.

"Look at us, debating investment philosophies, *here*." Bea waved her hand at the party. "We should be dancing."

"Anything that gets me closer to you, I'm all for."

They hit the dance floor where, to Bea's surprise, she found Milly and Lowell cutting a rug. Milly pulled Bea toward her and whispered in her ear, "Did you see him? He's over there." She nodded her head across the dance floor to a white-haired man in chino pants, a navy blazer, and spectator shoes. He looked more ordinary than almost anyone else at the party.

"Who?" Bea asked, wondering if Milly expected her to know him because he worked at Morgan or National City.

"Livermore!" Milly said, laughing.

"No!"

"Yep."

This man, this captain of industry, Bea's Wall Street idol, looked so plain and approachable that she immediately ran across the floor to meet him.

"Mr. Livermore, sir. You have such a fabulous home. And this party." Bea grabbed his arm, trying to seem casual and failing miserably.

He rolled his eyes as he turned in her direction, and then he looked at her. And she could swear his eyes were hungry.

"I'm Bea, Bea Abramovitz." She held out her hand to shake his, and he grabbed her and spun her toward him.

"Look at you, delicious little thing. How about a dance, Bea Abramovitz?"

Bea didn't really want to dance with Livermore, she wanted to talk to him about investing. About his trading rules. About how an outsider like she was, and he used to be, might become an insider like he was now. She tried to do this, unsuccessfully, as he twirled her toward and away from him, grabbing her a little more tightly than she would have preferred. As the song the band was playing reached its crescendo, he grabbed her waist and dipped her dramatically. With his hand tightly on the small of her back, he slowly drew her up to standing, pressing himself against her in a way that was incredibly inappropriate. Then he leaned in close and whispered, "You're too pretty for all this talk about Wall Street. It's not a place for gals anyway. If you want to get rich, just marry a banker." He slid his hand down to her behind, but as he tried to squeeze it, she slapped him away strongly. She took a large step backward, looking at him with fury.

"Mind if I take a spin with my fiancée?" Nate was at her side. Thank goodness he'd shown up when he did—she was ready to cause an awful scene.

"I don't see a ring on that finger. You better get it there before someone beats you to it." Livermore leered at Bea one last time, and then disappeared into the crowd.

"You okay?" Nate asked gently.

"I'm fine. Just disappointed to learn that one of my idols is nothing more than a lecherous heel."

"I told you. You know the best way to get back at him?"

"What's that?"

"Drink his champagne and gorge on his oysters and caviar. He owes you."

"And then some!" Bea laughed. She always appreciated Nate, but right now she was even more awestruck by him. She couldn't have designed a more perfect man if she tried.

The rest of the night was a whirlwind of fun. At midnight, the party officially ended with a phantasmagoric display of fireworks that Dorothy Livermore had arranged to have launched from their yacht, which was moored off the shore. The crowds were sloppy and silly as the cocktails continued to flow, and merriment moved from the dance floor to the sandy beach, where some of the wilder partygoers stripped down to their underthings (or nothing at all) and plunged into the salty water. By the time the eight friends headed back to their cars, Bea had almost forgotten the ugly incident with Jesse Livermore. Nate had not.

Pulling up in front of Abramovitz Grocers, Nate shut the engine and turned to Bea.

"What's going on with us, Bea?"

"Whaddya mean?" She wasn't thinking clearly after all the champagne, and it took her a minute to see he was upset.

"I mean, you heard Livermore: 'I don't see a ring on her finger.'" He lifted her left hand, and she thought how perfect that ring would have looked tonight.

"I know, Nate, you've been so patient. Things have just been more complicated than I anticipated. Now that I'm working for Jake—"

"Yeah, about that. Why are you working for him? You don't want to be a secretary, Bea. I know that. You had a real, professional job at Morgan. Why give that up for this? Does Jake have some kind of special power over you? Seems like you'll do anything for him, but what about me?"

"He's my brother, Nate. My twin. It's hard to explain but . . . anyway, if you had a problem with me taking the job, why are you telling me *now*, more than a month later?"

"I dunno." He looked down at his lap. "Look, I asked you to marry me in February. It's July. I know this is the twenties, and you're a modern woman and all that, but I thought you'd at least be wearing your ring by now. I'm starting to think you're never gonna put it on. All our friends are beginning to settle down, even your brother. I can see how sweet he is on Hen. I know I want to spend my life with you . . . but, it's been two years, if you don't want me anymore—" Nate turned away from her so she could no longer see his face, but she could hear the vulnerability underneath the anger in his voice.

Nate was right. Their friends were moving forward with their relationships while he and Bea were still running in place. And why? Because she couldn't tell him the truth about her job with Jake? It was absurd. But she and her brother were in a rhythm and doing so well, she might have a real chance at a bigger job in the department. Maybe even as a broker. She didn't see why she should be forced to choose between Nate and that, just because Jake refused to tell anyone about their arrangement. She wouldn't stand for it anymore. Jake needed to come clean about her role so they could both move forward with their lives.

"Nate, please know that I love you desperately. And I hate myself for making you feel like I don't. I want to build a life with you, more than anything. I just need a little more time." She grabbed Nate's lapels to pull him close to her and, as he leaned in, she looked deeply into his eyes. The gold flecks sparkled more than usual, the streetlight above reflecting the tears that were building. How could she do this to him?

To this man whom she loved so much. She did not want to lose him. She had to make this right. She kissed him, holding him tightly, like he might slip away if she let go; when she finally felt him soften into her, she knew that, for now, they were okay. She also knew that they wouldn't be for long.

CHAPTER THIRTY-SIX

After seeing what real success looked like at the Livermore party, Jake had new, grander goals. It had become popular for the more successful young brokers to rent or buy "starter" homes in Great Neck. These properties were adjacent to Long Island's grand mansions, like Livermore's, but not directly on the water; still, they offered sprawling lawns for parties, and salt air and sea breezes to cut the dense heat of summer in the city. Jake had already moved into his new apartment on Sutton Place, but now he also wanted to buy one of these weekend homes. He didn't have more than a down payment for either property, and Bea worried, as always, about Jake spending beyond his means. But her family was protected; they owned their building outright, and she had her own money now. Jake could do what he wanted with his. And what he wanted was to buy a weekend house and a ring for Henny that left no question about how successful of a man he had become.

Bea didn't care so much about jewelry, but when Jake asked her to leave with him in the middle of the workday to go to Tiffany's, she couldn't say no. This was Henny. One of Bea's best friends, about to be engaged to Bea's twin brother. Of course she wanted to help pick out the ring.

They stepped inside the store at Thirty-Seventh Street and Fifth and were immediately greeted by a salesgirl with whom Jake had, apparently, already made an appointment. All by himself. He'd become so reliant on Bea for administrative tasks she'd almost forgotten he still knew how to do things. As they were whisked past case upon case of glittering jewels, even Bea was mesmerized by the sparkle, the artistry of the settings, the colors of the gems. One piece was more elaborate and enormous than the next and, as she took it in, she thought of her mother's prized necklace; sometimes she thought her mother exaggerated its value, but she believed it would fit in perfectly in this room, among these treasures.

Toward the rear of the store, a pair of earrings stopped her in her tracks. They were pink teardrop-shaped stones, each larger than a cherry and surrounded by diamonds. They were extraordinary.

"Ah, our signature morganite." The salesgirl paused with Bea and Jake. "That stone was discovered by our chief gemologist and, of course, named after Mr. Morgan, an avid gem collector. Isn't the color just divine? You won't find anything like that anywhere else but at Tiffany and Company."

"This stone is named after J.P. Morgan?" Jake asked, intrigued. "I had no idea such a thing was possible."

"Anything is possible with enough money, I'd say." The salesgirl smiled and kept walking. Jake turned to Bea and raised his eyebrows with a look that said "I have a new goal" and made Bea shudder. When was enough enough?

They were led into a small, brightly lit room, where they were directed to sit in velvet chairs across from a small wooden table. The saleslady proceeded to open a safe and remove a tray containing six rings in a variety of shapes and sizes, all set simply in silver bands that Bea soon learned was a metal both sturdier and more precious than silver or gold, called platinum. She showed Jake and Bea each one, explaining the different characteristics of the cuts of the stones, the typical customer who was drawn to each style, and the impression they would make about the man who bought them. When she was finished, Jake asked:

"Do you have anything a little glitzier? My gal is a real sparkler, and she needs a ring to match. Don't you think, BB?"

"Well, I personally love the simple diamonds," Bea said, thinking wistfully about her own ring, which, after today, she knew was called an Asscher cut. Jake had been so preoccupied the past two weeks that she hadn't found a moment to ask him to come clean about her actual role at the bank. But she was determined to put their secret behind them so she could finally wear it and move on with her life too. "But, yes, Hen would probably like something more ornate."

"Marvelous, we are well known for our new art deco settings; perhaps you'd like to see one of those?" Jake nodded, and the saleslady picked up the phone to request them. She turned back to Jake. "These are more costly, of course, since they contain multiple stones, all set by hand, and then there are the details in the metalwork: filigree and bead work and the like. But they are absolutely unique and breathtaking. Each one a true work of art."

"That sounds just like my Henny. And, for her, money is no object."

"Well, there is always a limit to what is sensible to spend," Bea jumped in. She couldn't help it. Jake had gotten out of control.

"Ignore my sister; she's always so practical." Jake flicked his hand in Bea's direction and winked at the saleslady.

"And what is wrong with a little practicality?" Bea asked, suddenly defensive. "I just think you should—"

Bea was interrupted by the arrival of the second tray of rings. When they were set down on the table, she gasped. They were amazing, one more incredible than the next.

"You were saying?" Jake laughed. Then he pointed at a ring that was nothing short of art. A round diamond in the center was encircled by teeny ones, and each side was framed by a thin rectangular blue sapphire and a diamond, set vertically. Somehow, it managed to be striking yet not too ostentatious. Bea couldn't help but try it on herself and, as soon as she did, she and Jake agreed that this was the one. It was unique, modern, and unmistakably chic. It was perfectly Henny.

"I'll take it." Jake stood up and clapped his hands together, indicating that the deal was done. Bea looked at him, expecting to see some trace of nerves, but she saw only elation. His whole face was illuminated in one of his unabashed grins. She thought he might even start giggling. She couldn't believe it. He was about to spend the equivalent of what Bea had earned in a year at the wire on a single piece of jewelry. And he didn't have a bit of hesitation. He had become the archetype of new-money Wall Street and, as happy as she was for his—their—newly earned wealth, something about his comfort with it didn't sit quite right with Bea.

As they made their way in a taxicab back to the bank, Bea was full of questions, but the most pressing was, "When are you planning to do it?"

"I'm not sure yet. But probably soon. Now that I've moved into Sutton Place, I'm lonely. I want her there with me."

"Please, Jake, I'm not Mama. I know she's staying there already."

"Some nights, sure, but it's not the same. I want her there as my wife. So she knows it's our home, together. I've found that second place, on Long Island too. I'll probably surprise her with both once I close on that."

"Whoa, Jake . . . Don't you think you should slow down a little? Save some of the money you're making for a rainy day—a downturn?"

"BB, how many times do I have to tell you? There's no need. It's a new era. And this is just the beginning. There's no downturn coming, ever. It makes sense for me to have a place at the beach. Henny loves it there. We can have parties. Get a boat."

"You know, Jake, just because that's what the bank presidents and big stock operators are doing doesn't mean you have to too. You're already successful. Who are you trying to impress?"

"The world, BB. Everyone who is anyone. Sure, we have more than we had before. We have a comfortable life. Mama is finally happy. Papa has a store. But there is so much more money to be made. And as a team, we are unstoppable."

This was it. This was her moment.

"I've been wanting to talk to you about that. It's time to put this secret-team stuff behind us. You need to start giving me some credit for my ideas."

"I do? Why? Is someone onto us? You just started a few months ago."

"No, but . . ." Bea knew the best strategy with her brother was to appeal to his interests, make him see how this secret was impacting his life. "Once you and Henny are engaged, you won't keep this from her, and once she finds out . . . she has the biggest mouth of anyone."

"For sure." Jake laughed. "But she won't know."

"She won't?"

"Why should she?"

"But if Henny is your fiancée, if you're living in the same house . . . don't you talk about these things?"

"Not really. When work is done, we both want to leave it at our desks. We have better things to do than discuss our days."

"Well, that's not the kind of life I want to have, the kind of marriage." Bea was suddenly overcome by frustration and anger. Of course Jake was happy to start a life with Henny under the shadow of this ridiculous lie; it got him nothing to tell the truth. But it was hurting her. Suddenly she was stuck again, in her career and, because of that, in her love life. Her eyes pooled with tears.

"Whoa, BB. What's going on here? I thought everything was fine?"

"Well, turns out it isn't."

Jake reached over to her cheek and brushed away a tear. "Okay, okay. How can we make it better?"

Bea told Jake that Nate had proposed months ago and that she had said yes but only unofficially. She didn't want to start a marriage with Nate by lying to him. And she'd been certain that, now that she was actually working among the brokers, it wouldn't be long before things were more settled in her career. She'd asked Nate to wait for that to make things official.

"But why? You love him, he clearly loves you. He has enough clams to take care of you, and you've made a bundle too. Just get married."

"Jake, this lie, my stock picking for you in secret, this wasn't supposed to be forever. You've built a reputation as one of the new wunderkinder on Wall Street. It's my turn. Help me become a broker at National City, Jake. I'll still be there to advise you; I'll just have my own voice. My own clients. My own commissions. All the brokers on the floor are already impressed with how I read the tape. I think they'd accept me working alongside them."

"I think you're delusional. There are no female brokers. Period. And much as I wish I could, I don't have the power to change that."

"Then at least come clean about my role in your success. At least make me your investment assistant. We can be a team out in the open. Let me put this secret behind me, so I can get engaged and start my life alongside yours."

"Do you think just because we're twins, we have to do everything in lockstep?" Jake grinned. He was trying to tease her, but she was in no mood.

"Nate asked me to marry him in *February*, and I have been lying to him and holding him at bay because of you. I can't do it anymore. I won't."

"Okay, okay. No more secrets. But if I'm going to come clean, I need to do it in a way to optimize the outcomes for everyone."

"Listen to you sounding like a stock guy . . . 'optimize outcomes.'" Bea smiled feebly, feeling relief that Jake had agreed to end their charade. "So how do we do that?"

"At the end of the year, they're going to be giving out a bunch of promotions to the standout performers. I'm on track to be one of them, but I want to be sure. We need to do something big. You're always full of ideas. So how about we find the big one, BB? Something so huge, it gets the whole bank's attention. Something that will ensure I get noticed and then, when I say it was your idea, maybe, just maybe, you'll get to become a broker too. And if you don't, you'll have made so much money it won't matter anyway."

"I see several problems with your plan. First, it's not as if life-altering investment ideas come to me every day. I don't have any that I can think of right now. And even if I do come up with something, one big idea isn't going to change everything. I risked it all once, and I don't see any reason to do it again. Making money isn't about quick fixes."

"I disagree. Livermore can make a million in a day. And if he can do it, we can too. So, c'mon, find that big idea, BB. Look for the investments that make you a little nervous, fluttery even, the ones you have cast aside. The ones that feel too risky. That will be the ticket. That will get us both what we need to succeed."

"And what happens if I don't come up with anything?"

"You will."

"Jake, I can't keep up this charade. I need a definitive timeline, for my own piece of mind and for Nate's."

"Fine. At the end of the year, wherever we are, we can put this secret behind us. Deal?" He held out his hand, and as she went to shake it, he pulled her into a hug. "BB, don't worry. Everything is coming up diamonds!"

CHAPTER THIRTY-SEVEN

August

DOW MONTHLY AVERAGE: 240, +24 POINTS FROM JULY

Jake proposed in an elaborate ruse at the new house on Long Island. He told Henny and the gang that they were invited to a party out there, but when they showed up, he revealed that it was his house. Then he popped the question, and everyone celebrated with an extravagant alfresco dinner on his and Henny's new lawn. He spared no expense, hiring a three-piece jazz band and decorating with dozens upon dozens of the most fragrant gardenias—Henny's favorite flower. Henny was over the moon and immediately shifted her focus to planning her wedding.

"So," Nate said to Bea as they drove back to the city the morning after the big proposal, "now that Jake is all settled, and your mother has a wedding to focus on, why don't we go ahead and get engaged ourselves?"

"We can't steal the spotlight from Henny and Jake now! Let's wait until the end of the year. January will be here before we know it, and by then you'll be a vice president, and maybe I will be something more than a secretary."

"Oh good, you're finally planning to move on from being Jake's secretary?"

"Well, if I can. Why?"

"I just don't get it. When I met you, your goal was to be a career girl on Wall Street. You had such a fire about investing, it was one of the things I fell in love with about you. Since you've left the wire, it's like that spark is gone. Replaced by this need to take care of your brother. But Jake is doing just fine on his own, Bea. He doesn't need you. You have to take care of yourself too. Of us."

"What makes you think I'm not?"

"I just feel like, since you've been working for Jake—well, since he started at the bank, really—so much of your days revolve around him. You are allowed to have a life that is separate and apart from your brother. You are allowed to have your own home. Your own love. Your own happiness."

"I know that. And I do have one. Isn't that what we're talking about now? Planning for us to start our life together."

Sure, she and Jake took care of each other. But she was still her own person, chasing her own dream. The problem was that Nate didn't know that. Because he didn't know the truth about what she was doing for Jake. This secret arrangement was like a fog, slowly obscuring every corner of her relationship with Nate so nothing was as it seemed. If only she could tell Nate the truth now. But she had promised to wait. She was still looking for her big idea. If she was going to have any chance of finally being what she set out to be, an investor on Wall Street, this was it. "Nate, I hear your concerns. But we've already had this conversation. Don't you understand? Jake and me, this is just how we work. How we've always worked. But—"

"I know. I'm just fed up. We have our own life to live. Our own future to plan. I've been patient, but I'm finished waiting. So I'll give you until the end of the year, as you ask. That should be more than enough time to let everything be about Jake—his engagement, his new house, his success. I am happy for him. And, Henny, I want to celebrate them too. But not at the expense of us. So come December 31, either we get engaged, for real, or we're done."

"I don't know why you have to say that as a threat when that's what I've already promised you."

"I'm sorry, Bea. I'm not trying to act like a heel." He took her hand and ducked his head as he looked at her, contrite. "I just, I just love you so much."

"I love you too. And I cannot wait to be your wife. And I promise, by the time the year is through, nothing will stand in the way of the rest of our life."

Bea didn't have her big idea yet, but she had Nate. And she wasn't going to lose him. No matter what.

CHAPTER THIRTY-EIGHT

November

DOW MONTHLY AVERAGE: 293, +41 POINTS FROM OCTOBER, +95 FROM JANUARY

Bea felt like she closed her eyes for a second and when she opened them again the end of the year was upon her. Bea had yet to find an idea that made the bank take notice of Jake. It wasn't that they weren't making tons of money, it was just that everyone was. The markets had continued to soar through all of 1927, with the Dow nearing an unheard-of high of almost 300. A one-hundred-point gain from January.

In fact, stock prices were so high across the board that Bea had grown concerned about the stability of Wall Street. "New Era" thinking was that the market had reached a new point of stabilization. This prevailing wisdom was that, beyond some minor dips, stocks would only go one direction, up. But Bea was old-fashioned. She believed that what goes up must come down, and with the market reaching new highs all the time, she thought a drop was imminent. For the first time since she began investing, she was worried about keeping her money in the market.

There were some economic factors that supported her belief: the Federal Reserve was asking banks to stop loaning so much money to investors, because it was worried people were relying too much on funds they didn't have. So far, the banks hadn't listened. Broker loans continued to rise. There was a chance the Fed would raise interest rates to force the issue; if interest rates went up, borrowing money would be too expensive, which would lead to mass stock sales as leveraged owners had to dump stocks to cover their debts.

Right now none of this was happening. She and Jake were making money without even trying and, as wonderful as that was, she knew better than to trust something that was beginning to look an awful lot like a bubble. And that was when the idea she'd been looking for hit her like a bolt of electricity. If it was a drop in the market that she was worried about, then that was the big bet they should take. Bet for the market to temporarily fall and reset these out-of-control prices.

"I've got it!" she announced as she burst into Jake's office, slamming the door behind her.

"Got what?"

"The idea. This is it."

"Well, are you going to just stand there grinning, or are you going to tell me?"

"We short the market. All the big names. The blue chip stocks. As soon as we can."

"Are you crazy? The market has never been so strong. It would be suicide."

"Jake, remember when you told me that my big idea, the one that would really push us over the top, would be the one that made me nervous? The one that had been gnawing at the back of my mind for ages? The one that I dismissed?" Jake nodded, his eyes growing wide. "This. This is it."

"But how—"

"Look." She pulled out her latest notebook. "Nothing has happened in the last two months to account for such big lifts in these stocks. The prices keep going up, yet company earnings don't come close to matching the gains. Things can't keep going this way. Some economists have been saying as much, but it hasn't been reflected in the market yet. Except for here." She pointed to Peabody Energy, a coal company. "Commodity industry, old world. Even that has been on a tear. Until two weeks ago. Look what it did."

"Holy crow, it plummeted. But that's one stock, BB. This is the new economy. Overall, the market is just going to keep going up."

"What if it doesn't? What if we've hit the top? If we short the stocks that everyone thinks are the safest, the ones that will always rise with the market, we will be on the right side of a correction when it comes. And I'm telling you, it is coming. I've been analyzing this intensively, and I'm sure of it."

"Do you realize what this means? If you're right . . ."

Bea nodded. "I know, it could be bad."

"Yeah, which is why I just can't see it. No one would let that happen."

"But if they couldn't stop it? At least for a little while?" Bea watched Jake's face begin to light up.

"Just for a little while?"

"Yes. Jake, the Dow has jumped fifty percent over the course of this year. It's unprecedented. The market has to correct, to adjust to digest all the growth. So, in December, we get short into the correction, and once prices drop, we start buying again at a discount. By the time things stabilize, we will have made money on the down and the up."

"And you think you can really know when that is? Because if we bet on this, and you're wrong . . ." Jake's voice was almost a whisper.

"I won't be."

Bea hadn't taken this much risk with her own portfolio since her desperate attempt to make the money she needed to pay off Jake's debt. But she was so sure about this correction that she bet her entire savings on it. Jake did too. And he convinced many of his clients to follow suit even though the idea that the market was going to drop was contrary to the prevailing sentiment on the street.

And Bea was right. In the first week of December, the Dow plummeted nearly 10 percent, a classic correction. The Abramovitz twins were richer than they'd ever been in their lives, and that was before the commissions on all of Jake's clients' earnings. Before Jake's promotion. Before Bea finally, hopefully, got her shot to be an investor herself.

Jake was ready to lock in their profits and then start buying back stock now that the prices were deflated. But Bea insisted that they wait. She was certain this was just the beginning. It was simple supply and demand. The Fed hadn't yet touched interest rates, and the banks hadn't stopped excessive margin loans. If either, or both things, happened, then stock prices would have to fall more, because there would be no one to buy them—too much supply, not enough demand. It was so clear to her. And no one else saw it. She was lost in the excitement of recognizing something so contrary to popular wisdom, and she convinced Jake to stay short. It was the mistake that would cost her everything.

The beginning of December turned out to be a blip. The market recovered just as quickly as it dropped, ending 1928 at a new all-time high. Because they hadn't reversed their short positions, Bea and Jake were still betting that the market would go down as it started to go up. By the time they were able to get out of their bets, they'd lost everything. Everything Bea had saved, everything Jake had counted on to pay off his apartment, his house, Henny's ring, every penny they had made in the market, had all been obliterated.

Bea was in shock. She'd been through this once before. She'd grown up under the pall of what a loss like this had done to her mother. Yet she had been foolish enough to bet it all again. And she'd lost. She and she alone had made a catastrophic mistake that could take away all the financial security she'd vowed to herself to preserve for her family. She was overcome with guilt, shame, and confusion. She'd been so sure that the market was about to go through a significant correction, and she still didn't understand why it had rebounded the way it did. She didn't have time to make sense of why. Jake was in a panic, furious with Bea for pushing him to make such a devastating mistake, and desperate to fix it in the few days that remained before the year was over.

"What do we do now, Bea? We need to get this money back. What do we buy?" he barked at her on the last Monday of the year.

"I don't . . . I don't know." Bea had never frozen under pressure before; usually she thrived on it, but this time was different. This time the crisis was entirely her fault, and she still didn't understand how it had happened. What had she missed?

"That's not an answer," Jake snapped back. "I've been studying the tape all morning. GE still looks depressed. How about buying that? Same with wheat futures. If we buy those now, while they're low, we can ride the gains."

Bea still didn't think that was a smart idea. When she looked at their portfolio and at the market overall, she still saw overvalued companies. Yet stocks continued to rise. She couldn't think straight anymore. All her conviction and instincts were replaced with hesitation and indecision. "Maybe?"

"Maybe? C'mon, Bea. I've gotta fix this!" Jake stormed off and went into the pit outside his office, where he started talking with some of his junior brokers. Bea remained in the chair across from his desk, paralyzed. When he returned, ten minutes later, she was still there.

"I can't believe this. You lead us to the biggest blowup of our lives, of my career, and you're doing nothing? What's wrong with you?"

Bea knew Jake was counting on her. She didn't cause the problems in their family, she solved them. But not now. Now she was to blame. And nothing she had learned about the market or seen in the patterns of the stocks was giving her any clue how to make it better. For the first time she had no idea what to do.

"Bea?" Jake's voice softened slightly. "Look, I know you lost your dream here, too, but if you don't snap out of it and help me, I'm gonna lose my job. We need to act. Now. And maybe we can save ourselves."

He shoved a piece of paper in front of her. "These are my ideas so far. What do you think?"

Bea looked at Jake's notes, but it felt as if nothing she saw made it past her eyes into her brain. It was too much. She couldn't help Jake, and she'd likely ruined him. "I'm sorry, Jake. I'm so sorry. I just don't know. None of this makes any sense to me right now. All my instincts are still saying we should short and, clearly, that's not right."

"Clearly."

"Jake, I'm trying to figure it out, I really am, but—" she whispered, crestfallen and desperate.

"But you've lost your magic powers," he snapped. "Well, you're certainly not helping me like this. Least you can do is what you're actually paid for. Go answer the phones and clear my calendar. I'll find my own way out of this mess." He turned and stormed away. Those were the last words he would speak to her for the rest of the year.

Jake did not earn his hoped-for promotion after such a colossal blowup, but Nate, who had stayed the course in the market, got the one he had been working toward for years. He was now a vice president at one of the biggest banks in the country, and he and Bea went to Adolph's Asti to celebrate.

"I know this is hard for you, Bea, given Jake's big loss," Nate said, touching her hand across the table.

"It wasn't just Jake's loss, Nate. I had my entire savings in that portfolio too."

"I know. And I know how important it is for you to have your own money. But we will be fine. Frankly, I don't understand how someone as smart as you could participate in such a ridiculous position. Jake might be too green to know that betting against the market is always going to end up being a losing proposition. But you? You've been watching the market long enough to know that if you think things are weak, sit it out. Shorting it is such a risky and stupid move."

"But the market is so high, don't you think it's unnatural? Doesn't there have to be a real correction soon? What about the Fed raising rates?" She had been sure of this before, but now she was questioning everything.

"I don't. Look, Bea, I know you want to protect your brother at all costs, but this was a bad mistake. He's gotten lucky with shorts in the past, but they are always speculative. Charley wants me to put Jake on probation. He's worried that Jake is a risk to the bank."

"A risk to the bank?" Bea couldn't believe what she was hearing. Her mistake had been so bad that the head of one of the most respected banks on Wall Street thought she might be more of a liability than an asset. Well, Jake. "From this one bad pick? What about all his other wins? The rest of his year was so good. Doesn't that count for anything?"

"It does. It's the reason he still has a job."

Bea felt like she was going to be sick. She had nearly cost Jake his job.

"He'll be okay. Everyone gets knocked down sometimes. He's just lucky it happened in such a strong market that he can pick up and grow again. Okay?"

"Okay," Bea said, not feeling at all reassured but knowing that this was a special night for Nate; she needed to put aside her concerns and celebrate.

"I know the timing isn't ideal, but it is the end of the year, so—" He pulled the red ring box from his jacket pocket and placed it on the table. "Bea, I love you. If it's possible, even more than I did when I gave you this ring the first time. You have the biggest heart of anyone I've ever met, and the sharpest and most stubborn mind." He smiled and she smiled back. Even with the rest of her life falling to shreds, she had Nate. And that counted for a lot. "Beatrice Abramovitz, will you take this ring and finally commit to me? Show the world that we are going to get married?"

"I will!"

Nate placed the ring on Bea's finger and then came around the table to kiss her. Instead of going back to his seat, he walked to the piano and, before Bea knew what was happening, he was singing, just like on their very first date.

The waiter brought them a bottle of champagne. "The good stuff," Nate said. "Not quite as good as Livermore's, but close."

It had been a dreadful month, and she had a lot of work to do to redeem her mistake with her brother, but she had a wonderful man by her side, and she was hopeful again that she'd find a way.

Bea's happiness lasted exactly one more hour. She and Nate were starting to make plans for the year ahead when he made an unexpected request.

"So, now that you're officially my fiancée, do you think maybe you can stop being your brother's secretary?"

"Why? What does one thing have to do with the other?"

"Well, to be honest, I never really understood why you wanted to work there in the first place. I just figured becoming Jake's secretary was part of your keeping an eye on him, of taking care of him."

"It wasn't, but if that was the case, don't you think he needs that from me now more than ever? He's in such a tough spot." Bea couldn't believe what Nate was suggesting. Jake was in trouble, his investments were in shambles, and Nate expected her to wipe her hands and walk away? Even if he didn't understand that she was the one responsible, this was her brother.

"I can't leave him now. Jake is a mess. Everything he had was on a payment plan, and he can't even make the minimums. He could lose everything."

"Look, Bea, I feel bad for the guy, but that just tells me how reckless he can be."

"That's not fair! Everyone is buying with loans these days." Bea wasn't sure why she was defending Jake. She actually agreed with Nate on this point. Bea's personal loss had been devastating but was just her savings. She didn't owe anyone anything else. Jake, on the other hand, had built a grand life on mostly borrowed funds. Still, if she hadn't insisted that they hold their short positions, he would have had enough money to pay off all those debts and then some.

Bea's eyes filled with tears. She'd never been this wrong about the market in her life, and she'd ruined everything for her brother and herself.

"Bea." Nate grabbed her hand across the table. "Jake is in a bad place. That doesn't mean you have to be. I'll help him get back on his feet. Set him straight. But there's no reason for you to be working for him anymore. Let's start our lives."

"It's not just about Jake." Bea realized that if she couldn't tell Nate that she had been the one behind Jake's spectacular rise and cataclysmic fall, she had to at least explain why she'd taken the job in the first place. Why she felt a duty to stick it out now—to try to turn things around for both of them.

"Then what?"

"These months, while I've been working for Jake, I've been in the pit with the brokers. I've finally felt like I was part of the action that I came to Wall Street for. Jake and I had a plan. If he got promoted at the end of the year, which was a possibility before—"

"Before he had the single-biggest blowup I've seen in all my time at the bank."

Bea recoiled like she'd been slapped. But Nate didn't know what he was saying, or more, whom he was saying it to.

"Yes, before that. If he got promoted, I thought there was a chance he might be able to make me a junior broker."

"Did he tell you that?" Nate asked, derisively.

"Well, not exactly, but . . ."

"Look, I know you love the markets. And you're great at it." *Not anymore,* Bea thought ruefully. "But why in the world would you think Jake could make his secretary into a broker? Don't you think if there was any chance that you could be a broker at National City, I would have tried to help you?"

"Honestly, I didn't think about it. Jake's my brother, it's different. I'd never expect you to—"

"For goodness' sake, Bea, why not? I know how smart you are, how good you'd be at this. But Wall Street just doesn't work that way."

"Well, you've known from the moment we met that I am determined to stand on my own two feet in this man's world. Are you saying that I shouldn't even try?"

"No, I'm not saying that at all. What I am saying is that for such a smart gal, you seem to keep missing the obvious. There are simply no female brokers on Wall Street. If that's your goal, what you are waiting to have happen, then you'll be Jake's secretary forever. It's simply not possible." Bea watched Nate's face fall and his jaw clench. "I just don't understand this, Bea. I don't understand any of it. I know it's disappointing that Wall Street hasn't caught up to your talents or dreams, but I'm offering you a pretty wonderful life, and you don't seem to care."

"Of course I care, I just, I just need to stay with Jake a little longer. To get him back on his feet."

"I love you, but I can't compete for your attention anymore." He shoved the ring box across the table at her. "You can keep this. Consider it a parting gift." And then he pulled a wad of cash from his wallet, dropped it on the table, and left. He didn't even turn back to look at her as he walked out the door and away from her, forever.

Bea crumpled. For the first time in her life, she was responsible for everything falling apart, and she didn't see any way to put it back together.

CHAPTER THIRTY-NINE

Bea spent New Year's Eve alone with her parents. Jake and Henny had been planning a big party before Bea destroyed everything and, apparently, it was still on, but Bea was sure she wouldn't be welcome. Plus, given the state of her life, there was nothing about the upcoming year that she wanted to celebrate. In a matter of weeks, she had lost not only all her savings, and her last shot at Wall Street, but also the man of her dreams. Her entire future had evaporated, and she had no idea what to do about it.

First thing in the morning on New Year's Day, she was happily surprised to get a visit from Henny. She was still in her dressing gown when she answered the door.

"We missed you last night, Bea's Knees."

"I doubt that. And I don't think I am deserving of that name, especially not now."

"I disagree. Jake and I will survive, and so will you. You made a bad decision. I know that's hard for you because it's so unusual, but we all make mistakes." Bea looked up at Henny in surprise. How did she know Bea had been the one to want to sell short? Had Jake told her? And if he had, why didn't she hate her? "Oh, c'mon, Bea. I love Jake, but I know he'd never think of something that radical—shorting the biggest stocks in the market. That had to be your idea."

"And you're still here? Oh, Henny, I'm so sorry. I've ruined everything. Everything. Your future. Mine."

"Enough. I've spent the past week with your brother, crying my tears over losing the life we thought we were going to have. It will be a big adjustment, but if that's what it comes to, so be it."

"What do you mean *if*?"

"Bea, you know Wall Street. Jake made all that money in a single year; he can make it again. He's already put plans in place to start digging out of this hole when the market opens tomorrow."

"He has?" Jake hadn't made a single significant move in the market without Bea's direction. And yet he was okay. He had ideas. Why didn't she?

"Yes, ma'am. You'll see for yourself when you get to work tomorrow."

"I wasn't sure I should go." Bea looked away from Henny. "We lost everything because of me, and I don't know how to fix it. Jake and I haven't spoken. I don't think I have a place there anymore."

"For the love of all things sacred! Bea, money is not everything. Investing is not everything. I've been telling Jake as much all along. But he had this vision of the life he thought I expected. The one he wanted. Yes, he was riding high, and it was fabulous. But look around. You're not destitute. I told Jake, we can move into one of these apartments—or even his bedroom here—if we need to. I don't care about that nearly as much as I do family and friends."

"That's awfully big of you. But I don't think Jake sees it that way, and I'm not sure he ever will." Bea looked away from her friend, her sister-to-be, and fiddled with the tie on her silk robe to hide the plump tears that were building in her eyes.

"Oh, honey." Henny wrapped Bea in her arms. "No, he doesn't. Yet. But he will. Just give him some time. Let him lick his wounds. He's your brother. He loves and adores you. And he'll come to understand that sometimes the market is a gamble, plain and simple. No one wins all the time."

"Do you really believe that?"

"Heck yeah, I do. It's the truth."

"When did you get so wise about these things?" Bea pulled away from Henny just enough to wipe her tears and offer her a small smile.

"Well, first, I worked on Wall Street for four years before I got engaged and left. Most of Mr. Driscoll's brokers had their moments of failure. It comes with the territory. But also—" Henny's face changed, her usually rosy cheeks drained to white, and her easy smile was replaced by one that was straight and tight.

"Henny? What is it? Has something happened? To you?"

"Oh, Bea, I should have told you this ages ago. Honestly, I assumed you'd figure it out by now, genius that you are and all."

"What? What is it?"

"Don't you think it's odd that you've never met my parents?"

"Well, I had wondered about it, especially when Jake was making plans for your proposal. But I didn't want to pry. I figured if there was something you wanted to tell me, you would."

"It's funny, I'm usually an open book, but this, this is something I've been too ashamed to talk about."

"Henny . . . what?"

"I haven't spoken to my family in years."

"You haven't?" Bea was shocked.

"Papa wanted me to marry his partner's son when I was nineteen. I refused. I wanted to make my own way in the world. Live life on my own terms."

"I remember you saying that. And look at you now!" Bea said cheerily.

"This wasn't all by choice. When I said no to getting married, my parents kicked me out. That's why I live in Greenwich Village. That's why I'm always free to do as I please on Shabbat. Nate was the only person in my family who stayed loyal to me."

"Oh, my goodness, Henny. I thought you were strong before, but . . . you walked away from so much just to stand on your own two feet. I'm in awe of you."

"Now hang on, that's not the point of my telling you this now. Yes, I refused to let someone else tell me how to live my life, but eventually my father tried to make amends, and I wouldn't have it. I shut them out and, for a while there, it was really lonely. The best part of my life is all of you. Bea, I've realized that we all need people. We need family. I should have found a way to make my choices without sacrificing my parents and sisters. It's my biggest regret. So, I'm begging you, don't be a prideful, stubborn fool like me, Bea."

"It's not too late with your family, is it? The wedding? Won't they be happy?"

"Maybe. I told Jake about all this right after we got engaged, and he wanted to go to meet them immediately. But I want to be the one to reach out to them. I was going to tell them about the engagement in the New Year. Of course, now, well, I'm not sure it's the best time to do that."

"Because of me."

"No! Are you hearing anything I am saying? Stop blaming yourself. Surprise. You're not perfect. No one is. Not even Nate." Henny took Bea's hand and looked her squarely in the face. "Bea, I don't know exactly what happened between the two of you, but I do know he was a fool too. These men are stubborn fools. But we love them anyway. And I know he loves you. You are the only girl for him."

"I don't think that's true anymore."

"You're wrong. This has been hard for him too. Until Jake came along, there was no one like him—at National City or anywhere else. Even the best guy's bound to get a little competitive. But he's a good egg, and I know all he wants is to build a life with you."

"I'm not so sure about that."

"Well, I do. He loves you. He just doesn't want to have to compete with Jake for your attention and affection. And, really, he shouldn't have to. Bea, think about it. I know being an investor has been your dream, but is it possible that you're using that dream to hide from living the life you deserve? You should be loved, happy, and even taken care of by someone else some of the time. This is a new year. Can you try to find a way to make peace with yourself, with your mistakes, and move on?"

Bea had never thought about things this way before. She had seen her dream of being an investor only one way, as her path to respect and independence. Was it possible that, instead, it was impeding her ability to move forward in life? Surely it had made it impossible for her to be with Nate. But she loved the markets. She was great at picking stocks. Well, she had been, before. Could it be that her success in the market was nothing more than luck? She'd been horribly wrong about the market correction so, clearly, there was some dynamic at play on Wall Street that she didn't understand. And if she didn't understand it, she should never have tried to be a broker in the first place.

Tomorrow was the first trading day of 1929. She would go back to work to find out, once and for all, if she was meant to be an investor. If she was, then she would figure out what she missed in December and help Jake recover what they had lost. If she wasn't, she would accept defeat and walk away from Wall Street forever.

1929

The Year of the Crash

CHAPTER FORTY

January, nine months before the crash

DOW MONTHLY AVERAGE: 318, +18 POINTS FROM DECEMBER, +119 FROM JANUARY '28

Bea's first week back at work was agonizing. Jake had, ostensibly, forgiven her, but his feelings were tinged with an undercurrent of resentment that he couldn't hide and, as his twin sister, she would have felt even if he tried. Bea desperately wanted to fix things and attempted to approach the market with a fresh eye. She went back to studying stocks as she always had but, where patterns revealed themselves before, she now saw nothing. Well, not exactly nothing. Every data point led her to the same conclusion it had before. That there was a correction coming. Yet the market kept going up. No matter how she analyzed it, she couldn't understand why this was happening, nor could she correctly identify what to buy to rebuild her and Jake's portfolios. Her instincts were completely wrong, and she was lost.

Jake, on the other hand, had spent the final few days of 1928 buying every obvious stock in the market, and things had begun to turn around for him and his clients. Still, Jake was on probation at National City. If he made one more big mistake in the market, he would be out of a job. He'd used Henny's ring as collateral to secure his apartment and was trying to refinance the Great Neck house so he could keep that, too; if he lost his job, he would lose everything. Jake didn't want to take any more chances, and he stuck to tried-and-true stock picks, which was a safe way to go in an ever-rising market. There were no big ideas, no contrary positions to get him noticed, but he was holding on and rebuilding slowly. And that seemed to be enough for him.

At work, the dynamic between Bea and Jake had changed. He had no interest in even discussing stocks with Bea and simply treated her as his secretary. Bea complied. She was so ashamed by how horribly she had failed, so thrown off by her inability to understand what she was witnessing in the markets, even now, that she had become a meek and quiet shadow of herself. It was clear to Bea that a stock market career had been a false dream; it was time for her to leave Wall Street, and she had an idea that might actually help Jake in the process.

"Tell them it was me," Bea said, as she walked into Jake's office.

"What are you talking about?"

"Charley Mitchell, Nate, whoever it is that is holding this blowup over you. Tell them it was my idea."

"Why would I do that?"

"Because then they will know that you aren't the one with the bad instincts, you aren't the one who doesn't understand the market, you aren't the one who lost everything."

"But I am. Don't you see, BB, whether it was your idea or not, I went along with it. I believed you. And if I tell them that, I look like an even bigger fool."

A fresh wave of shame crashed over Bea. Jake was right. Of course he was right. And she hadn't even seen that.

"Well, then there's no reason for me to be here anymore." She hung her head.

"Why do you say that?"

"Because I was wrong. About all of it. I thought Wall Street, being a broker, was somehow my destiny. Clearly that's not the case."

"C'mon, BB. You screwed up. It was big and bad. But I'm okay. We can start over. I'm happy to have you as my secretary. You'll make good money and still be here, on the Street. With the brokers. No one gets it right all the time, BB. I'm sure you will again, at some point."

"No, Jake, you don't understand. I still can't see it. I keep looking at the market, at the patterns, at the economic indicators, and all I see is a crash. I can't make any sense of the data." She turned away from her brother for a moment to hide the hot pink shame that was spreading across her face. "I don't want to be a secretary. I want to be a stock picker, and if I'm no good at picking stocks, I have no reason to be on Wall Street."

"That's a little extreme, don't you think?" He leaned across his desk and took her hand. "Give it a little time, maybe?"

"I've given it enough time. I had my run. I was good at this, for a little while, but I guess that was just dumb luck. I need to find a new job, because my days on the stock exchange are over."

Part of Bea hoped that Jake would beg her to stay. To tell her that she was still one of the sharpest minds on Wall Street and he needed her. To call her a pint-sized genius like he used to. But he didn't. Because she wasn't. She had gotten it all wrong. And that left her no choice but to walk away. It was time for her to accept that dreams were just that, fantasies; from now on, her goals would be grounded in reality.

Bea started working at Abramovitz Grocers with her father. It had never been what she wanted, but she was good at it, and being where she was appreciated was a huge comfort right now. As Bea came to understand the rhythm of product sales, she began to develop a pricing and marketing plan to move more inventory. Bea found that when she thought about the store as a strategic business, she actually enjoyed the work. And her ideas were successful. The store's customers and revenue began to grow. People started coming from farther away, and Bea had a new idea. She would turn Abramovitz Grocers into a chain of stores. Open other locations. Make the Abramovitz name synonymous with fine produce across the city. Her mother loved the idea, while her father was reluctant to change things. But for the first time in a long time Bea saw a whole new path to success, and she was genuinely excited to follow it.

That evening, Bea met her friends at P.J. Clarke's. It pained her to be with the whole gang without Nate, but her friends had been insisting she stop hiding at home; tonight, with this new, big idea for the store, she was actually excited to see them. She scanned the room as she entered and saw Henny at their usual booth, already sipping a martini with Milly and Lowell.

"Jake not here yet?" Bea asked as she slid into the banquette next to Henny.

"Working late again if you can believe it." Henny laughed. "It's almost like that year-end hiccup was good for him. Got him to take his job seriously."

"It's pretty amazing how quickly he bounced back from that short sale fiasco last year," Lowell said. "Don't know what he was thinking with that nonsense."

"He thought the market was getting too high," Bea snipped. "You know, what goes up eventually has to come down."

"Right, but not these days. Not in the new era of finance. Everyone knows that," Lowell said casually. Bea felt the comment like a personal insult and was about to defend herself when Milly cut in.

"Well, I for one am glad to be finished worrying about all of that," Milly said excitedly. "No more stock market for me!"

"What do you mean?" Bea asked, confused. "You're leaving the bank?"

"I am. But for good reason." She lifted her hand from under the table to reveal an extravagant diamond ring. "We're getting married!"

"Oh, Milly, how wonderful for you!" Henny clapped her hands excitedly.

"What terrific news. A toast!" Bea lifted the martini that had been waiting for her when she arrived and drained it in three large gulps.

"Whoa, BB, slow down." Jake arrived. He nudged her over as he piled into the booth next to her. "What are we drinking to?" He motioned to the waitress for another round.

"Milly and Lowell are engaged! Isn't it spectacular? Now we can wedding plan together," Henny exclaimed. "Oh gosh, Bea's Knees. I didn't—"

"It's okay, Henny. It's not as if I'd forgotten about him." On the contrary, Bea hadn't been able to stop thinking about Nate. Especially now that she had left Wall Street for good and there was nothing keeping them apart. Except her stupidity.

"If it makes you feel any better, I saw Nate last week, and he was absolutely wrecked," Lowell added sympathetically, and Bea felt a flash of hope. "What happened with you two anyway? I was sure it was going to be wedding bells soon."

"They had a stupid argument because he's a stupid, pigheaded man," Henny jumped in before Bea could speak. "Mark my words, they're not done for good."

"I don't know about that," Bea quickly retorted, even though she hoped Henny was right. "Anyway, Milly, back to you. Tell us everything. You're leaving J.P. Morgan?"

"I am."

"Milly and I are planning to take a year off and sail around the world, after the wedding," Lowell said excitedly.

"Sail around the world?" Bea was shocked. She didn't think Milly even liked the water.

"Yes! Lowell is an excellent seaman, and while he and the crew do the sailing, I can sit on a deck chair and read. What could be more fabulous?"

"Milly's being modest. She's also planning to start writing. She's terrific at it, did you know that? She's going to chronicle our adventures as we go!"

"Sounds wonderful!" Bea said enthusiastically. "But I thought you loved Morgan? You were living the dream!"

"In the beginning I thought it was great but, over time, I realized that most of the job was listening to demands and complaints from women like my mother. There wasn't much thinking about actual investment strategies." Milly took a sip of her drink. "Honestly, Bea, I think you might have saved yourself getting out of banking."

"Funny you say that because, for the first time, I might agree."

"You do?" Jake and Henny asked in unison.

"I do. I'm actually enjoying working at the grocery. And the store is doing so well; our reputation is growing beyond the neighborhood. I'm thinking we should expand. You know, open more locations?"

"It's a brilliant idea, Bea! You've got such a head for numbers and business, you can turn Abramovitz Grocers into an empire. The Brodsky's of grocery stores." Henny waved the toothpick from her martini in the air with a flourish and then popped one of the olives into her mouth.

"You know, I've noticed that we don't have anything close to what Papa is selling near Sutton Place. And with the skyscrapers going up all the time, the demand is sure to grow," Jake said encouragingly.

"Oh, and we'd love to have a grocery like that in Gramercy Park too!" Milly chimed in.

"Both great ideas. My next step is to walk around a few neighborhoods and see what the competition looks like; then I'll find my target and go for it." Bea smiled. And for the first time in a long time, it didn't feel forced.

"Well, since this seems to be the evening of big announcements, I have one too." Henny traced her finger around the rim of her glass nervously. "I spoke to my parents."

"You did! Oh, Henny, that's wonderful. And how was it? How were they?" Bea asked, excited.

"It was nice, actually. Well, more than nice. It was tops. We went to see them. They loved Jake, of course, he could charm the peel off a banana, and they want to meet you too. And your parents. They're hoping you can come for Shabbat. Maybe next week? Or the following?"

"Of course! Mama will be beside herself to get to have Sabbath with the famous Brodskys." Bea exaggerated her voice in mock awe.

"They want to meet you too, Milly Moo. And you, Lowell, and Sophie and Sal and—well, our whole gang." Henny prattled on excitedly, and Bea was filled with warmth for her soon-to-be sister.

"They do, but I told Henny we should get the family part settled first. Before the wedding," Jake added.

"Of course. How wonderful for you both." Milly smiled at Henny and Jake.

"Looks like lots of good news all around tonight." Jake raised his glass. "To Milly and Lowell, Henny and me, and Bea the grocery magnate."

"To fresh starts and new adventures," Bea added with a wistful smile.

CHAPTER FORTY-ONE

February

DOW MONTHLY AVERAGE: 318, NO CHANGE FROM JANUARY '29, +123 POINTS FROM FEBRUARY '28

Bea didn't find out until Thursday morning that Nate and his family would also be at the Brodskys' Shabbat dinner the next evening, and she was in a panic. She hadn't been able to get him out of her mind and, after what Lowell said about Nate being a wreck without her, she'd been hoping he might feel the same. She had considered reaching out to him. She wanted to apologize, to ask him to start over, but every time she picked up the telephone to dial or considered going to see him in person, she panicked. And since he hadn't tried to get in touch with her, she assumed she'd lost her chance. Now she'd be seeing him for the first time since that awful night. In front of her whole family, and Henny's, and his. She didn't know what to do. She hoped Sophie would have some advice.

"Maybe he won't come," Sophie said as she pulled a pin from her mouth and inserted it into a pleat.

"If he wasn't coming, then Henny wouldn't have told me, would she?"

"I don't know, maybe she wants you to be prepared just in case. It's been almost two months, Bea, and he is Henny's cousin. You're going to see him eventually. Might as well get the first awkward time over with, no?"

"But what do I say to him?"

"What do you want to say to him?"

"That I miss him. That I'm sorry. That I was a fool."

"So say that."

"But he ended things. He walked out on me in a restaurant. And he hasn't even tried to get in touch with me again."

"He was hurt, Bea. And rightly so. This is a genuinely good man who adores you. And he was begging you to start a life with him, a life that most girls would give an arm or a leg for."

"Yes, but he wanted me to abandon Jake to do it."

"Not being your brother's secretary is hardly abandoning him, Bea. I never knew why you agreed to that in the first place. It wasn't like you."

Sophie didn't know that Bea had been behind Jake's success (and his failure). She didn't know the obligation Bea felt to Jake, and to herself, to fix her mistake. And there was no point in telling Sophie now. It was all behind her. Part of her past. Her future was the grocery.

"Jake needed me. I wanted to marry Nate, I just wanted to help Jake at the same time. And Nate didn't want that."

"Nate doesn't seem like the type to have made demands on you like that. Did you ever consider that maybe he just wanted you to put him, your relationship, first for once? Bea, you've spent your life taking care of Jake. When does it get to be your turn?"

"It would have been, soon. I just had to get things back on track first."

"Oh, Bea, don't you see? Life is messy. It doesn't always come together exactly in the order we want it to. Like this pleated skirt here. If I waited to pin it until every fold was in place, it would never work.

It would fall apart. You have to take things as they come up, one fold at a time. Otherwise you risk being left with nothing."

"So are you saying that without Nate, I have nothing?"

"Of course not. You have a lot. Me and Sal, Jake and Henny, Milly and Lowell."

"And the grocery. I'm scouting new locations. I'm going to make Abramovitz a name in fresh food, like Brodsky's is in clothing, or like Romano will be one day in fashion design."

"From your mouth to God's ears." Sophie laughed. "Bea, I just want you to be happy. I know that Nate made you happy. You're doing something different now, not even working for Jake anymore. Nate put it all on the line for you; maybe you need to do the same. You still love him, Bea, so tell him. Give him another chance."

As usual, Sophie saw what Bea had failed to. Nate only ever wanted to feel that she was as devoted to him as he was to her. And she had been, but he didn't know it because she'd let a stupid secret stand in the way of their future. Tomorrow night she would apologize and beg him to take her back. She wasn't focusing on unattainable dreams anymore; she was going to let herself be happy. And nothing made her happier than Nate.

When the Abramovitzes arrived at the Brodskys' the following afternoon, Jake, Henny, and her parents, Mort and Helen, greeted them at the door.

"Mama, Papa, this is Jake's family. Remember Mrs. Abramovitz only speaks Yiddish or Russian." Henny was trying to be considerate, but Bea thought it made them sound horribly provincial.

"We translate for her, when necessary," Lew said quickly, dismissing Pauline's lack of English as an issue. Bea sensed that he was as anxious to impress these people as Pauline was.

"Mr. and Mrs. Brodsky, it's wonderful to finally meet you. I do so adore Henny and am just thrilled that she's going to be my sister soon!"

"You're just cute as a button, isn't she, Mort?" Henny's mother said, as she looked Bea up and down. "So petite, like a little fairy. Oh, I could have some fun dressing you."

"Um. Thank you . . . ," Bea said, forcing a smile. She saw where Henny got her bubbly personality.

"Mama, Bea might be a doll, but she's nobody's toy. She's one powerful little thing, I promise you that. Smartest girl I know." Henny gave Bea a squeeze.

"Yes, I hear you are helping your father expand his business," Mort said pointedly, looking at Henny as he spoke.

"I am, yes. I was working on Wall Street. Well, you know that, of course, because that's where I met Hen—Henrietta—when she was working there too."

"Wall Street, that's no place for girls. I've been telling Henrietta that for years. Took finding your brother to finally convince her to listen to me."

Bea watched Henny's face flush as she opened her mouth to defend herself and then closed it again.

"Come, let's go sit and have a nosh before prayers," Helen said in perfect Yiddish as she linked her arm in Pauline's. "I just love your scarf. Is that silk? We'll have to go shopping together soon." Bea watched Pauline stand a little taller as she left the hallway. The men followed, and she turned to do the same, but Henny pulled her the other way.

"Let me give you a tour first. Show you my bedroom and the rest of the house." Jake turned to join them, but Henny ushered him away toward the others. Bea was surprised, but happy to see more of where Henny grew up. It made her smile to picture Henny as a little girl here. It seemed like a happy home.

As soon as they were out of earshot of the group, Henny leaned in close to Bea. "I'm so sorry, hon. I had no idea until they arrived five minutes ago."

"No idea about what?" Bea felt a chill of fear run down her neck.

"Nate's brought a date." Henny looked at Bea wide-eyed and apologetic all at once. "If you want, I'll call you a taxi and say you've come down with something? You can hide out in my bedroom until it comes."

Bea was crushed. She had come tonight hoping for a reconciliation with Nate. And instead, he had already moved on. And so much so that he was bringing her to Shabbat dinner? Didn't Lowell say he was falling apart without her? Instead, it seemed he was already building a new life.

"No, it's all right. If Nate has a new girl, I'm going to have to meet her eventually. Might as well do it now, in the most embarrassing possible moment, when all our families are here." She tried to sound light and breezy even though inside she was crushed. She wasn't going to cower in a corner, much as she wished she could.

"I'll tell you something, I would never have expected this of him. He's a real heel for bringing her here tonight. He didn't warn anybody. Not even his parents. Just showed up with her on his arm. And one thing's for sure, she's no looker like you. Probably boring too."

"Probably." Bea smiled falsely and took a deep breath. She had had a lot of tough breaks lately, but this night just might take the cake.

Bea did her best to avoid Nate and his family all evening. It wasn't difficult, as they seemed clearly embarrassed that he had brought an uninvited guest. Especially on such a special evening. Even Pauline was kinder than usual to Bea. She bragged to the table about all of Bea's new innovative ideas for the grocery and praised her for having stuck it out so long on Wall Street.

When Nate was in conversation with someone else, Bea stole glances at him and his new girl. She never seemed to speak; she just sat and nodded, smiling. Nate didn't even laugh around her. *That couldn't be what he wanted, could it? Not if he had once wanted Bea. Why had she been so foolish? Taken him for granted?* Well, it didn't matter now, because he had obviously moved on. Although, several times over the course of the meal, Bea was sure she could feel Nate looking at her. Maybe he missed her too?

After coffee and cake, the Abramovitzes stood to leave. Bea was waiting in the hall for Jake to collect their coats when she caught Nate's eye. He was standing alone at the edge of the living room. This was her chance to talk to him. She didn't care if he had a new girl; she'd apologize anyway, lay it all on the line. She started to walk in his direction but, before she reached him, his girl intercepted, linked her arm in his, and pulled him back into a conversation with his parents. Bea's heart sank. It was too late. He was otherwise spoken for. She had made a lot of mistakes, but letting the love of her life slip away was undoubtedly the biggest yet.

Early Sunday morning Bea was sitting at the counter of the shop, going over their orders for the upcoming week when she saw a silhouette in the window. The shop wasn't set to open for two hours, she wasn't expecting any deliveries, and her parents were upstairs having breakfast. *Who was here?* She walked to the door, and her heart raced as she recognized the tall figure standing on the other side of the glass.

"Nathan Greenberg," she said guardedly as she opened the door a crack, sticking only her face outside. "Something I can do for you?"

"Bea, I'm sorry. Friday night was awful. I wanted to come down first thing Saturday, but I figured you'd toss me right out."

"Well, I might have." *He wanted to come see her! He was apologizing. Maybe she still had a chance with him after all.*

"Can I come in?" He put his hand on the frame of the door to open it, and Bea backed away slightly. "It's freezing out here, and I really want to talk."

"Well, I don't know, how would your girl feel about that?"

"She's not my girl; she's one of my buddies' secretaries. I didn't want to show up alone so . . ." *He didn't have a new girl!* "Bea, what I did on Friday was rotten."

"You'll get no argument from me on that." Bea released the door and walked to stand behind the counter, leaving Nate on the other side like a customer. Having him here, now, acting sweet and soft and like the Nate she had loved for so long, she wanted to embrace him. A physical barrier would help keep her impulses in check.

"I should never have done it. I know that. Knew it then too. I was just so worried about seeing you again."

"You were worried?" She felt a flutter in her chest.

"Of course. You broke my heart."

"Did I really? You're the one who left me sitting alone in a restaurant."

"Yes but . . . forget it. I shouldn't have done that, but it was because I thought you were done with me."

"I wasn't. Not at all. Nate, I had my priorities all wrong. I was so focused on becoming a broker, on helping Jake dig out of his hole, that I lost sight of everything else for a while."

"I can't argue with that. And Jake seems to be doing just fine this year, thankfully."

"I know." It hurt Bea a little to hear Nate say this. Even though she was well aware of Jake's success without her, his continued achievement in the one place she had failed still stung. "Anyway, I'm here now." She motioned to the grocery. "I'm looking for new locations to expand. Making my mark on the business."

"That's terrific, Bea. It really is. I have no doubt you will turn this into a thriving chain of stores." Nate smiled, and Bea wanted to jump across the counter and wrap her arms around him.

"So, is that all? You came all the way down here on a cold Sunday morning just to apologize? You know you could have done that on the phone." Bea had been doodling on a sheet of paper while they were talking—it soothed her nerves. But now she stopped and looked up. Nate was gazing at her with a gentle, open expression. His eyes were pleading and hopeful and possibly still full of love. She hoped still full of love.

"No, that's not all." He moved around the counter so he was standing right in front of her, and grabbed her hand. Her whole body warmed, and she began to ache for him. "The thing is, Bea, the way it all ended between us . . . I'm not proud of this, but I was jealous of Jake, of the fact that you seemed to care more about him, and work, than me. I was a chump."

"Well, I wasn't a peach either. You were so supportive of me. So patient. And I never gave you any credit for that. I just kept asking you to wait. Can you ever forgive me?"

"Forgive you? Bea, from the day that I met you I haven't been able to picture my life any other way than with you in it. These past months have been the worst of my life. Us being apart, it just doesn't make sense to me. And it seems like all the things that were getting in our way were so small and silly. You had this idea that you had to make something of yourself, on your own, before you could make a life with me. But don't you see? You already have."

"Have I?"

"Of course. I know it's been frustrating for you. You have a passion for the markets, more than most of my brokers or almost anyone I know on Wall Street. But don't think for a minute that 'Bea the Investor' is any more or less of a woman than the Bea sitting before me today. You are a brilliant, capable, independent woman no matter what you do. And I wouldn't want it any other way."

"Oh, Nate." Bea's vision grew blurry as her eyes filled with tears. "Thank you."

"Bea, I think I've loved you from the first moment that I met you. And I know I'll love you for the rest of my life, whether it serves me or not. Is there a chance that you will give us another try? Bea, will you marry me?"

For the third time in their relationship, Nate was popping the question. But this time was different. This time her dreams had changed. This time she understood what was really important, and her vision of the future aligned with his. This time she had grown up.

"I love you, Nate. I've never stopped loving you. Of course I will marry you." He pulled her to him. She was overwhelmed with happiness to feel his solid body again. Intoxicated by the scent of him. They kissed, and it held all the wonder and the excitement of the very first time while also feeling like the most natural and inevitable kiss of her life. She was elated. And then a thought crossed her mind and she pulled away.

"There's just one thing." Bea took in Nate's smile, his handsome, loving face; she had been dreaming of this moment. But she still had this secret. Could she start a life with Nate without telling him what she'd really been doing for Jake? Maybe this was her chance to clear the slate and start fresh. But what if he changed his mind when he found out?

"Are you kidding me?" His face tensed and she started to panic. She couldn't tell him. She finally had him back, and there was no reason to ruin their chances at happiness by revealing something that was no longer relevant to their lives. Jake was on Wall Street. Bea wasn't. She never would be again. The past was the past. It was time for her to leave it behind and walk toward her future with the man she loved.

"The ring is in the back of my top bureau drawer. Can you go upstairs to get it and ask my parents first? Then come back down here with them, and we can do this one more time."

CHAPTER FORTY-TWO

May, five months before the crash

DOW MONTHLY AVERAGE: 297, –22 POINTS FROM APRIL, –20 FROM JANUARY

Milly and Lowell had gotten married at the beginning of the month, in a beautiful (if quickly planned) wedding. Her family hadn't wanted to waste any time with a long engagement and put on the wedding of the season only a few months after Lowell had popped the question. Milly, who didn't like being the center of attention, was happy with a short engagement. Less time for fuss. And now all the focus was back on Henny. Her wedding party had grown since her reconciliation with her family and now included not just Milly and Bea, but also Henny's two younger sisters, Deena and Edith, and Nate's sister, Lizzie. Sophie was, of course, making her dress, as she had Milly's and would Bea's.

After Henny's first full fitting, at Sophie's new studio on Delancey Street, Lizzie had arranged for the whole bridal party to have lunch uptown, at the very exclusive Colony restaurant. The Colony was bustling when they arrived, full of women who were resting their tired feet and refueling after a morning spent shopping. Bea knew that many considered this an ideal day and, while being able to take lunch in this leisurely manner was undoubtedly an extreme luxury, these activities would never be her first choice. She was grateful that she had the grocery to occupy her time now. She had found an ideal second location on Madison Avenue, near Nate's apartment, and negotiations for the building were keeping her busy. In quiet moments she still felt the absence of working on Wall Street; she missed the pace and the way it made her brain hurt to process so much data all the time. But expanding the grocery into a chain would be a significant accomplishment, and she was happy to be putting her focus there.

As soon as the girls were seated, Henny turned to Milly and asked with enthusiasm, "So, Mrs. Forester, how does it feel to be an old married broad?"

"She's hardly old!" Bea jumped in.

"It feels terrific." Milly smiled, looking truly blissful.

"Are you bored at all, now that the wedding is behind you?" Bea asked. No matter how much money she had, she would always want to work somehow, and she still had a hard time understanding that Milly didn't feel the same.

"It was such a beautiful ceremony," Sophie gushed, cutting in.

"And a wonderful party," Bea added, realizing she should have said something complimentary about the wedding. She was a dolt.

"Thank you," Milly said sweetly. "And, no, I'm not bored at all. I've been too busy planning our trip. I've been researching every port, so we know exactly what to do when we arrive. And to have some color for my writing."

"I'm confused. Don't you work in the stock market, Milly?" Lizzie asked. Bea was surprised that Lizzie, of all people, would be interested in Milly's work or the market.

"I did, but not anymore. I used to be in the ladies' department at Morgan Bank."

"Oh, phooey." Lizzie pouted her lips as she said this. "I do a little investing myself, and I was thinking that I might switch my accounts. You know, go to one of the big banks. I asked my brother to help but, of course, he was useless. Nate just told me to find a nice women's department. I want someone I know!"

"Well, I could introduce you to someone at Morgan if you wanted?" Milly offered.

"You'd leave Abe?" Henny's sister Edith asked Lizzie, then she turned to the table and explained. "We have a great broker, Abe Friedland, and he has an office in Queens."

"We all use him," Henny's other sister, Deena, chimed in. "We just pop in whenever we're bored!"

"And we've made such a bundle it's like we have jobs!" Edith added.

"This new era of stocks is incredible, isn't it?" Lizzie said. "Once you learn not to worry about the little jumps up and down, you can't help but make money!"

"Oh, I know," Edith added. "Papa had to hide the newspaper from us because we were getting too upset when a stock fell for a day. But that's the incredible thing, they always go back up!"

"Yes, they do. Investing is the surest way to make money these days," Lizzie said with authority. "I guess I'll stick with Abe too."

Bea sat stunned. She'd expected the conversation at lunch to be all about weddings: Henny and Jake's, Milly and Lowell's; her own plans. She never anticipated that this group of girls would give even a single breath to investing. Yet, here they were, talking about the market like it was the latest Paris runway show.

Bea supposed she shouldn't have been surprised; the market had become a popular subject in the media, even the *Ladies' Home Journal* had pieces about investing. But this idea that it was a path to easy money, Bea knew firsthand that wasn't true. Sure, it had mostly been that way lately, and these girls had so much money that, even if they lost some, they'd likely be just fine; but still, the way they were thinking was dangerous. How did no one see that?

"If you're all investing, you need to be careful." Bea couldn't help herself. "Maybe now more than ever, with the market being so unpredictable."

"It's not that unpredictable," Lizzie said dismissively. "Plus, the big banks will bail us all out if things get bad. Like back a few weeks ago, when it took a dive and the head of Nate and Jake's bank—what's his name again?—anyhoo, doesn't matter. The head of National City fixed it. And everything is peachy again."

"Charles Mitchell, that's the president of National City," Milly said.

"Ah yes! Charley Mitchell, that's the name I was looking for."

"He didn't fix it, though," Milly added. "I'm not following closely anymore, but from what Lowell said, there was another scare about the Fed raising interest rates, which spooked investors; Charley pledged twenty-five million dollars in credit to demonstrate his confidence. You know, so people could borrow more to buy more. That's what stopped the slide."

Bea nearly dropped her fork. She had stopped following the daily movements of the markets, as well as most of the financial news. She found she grew too obsessed with the drop that never happened and was much happier when she didn't pay attention. But if what Milly had just said was correct, it was another sign that things weren't as stable in the market as people believed. She was about to say as much when Henny changed the subject.

"All right, enough! This is my bridal lunch, not a stock salon, for heaven's sake! I don't let Jake talk as much about the mind-numbing market as you all have so far. Can we puh-huh-lease change the subject to something more droll?"

"Great idea," Sophie said. "Hen, why don't you tell the girls what we're thinking for their dresses? And then, maybe you can give us all a few clues about the details of the wedding. I made the dress and even I haven't heard much about what you're planning!"

Sophie successfully shifted the rest of the lunch talk to weddings and, as Bea listened and tried to remain enthusiastic, her mind was turning over what she'd just learned. The signs that she had seen in December were only getting stronger. Maybe it wasn't that she had been wrong about a correction altogether; maybe it was just that she had been wrong about when it would happen. But she had no reason to believe she could predict that better now than she had before. What could she possibly do?

CHAPTER FORTY-THREE

Bea and Sophie took a taxi downtown together after lunch and, as soon as they sat down in the back, Sophie turned to her with concern.

"Okay, so tell me. What is it? Everything okay with Nate?" Sophie asked. "You didn't say much about the wedding."

Bea nodded. "Everything with Nate is fine. More than fine. I was distracted by the market."

"The market? The stock market?"

"Yes. You heard the girls today. They think the market will go up forever, and it's just not possible, and I think something bad is coming and—"

"So what? You're not working on Wall Street anymore, you're not invested. Why do you care? Is it Nate? Are you worried about his money? Jake's?"

"No—well—yes, but it's more complicated than that."

"I can do complicated. Explain."

Bea had never told Sophie the truth about her time working for Jake, but she didn't think her concerns after today's lunch would make sense if Sophie didn't understand why Bea really left Wall Street. It was time to confess.

"When we get to your house." Bea didn't want to share this information in the back of a taxi.

As soon as they were settled inside, Bea started to explain. "There's something you don't know about my time at National City with Jake. Something big."

"Chianti big?" Sophie asked. Bea nodded and Sophie held up her finger before going to the fire escape, where Sal kept his homemade wine. She came back with two full glasses of muddy purple liquid. "Okay, so what is it?" she asked as she handed one to Bea.

"Do you know why I left banking at the beginning of the year?"

"Yes. You left because you couldn't get the job you really wanted, because no one would take you seriously even though you were surely the smartest person there, and because you were sick and tired of being Jake's secretary."

"Well, yes. But I really left because . . . because I lost everything for me and Jake."

"What are you talking about? You're all doing great, far as I can tell."

"We are now. But all that time that I was Jake's secretary, I wasn't just a secretary."

"What do you mean?"

"I was the one making all the investment decisions. I was the broker. Jake just did what I told him to."

"He was okay with that?" Sophie asked as her eyes widened.

"More than okay; it was what he wanted. It was no different than when I used to do his homework for him, all he cared about was being successful."

"Right, okay." Sophie seemed to be turning over this new information in her mind. "So . . . you weren't okay with that?"

"Well, I was for a while, but once I was there, it seemed like it should be easy for me to become a broker. I knew it wasn't possible anywhere else, but working for Jake . . . I was already acting as a broker, it was just that no one knew it. And Jake wanted to keep it a secret."

"And you didn't? So that's why you left?"

"Not exactly. Jake wanted to do something big before the end of the year, to really get the attention of the top guys at National City, and he was counting on me to find it. I thought the market was going to drop. And last year it did. We had made a bundle, but I didn't think the fall was over. I made Jake wait for it to drop even more instead of taking our profits. It never did. It went up. A lot. And we lost. Badly."

Sophie took a sip of her wine, and Bea watched her face change as she suddenly realized what Bea was saying. "So, when Jake was in a panic at New Year's about losing everything . . . and you didn't show up . . . and then you stopped working for him . . . that was because of this? Because you got something wrong, *one* time?"

Bea nodded as she blinked to try to clear the tears from her eyes. But it was no use, they just kept coming. The shame of her failure was all tied up in her secret, and she'd been alone with both for too long. Sophie put down her glass and placed her hands on Bea's arm.

"Bea. You made a mistake. I know you're not used to it, but it happens. You walked away from Wall Street because of that? Because of *one* error?"

"It was more complicated than that. If we had gotten this right, Jake was going to get promoted and, hopefully, promote me. And I was going to come clean about what I had been doing for Jake to Nate."

"Did you?"

"No."

"Look, I don't know enough about that world to know whether what you're saying about the market is right or not. But I do know that if you are this upset, it is more complicated than a worry about stocks. You're treating what you did for Jake as some huge secret. But all I hear is that you helped your brother get started. Is it possible that you are so concerned about the market and everyone else in it because you've twisted that up with this old secret? Whether you want to work on Wall Street or not, you should tell Nate the truth."

"I can't do that, Sophie. The time to tell him has passed. I almost did when he proposed, the last time." Bea smiled. "But I decided that there was no reason to. He doesn't ever need to know. It is in the past. What would be the point now?"

"The point would be to free yourself. To be able to talk to your bank vice president fiancé about the stock market. To, maybe, do what it sounds like you really want to do, which is go back to Wall Street."

"I failed on Wall Street. And I'm happy at the grocery."

"If I remember right, Jake made a bundle last year before that one bad moment, which, I will add, he quickly recovered from. So you hardly failed. You need to be okay with that, Bea. Accept your mistake as only one small part of your life. It sounds like that will be easier to do if you tell Nate the truth. Show him what you're really capable of, what a sophisticated investor you are."

"But I'm not. Not anymore. Even if I did tell Nate, tried to go back to Wall Street, what's the point? No one would hire me, remember? Anyway, after all that we've been through, how would Nate ever trust me if he found out about my deception?"

"I wish I had the answer for you, Bea, but I don't. Life is about compromise, trade-offs. We all have to make them. We give up some things, we get others. Look around, do you think I want to live in the basement apartment underneath Sal's parents? I'd love to have a space of our own. But Sal and I are building businesses, we want to go to Italy, we need to save money. So this is what we do. We make choices and we learn to live with them, to make peace with them. That's what growing up is. You know what your options are. So make a choice. Just make sure that whatever it is, it's one that truly makes you happy."

Bea and Sophie talked for a little longer, and as they did, Bea gained the clarity she was seeking. It wasn't about going back to Wall Street; it was about the unresolved question of why she had been so wrong. And she'd solved that, sort of, today at lunch. It had been about timing. The market did fall in December, just not as much or for as long as she thought it should. It was time to let that go. She had a job that challenged her. She had a man who loved her and supported her new career. She'd already made her choice. She had a new life. She just had to forgive herself so she could start to enjoy it.

CHAPTER FORTY-FOUR

July, three months before the crash

DOW MONTHLY AVERAGE: 348, +16 POINTS FROM JUNE, +30 POINTS FROM JANUARY

Lew and Bea stood at the front door of their house, waiting for Pauline. "Mama, we're going to be late!" Bea called up the stairs in the direction of her mother's dressing room. Bea and Jake were turning twenty-four, and Henny was hosting a birthday dinner for the two of them and their families on Sutton Place. Jake had wanted to host everyone on Long Island, but Henny refused because they were having the wedding there in a month, and she didn't want to risk ruining the lawn.

Bea was looking forward to the evening. She finally felt like her life was on track. She'd finalized the purchase of a building near Nate's apartment (soon to be hers as well), on Madison Avenue, and was now looking to buy a second one off Gramercy Park. Like her family's home on the Lower East Side, each of these properties had apartments above the storefronts that could generate rent. Nate had happily funded the purchases but assured her that, in his mind, the properties were truly hers and her father's. It was hard for her to accept his help, but doing so was part of her push to grow up. To be an adult and embrace the gifts in front of her.

"All right, no need to yell. I'm here! Had to find this." Pauline held out a silver mesh bag. "I bought it shopping with Helen, and she made me promise I would carry it when I saw her next. It is imported from Paris!"

As usual these days, Pauline was dressed like she was going to visit royalty at a European palace. Her hair was elaborately curled, and every part of her body that could hold jewelry was adorned with something. Every time Jake had a particularly good month, he bought her some sort of bauble, and at this point she had amassed quite a collection. Still, her wedding necklace was her most prized possession and, whereas her wrists were piled with bracelets and nearly every finger had on a ring, that sat alone on her neck.

The party was already in full swing when Bea and her parents arrived. At this point, most of the city seemed to behave as if there was no such thing as prohibition, and everyone in attendance raised their cocktails to toast Bea when she walked in. Nate was immediately at her side and, as she looked around the room, she felt momentarily overwhelmed. When had her family gone from just their small unit of four to a group so large? Nate's parents were there, and Lizzie and her husband, the Brodskys, including Deena and Edith, Milly and Lowell, Sophie and Sal, and even Mr. and Mrs. Romano.

"Happy birthday, old lady!" Jake teased as he handed Bea a drink and raised his in a toast, throwing his arm over her shoulder.

"If I'm an old lady, you're an older man!" She nudged him, smiling. "Remember, you came out first."

Bea mingled with her friends and family. At one point she was cornered by her mother and Nate's mother, Arlene, as they feverishly discussed wedding plans.

"Are you sure you don't want to have the wedding sooner, Bea?" Arlene asked with concern.

"October is perfect," Pauline jumped in. "We will be busy with Yaacov and Henrietta until the end of the summer. And then I will have a few weeks to recover before we have another wedding."

"Yes, but the October weather is more unpredictable. And with the party outside . . . plus, you have the new store opening in October too. It just seems like a lot for you, Bea." Arlene looked at her pointedly. It had been years since Arlene had had a wedding to plan, and she yearned to be as occupied by it as her sister—Henny's mother, Helen—was now.

"Beatrice can handle it. She can handle anything." Pauline smiled with pride. Since Bea had left Wall Street and gotten engaged, her mother had been treating her differently. She almost felt like Pauline respected her for her abilities instead of simply dismissing her as she had in the past. Bea's life was finally on an excellent path.

The sound of metal on crystal filled the air, and Bea turned to see Henny standing on her coffee table, tapping her champagne glass with a knife. "Hi, guys and dolls, and thank you for coming tonight to celebrate two of the most marvelous people in the world! Bea, a best friend and another sister all in one, and Jake, a handsome, successful almost-husband. I hit the jackpot with these two. Everyone—" Henny lifted her glass in the air. "A toast. To Jake and Bea, the fabulous Abramovitz twins."

Henny stepped down from the table, grabbed Bea, and gave her a big kiss on the lips before turning to Jake and doing the same. Then she directed the group to the dining room for dinner. As people slowly made their way to the table, Jake held Bea back.

"Can we talk for a minute? Before the party continues and I don't have my wits about me?"

"Of course."

"I just wanted to say, again, how happy I am that you have such big plans for the grocery. And also to thank you for all that you did for me last year. I wouldn't have any of this without you, and I think that got lost in the short selling hullabaloo." Bea felt a flood of gratitude.

She hadn't realized how badly she wanted to hear this from Jake until he said it. It meant a lot.

"Thanks, Jake. But that's all behind us now. Like your view." Bea motioned to the window. "Water under the bridge."

"You have such a big heart, BB. You're just the tops."

"I love you too, Jake." Bea started walking to join the others at the table, but Jake hadn't moved. "Is there more?"

"Well, I'm sure you've seen what's been happening in the market lately. The volatility has been crazy—"

"I try not to pay attention to the market anymore."

"Not at all? Not even in your notebooks, for fun?"

"Not at all. I can't, Jake. It just makes me too frustrated. And worried."

"Worried?"

"Yes. I've pored over what happened at the end of last year, and all I can think is that it was just a timing issue. I assumed too much of a drop too soon. But, last I checked, all of the indicators for a correction were still there; you just said the exchange is more volatile than ever, brokers' loans are still on the rise, the Fed is still threatening to raise rates . . . all I see is an eventual slide. And no one else seems to see what I do."

"Maybe that's a good thing, BB."

"How?"

"Well, I've just been thinking. I'm doing swell when the market is on the ups, like it is now. But back in May, when it dropped huge, I struggled. And I know that if I'd had you around, to predict the drop and tell me what to short, I would have made a bundle. You know how to play the downs, BB. I don't. And riding the market while it's on a tear is fine, but it's not gonna make me a big-time operator, you know?"

Bea should have told Jake that he was plenty "big-time" already, but she was distracted by the specifics of what he was saying. "How much did it drop in May?" Bea felt an anxious knot start to form in her chest. Maybe the correction she'd been anticipating was about to happen.

"It fell below three hundred. It was bad for a minute there. Nate didn't tell you?"

"No." Now that she didn't work on Wall Street, they hardly spoke about stocks. "And where is the Dow now?"

"Do you really have no idea?"

"I wouldn't be asking if I knew, Jake."

"Almost three fifty."

"So you're telling me that the Dow has jumped fifty points in the past two months? You know these wild swings are a sure sign of instability, Jake. This could be bad. This could be really bad."

"Nah, it's just the market. Goes up and down. Like they said in the *Wall Street Journal*: 'The market has big reactions, but it always comes back, because business refuses to slump with the market anymore.' The foundations are stable."

"Then why are we out here talking about this now? Everyone is in there waiting for us." He had gotten her all riled up, and now he was dismissing her concerns. She turned to walk toward the dining room.

"Hang on a second. I have a point. Come back, BB. Please? Come work with me again?"

"With you how?" Bea asked.

"As my personal assistant. I'll keep my current gal to do the administrative stuff so you can focus on the ticker. It moves so much faster now that they have the high-speed model, and your brain is the only one I know that could keep track of all those numbers, let alone analyze them on the spot."

"Your personal assistant? So you mean make your picks for you, in secret? Again?"

Bea couldn't believe he would even suggest this now. She had finally let go of her Wall Street dreams and found her own work. She was doing big things for the family business. How dare Jake ask her to set that aside just to hide in the shadows again?

"Well, yes. But it's not a big deal. I'd cut you in with an even bigger percentage."

"It's a big deal to me. It's everything. I can't, I won't start my married life with secrets. And you shouldn't either. But if the market is as volatile as you say, you should start to look for shorts. You need to get ready. You—"

"Hey, you two—we're waiting for you! What's holding you up?" Henny came looking for them.

"Sorry, love. Bea and I just had a little business to discuss. We're coming."

"Ooooh, I hope it was about a wedding surprise." Henny winked at them. "I have been eyeing those sapphire earrings at Cartier—you know, something blue." She giggled, and they followed her into the dining room.

Bea sat down at her place next to Nate. "Everything okay?" he whispered as he grabbed her hand under the table. "You look pale."

"Swell. Just a little too much champagne and no food." She took a sip of water, hoping that it would also wash down her feelings. "Can I ask you something?"

"'Course. What is it?"

"Did the market take a dive at the end of May?" Bea tried to sound nonchalant even though Jake's comment had her mind in a tilt.

"I thought you didn't care about the markets anymore." Nate laughed. "We haven't talked about them in ages. It fell, but it came right back up and then some. Don't worry, all our money is just fine." She was astonished that he didn't understand. If the market had dropped this dramatically, so suddenly, any rebound might be temporary. The bigger correction she'd been waiting for could actually be coming. How did Nate not see it?

Maybe she needed to start watching the market again, just in case. Just to be safe.

CHAPTER FORTY-FIVE

August, two months before the crash

For the next month, Bea charted stocks. She learned nothing. The market just kept going up. It was now at a new all-time high of 380, which was a 20 percent gain from the unprecedented high of 318 when the year began. These unchecked gains made no sense to her, but since she now had plenty of other things to keep her mind occupied, between her work on the new grocery locations and the upcoming weddings—Jake and Henny's in a few weeks and hers in October—she set her notebooks, and her worries, aside.

By the time Henny's wedding week finally arrived in late August, the schedule of events and indulgences was so expansive that she didn't have time to think about anything but the happy couple's upcoming nuptials. They had had lunches, dinners, shopping sprees, and nights on the town, and even a full day of beauty behind the famous red door at Elizabeth Arden.

The actual wedding was a beautiful and extravagant backyard affair. The Brodskys had spared no expense for their eldest daughter's day, and every detail was exceptional. From the lush chuppah, which dripped with lilacs and gardenias, to the seven-piece band that played late into the night, to the long, elegant banquet tables set with cut crystal and china in a pattern that matched the flowers, the evening was a lively, beautiful, joyful celebration. It was made even more so by the all-encompassing love between Jake and Henny, and the elation of both families at their pairing. It was just the tonic Bea needed to purge concerns of the market from her mind. Wall Street was her past. This, the joy of love and marriage, embracing a bigger, broader family and, hopefully, creating a new one of her own. This was what was important. This was what really mattered.

September, one month before the crash

DOW MONTHLY AVERAGE: 343, –37 POINTS FROM AUGUST

It was the first week of September, and in a month, Bea would be marrying Nate. While the market had fallen from August, it was still up a dramatic twenty-six points from the beginning of the year. Things were stable enough that Bea felt free to focus all her attention on being a bride. Well, that and opening the second location of Abramovitz Grocery, now to be called Abrams, the week after she wed.

Pauline and Arlene had planned wedding festivities that filled an entire weekend, including a lavish Shabbat dinner and a Saturday luncheon both thrown at Bea's house by Pauline, a tented evening party in Nate's family's backyard, and a Sunday brunch at Jake and Henny's. It wasn't exactly the small, casual affair Bea had envisioned, but she was so happy to be marrying Nate that she gave in to most of both mothers' wishes. Concurrently, she worked double time getting the second location of the store ready to open. She didn't care about flowers or linens or most of the details that Pauline and Arlene spent their days focused on; instead, Bea's time was spent in the new shop on Madison Avenue, overseeing the installation of displays and the new refrigeration units, selecting paint colors, and making sure the logo on the window was big enough to see a block away.

Bea was happy. She was busy. And she had all but forgotten about stocks. She didn't even know that on the Tuesday after Labor Day (which also happened to have been the hottest day of the year), the market had hit 381, a new record. She also missed the headline in the paper on September 6, which most clearly validated her fears:

STOCK PRICES BREAK ON DARK PROPHECY

Millions of dollars in the open market value of securities wiped out in less than an hour. Economist Roger Babson says, "Sooner or later a crash is coming, and it may be terrific."

If she had, maybe she would have taken more notice sooner, but she didn't. So she went into her wedding week blissfully unaware.

There was a lot of hoopla around getting married that Bea thought was silly, but she was excited for today, her final fitting with Sophie for her wedding dress. She had intended to do her fitting alone, just her and Sophie. But Pauline insisted she be there, and that they include Arlene, Nate's mother, who wanted to bring Nate's sister, Lizzie. Sophie's mother, Mrs. Romano, was dying to see her daughter's masterpiece for the girl she'd known since she was a baby, so Bea invited her to join them. And with such a large group, of course Bea then wanted Henny and Milly. So here she was, one week before her wedding, about to have the final fitting of her dress in front of a crowd.

The dress was perfect: a simple top of sheer ivory organza with a slip-like silk camisole underneath that fell to a drop waist draped in ivory silk from back to front, where it gathered to a point, accentuated by a cluster of crystals. The knee-length skirt was made of the same silk, ornamented only by a scattering of small silk roses, that would sway fluidly with Bea as she walked. Sophie knew Bea so well she hadn't even had to consult her on the design. She stood behind the curtain about to put it on when Lizzie started talking.

"Have you been on the wild roller-coaster ride this month?" Bea heard her ask.

"Is there a new attraction at Coney Island?" Milly questioned innocently.

"Coney Island! You're a funny one, Mildred. No! I'm talking about the market, silly."

"Oh, we've taken our money out of the market. We're getting ready for our trip, and Lowell and I can't be worrying about checking in on our portfolio at every port. We'll get back into it when we return, but we've already made so much. And Lowell is happy for the break." Milly and Lowell had initially intended to set sail around the world in September but postponed another month as soon as Bea and Nate set their wedding date.

"Well, you've missed a crazy ride. Stocks have been all over the place. Up and down and up and down and—"

"Stocks move, Lizzie, that's what they do. If you're going to invest, you've gotta expect that," Henny said. "Milly, when, exactly, does your voyage begin? So romantic! Taking a boat around the world."

"The idea of it makes me feel sick," Lizzie said.

"You get used to it," Milly said kindly.

On the other side of the curtain, Bea was standing in her underthings, dress in hand, listening intently. She'd grown comfortable that the markets were stable enough, at least for now. If there was cause to worry after her wedding and the store opening, she'd revisit the stock market then. But the way Lizzie was talking made her wonder if she had that kind of time.

"Beatrice, what is taking so long? We are all waiting out here," Pauline prodded.

"Really, Bea's Knees! Did the dress swallow you up in there?" Henny asked.

Sophie poked her head in. "Is there a problem with the fit? I know your measurements as well as my own! Did I mess something up?"

"Not at all. I just got lost in thought for a moment." Bea slipped the dress on as she spoke and came out of the dressing room to the anticipated oohs and aahs from her friends and family. She admired herself in the glass and was overwhelmed. She was about to be a bride. Her nose started to tingle with impending tears of joy. After everything she and Nate had been through, they were finally going to start their life together.

"Sophie, you are quite a talent. I really need to have you make my dresses for the upcoming party season," Lizzie said casually. "If I can afford it after the disaster of my stock portfolio last week." She laughed and Bea's elation was replaced by concern. How bad was the market? She needed to look at a newspaper to find out.

"I'm suddenly feeling a little woozy," Bea said, as she hurried back behind the curtain to take off her dress.

"Are you all right? Do you need to lie down?" Sophie asked, concerned. "Do you hate the dress?" she whispered, looking worried as she stepped into the small dressing area with Bea.

"Oh, goodness, no. Soph, it is perfect, even more perfect than I could have possibly imagined. I just—"

"You just heard Lizzie talking about the market, didn't you? And now you're thinking about it? Vexed by it?" Bea nodded, guiltily. How did Sophie know her so well? "Listen, my opinion may be unpopular, and we're not invested in stocks because Sal doesn't believe in it, no matter how hard Jake has tried to convince him, but I think if you are still this worried, there is a reason. You're smart about these things, Bea. I don't believe that this is some delusion of yours. Talk to Nate. Tell him what you're concerned about. That's what husbands are there for. If they're worth anything, that is!"

Sophie was right. Bea wasn't some uninformed speculator getting swayed by every move the market made. She had been studying this for years now. And she knew what she was seeing, whether others agreed or not. She would talk to Nate. If what Lizzie was saying about the market was true, he would surely share her concerns.

"Thank you, Soph." Bea slipped on her regular clothes and gave Sophie a hug.

"I'm so sorry, everyone. I just realized that I need to take care of something. Thank you oodles for coming. Mama, I'll be home late tonight, and, the rest of you, see you Friday night for the big prewedding Shabbat."

Bea raced home to collect her notebooks and her father's discarded newspapers and then drove up to Park Avenue. It was only four thirty when she arrived, and Nate wasn't yet home, which gave her a chance to go back over her charts and add in new data since she'd last looked in mid-August. She was making notes about some of the overall market indicators when Nate finally walked in.

"Bea. Did we have a plan that I forgot about?" He looked tired. She wondered if all the movement in the market was starting to drain him.

"We didn't. I just had my final dress fitting and—"

"And you got so excited about this weekend that you had to come see me immediately?" He smiled and sat down next to her on the sofa. "What's all this?"

Bea suddenly saw the room through Nate's eyes. She looked like a madwoman: newspapers, her notebooks, and paper scraps with charts and scribbles were spread all over the coffee table; she had a pencil behind her ear and another, she now realized, gripped between her teeth. She might as well be Evangeline Adams, the stock market astrologer, making silly predictions like her latest claim: that the market "could climb to heaven." If that didn't exemplify the ridiculous popular opinion that had brought the country to this dangerous place, Bea didn't know what did.

"These are my notebooks," she said sheepishly, placing the bite-marked pencil down and collecting her things into a neat pile.

"The infamous notebooks. I thought you had packed those away ages ago?"

"I had. Well, I tried. But—Nate, for most of this year, I have been singularly focused on our wedding and our life together. But there have been a few moments when the market has had me very concerned. Back in May, at Henny's bridal lunch when the girls were all talking about stocks like they were experts. And then at my birthday when Jake told me about the sudden drop in the Dow . . . and then, today, at the fitting, Lizzie was going on about wild swings in the market. I've been combing papers from the past month, and I just saw what Roger Babson said on September 6 . . . I know how you feel about short selling, but I'm worried. I think Babson is right; a correction is coming soon, and it's going to be much worse than anyone is anticipating."

"What makes you think that, exactly?"

"There are so many factors. First, the volatility. Prices have been swinging violently for a while. Look at this." She held up a chart in her notebook. "I've been watching AT&T for several years, and in the middle of September it suddenly jumped fourteen points out of nowhere. I combed through the papers and there was no reason. No news."

"Okay, well stocks sometimes behave erratically because of selective buying. But that's the kind of thing that only makes sense when you're in it every day at a bank, in the trenches. Honey, talk of the market is everywhere. Heck, there's even a song on the radio about it right now." Nate started humming "I'm in the Market for You." "I know you love to analyze stocks, but it is easy to have these big ideas, and worries, when you're not as close to it."

"Okay, so you're there, seeing things as they come. Don't you think it's time we protect ourselves? Get out or, possibly, get short?"

"No. And neither do Charley or Tommy Lamont. And, as the heads of two of the biggest banks on Wall Street, I'd say they stand to lose a lot more than the rest of us if the market went south, right? If there is a correction, National City and Morgan are ready to bail the market out. They've done it before. So you can stop worrying."

"But . . . have you looked at all the data? The macroeconomic factors? Brokers' loans are climbing again, and the Fed really might actually raise rates this time. Numerous stocks are clearly overpriced relative to their earnings; agricultural commodities like wheat and cotton prices are dropping."

"You've clearly been doing a lot of homework. But, again, I will tell you that you are getting caught up in unrealistic panic. Yes, brokers' loans are on the rise again, but rates are still low, and money supply is ample. Some stocks may be overvalued, but that is always the case. Overall business conditions for major companies are stable. Agriculture might be slow, but retail is expecting a record season this Christmas, which will more than offset it."

Bea processed the things Nate was telling her. They were strong counterpoints to her concerns, and she might have been convinced by them at one time, but not anymore. "I hope you're right, but do you think it's also possible that you are just too close to this. I've stepped away from the markets for a while, and when I put it all together now the picture is so clear. I think we should be prepared if things start to turn. I've mapped out some strong shorts—"

"You've mapped them out?" Nate opened his eyes wide, surprised. "Bea, I know how smart you are, and that you've had success in your own portfolio, including that incredible call that saved your family after the Julian Pete disaster . . . and yes, you were a broker's secretary for a while, and were there when Jake was making all those foolish short sales. But you must realize that's not the same as doing this every day, as your job."

All at once, something inside of Bea shifted. Nate might not have meant to do it, but with this casual dismissal, he had turned something in her. He had treated her the way every person on Wall Street had from the first day she arrived, four years ago, when she had stood hopefully in front of Mrs. Halsey and naively thought being smart was enough to get her hired. Something bad was happening in the market, and she didn't want to pretend it wasn't anymore. She wanted to help protect them. Nate needed to understand what she was capable of, and the only way he would is if she finally told him that she was behind all of Jake's trades for his first year at National City. She thought she could put that secret behind her forever, but now she knew she couldn't; it was the only proof she had that she'd actually been good at this once.

"You're wrong," she said under her breath.

"I'm what?" he asked lightly.

"You're wrong," she said with more force. "I do know how to do this. To invest. To play the market long and short. To make a fortune. To lose one too."

"Honey, are you okay? Is this some kind of prewedding jitters? You're not making any sense."

"You know how, when Jake started, he became this Wall Street legend, almost immediately?"

"Well, I don't know if I'd go that far, but yes, I remember he was unbeatable in his picks for a while."

"Exactly, for a while. When I was there."

Nate looked at Bea, perplexed.

"It wasn't Jake."

"What do you mean it wasn't Jake? Did he hire an actor to play him?" Nate laughed, still not understanding what Bea was trying to say.

"Jake didn't pick a thing. He did what I told him to do. It was me. I was the one with the perfect track record. I was the one deciding to short before the dips and to get long again before the upticks. I was the one who called every extraordinary bump and every unexpected drop. Jake didn't do a thing except execute my ideas."

Nate's face froze as he tried to process what Bea was telling him. "I don't—how can that be?"

"That's why I went to work for him. I never wanted to be a secretary, not for a single minute. You know I tried everything to be able to invest for a living, and it was all dead ends. No one would give me a chance. Jake wanted my help and, by helping him, I got to do what I had always wanted."

"Are you saying that Jake didn't make any of the investment decisions? That you—"

"Yes. I'm saying that, behind the scenes, I was the broker. I was making all the calls. I was the one who thought the market was going to collapse last December, who shorted all the big stocks. The one you called a reckless fool. And I spent most of this year believing that I was just that. But not anymore. I know I am right. I was right then; I just had the timing wrong. A crash is coming! You have to believe me."

Bea watched as the recognition of what she was saying slowly shifted Nate's face from light and soft to angry and rigid.

"For all that time, all those months, you were *lying* to me?" His words faltered, and his voice suddenly sounded hard. He was furious. And how could she blame him? She'd known this lie had the potential to go off like a bomb in their relationship.

"I didn't want to, Nate. Please know that. I wanted to share everything with you. But I was also desperate to make my own way in this business. You knew how badly I tried to be taken seriously on Wall Street. You watched me struggle to get a job on my own. You just didn't know that, for a little while, I actually had one. When I worked at the wire, once they saw what I could do, they gave me a job that no woman had ever had. I really believed that if I did this for Jake, he would eventually give me the credit I deserved, and I'd get to work as a broker. I never wanted to keep this from you, but it was Jake's only condition. Jake's disastrous short was supposed to be our big win, and I made him agree that, subsequently, we would put an end to the ridiculous deception. I was planning to tell you, but then I blew us up, everything went wrong, and . . ."

"Enough." Nate held up his hand and stared at Bea, his face collapsing in disappointment. She had momentarily deluded herself into believing that Nate might see this the way Sophie did—as a small moment in the past—but he didn't. Instead, her worst fear seemed to be coming true: Nate would not forgive her for this deception.

"This was such a huge part of your life, almost all of it, for a year . . . and you kept it from me? I thought we shared everything, Bea! That was the foundation of our whole relationship, what makes—made—it so special. Is everything I believed about us one big lie?"

It was true that there was a part of Bea's life Nate hadn't shared at all. He hadn't known her pride when she made the right calls on a stock, or the agony when she failed so tremendously. He didn't know the nuances of her concerns over these past nine months. He didn't know her as a market maven. But that was such a small part of who she really was. He knew the truth about everything that mattered. He knew how much she cared about her family and friends. He knew how driven she was to succeed at whatever she set her sights on. And he knew how big her heart was and how much of it was devoted to him.

"No! We are the truest thing in the world. That secret, it was just a moment in time. I was wrong to ever keep it from you. I know that, but I thought I had to. I believed I was protecting Jake. Protecting you. Protecting myself. And now . . . well, it's so far in the past that I could have just let it be forgotten. But I didn't want that. I don't want that. I want our life together to start with honesty. As a true partnership. That's why I am telling you now. So you know what I'm capable of and, together, we can figure out how to navigate what's coming.

"For the past few years, I thought being a broker would be my greatest achievement. I wanted to be so good that, even though I'm a poor Jewish girl from the wrong part of town, my talents would be recognized. I wanted to be seen for my brain, not my gender or my background. But my dreams have changed. My dream is you, us, a family, a chain of grocery stores. I don't need to make it on Wall Street, because I already have everything I want right here, right in front of me.

But I'm scared, Nate. I've had a very bad feeling about this market for a long time. And everyone keeps telling me I'm wrong, that I'm fixated for all sorts of other reasons. When I called it so wrong in December, I believed them. But not anymore. I think something catastrophic is going to happen and, if there is anything I can do to help save us, I want to do it. Together, with you."

Nate shook his head as he walked into the living room and collapsed into one of the two new leather chairs Bea had picked out. Nate had asked Bea to help redecorate this room in the style she wanted, so when she moved in, she'd be happy with it. She'd updated things to be more streamlined, more modern. She had pictured the two of them on a Sunday morning, sitting side by side on these chairs in their robes, passing sections of the newspaper to each other. Reading aloud interesting tidbits. She had liked that the chair's chrome frame had padded armrests, had imagined herself using them someday to cushion her arm as she nursed their babies. She looked at this beautiful room, the even more beautiful man sitting in it, and wondered if she might be seeing them for the very last time. She began to sob.

Nate sat in silence as Bea cried in the foyer. She wished he would get up to comfort her, yearned to feel her small body cocooned inside his embrace, but she'd made sure that wouldn't happen with her deception. She'd made it impossible for him to feel anything but anger toward her. Anger and disappointment and betrayal.

When what felt like forever (but was actually closer to one or two minutes) had passed, she took a deep breath and went to him instead. "I know I've hurt you. But I didn't keep this from you because I don't trust and value you. I'd made a promise to Jake that I believed was harmless and temporary. I got into this mess without immediately understanding the consequences and, by the time I did, it was too late. But now I'm standing here, finally telling you the truth. I know I never should have lied to you at all. I'm so sorry, Nate. Please. I love you. We're getting married in a few days." She hoped this was still true. "Can't we put this behind us?"

"I don't know, Bea." His voice was flat, and she felt like she was buried under one thousand pounds of sand with no way to get free. "You're standing here telling me that you think I'm not good enough at my job to recognize whether or not we are about to have a cataclysmic crisis in the market. That, because of it, you've deigned to let me in on your little secret, the one that makes me look like a chump for bringing your brother to National City in the first place, and for trusting your lies. You're saying that I am so bad at what I do that you need to come out from hiding and help save me. And I'm supposed to smile and thank you. I'm supposed to marry a woman who thinks so little of me?"

"No! That's not what I'm saying at all. Don't you see, it's just the opposite? I made a mistake deceiving you, a huge mistake. You are the smartest person I know. I'm certain if you look again at the data, you'll come to the same conclusion. I'm coming to you, exposing myself, risking everything, because I believe that if there is any hope of fixing any of this before it is too late, it lies with you. I just want to help. To be in this and everything else right next to you."

"I need some time to think. Please, just go. I want to be alone right now."

Bea felt like she might be sick. She couldn't let it end this way. "Please, Nate, I love you. You love me, too; we're about to get married."

Nate stood up and started pacing the length of the living room.

"I know it feels like an enormous betrayal right now. It was. But I promise you it is in the past. I was a fool, in so many ways. Can't you forgive me? Put this behind us? You are my future. All I want in the world."

"I'm not sure. And I'm not going to figure it out with you here right now. Go home, Bea. I'll talk to you when I'm ready."

Bea was too devastated to tell anyone what had happened, not Jake, not Henny, not her parents. Maybe if she didn't say anything about it, it wouldn't be real. She wouldn't be days away from her much-awaited and long-planned wedding, wondering if it was going to even happen. She spent the next day trying to focus on the store, but every time a tall figure passed the window, she ran to see if it was Nate. By the end of the day, she'd given up hope that he might come to see her in person. It finally hit her that the wedding actually might not happen. That she had truly ruined everything. Again.

She had locked the front door and was covering the displays when she heard a knock. Her breath caught. She turned slowly, not wanting to know if it wasn't him. But it was. Nate was there, standing right on the other side of the glass door. His expression was so flat that she couldn't tell what he had come to say, and her whole body seized up into a tight ball of fear. She opened the door and let him in.

"Damn you, Bea," he said as he walked inside, pacing between the displays. "I am so angry at you." He turned to look at her. "What you and Jake were doing was a brazen and irresponsible deception."

"I know." She hung her head as tears trailed down her cheeks, waiting for him to deliver the final blow.

"But I love you."

Everything froze, even Bea's pulse. *Did he just say what she thought he had?* She looked to him for validation and saw that familiar smirk. She was overcome with relief. She ran and threw her arms around him, squeezing tightly.

"I love you too. More than anything."

They stood there for what felt like hours, holding still in this embrace. Bea was almost afraid to move lest it break the spell of this miracle. But she also needed to know for sure that she could relax again. "So we're still getting married?"

"Yes." Nate smiled. "I reserve the right to be mad about this for a while longer. But I still don't want anyone in the world more than you."

For a moment she thought she had lost Nate forever, but now he knew everything, and they were still getting married. She didn't have to hide anything anymore.

CHAPTER FORTY-SIX

October 5, Saturday, twenty-four days before the crash

Dow Daily Average (Friday): 325, –20 points from prior Friday

Bea's wedding day had arrived and, as she got ready with Sophie, Henny, and Milly in her bedroom, she was overcome with elation and relief. It had been a tumultuous week, a tumultuous few years, really, but today she was finally going to marry Nate. He hadn't mentioned the market again, and Bea felt it was better not to bring it up. He knew her concerns, and after coming so close to losing him, she realized their relationship was more important than whatever might happen on Wall Street. Her focus was on her new, married, life. Her new husband. The only man who had ever made her heart leap from her chest. The only person capable of rendering her speechless. The man she was meant for and who was meant for her.

When she entered the dining room of the Abramovitzes' duplex, flanked by her friends, she was filled with so much joy she felt like she was floating. Nate was already sitting there, but he stood as Bea entered the room. Her whole body pulsed from the ferocious pumping of her heart as their eyes locked. Standing there, in his tuxedo smiling at her, she marveled at her good fortune. She got to spend the rest of her life with this man, the love of her life. Her *basherter*, her soulmate. She moved to his side and, as he kissed her chastely on the cheek, he whispered in her ear, "You are the most beautiful woman I've ever seen." She squeezed his hand tightly, and they sat down to sign the ketubah.

Even though they would have a ceremony in the Eldridge Street synagogue afterward, this moment, when they both signed the traditional Jewish wedding contract in front of their rabbi and closest friends and family, was the one that mattered. This was the moment of the wedding day when Bea and Nate saw each other for the first time, and when they committed to spend their lives together. From here, the rest was just celebration.

After they signed the ornately decorated contract and drank a ceremonial glass of wine, Henny popped the cork on a bottle of champagne for a toast. Then they gathered their things and walked together to the temple, where it felt the entirety of the Lower East Side and Kew Gardens was waiting to watch them wed.

The ceremony took place under a rose-covered chuppah (the flowers chosen by Pauline) inside the temple. For the most part it was a traditional Jewish wedding: Bea circled Nate seven times to symbolize the wall of love they had built around them, the rabbi recited the many blessings, and Nate and Bea exchanged simple gold bands. But when it was time for Nate to break the glass, the representation of their lives commingling as one from this moment forward, he took Bea's hand. "You are my partner, Bea. In every way. Let's start this marriage together."

They counted to three and stomped on the crystal goblet. Then Nate grabbed Bea's waist and kissed her like no one else was there. "I love you, Mrs. Greenberg." He smiled as he drew back and looked at her with adoration.

"And I love you, Mr. Greenberg."

Pauline threw a "small" luncheon following the ceremony for the wedding party and family which, thanks to the extended Greenberg and

Brodsky clan, was still more than forty people, and then Bea collected the last of her things and officially moved into Nate's apartment. They had all of an hour alone to "reflect on their union," as was traditional, and they spent it in bed. Bea lay next to Nate, her husband, and felt ecstatic.

"Are you sure we can't just call it a day and start the honeymoon right now?" she asked as she lay on his chest, his hands twirling her curls.

"Our mothers would murder us. We'll get our honeymoon at the end of the year, once the new store is up and running."

"I wish we could go away and hide from the world for weeks, starting right now," Bea said dreamily. In that moment she really did. But she had a store to open, and now that Nate was a vice president, he was needed at the bank more than ever, so they had agreed that they would both enjoy their time more if they waited until the end of the year, when things would surely quiet down.

"Me too. At least we have the rest of the weekend, but now"—Nate tickled her playfully as he pushed her off his chest—"we have to get dressed and go to my parents' for our party."

The weather was crisp but clear, and the Greenbergs' party took place under the stars. Everyone was kept warm by the dancing and the booze—Nate's family took prohibition about as seriously as the rest of the city—and Bea was several drinks in and feeling footloose and fancy-free when Jake pulled her back to the bar for a toast.

"Look at you, BB, all grown up. I haven't had a minute with you alone all day!" He swayed a little as he spoke, no doubt because he was on at least his fourth martini.

"Yep, look at the two of us. A pair of old marrieds. And to cousins, no less. It's almost like a farce on Broadway."

"Sure, sure. Whatever you say. You know I hate theater." Jake laughed. "See—I told you everything would work out!"

"What do you mean?"

"You were so worried about our 'big secret' . . . and you thought I couldn't do it!" He was slurring his words. Bea took his glass and placed it back on the bar, leading him to a table to sit.

"Do what?"

"Be a broker on my own."

"I never thought you couldn't. I just knew I could. And I wanted to. So badly."

"Eh, it's boring. You've got the fun job, buying buildings, opening new stores."

"You really think so? You could have been doing this."

"Nah, I needed the big money. Gotta make money, BB. Lots and lots of money. And look at me now. A rich man!"

"Indeed. You've done well, Yaacov," she said in mimicry of their father.

She felt a flash of worry, her uneasy feeling about the state of the market returning suddenly, but then Jake grabbed her hand to pull her from her seat. The band was playing "When You're Smiling," and the crowd was doing the Lindy Hop. "Let's dance. It's your wedding day, little sis, and we've got so much to celebrate!"

October 14, Monday, fifteen days before the crash

Dow Daily Average: 351, +5 points from prior Monday

When the doors to Abrams Grocers Madison opened at 7:00 a.m. on Monday morning, there was a line to get in. Apparently the neighborhood was desperate for fresh produce. Lew and Bea worked side by side all day, helping customers select the best items, offering recipes for some of the more exotic items they stocked, and reminding people that their produce was fresh "every single day." Pauline joined them midday, dressed to impress, as always, in green velvet, and chatted with the customers about her genius son in the stock market and even, occasionally, about her clever daughter, who knew this was a good place for a store. When they closed at 5:00 p.m., all three of them were both elated and exhausted.

"Mazel tov, Beatrice. I wasn't sure these uptown types would want a store like mine, but I was wrong. Did you hear that woman this morning? All perfect looking with her makeup and her hat and gloves. 'I saw your ad in the paper and marked my calendar! Do you know how far I used to go to get a good head of lettuce? Now I can just walk around the corner.'" Bea laughed at Lew's attempt to make his voice high and feminine. "And the man in the suit who bought the one banana. 'I eat one of these on my way to work every single day. And this is the best-looking bunch I've ever seen. Not even one bruise or spot. I'll be back tomorrow.'"

"It was a great day, Papa. And, did you see, not a single person tried to haggle on price? I told you they do things differently up here."

"I saw. Of course I saw. I also saw that you marked everything ten percent higher than downtown." He raised an eyebrow at her.

"As she should," Pauline broke in. "These people can afford it."

"They can. But it also makes business sense—real estate costs more here, so we need to match our prices to our location to keep our margins healthy. Didn't seem to hurt sales, did it?" Bea motioned to the nearly empty shelves. Almost everything they had put out for the day was gone.

"It really didn't. *Shayna*, you are a marvel. Do you know that? You have made my dreams come true. My name on the door of not just one, but two, stores." Lew's voice shook slightly, and Bea could see his eyes getting watery.

"And, soon enough, three." Bea nudged him lovingly.

"Beatrice, you have done a wonderful thing for your papa. For our family." Pauline pulled her in and embraced her awkwardly. "You see, everything worked out in the end. Just like I told you. Your Nathan and your brother have made us all rich, and you and your papa have a grocery chain. The House of Oppenheim has been returned to all its glory."

"I think you mean the House of Abramovitz," Lew corrected proudly.

Bea smiled. She was overwhelmed. It wasn't much, but this might have been the greatest praise she had received from Pauline in her whole life. It was a genuine acknowledgment of her abilities, of the success of something she had put her mind to and made happen. It was a terrific day. Bea went home feeling gratified and proud. Turns out she didn't need Wall Street to make her mark after all.

CHAPTER FORTY-SEVEN

October 16, Wednesday, thirteen days before the crash

Dow Daily Average: 336, –11 points from prior Wednesday

Bea was getting ready to leave for the store when the headline of the morning paper stopped her in her tracks: STOCKS FALL AGAIN IN THE BIGGEST DROP IN WEEKS. For the past month, since she came clean to Nate, she had been happily consumed by her wedding and the grocery, and while she still had some concern about the health of the market, she had put it to the side of her mind. But this headline brought it right back front and center. She grabbed the paper and started to scan the article as she walked out the door. By the time the elevator reached the lobby, she was panicked again. The market had been bouncing all over the place. Fundamentals were getting worse. She couldn't ignore this anymore.

At the store she worked with her father and the new manager they were training, through the morning rush. When things calmed down, she decided it was her chance to sneak out. "Papa, I completely forgot that I have an errand to run. Will you two be okay if I'm gone for a bit?"

"Yes, yes, Beatrice. We'll be fine," Lew answered distractedly while trying to restack a pile of grapefruits.

Bea didn't wait for him to even look up before she grabbed her purse and was out the door and into a taxi. She needed to go see Jake.

As soon as Bea told the taxi driver she was going to Wall Street, he started to chat. He had a heavy accent that Bea had heard before, in her immigrant neighborhood, but couldn't quite place.

"Been a rough few days in the market, you know? But it'll turn around. It always does," he said with authority. "In the long run, you can't lose."

The hairs on the back of her neck stood at attention. "I'm not so sure about that."

"Do you know if RCA goes up another ten points, I'll have made enough to buy this cab?" He continued talking, and Bea was now listening intently. "Free and clear. Even after I pay back what I borrowed. America is really the land of prosperity."

"But what if it doesn't?" Bea asked, her fears intensifying.

"Lady, trust me. This is a sure thing. In fact, you should try to buy some of that RCA yourself."

He continued to talk, not listening as she tried to interrupt to warn him. What he was saying terrified her. It was one thing for professional investors to believe in the ongoing strength of the markets—they were sophisticated (and, likely, rich) enough to withstand a downturn when it came. But this was a regular working-class person. Bea was sure he didn't have the money to risk and, furthermore, he had bought on margin, borrowing most of what he had invested. This was a sure sign of a bubble waiting to burst; it was supply and demand in action: if loans were so easy to get that every man in the country could buy in, there would soon be no one left to buy more. And once there wasn't anyone to buy, prices would start to plummet. These amateur investors would be wiped out. This was as sure a sign as any she'd seen. A correction was imminent and the thought of what that would mean for the people she loved, let alone the average American, filled Bea with panic.

She arrived at the National City Building with an even stronger sense of urgency. She tapped her foot impatiently as the elevator slowly rose to the eighth floor, and then she suddenly felt clammy. This was the first time she'd set foot in this office since she and Jake had worked together last year. She hadn't considered how it would feel to return. As she walked to the back corner, where Jake's office was, Bea was hit with a sharp pang of loss. How she loved the energy, the sounds of brokers talking, the ticker clicking, the smell of chalk on the board as the boys wrote the latest quotations. She quickly shook it off. This dream was long dead. That wasn't why she was here. She knocked once before opening Jake's door.

"BB! Did we have an appointment?"

"Do I need an appointment to visit my favorite brother?" She smiled, trying to disarm him with her syrupy sweetness.

"Oh boy. What's happening? You're never sweet unless there's trouble. Everything okay with Nate?"

"Yes, Jake. Everything's okay."

"Is it Henny? Did she send you here to tell me about some piece of jewelry she wants to be surprised with?"

"Would she do that? Do you think I would?"

"Not really . . . but—"

"Jake, I'm here to talk business."

"Business?" He looked at her, perplexed.

"Jake, remember at our birthday party when you asked me to come back?"

"Yep. You shot me down completely. And good thing, too, because we're both doing great."

She smiled stiffly and nodded. "Have you been okay this week? In the market? I see it's been dropping for days."

"It's just bounce. We're off today, but it'll come back."

"Are you sure? I know Charley Mitchell says everything is fine, but . . ."

"But what, BB?" He looked at her, her face all serious and concerned, and he started to laugh. "Are you kidding me? Are you back on your grand predictions of a crash? I thought you gave up on being the prophet of doom, that you put away your crystal ball."

"Crystal ball? You know how I work, and it's not like that." She opened her satchel and pulled out a notebook. "Look at this; this is the past nine months. I should have made this graph before. Do you see the overall trend line? It's heading down. The fall has already started. You need to get short or get out."

"C'mon, BB, we've been through this. I don't care what the 'overall trend line' says," he mimicked her in a mocking tone. "Everything is fine. Just like it was fine eleven months ago, when you were so certain of a fall. BB, I think you've lost your marbles. The market is secure."

"But it's not, Jake, I know it. How about this? The taxi driver who brought me down here was giving me stock tips. Stock tips, Jake!"

"Good for him! Putting his money to work."

"No, it's not! Not now. Jake, there's no bigger sign of a bubble than when people who don't understand the market suddenly become speculators. Stock sales are out of control and money is spread too thin. This 'permanent prosperity' that everyone keeps talking about seems like it's a run-up before a drop, and if it is—"

"Jeez, BB, you're getting hysterical over nothing."

"Nothing? When this crash comes, it's going to be big. The market has been too high for too long. Look at what happened in Florida in '26. Everyone was wiped out."

"They were hit by a hurricane."

"That just hastened the collapse. And this is bigger than Florida. This is the entire American financial system as we know it. Don't you see? You could lose everything! We *all* could lose everything!"

"Beatrice." He never called her by her first name, unless he really wanted to make a point. "Have you hit your head or something? You're really taking a dive off the deep end." Jake stood from his desk and walked over to the ticker in his office. He ripped off the tape and put it in front of Bea. "What do you see?"

She looked at him blankly.

"Tell me, what do you see? Do you see lots of down arrows, red marks, losses?"

Bea shook her head. Right now, the ticker looked very positive.

"Exactly. No. Stocks are going up. People are buying. The market is strong. You need to stop worrying."

"I wish I could, Jake. But I can't. Look, you don't have to listen to me, but I know I'm right. If I give you my money, what we got at the wedding, can you at least short these stocks for me?" She showed him a list of companies in her notebook. "Act as my broker?"

Jake shook his head.

"Why?"

"First of all, you're not a client. Second, I already told you we aren't taking short positions right now. It's all about staying confident in the market. If you really can't let this go, you should talk about it with your husband. Although I can promise you Nate will laugh you right out of the room."

"Yes." She sighed as her heart sank. "He will. Actually, I'd appreciate it if you didn't mention this to him at all."

Bea's theory about a crash was one thing she didn't discuss with Nate. In fact, since their fight, she had made a point of not discussing the market with him at all. He had more market experience than she and Jake combined, and he believed the official thinking of Wall Street, not Bea's notebooks.

"Listen, BB, I don't mean to be a jerk, but it's the middle of the trading day, and I've got work to do. Relax, everything is going to be fine."

"If you and Nate say so." She smiled falsely as she stood to leave. She wished she could trust that everything was going to be all right. But the data said otherwise. And she knew that, in the end, the data never lied.

CHAPTER FORTY-EIGHT

October 18, Friday, eleven days before the crash

Dow Daily Average: 333, –19 points from prior Friday

Bea had planned to have her parents, Jake, and Henny over for Friday-night dinner. Until she saw the paper on Wednesday, she'd been looking forward to the evening; it would be the first traditional family meal in her new home, and a celebration of the success of the Madison Avenue store with her family. Now she was preoccupied again by fears of a crash—fears that she would have to keep to herself, since she was still the only one.

From the moment everyone arrived, spirits were high, and they gleefully lit the candles and made their way into the dining room for dinner.

"Bea, your china looks divine in here! Aren't you glad that you went so modern?" Henny had been the one to persuade Bea to select an art deco pattern instead of the more old-fashioned floral Pauline was in favor of.

"I am, it really looks great in the room. Makes the place feel more fun."

"It is pretty, Beatrice," Pauline said kindly. "Even though I still think you should have selected the more classic pattern." She shot Henny a dismissive look, and Bea was thrown off. She was used to being the one on the receiving end in these moments, but Pauline had been gentler with Bea lately. Opening the new store had really meant a lot to her mother.

"Leave it to the ladies to get heated about dishes, right, Nate?" Jake cut in, protecting Henny from Pauline's impending ire. "We've got bigger things to think about."

"We do, thank goodness," Nate said as he poured wine for everyone.

"Been quite a week in the markets, huh?" Jake said casually.

"Yeah, but I'm not worried," Nate replied. "Charley said it best: 'The market had a good shakedown, for which it was due, but prices are stable and strong.'" Nate patted Jake on the back as he retook his seat at the head of the table.

"Where did the Dow close today? I didn't have a chance to look at the papers," Bea said, growing more anxious.

"Three thirty-three," Jake said matter-of-factly.

"So an eight-point swing from yesterday, and a nearly twenty percent decline from just a week ago? Nate?" Bea looked at him pleadingly. "You can't really think this is nothing anymore. The swings are wild. Too wild."

"Since when are you tracking the daily movements of the market again?" Nate asked, an undercurrent of irritation in his voice.

"You don't know? She's worried the whole financial world is going to collapse. Funny, she's the only person around who thinks so," Jake teased. "She even came to see me to beg me to start selling short."

"Jake." Bea squinted her eyes disapprovingly at her brother. She'd specifically asked him not to tell Nate about their meeting.

"You what, Bea?" Nate barked at her.

"Jake is exaggerating, as usual. I told him about my concerns in case he wanted to take some precautions."

"Beatrice, I thought you were leaving the stock market to Jake and Nate. Focusing on the store," Lew said, a sharpness to his tone.

"And a very successful one so far!" Pauline said, seeming to want to shift the conversation. "A toast. To Beatrice and Lew."

"To Bea and Papa." Jake lifted his glass, too, clearly trying to unwind the growing tension at the table. "And the success of Abrams Grocery Madison!" They turned and clinked glasses one by one as Bea's housekeeper brought out dinner.

"Looks delicious, Bea." Henny smiled across the table. Bea knew she was also trying to smooth things over, seeing that Bea was unsettled by Nate's uncharacteristic ire.

"Wish I could take credit; I just told Grace what to make."

"Well, you give excellent direction." Henny laughed.

"She sure does," Nate said. There was an edge to his voice. "Apparently her favorite thing to do."

"That's not true. I just—"

"You just what? I thought we were past this."

"We were, we are."

"Yet you went to see Jake, behind my back, at my place of business, and asked him to make changes based on your instincts? Don't you see how bad that looks for me?"

She'd made a mistake going to Jake. She saw that now. But she also felt humiliated being chided in front of the whole table.

"I went to him because I knew you wouldn't listen," she snapped. "I'm worried. Really worried. Every time I look at the numbers, they simply don't work. The market is moving in the opposite direction than all the economic indicators say it should. It makes no sense. And we all have so much—nearly everything—in the market. I just think it might be smart to protect ourselves a bit."

"We do not need protection. We are fine," Nate said curtly.

"More than fine," Jake added.

"All right, all right. If you say so." Bea wanted the conversation to end. She felt bullied with Nate and Jake together. Even her father seemed to blindly believe them. But she didn't. She hadn't changed her mind. Time was marching forward, and with every bump in the market, she feared a big drop was closer. This wasn't about making the right pick for the sake of winning anymore. This was about protecting all of them from potential ruin. She had to find a way to save her family. She just wasn't sure how.

October 20, Sunday, nine days before the crash

Market closed

Bea was drinking coffee in her dressing gown when she heard a knock on the door. Nate was still fast asleep. He woke so early during the week that he used Sunday to catch up on his rest. *Who would be coming over at this hour?* she wondered.

She opened the door to find her mother standing there. "Mama, is everything all right?" Pauline was dressed in a plain skirt, a blouse, and a silk scarf tied around her hair, casual for her these days. She walked quickly past Bea and into the living room.

"Is Nathan here?" She looked around nervously.

"Of course he is. It's Sunday morning. He's still asleep."

"Good. We need to talk without him. Without any of the men." She sat on the sofa with her bag still in hand and patted the seat next to her for Bea to join.

"Mama, what is going on?" Bea asked anxiously as she moved to follow her mother's orders. Suddenly she thought better of it. She should remember her manners, or she'd get an earful as soon as she sat down. "Can I get you anything? Our girl is off today but—coffee? Some cake?"

"*Neyn.* Come, sit. I need to do this now, quickly." Bea suddenly felt overcome with concern. She had never seen her mother behave this way in her entire life. She worried something was terribly wrong.

"Is it Papa? Did something happen?"

"Of course not! Your father is fine. Just let me speak!"

She sat down next to Pauline and looked at her searchingly.

"I have always believed your brother would be a *macher* one day. He is my only son, and I've known since you were children that it was his destiny to restore wealth for our family, to return us to the life we had to leave behind in Russia, to raise the House of Oppenheim—Abramovitz—up again. And he has lived up to my expectations. And then some."

Bea was suddenly irate. Had her mother really come here on a Sunday morning, her first alone with Nate since the wedding, to crow about all of Jake's success? Hadn't she done enough of that every day of Bea's life? She opened her mouth, about to snap at Pauline when her mother continued.

"But you, you have accomplished so much more." Bea's eyes opened so wide she was certain she looked like a character in a comic strip. "Beatrice, you think I don't see everything you've done for our family. The sacrifices you've made for your brother's success, your father's happiness. I know how smart you are, I just never told you that, because I also know the world, and unfortunately to be a woman with a brain like yours . . . can be a curse more than a blessing. I know you've struggled trying to make your mark in such a man's world. I hoped, with Nathan and the grocery, that you had found your way. That it would be enough. But I see that you haven't yet found peace."

"I'm fine, Mama. I'm happy. I love working with Papa at the store, and I have the third building contract in negotiation now. I—"

"You are smarter than any of these men. You have been saying you are worried about our money, about the stock market. Yes?"

Bea sat for a moment in stunned silence. She'd spent her life feeling like nothing she did was enough, like all her sacrifices, all her efforts, were simply taken for granted. She thought Jake was the favorite child, and Pauline's only use for her was to help cook, clean, and serve her. Yes, she'd gotten some recognition from her mother when they opened the second

Abrams store . . . but this, this was different. This was her mother telling her that she saw and heard Bea, that she fundamentally understood her.

"Yes. I have. I am. Mama . . . I didn't think you cared about those things."

"I pay attention to much more than you think I do. I know you and Yaacov think I'm just some old-fashioned Russian who won't embrace America, but I see the new world clearly. Yes, I left a part of myself behind when we left Russia, and I've struggled. But we have a good life now. You and Yaacov and your father and me. And I don't want any of us to lose it again."

"I don't want you to, Mama!"

Pauline reached into her purse and pulled out a black velvet box. Not just any old black velvet box, but *the* black velvet box.

"Here." She handed it to Bea.

"Mama?" Bea didn't need to open the box to know what was inside, but she did it anyway. Every diamond in her mother's necklace sparkled in the dappled morning sunlight streaming through the living room window. Bea's eyes filled with tears. "Your necklace? Mama, why?"

"If you believe the market is going to fall, I believe it too. I've listened to you and Yackie enough to know that you can make money when the market falls. So do what you need to do with this to protect us. I know it's not much, but hopefully, it will be enough. Now"—Pauline stood and smoothed her skirt—"I should leave before Nathan wakes. Don't get up." She patted Bea's shoulder gently before turning and walking out the door.

Bea sat and stared at the necklace. It might no longer be the only valuable jewelry her mother owned, but it was by far the most precious. By giving it to her, Pauline was telling Bea that she trusted her to do what none of the men in their life had been able to. She trusted her to save them. Her mother's trust was the final push Bea needed. She put the necklace in the drawer with her underthings for safekeeping. If Pauline believed in Bea, trusted her to protect their family, then she had to do what she thought was right. Tomorrow, she would do just that.

CHAPTER FORTY-NINE

October 21, Monday, eight days before the crash

Dow Daily Average: 321, –12 points from Friday, –30 points from prior Monday

By nine thirty Monday morning, Bea was on her way to Queens. She had already been to the grocery to tell the new manager that she'd be out for most of the day and then stopped at her savings bank, where she dropped the necklace in the safety-deposit box and gathered the documents she needed. Now she was on her way to see Lizzie. She wished desperately that Milly hadn't already left on her boating adventure, because she could have really used her help. Lizzie was a distant second choice. But she felt like time was running out, and she needed to act fast. She just hoped it wasn't already too late.

Bea had never been to see Lizzie unannounced, and her new sister-in-law was surprised by the unexpected visit. She was even more surprised when Bea said she couldn't even stay for coffee and asked Lizzie to direct her to her stockbroker's office.

"I'm not sure he's taking new clients. Last time I was there, I waited almost an hour to see him. Everyone in the neighborhood is investing these days." Bea's face fell. She needed a broker, and she needed one today. "Honey, you look sick. Can't you just get Nate to do it for you? Or your brother?"

"No!" Bea watched Lizzie recoil and realized how worked up she was. She needed to calm down, especially in front of Nate's sister. She smiled and said sweetly, "They can't be bothered with my little investment. This is just for fun."

"Oh, I hear you." Lizzie winked. "You know what, I've been meaning to go down there myself. I'll bring you. If I tell him you're family, I'm sure he'll help you."

Bea was flooded with relief. "Thank you!" She threw her arms around Lizzie's neck and hugged her tightly.

"Wow, you're really excited to start investing," Lizzie said as she pulled away from Bea, looking at her askance.

"You have no idea."

Abe Friedland was exactly what Bea had expected: a middle-aged man trying to project the image of a young Wall Street broker. He was dressed in a shiny three-piece suit, his protruding belly straining the buttons on his vest. His hair was tamed by a dark pomade, still too light to cover the large patches of gray in his temples. His craggy face, surely clean shaven that morning, already carried a shadow of salt-and-pepper stubble, and his eyes were ringed with dark circles that belied long days hustling. When he reached out his stubby hand to shake Bea's, it was adorned with not one but two gold rings. The one on his pinkie sparkled from a large, glassy-looking diamond. He was the kind of broker Bea would normally warn people to stay away from, yet here she was about to hand over everything she had, in the hopes that he would save them if things went as badly as Bea feared they might.

"So, Mrs. Abramovitz." Bea hadn't given him her married name, having convinced herself that this would somehow hide her activities, despite having come to the office with Lizzie. "What can I do for you?

Mrs. Schwartz is one of my best clients—that Elizabeth loves the market, am I right? Anyway, it's a good thing you know her, because I ain't got time for new gals investing with me. 'Specially if they're green in the market."

"Well, Mr. Friedland, you don't need to worry about that with me."

"Oh yeah? Who you been workin' with?"

"I have some friends on Wall Street."

"Right, right." He winked at her. "Well, Friedland and Partners isn't some sleazy bucket shop. We're on the up-an'-up, I'll tell you that. Just look at the gals in here—real classy types. Like you."

Bea didn't see any reason to explain that she had never in her life invested with a bucket shop—she wouldn't be that foolish. Nor did she need to explain that while she appreciated that he perceived her to be "classy," she didn't believe for a minute that having money to buy nice clothes had anything to do with real class. No, she was here for business. And the sooner she could take care of it and leave, the better.

"Mr. Friedland, I am interested in taking short positions with the following stocks." She pulled a list from her bag and handed it across the desk. Abe Friedland looked at it, casually at first, and then his jaw dropped.

"Lady, are you nuts?" He looked up at Bea, and then he started to chuckle. "Ahh, you're pulling my leg. Testin' me, right? You've heard talks about the panicked bears and you're poking around to see if I buy into it? You really want me to buy these for ya?"

"I do not. I want you to short them, on as much margin as you can get. And I want you to use this as collateral." She took two pieces of paper from the bag and handed them across the desk. The deeds to their East Broadway building and the new one on Madison Avenue. The two deeds were worth more than $100,000, and as he read them, Abe sat up straight in his chair like he'd been hit with a jolt of electric current. "Honey, this ain't play money. You'll be in deep if this goes south. Your husband know about this?"

"Of course." She didn't need to explain herself to him. Or to anyone else, for that matter. "Will you do it? Or should I find another broker to offer an easy thousand dollars?"

"I'll do it, I'll do it. But, Mrs. Abramovitz, you sure you know what you're askin' me here? These are some of the biggest, most profitable companies on the exchange. These are sure bets to buy. You know that shorting them means you need 'em to go down to make money, right?"

"Yep. I sure do." Bea smiled. "So, can I count on you to do this for me, Mr. Friedland? Today, if possible?" She stood up to go, waiting for Abe to do the same. But he just sat there studying her list and twisting his pinkie ring. "Mr. Friedland?" she asked again, stretching her hand out to shake his and snap him out of his surprised stupor.

"Huh? Yeah. You got it, lady. If this is what you want me to do, I'll do it. Good luck."

"Thanks. I'll take all the luck I can get."

Bea turned and walked confidently out of his office, her heart pounding triple time. For the first moment in her investment life, she hoped with all her being that she had just bet wrong. If the market didn't collapse, as she was anticipating, and instead continued to rise, then they would still have more than enough money to buy back the buildings she had just sold, but if she was right . . . she really didn't want to be right.

CHAPTER FIFTY

October 24, "Black Thursday," five days before the crash

DOW DAILY AVERAGE: 299, –22 POINTS FROM MONDAY, LOWEST VALUE SINCE MAY

It was ten fifteen in the morning and Bea was at Abrams Grocery when the telephone rang.

"BB, you've gotta come down here!" Jake was on the other end of the line in a panic.

"What is it? Are you all right?"

"No. I'm not all right, not all right at all. There's an angry crowd outside the exchange. People yelling and holding signs. Police everywhere. The market's collapsing. I need to get out fast. I need your help. Please come—sell! No, I said sell it all!" Jake barked at one of his brokers. "Just come, Bea. I need you."

Bea made her way to Wall Street as fast as she could. Her hands were shaking as she ran down the corridor toward Jake's office. Stocks had been weak yesterday. Investors were starting to get nervous. This was it. This was what she had feared for months. And no one was ready. It was going to be a bloodbath. Jake was pacing back and forth among the brokers in the smoke-filled area outside his office. She hadn't seen him looking this disheveled since he came home from California. *Was that really only two years ago? It seemed like two lifetimes.*

"How are things moving?" she asked as Jake rushed past her barking orders at his junior brokers.

"They're not. No one is buying at any price. We can't find any bids for our shares. It's a disaster, BB. We're going to lose everything!"

"Well, then you're doing what you have to do. Take any price you can get; some money out is better than none."

Bea spent the next two hours in the pit, working alongside Jake's brokers to try to sell any position they could. At one thirty, trading abruptly halted completely. When it resumed, a few minutes later, the free fall was suddenly and inexplicably stopped. Investors started buying again, and prices began to rise. The market had miraculously recovered.

"What just happened?" Bea asked Jake, who looked as perplexed as she was.

"I have no idea. But thank goodness it did."

"Jake, if this isn't a sign of how unstable the market is . . ." As Bea spoke, Jake got a call and went into his office to take it. He came out smiling.

"Gents, we are in the clear thanks to our boss Charley Mitchell and his friend Lamont at J.P. Morgan. They stepped in themselves and started buying to stop the panic. They're all buying like mad, and investors are starting to follow. The sell-off is over."

Jake's brokers started to embrace one another, tearing up their sell orders and throwing them in the air like confetti. Jake turned to Bea, smiling, and said casually, "Thanks for your help today, little sis. Looks like we're all okay after all."

"Hang on, don't you think—" Bea tried to tell Jake to pay attention, that this was proof that she was right. The past two hours had been harrowing, and Jake needed to be ready if this were to happen again. But he was already lost to her, back in his office on his phone.

Bea had tried to find Nate when she was at National City, but he was down at the exchange. She was anxiously waiting for him when he got home that night.

"Are you all right after today? Are we all right?" she asked as she was taking his coat and hat.

"You already know about that?" He looked at her, slightly surprised.

"Well, yes. It's right here in the afternoon paper." She shook the headline in his face. "But, actually, Jake called me in a panic this morning. I was with him, trying to help. Until suddenly everything turned around. I looked for you, but . . . do you know what happened?"

"'Course I do. This morning was unbelievable. Even I thought we were sunk for a minute there. Started hearing your voice in my head, warning me. But then the head of the entire stock exchange set everyone straight. You should have seen the looks on everyone's faces when Dick Whitney walked out onto the floor and bought ten thousand shares of U.S. Steel. It was like time froze. Then Charley and Lamont joined in, and the buying resumed. How's that for a vote of confidence in our economy?"

"Is it really? Or was it just a trick to manipulate the market? Stem the fall?"

"It doesn't matter, because it worked. Prices stabilized. Slips went from sell to buy. It was a momentary panic, but it's over."

"I sure hope so." And she did. Bea had been waiting for a day like today to come, but she hadn't realized how it would actually feel. The chaos of it. The helplessness. The utter hysteria. She really hoped that this was it. That the correction was over. The Dow had hit 380 at its high, and now it was back at 300; hopefully this was the bottom because, after seeing what happened today, she wasn't sure any of them would survive something worse.

The market held steady the Friday after the big scare and, while Nate and Jake had lost money, they still had enough that they would be fine. As long as things turned around. No one knew about Bea's short sales, but she took some comfort in knowing that they would provide a cushion, as long as Abe Friedland had actually executed her trades and not dismissed her as a crackpot. She hadn't been able to confirm that he had followed her direction because every time she tried to phone him, his lines were busy. She contemplated going back to see him, but by the time things settled on Friday, it was almost Sabbath. She'd simply have to wait until Monday to find out.

CHAPTER FIFTY-ONE

October 28, Monday, one day before the crash

Dow Daily Average: 260, –40 points from Friday

Monday morning, as soon as Nate left, Bea tried to call Abe Friedland. She was glad that they had hit the bottom of the correction, and she wanted to tell him to liquidate her positions before things started to improve. His lines were busy. She tried again before she left for the grocery, but she still couldn't get through. It wasn't urgent that she unwind her shorts this minute, but she was still rattled from the prior Thursday and, right now, she wanted to be out of the market altogether. She needed to go see him in person.

When she arrived at his office, she saw a line of women that stretched for blocks. She took her place at the end.

"Jonathan said he's taking everything out of the market today. It's just too risky now. We're not gamblers, you know? So if he's doing it, I certainly need to," Bea heard one of the women in line say to another.

"Oh, I know. Roger wasn't sure on Friday, but he woke up this morning and said he was pulling everything he could today. He just doesn't trust it right now. Better to be safe. If Abe will ever get to us."

Bea got a chill of fear. These women and their husbands were the exact kind of people who had been invested in the market. Who had driven the bubble. If they'd lost confidence and were getting out, the bottom hadn't come yet. Things were going to get worse.

She didn't need to see Abe today; she needed to talk to Nate and Jake. As she rode the train back to the grocery, her unease grew. Chatter about the market was everywhere. She contemplated going straight to Wall Street, but she had already left the manager alone at the grocery for several hours; she should at least check in.

Something felt off the moment she stepped inside the store. Their usually casual, cheery customers, who tended to round up the change on their purchases, were counting every penny to pay. People seemed on edge and uneasy. She tried to call Nate's desk, but the lines were tied up. Same with Jake. This was not good.

Bea knew the markets had taken another hit before she saw the afternoon paper, but she was stunned to see the Dow had fallen another forty points over the course of the day. The country had lost faith in the new economy, and people were pulling their money as fast as they could get it out. This was an epic failure of the financial system, vaster than anything Bea ever could have imagined. It was a true catastrophe. Bea was stunned. She thought about the chaos at Jake's desk last Thursday and wondered what was happening on Wall Street now. Was there anything she could do to help?

There was a silver lining to this additional plummet: she still hadn't reached Abe Friedland. Presuming her short sales were actually in place, she would have made enough money to make up for any losses suffered by her immediate family. She would save them. But she had yet to get confirmation from Abe. Feeling helpless, she went back home and pulled out her notebooks to look at the data. Should she have anticipated something this dramatic? Was there anything more she could do? She paced restlessly for hours, waiting for Nate to come home so she could understand what had really happened today. What this meant not just for them but for the country overall.

Nate didn't get home until almost sunrise and, when he finally stumbled in the door, Bea knew more than the worst had happened. Bea had never seen him—her strong, steady husband—look so broken. His shirt was untucked with two buttons missing at the collar, where his now-absent tie had been. His hair was a mess of untamed waves, sticking up in every direction. Bea feared he might actually collapse on the spot, and she raced to help hold him up.

"We're ruined." He began to weep as his knees started to buckle underneath him. She held him up with all her strength and brought him to sit in the living room.

"You need some food. Something to drink," Bea said softly as she took Nate's coat and went into the kitchen. She came back, handing him a bagel—it was nearly morning, after all—but he waved it away.

"I can't eat. I can't do anything. You don't understand what it was like today."

"I saw the papers."

"That doesn't begin to describe it. We couldn't put through trades when they came in; the whole floor of the exchange was just red slips, all sellers and no buyers. And they were coming so fast. So fast. The ticker couldn't keep up. We had to work through the night just to catch up on it all. I didn't have a minute to even try to save our positions. People are redeeming in such numbers that I don't even know if the bank will survive. The bank! Everything we have is in that bank."

Bea's heart broke to see her husband this way. No matter what she had thought might happen, she'd never expected something as disastrous as this. There was no way anyone could have anticipated this. It was so bad that she didn't even think about the fact that if Nate hadn't been so dismissive of her, he might have been better prepared. All she could do in this moment was try to console him.

"Maybe it will get better tomorrow. Turn around?"

"Well, it can't get worse. I've never seen a slide like this in my life. It's unprecedented. If the market opens strong tomorrow, maybe faith will be restored. Maybe we will be able to eke out something so we can salvage our lives."

"We will be okay. We will manage." Bea wanted to say more. If her short sales hadn't gone through, they would still have the deeds on the buildings. They could move in above the store. They would be all right. And if Abe had carried out her wishes . . . she almost couldn't dare to hope for it.

Nate looked up at Bea and then across to the table where her notebooks lay open.

"You knew. You saw it. I was so sure of myself, of the market, I . . ."

"Not now, Nate." Bea grabbed his hand. This was her moment of validation, her comeuppance, and it was supposed to feel good. But it didn't. Not with Nate so destroyed. Not with all these looming questions about National City. About the country. Her being right didn't matter now. Now they just had to focus on getting through to tomorrow. "There's no point in dwelling on the past. We've simply got to deal with the present. This must be the bottom. Right?"

"Has to be."

"So, as soon as the market starts to go up, you'll start recovering your losses. We'll be okay."

Nate shook his head. "We've lost so much. It's unrecoverable."

Bea wasn't sure she should tell Nate about her bet with Abe until she knew for certain that it had happened. But he was so downtrodden, and he needed to get some sleep before the market opened in a few hours. If she could give him a bit of hope, maybe that would be enough to get him through the upcoming day.

"Nate, remember when we fought, at Shabbat, about my fears about the market?"

"I know, Bea, I know. You saw what the rest of us fools refused to see. You knew this was coming. You tried to warn me. To protect us. My stubborn blindness put us in this position. I'll never forgive myself."

"Stop. That's not my point. Let me finish."

"Okay, I just want you to know how sorry I am. Instead of listening to you, my wife, my partner, the most brilliant person I've ever met, I assumed that I knew more. I didn't mean to, but I see now that I did. I ruined us."

After so many months of being told she was crazy, it should have felt good to hear Nate say this to Bea now, but it didn't. It did, however, make it easier to tell him that she had ignored his admonitions, gone behind his back, and bet against him.

"We might not be ruined."

"C'mon, Bea. Don't try to give me a pep talk. I don't deserve it."

"No, that's not what I mean. A week ago, I did something."

Nate's face froze. "What did you do?"

"I went to Lizzie's broker in Queens."

"That guy? He just does whatever the masses are doing. What'd you go to him for?"

Bea quickly jotted down the stocks she had asked Abe to short, their prices at the time when she asked him to do it, and their prices today. She handed the paper to Nate.

"I had him short these."

"You what?"

"I took the deeds to the buildings, plus the money from our wedding gifts, and I gave it to him. I asked him to buy on as much margin as he could and to short all these stocks."

"He must have thought you were insane."

"He did."

"But . . ." Nate studied the paper in his hand, and Bea watched him calculating in his head. "Holy cow, Bea, you saved us!" He jumped up and lifted her in the air, swinging her in a circle. "We're rich! Millionaire rich. Bea Abramovitz Greenberg, you are the smartest woman on Wall Street. You see the market more clearly than anyone else. You knew what was coming, and if I'd listened to you, I might have protected us, my clients. Instead, I dismissed you. And you saved us anyway."

Bea felt momentarily overcome with relief and joy as the reality of what she had hopefully done began to sink in. Still, she didn't know for certain.

"Hold on, I don't know that yet."

"What do you mean?"

"Well, Abe was pretty skeptical of my request. There's a chance he didn't put the transactions through at all."

"You haven't checked?"

"I've tried, but his line has been tied up since last week. I went to see him yesterday morning and customers were queueing for blocks. I couldn't get in."

"All right, well, in a few hours we can go down there . . . first thing, before he's even open."

"I can go. You need to be at the bank. If there is anyone who can help salvage this mess, it's you. They need you."

Nate leaned down to put his forehead against Bea's. "They need you. And I need you too. Can you ever forgive me for being such a fool?"

"Yes." She kissed him. "I can. But let's not worry about that right now. Now we both need to get some sleep before the market opens. We need our wits about us. Hopefully things will turn around, stabilize. I'll go see Abe. Let's get through this upcoming day, and then we will see where things stand."

Finally, Bea felt completely seen. She had stuck to her beliefs even when everyone told her not to, and they were going to make it through this disaster intact. Bruised but okay. By tonight it would all be better. By tonight the rest of their lives would begin.

CHAPTER FIFTY-TWO

October 29, "Black Tuesday"

DOW DAILY AVERAGE: 230, –30 POINTS FROM MONDAY, –71 POINTS FROM FRIDAY

Stock Prices Collapse, Dropping $14,000,000,000 as the Country Panic-Sells

For the second time in four days, the market turned to pandemonium as investors rushed to liquidate their holdings. The latest sell-off came in aggressive and swift, after a rally Friday and Saturday that created a false sense of confidence for investors. The nationwide declines are so extreme that actual losses look to be the greatest in the history of the exchange.

Nate was gone when Bea woke up, but the paper outside her door told her everything she needed to know. Tuesday was not going to be better than Monday; in fact, today might be worse. She picked up the phone to try Abe again. The more the market fell, the more desperately she wanted assurance that he had executed her shorts. But it was no use. The lines were jammed. She dressed as quickly as she could and was about to walk out the door to go see him in person when her phone rang.

"Oh, Bea," Henny sobbed on the other end of the line. "We're sunk. Everything is gone, our apartment, the house. Jake's lost everything."

"Are you sure?"

"That's what Jake said last night. He said if things didn't turn around today, we'd be wiped out. And the papers this morning . . . I keep trying to call him, but I can't get through."

"The lines are all tied up. Listen, Henny, try to stay calm." Bea got an idea. "Last week I went down there and helped Jake put through sell orders. I don't know if it will make any difference, but why don't I see if I can help."

"Oh, Bea, you're incredible. If there's anyone who can save us right now, it's you." Henny had no idea, Bea thought. "Call me as soon as you get back. And good luck!"

Bea hung up the phone and went downstairs. She'd planned to drive to Wall Street, but the traffic was at a complete standstill. At this rate, by the time she got there, the day would be done. She'd jump on the train instead.

When she exited the station at Wall Street, she encountered a scene of chaos, panic, and despair. Packs of men stood outside the doors of the exchange, waving trading slips, hoping that someone, anyone, would give them pennies for the dollars they had had just days before. But there was no one to buy. The market was in free fall, and everyone was a seller. Bea tried to fight her way toward National City, but she made no progress against the thick crowds. There was nothing she could do.

Bea heard a voice say something like "look out, another jumper," and then she heard screams and a thud as she watched a man leap from his window to his death on the street below. This couldn't be real. She had to be asleep, still dreaming. But she knew she wasn't, because even in her worst nightmares she could never have imagined something this horrific. For a moment her mind flashed to Jake. Might he jump too? She tried again to get to him, but it was useless. All she could do now was go home and wait. Wait and hope that they would all survive the day.

When Bea got back to her apartment, Henny and her parents were waiting, anxiously, in her lobby. It seemed that news of the crash had taken over the city and, after trying unsuccessfully to reach Jake, they came uptown to her. She sparingly described the scene on Wall Street. The last thing she needed was Pauline or Henny worrying that Jake was among the hopeless men jumping from windows. Bea would shoulder that particular concern herself.

As soon as they were inside the apartment, Henny went to the bar to make them all a drink, and Bea went to the kitchen to ask Grace to bring them something to eat. Pauline cornered her as she was coming out.

"Beatrice, are we all right? Did you do it?" Her mother was agitated but hopeful.

"I don't know yet, Mama. I hope so. I tried. But I don't know if the broker I went to did what I asked. I've been calling him for days and I can't get through."

"Can't reach him? But you're a client. Shouldn't he—"

"It is bedlam right now, Mama. I tried to see him yesterday, and there was a line that would have taken me all day. And if his office is anything like what I saw on Wall Street—" Bea stopped herself from saying more. "I'll go see him tomorrow. Hopefully by then things will have settled."

"But my necklace?"

"Your necklace will be fine, Mama. That I can promise you."

Day turned to night with no word from Nate or Jake. And then there was a knock at the door. Well, less of a knock and more like a scratch. "BB, Henny?"

"Jake." Henny had left Jake a note that she was at Bea and Nate's. She leapt up and ran to let him in.

As soon as Henny opened the door, Jake enveloped her in a defeated embrace.

Bea took in his appearance with concern. His eyes were bloodshot and ringed with purple; his hair was hanging in his face and so greasy the blond almost looked black. His rumpled shirt was stained with perspiration, and if he'd had a jacket when he went to work that morning, he didn't now.

"Jake." Bea went to the door. "Come, sit down."

"We'll get you some food and a stiff drink," Henny said with all the false cheer she could muster.

Jake shuffled into the living room, the tips of his untied shoelaces clicking on the ground as he moved, and Pauline stood up, gasping.

"Yaacov! My *yingele*." She ran to try to soothe him, but he rebuffed her and sat down in a chair.

"It's over. We're destroyed." Jake's eyes filled with tears. "I've ruined us."

"I went to Wall Street today, Jake, it's not just us. It's everyone," Bea said softly. "This is a calamity of unrivaled proportions. Bubbles have burst before but—"

Jake started to cry harder. "We had so much. Everything. More than we needed. And now it's gone. Mama, Papa, I destroyed your dreams. I—"

He paused as they heard the sound of keys in the door.

"Nate." Bea ran to the foyer.

"And we thought yesterday was bad," Nate said, as he dropped his things at the door, trying to smile through his obvious misery. "Did you talk to Abe?"

Bea shook her head. "Everyone's here. Mama and Papa. Henny and Jake. Come sit."

Nate entered the room, and, at the sight of her cousin, Henny broke down and started to weep. "Nate, is this really happening? Is it really over? Have you talked to your parents? Lizzie? Are they okay?"

"No one is okay, Henny," Jake snapped at her. "The entire country's financial system just fell apart. Everyone is wiped out. Decimated. Done for."

"That can't be true. Is it that bad, Nathan?" Pauline asked.

"It might be. Some of the banks are failing. Even people who just have savings accounts may be wiped out. And the investors . . . there has never been anything like this. Ever." He turned to Bea. "All this time, you saw it."

"We were fools," Jake added. "Arrogant, ignorant fools. If we had listened to you, Bea, we'd still have our lives. Our homes."

"Enough," Bea said firmly. "Enough of all of this. Yes, I saw this coming. I told you to be careful and no one listened to me. You were wrong. You made mistakes. But most of the country did the same. This crisis is much bigger than the wealth that we in this room had and lost. We have our health. We have each other. We will manage through this." Bea believed this to be true even if she hadn't made a cent in her short sales. They would move back into the tenements if they had to. If they stuck together, they would find a way to rise up from this.

"Well, I can tell you one thing for certain," Nate said, grabbing Bea's hand tightly. "If we survive this, and if you can really find it in yourself to forgive me, I will never dismiss your instincts again."

Bea was about to respond when the phone rang.

"Mrs. Abramovitz?" Bea would now know that voice anywhere.

"Mr. Friedland." Bea's pulse quickened. "Mr. Friedland. Thank you for calling. I—"

"Mrs. Abramovitz, thank you! You saved my life."

"I did?"

"Yes, ma'am. I thought you were cuckoo when you came to see me. Two deeds and a wad of cash as collateral to short the hottest stocks in the market. And with so much leverage."

"Yes, you said so at the time. I was afraid you might not put my orders through."

"I almost didn't. Thought you were just another one of these dizzy housewives looking to get the thrill of a little risk. But you! You some kind of seer or somethin'? When I placed your orders, I decided you were so bananas that I would bet a little myself. I'd made so much this year, I figured—why not play along with this *meshuggeneh* dame? I only did a little, mind you . . . nothin' like the kinda clams you bet . . . but still . . . the whole world collapsed yesterday—every one of my clients, wiped out. I've been up two straight days trying to sort through all the losses. Except for you . . . Mrs. Abramovitz, do you know how much money you made?"

"Well, no. I don't know exactly when you put in the orders, and how much margin you were able to secure, so—"

"Lady, I did exactly what you asked. The day you asked."

As if in slow motion, a smile unfurled across the width of Bea's face as she did the quick calculations in her head. The market had dropped nearly one hundred points since she went to Queens a week and a half ago. If Mr. Friedland had done as she directed . . .

"Mrs. Abramovitz, if you were rich before, now you're filthy rich! Heck, I'm rich just from doin' what you said with my own little gamble."

Bea felt her knees weaken underneath her. The floor started to rock. This was real. She had done it. She had saved them all.

"Mr. Friedland, I could kiss you! And it's Mrs. Greenberg. For future reference."

"Whatever your name is, the feelin' is mutual."

Bea returned the receiver to the stem of the phone and turned to look at the confused faces of her family sitting all around her living room. It was over. Everything she'd feared had happened. She took in her husband and her brother, who had been so dismissive, suddenly at their wit's end, lost and desperate. And now, thanks to her, they would be taken care of forever.

"There is something you all should know," she said with a smile.

"Abe?" Nate asked, the quiver in his voice demonstrating the anxiety that everyone else in the room surely felt. Bea nodded, and a smile spread across his face.

"I shorted the market. A week and a half ago."

"You did?" Jake asked. "With what money?"

"With my money," Pauline said proudly. "I gave her my necklace."

"Your necklace, Mama?" Jake looked dumbfounded; he knew as well as Bea that that had been Pauline's most prized possession.

"I didn't actually use your necklace, Mama. I know how much it means to you. I took the deeds to the Madison Avenue and East Broadway buildings instead. And the money from our wedding gifts."

"Weren't those buildings worth—" Lew paused, trying to calculate the possible returns.

"Over one hundred thousand dollars. And I used margin. We are all fine. More than fine, we're set for life."

"How set?" Jake asked sheepishly.

Bea went to open her mouth, but nothing came out. She needed a moment before she could speak. The number was so enormous she still didn't entirely believe it was real. And then she said it out loud for the first time.

"Five million dollars set."

Henny screamed and jumped on Bea. Jake joined her. Her parents hugged, crying, and Nate just sat in his chair, stupefied.

"Nate?" Bea asked gently as she'd pried herself out from the Jake and Henny scrum. "Are you all right?"

"All right? Oh, Bea, I'm more than all right. I'm awed, humbled, grateful. I'm sitting here realizing that all the time I thought I was treating you fairly, I wasn't even giving you a fraction of the respect you deserved. You are the most spectacular woman in the world. And I vow to you, right now, to spend the rest of my days making sure you know it."

"As you should." Pauline stood and took Bea's hand. "I'd say it's a miracle, but it isn't; it's you. Beatrice, you saw the truth when no one else did, and thanks to your wisdom and insight, you've saved us all. We will never forget all that you've done to protect the House of Oppenheim."

"And Abramovitz," Lew, Jake, and Henny added, almost at the same time.

"And Greenberg," Nate said. "Perhaps we should just call it the House of Beatrice."

All at once Bea smiled and started to cry. This had been one of the hardest days of their lives. But, somehow, amid all this misery, her family had become stronger than ever before. She knew that, for so many, the worst was just beginning. And she also knew that, from this moment on, it would be her mission to help as many as she could to make their lives a little bit better.

EPILOGUE

January 1930

Dow Monthly Average: 267, +19 points from December, −50 from January '29

In the wake of the crash, it was hard to feel anything but distraught. More of the country had been invested in the stock market than ever before, and that meant more people than ever went from having money to having nothing. In the streets, men who had once been driven by chauffeurs were selling their cars for a few dollars just to buy food. They were the lucky ones—they had cars to sell.

It was strange, in this new environment of utter devastation, to be richer than their wildest dreams. Bea's family had been among the very few to profit fantastically from the worst days in the history of the American economy; still, she took solace in the fact that she hadn't done what she did out of greed, but to protect her family. There were men, the great Jesse Livermore one of the most notorious, who had profited immensely from the crash and sat home counting their money and gloating. But that was not Bea or her family. The instantaneous shift from riches to rags and back again had changed them all forever.

The whole family approached their wealth with a newfound altruism, giving wherever they could. Jake didn't even try to return to banking. Just as Bea's passion was Wall Street, Jake's was selling, so he joined Lew at Abrams Grocery, where he happily excelled. It was his idea to have special "penny hours" every evening where they would sell whatever remained from the day for a penny, to those who could hardly afford anything at all. Usually, in the morning, Jake set aside some of the best produce, which their manager would "happen" to discover at the end of the day.

Bea had offered to buy Jake and Henny's Sutton Place apartment for them to live in (collecting rent whenever they could afford to pay it), but they now believed that it was more than they needed, and moved into one of the apartments on Madison, above the grocery. Pauline and Lew moved into the other, insisting on converting the East Broadway property back into multiple units that they leased, for almost nothing, to those who had lost their homes. Anyway, Pauline wanted to be close to the rest of the family.

Thankfully Mort Brodsky's distaste for Wall Street meant that they had very little of their money in the market. But they, too, wanted to help those who had not been so lucky. They reconfigured several of their stores with "secondhand" sections and hired Henny to develop a new line of fashionable, affordable clothing that would launch the following year. She made Sophie her head designer.

The market recovered a bit. It had dropped so low that there were many stocks ripe to be purchased. As soon as the dust settled, Bea began investing. But this time, she did it out in the open, with Nate by her side. National City had survived, but he no longer wanted to be part of something that had been so central to perpetrating such a disastrous event for the country. Instead, he set up a small brokerage house with Bea as his partner. They took clients with any level of wealth and advised them on conservative investment approaches. They wanted to help people really understand investing, without the illusion of permanent prosperity that had left so many with nothing. And they were so good at what they did that no one ever questioned the fact that the best ideas came from a woman.

Bea thought about where she was in her life today. For someone who prided herself on seeing patterns and forecasting responses, she hadn't expected any of this. She placed her hands on her swollen belly and smiled. It turned out that some of the most magical things happened when you stopped predicting and just started living.

AUTHOR'S NOTE

I'm the last person you'd ever expect to write a book about Wall Street. I do have an MBA, but before business school, I didn't know the difference between a stock and a bond. And even once I did, the market never particularly interested me. I've always cared more about the "why" behind a business than what the public thinks it's worth at any given moment, as reflected in the price of its stock. But in January 2021, something happened on Wall Street that got my attention.

The stock of a video game retailer, GameStop, suddenly began to soar. This was a company whose business fundamentals weren't great, in an industry (brick-and-mortar retail) that was declining, and the institutional (a.k.a. professional) investors had done what, after reading this book, you might expect: sold short. These kinds of investors select stocks based on long-term, in-depth analysis of companies and industries, data that they track and analyze over many years.

Meanwhile, we were still in a world of COVID isolation, and more and more individuals had begun to invest from home. A subset of these amateur investors, who communicated through a group on Reddit, decided that GameStop was a symbol of all that was wrong with capitalism: the rich fat cats getting richer at the expense of those who were already struggling. So they set out to prove the professionals wrong and started buying the stock. Briefly, they created so much momentum that GameStop stock skyrocketed, forcing the more sophisticated investors—the short sellers—to cover their losses and buy back the stock at a much higher price than they'd anticipated. This led to huge losses for them that, for a few days, created chaos across the whole market.

So far this just sounds like another stock market cautionary tale, right? But this was different. The Reddit investors saw this as a Robin Hood story, where by driving up the GameStop stock price, they were demonstrating to the big guys that anyone could move the market and get rich, and that they could do it by taking from the hedge fund villains who already had way too much.

In the case of GameStop (and AMC, which followed shortly after), the Reddit group was not investing out of altruism. They did it to make money, just like the professional investors. So why was it okay for the amateurs, but not for the professional short sellers?

I suddenly spent a lot of time thinking about this dichotomy. Why is it assumed that *rich* equals *bad*, and *poor* equals *good*? And, specifically when it comes to investing, why are short sellers categorically cast as evil? I grew fascinated by the complex morality of wealth.

"I wish there were a way to write about this," I said to my husband. "But I write historical fiction."

And then he told me about Jesse Livermore, a Wall Street legend who famously shorted the Crash of '29 and made a fortune. And the seed of *The Trade Off* was planted.

I had no idea that short selling even existed in the 1920s—I assumed it was a much newer trading strategy (not that I thought much about it at all before GameStop). I also had never heard of Jesse Livermore, but apparently, anyone who has ever worked in banking knows his name. He is heralded as one of the best traders in the history of Wall Street, and many of his revolutionary investment rules are still used today. He made and lost several fortunes over his career and, by shorting the Great Crash, profited tremendously (to the tune of $100 million).

Initially, I thought I might base my novel on him. Livermore was a poor outsider who pulled himself up from nothing to become one of the most powerful Wall Street insiders of his time. But in my research, I quickly learned that while Livermore started from humble beginnings, he was ultimately a ruthless investor who—like all the other big operators of the period before regulation—colluded whenever possible to manipulate stocks to move in the direction that benefited their portfolios. He reinforced every negative stereotype of the evil Wall Street guy. This was not my hero.

I knew there were successful investors who were also fundamentally good people. Ones who took stock positions (long or short) based on their analysis of the market and their ability to play the game strategically. They weren't driven by financial gain at the expense of others, and they might have been short sellers simply because economic conditions indicated that was the right strategy. This was who I wanted my protagonist to be. And since I also like to write about strong women making their place in men's worlds, I decided my short seller should be a woman.

There were some women who worked on Wall Street in the 1920s, but most of them were either extreme eccentrics or very-well-connected socialites. Further, despite that some of the biggest investment banks of the time were run by Jewish men, I didn't come across any Jewish women in high positions in banking in this era. Enter Bea. A girl with all the smarts and none of the advantages. A perfect heroine.

I anchored my story on real places and events. The Julian Petroleum oil scandal did, indeed, happen in Hollywood and was a Madoff of its day. The Livermores really did throw outrageous parties at their home in Great Neck; Dorothy, Jesse Livermore's first wife, was a Ziegfeld Follies dancer before they wed, and Livermore himself was a notorious womanizer. The newest and most advertised attractions at Coney Island in that era were, in fact, shows that would be deemed culturally insensitive by today's standards. And the Cotton Club in Harlem was known for its all-white clientele. Richard (Dick) Whitney, then vice president of the New York Stock Exchange, temporarily saved the market from the Black Thursday sell-off on October 24, 1929, by personally buying ten thousand shares of U.S. Steel. Charley Mitchell was the head of National City Bank, and his strategy was to bring banking to the people, which, unfortunately, got many unsophisticated investors in over their heads leading up to the crash.

Finally, what is now JPMorgan Chase was, indeed, called the House of Morgan and seen as the center of the financial universe in that era. As far as the specific sexism and anti-Semitism that Bea encountered are concerned, I have no evidence that this particular bank was unique in its hiring practices or treatment of women or Jews. The House of Morgan could have been a stand-in for any of the big banks on Wall Street at that time. Banking was first and foremost a man's world, as evidenced by the first quote in my epigraph, taken from an actual pamphlet written by Mary Vail Andress, the first woman to hold an executive position at a bank. (Note that she wrote it in 1928, a year after Bea meets with her in my novel, a small modification that I made to fit my story.)

Sadly, banking has remained slow to include women: the first woman to get her own seat on the New York Stock Exchange didn't do so until 1967, and even today, being female is considered "diverse" at the big investment banks.

For those of you who are data nerds like me, I'll add a bit about the actual market statistics. The stock market in the 1920s wasn't just a straight line up until it fell. It had many swings up and down until the big gains before the crash (which happened over four days, as I describe). This novel follows these fluctuations, represented by the Dow Jones Industrial Average. I was lucky enough to get this data (thank you to my husband!) parsed daily, weekly, and monthly from 1925–1930, and it became my bible. I studied it every time I sat down to write. I spared you, the reader, much of the detail, but if you're wondering how much the market rose, and how dramatically it crashed, I have charts on my website, www.samanthawoodruff.com.

I read a lot to research for this novel. What follows is a short list of the many sources that were helpful to me in painting a picture of the era. To understand the early days of women on Wall Street, my first stop was *Ladies of the Ticker* by George Robb. I reached out to George after reading his book and discovered that he is not only a brilliant academic but also kind and generous with his time. He became a sounding board and adviser to me as I tried to accurately capture what it might look and feel like to be a woman on Wall Street in this era. For the details of the financial and economic side of the crash, I relied heavily on *Rainbow's End: The Crash of 1929* by Maury Klein. I read several books on Jesse Livermore, including the famous fictional biography *Reminiscences of a Stock Operator* by Edwin Lefèvre, which is apparently required reading for traders at many banks to this day, and *Jesse Livermore: World's Greatest Stock Trader* by Richard Smitten. Finally, the foundation of my portrait of the life of Jewish immigrants in the early part of the twentieth century was from the seminal *World of our Fathers* by Irving Howe and supplemented heavily by images and descriptions from the Tenement Museum and Eldridge Street synagogue.

This is a work of fiction. While I did my best to remain true to the historical record as it pertains to people, places, and things, the specifics of my characters and story are invented, and any misrepresentations of facts are my own errors. There are a lot of nuggets from my own life sprinkled unexpectedly throughout this story. My paternal grandparents were Lew and Pauline, and the real Pauline's mother's history was the inspiration for the fictional Pauline. My grandpa Lew was a printer (like Nate's father), and he often encouraged me to follow in the family business with the line "there should be more women in printing." Grandpa Lew, does writing count? My great-aunt Henrietta, who passed away while this was a work in progress, apparently often touted her importance to her children by exclaiming that she hailed from the "House of" her maiden name.

Finally, at the time of this writing, anti-Semitism is on the rise, following the events of October 7, 2023. I cannot conclude this note, in a book about a Jewish woman persevering against prejudice and false cultural assumptions, without wishing for a kinder, gentler, more loving and accepting world for all people. And for we Jews, and all who face persecution just for being who you are, to finally reach a place where fear is truly a thing of the past.

ACKNOWLEDGMENTS

To those of you who have read this far . . . thank you! Thank you for caring enough to sift through my ramblings and asides in the previous note. Thank you for your interest in Bea and her family and friends. Thank you for caring about the plight of a woman who wants to excel in a man's world. Thank you for buying this book. This is only my second novel, and I still consider myself a newbie to the world of writing, but oh, how I love it. And I wouldn't be able to call it my job if it weren't for you.

I love everything about writing novels (sure, some days I feel isolated and alone and in a dark tunnel where I am trying to vomit up characters that feel real), but one of the best parts has been my new professional community. To the Bookstagrammers, bloggers, BookTokers, podcasters: You are our champions. Thank you for your public enthusiasm for books and reading. Special thanks in this category to Andrea Peskind Katz at Great Thoughts, Great Readers; Lauren Margolin, the aptly named Good Book Fairy; Suzy Leopold, virtual-book-tour whiz; Anissa Joy Armstrong; Katie Taylor at the Grateful Read; and the indefatigable author and champion of authors Zibby Owens. To the multitudes of you who I didn't have space to name: I love and appreciate you.

To my local booksellers, Rachel at Diane's Books and Jen, Greer, Barb, Sam, and Rachel at Athena: thank you for keeping our community reading, and for your incredible support for all us writers in the community.

I never cease to be astonished by how many smart, talented women are writing novels as second careers. And how generously they support one another. And that I now get to call so many of these women my friends. Annabel Monaghan and Eileen Moskowitz Palma, my gratitude and love starts with you, two of the only people who know how dirty of a sex scene I can write. My Lake Union sister and instant book BFF Rochelle Weinstein, you have been an almost daily sounding board on topics far and wide—love you to pieces and grateful for your friendship. My writing group: Jackie Friedland and Brooke Lea Foster, ditto to you. Even when we weren't meeting, I knew you had my back. Your insights and edits along this journey made this book what it is today, and also, I just kind of think you're both amazing. Lisa Barr, you're a true wonder woman with a huge heart, a sharp mind, and infinite energy. Love you so much. Also, does "calendar" remind you to check in with a "Hi, honey, how are you doing?" at just the right moment? Amy Blumenfeld, you're a soft-spoken genius. Finish that book so we can celebrate it. I would stop there, but the list of women I wouldn't know if not for writing and who make my life so much richer goes on: Fiona Davis, Karen Dukess, Daisy Alpert Florin, Avery Carpenter Forey, Jane Green, Jane Healey, Paulette Kennedy, Lynda Loigman, Amy Poeppel, Kaira Rouda, Susie Schnall—every one of you wows and inspires me. A special note of gratitude to a few women whom I consider to be historical fiction royalty, Pam Jenoff and Allison Pataki, for dropping what you were doing to read and review this novel in the midst of your own life and deadlines, for me, someone you didn't even know. Ditto to one of my new BFFs, Sara Goodman Confino (love her and her books!).

Kathy Schneider, agent, editor, adviser, friend—thanks for taking a chance on me back when I was just a girl with a story about lobotomy, for always having my back, and for never making me feel like I'm annoying you, even when I surely am. Oh, and for naming this book! Thank you to everyone else at Jane Rotrosen Agency who has supported Kathy (and therefore me) on this journey. Chantelle Aimée Osman, my terrific editor, thank you for your willingness to talk through plot points and character arcs all along the way, for stopping me from trying to include the Florida real estate bubble in this already weighty story, and for pushing my writing and storytelling to a place with so much more depth and dimension. Also, for not flinching at my early-weekend-morning emails with yet another list of potential titles for this book (fifty-plus in total)! Charlotte Herscher, developmental editor extraordinaire, every time I revised my text to address one of your little comment flags, I ended up saying, "Oh, that's what was supposed to happen in this scene." Danielle Marshall, thank you for stepping in to take care of me in the transitions, and for seeing the potential in this story. To the rest of the team at Lake Union and Amazon Publishing (Darci Swanson, Jen Bentham, James Gallagher, Jill Schoenhaut, and others I don't know by name but still appreciate greatly): thank you for all your hard work to bring this book to the world. To the marketing folks—you entertained a lot of titles for this one. Sorry for that, and I think we landed in a good place. Suzanne Williams at Shreve Williams PR, we are just starting our journey together, but I hope it will be a long one, because you're amazing.

George Robb, author of the fascinating book *Ladies of the Ticker*, thank you for taking so much time to talk with me. Your insights were invaluable in shaping so much of Bea's world on Wall Street, as well as informing some pretty critical plot points.

Beyond the writers' world, thank you to my besties who have cheered me on, come to my events, bought my books, and understood when I couldn't see you or pick up the phone because I was writing. Carrie, Dom, Karen, Kim, Mel, Shelby, Stef, Hillary: love you all so much.

I am extremely fortunate to have behind-the-scenes support that enables me to lock myself away and write when needed. Taryn Greene, Hester Culcay (Balvy), and Lindsay Kraut, thank you, thank you, thank you for keeping my world on its axis and for everything else you do.

My family: Elaine, Julia, Justin, Doug, Patti, Leslie, Alana, Mark, Amy, Joey, Kelly, Mike, and Sheri, thanks for your support and enthusiasm. My dad, Bob, and stepfather, Steven, are the perfect end-stage editors, so thanks for your eagle eyes; if you know my dad, ask him for a book, and he'll give you a signed copy: "I hope you enjoy my daughter's book.—Bob Greene."

Lila, my strong and inspiring daughter, who is funny, charming, curious, and beautiful inside and out—and unapologetically great at math (except, perhaps, geometry). May you continue to beat me at every game we play forever. Alex, my (no longer little) boy, who is full of compassion, exuberance, and love . . . for football, drums, his family, and his many reptiles. May your passions continue to grow as quickly as your feet. Jack, my husband, research assistant, and biggest champion. Thank you for your unwavering love and support, and for teaching me everything I didn't learn in business school. This book would have made no logical sense without you. And finally, Mom. You are my number one beta reader, my plot puzzler, my person. Thank you for being my biggest fan and for teaching me early in life that girls can do anything.

This is a lot of acknowledgments. And I could go on. But I won't. I'll just circle back to the start and reiterate—readers, none of this would exist without you. Thank you.

DISCUSSION GUIDE

1. What was your first impression of Bea Abramovitz? Did that impression change over the course of the novel?
2. How did the fact that Bea was a twin impact her journey? How did it impact Jake's?
3. How did her parents' immigration experience impact Bea's relationship to wealth and money? Jake's? How did that evolve throughout the story?
4. Early in the book, we learn about life on the Lower East Side. Was there anything about Bea's childhood home or life that surprised you?
5. Discuss the different ways in which the Abramovitz family responded to their shifting financial situation. How did it change each of them (Lew, Pauline, Bea, and Jake)?
6. Bea and Sophie have a unique friendship. Describe the role Sophie played in Bea's growth over the course of the novel.
7. How did Bea's newer friendships with Henny and Milly shape her along the way?
8. Do you think this book had a clear villain? If so, who?
9. *The Trade Off* takes place during the Roaring Twenties; how did the novel demonstrate the social and cultural expressions of excess that came with an ever-rising stock market?
10. Can you think of moments in more recent history where

the country's economic state has influenced other aspects of the culture? When? What happened?

11. The Great Crash of 1929 is a well-documented historical event. Did you learn anything new about the crash? About the stock market in general?
12. In the author's note, Samantha Greene Woodruff says she wanted to write a story that explored the "complex morality of wealth." Did she accomplish her goal?
13. The world of banking was closed to women like Bea, yet she persevered. What would you have done in Bea's situation? Can you think of a moment when you've pushed forward against seemingly impossible odds?
14. Perseverance and trusting oneself are two prevalent themes in this novel. What other overarching ideas did you notice? What did you take away from the book overall?
15. What message(s) do you think the author wanted you to take away from this novel?
16. Do you see any similarities between the underlying themes in *The Trade Off* and in the author's first novel, *The Lobotomist's Wife*?
17. Does *The Trade Off* remind you of any other books that you have read? In what ways?

ABOUT THE AUTHOR

Photo © 2021 Julia Daggs

Samantha Greene Woodruff is the author of Amazon #1 bestseller *The Lobotomist's Wife*. She studied history at Wesleyan University and continued her studies at NYU's Stern School of Business, where she earned an MBA. Sam spent nearly two decades working on the business side of media, primarily at Viacom's Nickelodeon, before leaving corporate life to become a full-time mom. In her newfound "free" time, she took classes at the Writing Institute at Sarah Lawrence College, where she accidentally found her calling as a historical fiction author. Her writing has appeared in *Newsweek*, *Writer's Digest*, *Female First*, *Read 650*, and more. Though she grew up in the New Jersey suburbs, Sam now lives in Greenwich, Connecticut, with her husband and two children, their two dogs, and a small reptile zoo. When not writing, Sam practices yoga, hikes, and occasionally indulges her love of singing with mandatory family karaoke nights. For more information, visit www.samanthawoodruff.com.